D0452006

Big Stone Gap

BIG STONE GAP

A NOVEL

Adriana Trigiani

BALLANTINE BOOKS

NEW YORK

2015 Ballantine Books Trade Paperback Edition

Copyright © 2000 by The Glory of Everything Company
Reading group guide copyright © 2001 by The Glory of Everything Company and Penguin Random House LLC
Recipes and script excerpts copyright © 2015 by The Glory of Everything Company

Originally published in hardcover in the United States by Random House, an imprint and division of Penguin Random House LLC, in 2000, and subsequently in trade paperback by Ballantine Books, an imprint of Random House, a division of Penguin Random House LLC, in 2001.

Production photographs © Antony Platt, courtesy of Picturehouse

ISBN 978-1-101-96744-7
eBook ISBN 978-0-345-46361-6

Printed in the United States of America on acid-free paper

randomhousebooks.com
randomhousereaderscircle.com

9 8 7 6 5 4 3 2 1

For Tim

BIG STONE GAP

This will be a good weekend for reading. I picked up a dozen of Vernie Crabtree's killer chocolate chip cookies at the French Club bake sale yesterday. (I don't know what she puts in them, but they're chewy and crispy at the same time.) Those, a pot of coffee, and a good book are all I will need for the rainy weekend rolling in. It's early September in our mountains, so it's warm during the day, but tonight will bring a cool mist to remind us that fall is right around the corner.

The Wise County Bookmobile is one of the most beautiful sights in the world to me. When I see it lumbering down the mountain road like a tank, then turning wide and easing onto Shawnee Avenue, I flag it down like an old friend. I've waited on this corner every Friday since I can remember. The Bookmobile is just a government truck, but to me it's a glittering royal coach delivering stories and knowledge and life itself. I even love the smell of books. People have often told me that one of their strongest childhood memories is the scent of their grandmother's house. I never knew my grandmothers, but I could always count on the Bookmobile.

The most important thing I ever learned, I learned from books. Books have taught me how to size people up. The most useful book I ever read taught me how to read faces, an ancient Chinese art called *siang mien,* in which the size of the eyes, curve of the lip, and height of the forehead are important clues to a person's character. The placement of ears indicates intelligence. Chins that stick out reflect stubbornness. Deep-set eyes suggest a secretive nature. Eyebrows that grow together may answer the question *Could that man kill me with his bare hands?* (He could.) Even dimples have meaning. I have them, and according to face-reading, something wonderful is supposed to happen to me when I turn thirty-five. (It's been four months since my birthday, and I'm still waiting.)

If you were to read my face, you would find me a comfortable person with brown eyes, good teeth, nice lips, and a nose that folks, when they are being kind, refer to as noble. It's a large nose, but at least it's straight. My eyebrows are thick, which indicates a practical nature. (I'm a pharmacist—how much more practical can you get?) I have a womanly shape, known around here as a mountain girl's body, strong legs, and a flat behind. Jackets cover it quite nicely.

This morning the idea of living in Big Stone Gap for the rest of my life gives me a nervous feeling. I stop breathing, as I do whenever I think too hard. Not breathing is very bad for you, so I inhale slowly and deeply. I taste coal dust. I don't mind; it assures me that we still have an economy. Our town was supposed to become the "Pittsburgh of the South" and the "Coal Mining Capital of Virginia." That never happened, so we are forever at the whims of the big coal companies. When they tell us the coal is running out in these mountains, who are we to doubt them?

It's pretty here. Around six o'clock at night everything turns a rich Crayola midnight blue. You will never smell greenery so pungent. The Gap definitely has its romantic qualities. Even the train whistles are musical, sweet oboes in the dark. The place can fill you with longing.

The Bookmobile is at the stoplight. The librarian and driver is a good-time gal named Iva Lou Wade. She's in her forties, but she's yet to place the flag on her sexual peak. She's got being a woman down. If you painted her, she'd be sitting on a pink cloud with gold-leaf edges, showing a lot of leg. Her perfume is so loud that when I visit the Bookmobile, I wind up smelling like her for the bulk of the day. (It's a good thing I like Coty's Emeraude.) My father used to say that that's how a woman ought to be. "A man should know when there's a woman in the room. When Iva Lou comes in, there ain't no doubt." I'd just say nothing and roll my eyes.

Iva Lou's having a tough time parking. A mail truck has parked funny in front of the post office, taking up her usual spot, so she motions to me that she's pulling into the gas station. That's fine with the owner, Kent Vanhook. He likes Iva Lou a lot. What man doesn't? She pays real nice attention to each and every one. She examines men like eggs, perfect specimens created by God to nourish. And she hasn't met a man yet who doesn't appreciate it. Luring a man is a true talent, like playing the piano by ear. Not all of us are born prodigies, but women like Iva Lou have made it an art form.

The Bookmobile doors open with a whoosh. I can't believe what Iva Lou's wearing: Her ice-blue turtleneck is so tight it looks like she's wearing her bra on the outside. Her Mondrian-patterned pants, with squares of pale blue, yellow, and green, cling to her thighs like crisscross ribbons. Even sitting, Iva Lou has an unbelievable shape. But I wonder how much of it has to do with all the cinching. Could it be that her parts are so well-hoisted and suspended, she has transformed her real figure into a soft hourglass? Her face is childlike, with a small chin, big blue eyes, and a rosebud mouth. Her eyeteeth snaggle out over her front teeth, but on her they're demure. Her blond hair is like yellow Easter straw, arranged in an upsweep you can see through the set curls. She wears lots of Sarah Coventry jewelry, because she sells it on the side.

"I'll trade you. Shampoo for a best-seller." I give Iva Lou a sack of shampoo samples from my pharmacy, Mulligan's Mutual.

"You got a deal." Iva Lou grabs the sack and starts sorting through the samples. She indicates the shelf of new arrivals. "Ave Maria, honey, you have got to read *The Captains and the Kings* that just came out. I know you don't like historicals, but this one's got sex."

"How much more romance can you handle, Iva Lou? You've got half the men in Big Stone Gap tied up in knots."

She snickers. "Half? Oh well, I'm-a gonna take that as a compliment-o anyway." I'm half Italian, so Iva Lou insists on ending her words with vowels. I taught her some key phrases in Italian in case international romance was to present itself. It wasn't very funny when Iva Lou tried them out on my mother one day. I sure got in some Big Trouble over that.

Iva Lou has a goal. She wants to make love to an Italian man, so she can decide if they are indeed the world's greatest lovers. "Eye-talian men are my Matta-horn, honey," she declares. Too bad there aren't any in these parts. The people around here are mainly Scotch-Irish, or Melungeon (folks who are a mix of Turkish, French, African, Indian, and who knows what; they live up in the mountain hollers and stick to themselves). Zackie Wakin, owner of the town department store, is Lebanese. My mother and I were the only Italians; and then about five years ago we acquired one Jew, Lewis Eisenberg, a lawyer from Woodbury, New York.

"You always sit in the third snap stool. How come?" Iva Lou asks, not looking up as she flips through a new coffee-table book about travel photography.

"I like threes."

"Sweetie-o, let me tell you something." Iva Lou gets a faraway, mystical twinkle in her eye. Then her voice lowers to a throaty, sexy register. "When I get to blow this coal yard, and have my big adventure, I sure as hell won't waste my time taking pictures of the Circus Maximus. I am not interested in rocks 'n' ruins. I want to experience me some flesh and blood. Some magnificent, broad-shouldered hunk of a European man. Forget the points of interest, point me toward the men. Marble don't hug back, baby." Then she breathes deeply, "Whoo."

Iva Lou fixes herself a cup of Sanka and laughs. She's one of those people who are forever cracking themselves up. She always offers me a cup, and I always decline. I know that her one spare clean Styrofoam cup could be her entrée to a romantic rendezvous. Why waste it on me?

"I found you that book on wills you wanted. And here's the only one I could find on grief." Iva Lou holds up *As Grief Exits* as though she's modeling it. The pretty cover has rococo cherubs and clouds on it. The angels' smiles are instantly comforting. "How you been getting along?" I look at Iva Lou's face. Her innocent expression is just like the cherubs'. She really wants to know how I am.

My mother died on August 2, 1978, exactly one month ago today. It was the worst day of my life. She had breast cancer. I never thought cancer would get both of my parents, but it did. Mama was fifty-two years old, which suddenly seems awfully young to me. She was only seventeen when she came to America. My father taught her English, but she always spoke with a thick accent. One of the things I miss most about her is the sound of her voice. Sometimes when I close my eyes I can hear her.

Mama didn't want to die because she didn't want to leave me here alone. I have no brothers or sisters. The roots in the Mulligan family are strong, but at this point, the branches are mostly dead. My mother never spoke of her family over in Italy, so I assume they died in the war or something. The only relative I have left is my aunt, Alice Mulligan Lambert. She is a pill. Her husband, my Uncle Wayne, has spent his life trying not to make her angry, but he has failed. Aunt Alice has a small head and thin lips. (That's a terrible combination.)

"I'm gonna take a smoke, honey-o." Iva Lou climbs down the steps juggling two coffees and her smokes. In under fifteen seconds, Kent Vanhook comes out from the garage, wiping his hands on a rag. Iva Lou gives Kent the Styrofoam cup, which looks tiny in his big hands. They smoke and sip. Kent Vanhook is a good-looking man of fifty, a tall, easygoing cowboy type. He looks like the great Walter Pidgeon with less hair. As he laughs with Iva Lou, twenty years seem to melt off of his face. Kent's wife is a diabetic who stays at home and complains a lot. I know this because I drop off her insulin once a month. But with Iva Lou, all Kent does is laugh.

I like to be alone on the Bookmobile. It gives me a chance to really examine the new arrivals. I make a stack and then look through the old selections. I pick up my old standby, *The Ancient Art of Chinese Face-Reading,* and think of my father, Fred Mulligan. When he died thirteen years ago, I thought I would grieve, but to this day I haven't.

We weren't close, but it wasn't from my lack of trying. From the time I can remember, he just looked through me, the way you would look through the thick glass of a jelly jar to see if there's any jelly left. Many nights when I was young I cried about him, and then one day I stopped expecting him to love me and the pain went away. I stuck by him when he got sick, though. All of a sudden, my father, who had always separated himself from people, had everything in common with the world. He was in pain and would inevitably die. The suffering gave him some humility. It's sad that my best memories of him are when he was sick. It was then that I first checked out this book on Chinese face-reading.

I thought that if I read my father's face, I would be able to understand why he was so mean. It took a lot of study. Dad's face was square and full of angles: rectangular forehead, sharp jaw, pointy chin. He had small eyes (sign of a deceptive nature), a bulbous nose (sign of money in midlife, which he had from owning the Pharmacy), and no lips. Okay, he had two lips, but the set of the mouth was one tight gray lead-pencil line. That is a sign of cruelty. When you watch the news on television, look at the anchor's mouth. I will guaran-damn-tee you that none of them have upper lips. You don't get on the TV by being nice to people.

On and off for about four years straight the face-reading book was checked out in my name, and my name only. When I went up to Charlottesville on a buying trip for the Pharmacy, I tried to hunt down a copy to buy. It was out of print. Iva Lou has tried to give me the book outright many times. She said she would report it as lost. But I can't do that. I like knowing it's here, riding around with old Iva Lou.

I guess I'm staring out the windshield at them, because they're both looking at me. Iva Lou stomps out her cigarette with her pink Papagallo flat and heads back toward the Bookmobile. Kent watches her return, drinking her in like that last sip of rich, black Sanka.

"I'm sorry. Me and Kent got to talking and, well, you know."

"No problem."

"Face-reading again? Don't you have this memorized by now? Lordy."

Iva stamps the books with her pinky up.

"See you next week." I wave to Kent casually, just to make him feel that there is absolutely nothing wrong with talking to single, available, willing Iva Lou and sharing a smoke. He smiles at me, a little relieved. I think most folks in Big Stone Gap know their secrets are safe with me. (God knows I don't get any pleasure in knowing that the town manager performs self-colonics.)

I have a delivery to make. I promised Mrs. Mac—MacChesney is the full surname—that I would bring her a new prescription to tame her high blood pressure. She is known around here as "Apple Butter Nan" because nobody cans it better. Her house is way up in Cracker's Neck Holler. There are lots of twists and turns to get there, and I sort of fly around the curves like Mario Andretti (another great Eyetalian). There's an element of danger in mountain roads—there are no guardrails, so it's you and your rack-and-pinion steering. If you lose your concentration, you could go over the mountain. One foggy night the Brightwell brothers lost control of their truck and drove off the cliff. Luckily, the trees broke their fall. A state cop found the boys hanging in the branches like fresh laundry the following morning. They lost their truck, though. On impact, it fell off of them like pants. Now it rests at the bottom of Powell Valley Lake.

The Gap, or "down in town" as the holler folks call it, is in the valley. The hollers are little communities nestled in the sides of the Blue Ridge Mountains. I couldn't give you directions to places up in the mountains, but I could take you there. There are no signs anywhere; you have to know your way. When you climb to the highest peak around here, you can see the borders of five states: Virginia, Kentucky, North Carolina, Tennessee, and West Virginia. You can't actually see the divider lines of course; you just know that you're looking at five states because there's a plaque that says so and because we were taught that in school. Tiny Miss Callahan, my fourth-grade teacher, would be very happy that I retained this information and shared it.

Each holler has its own name and singular history. Families found pockets that suited them in these hills and never left. Where people settle tells a lot about them. This is the only place I've ever lived, except for college. I went away to school, all the way up to South Bend, Indiana, to Saint Mary's, a small women's college. It was just big enough for me. When I got my B.S., I came home and took over management of the Pharmacy. I was needed here. My father had gotten sick and had to quit, and Mama couldn't handle it alone. It wasn't that she was a weak woman; she just couldn't handle change.

I've made it up to Cracker's Neck in record time. The MacChesney homestead sits in a clearing. It's a square stone house with four chimneys. Hearth fires smell better in stone houses, and Mrs. Mac always has one going. I park and wait for the dogs to circle. We have hundreds of wild dogs in the mountains, and they travel in packs. Most aren't rabid, and when they are, they get shot. I count six thin dogs sniffing my wheels. Buying time, I unzip my window and toss out the sign that identifies me to customers. It's a white plastic square that says: THE MEDICINE DROPPER. (I sprung for the extra artwork, a silhouette of a nurse in a rush.)

I usually find the guts to get out of the Jeep when I see Mrs. Mac peeking out of her window. The last thing I want to appear to customers is chicken. Truth is, I appreciate her watching out for me as I open the door and swing my legs out. Ever so casually I pull myself to a rigid standing position and walk confidently through the yard to the front door, like Maureen O'Hara in every movie she ever made with John Wayne. Maureen O'Hara is short-waisted like me. She is my inspiration in wardrobe and courage. I've even taken to wearing my hair like her—simple and long in a neat braid. I pack less punch though; my hair is brown, hers lustrous red.

The porch is freshly painted gray without a speck of dirt anywhere. The firewood is stacked neatly to the side of the house in a long row, in a lattice design. I try not to have favorites, but Mrs. Mac and her orderly home definitely top my list.

"Took you long enough!" Mrs. Mac exclaims as she snaps open the screen door.

"Iva Lou and I were chatting."

"I done figured that." Mrs. Mac points to the fire. "Is that a good un, or is that a good un?" The flames lick the grid in hungry yellow bursts.

"That is the best fire I have ever seen." And I mean it.

"Come on back. I made corn bread."

I follow Mrs. Mac to the kitchen, a sunny, spacious room with exposed oak beams on the ceiling. I hear a noise behind me. Praying that it's not another dog, I slowly turn and look, first low, then eye level. It's not a dog. It's a man. Mrs. Mac's son, Jack MacChesney, in his underwear, a faded-to-pink union suit that sticks to him like a leotard. We look at each other, and both our faces turn the color of his underwear before it faded—blood red.

"Jesus Christmas, Jack. Put some clothes on," Mrs. Mac demands.

"Yes, ma'am," he says to his mother, as if on automatic. "Good morning, Ave Maria," he says to me, and goes. I can't help it, I watch the man go. He has a fine, high rear end. I wish I did. I pull my belted CPO jacket down over my flat behind and follow Mrs. Mac into the kitchen.

Mrs. Mac and I cross the kitchen to the big table by the windows, where she pours me a cup of hot black coffee that smells like heaven. She serves me fresh cream and snow-white sugar, which I dump into the mug. "So what's happening in town?" Mrs. Mac asks. She has a mountain-girl face—a fine nose you could draw with a compass, shiny green button eyes, Cupid's-bow lips, smooth cheeks. You can tell that she was a great beauty in her youth, and she still is.

"Is 'Nan' short for anything?" I ask her.

"What? You mean my name?" Mrs. Mac cuts the corn bread in the iron skillet into neat triangles. "My mamaw's name was Nan. My middle name is Bluebell because that field was covered with 'em when I got born." She points out the window with her spatula to indicate the field in the back.

"Nan Bluebell. Pretty. What was your maiden name?"

"God-a-mighty, you got a lot of questions this here morning. Gilliam. Nan Bluebell Gilliam."

"I like it," I say as I sip my coffee.

Jack stands in the doorway. He lingers there for a moment, as if to assess the situation. Or maybe he doesn't want to interrupt our conversation. In town he is known as Jack Mac. He's a little over six feet but seems shorter because he's all neck and torso. His face is round and soft, with a determined chin. He has thin, straight eyebrows and hazel eyes. He has even lips—the top and bottom match (very rare)—and a nose that suits his face; it's a strong nose, one that doesn't break where it's connected between his eyes but shoots out like a clean wedge. He has a defined jawline, which means he goes after what he wants in life and gets it. Jack Mac is dressed now, in a flannel shirt and old blue jeans. His hair is slicked down wet; in the sunlight it is gray and going. Jack Mac and I are the same age, but he looks a lot older than me. I don't think he said two words in four years of high school; he's one of those quiet types.

Mrs. Mac pours her son coffee. "Sit down, youngun," she says to him with great affection. "I was just asking Miss Ave here about the goings-on in town."

"Jack Mac ought to know more than me. After all, musicians get all the dirt."

"We do, eh?" Jack Mac says and laughs. "You're the big director, you're in charge of the flow of information."

Jack Mac is referring to my "job" (volunteer, of course) as director of our musical Outdoor Drama, *The Trail of the Lonesome Pine.* A mountain love story, or so the poster says. The Drama was put together sixteen summers ago. There's a lot of dramatic and musical talent in the area, so local leaders decided to capitalize on it. We figure tourism will be a good business alternative if the coal mining dries up. The Outdoor Drama draws audiences from all over the mid-South.

"Well, I don't want to say anything," I begin ominously, "but a certain Sweet Sue Tinsley is quite smitten with a certain picker in the pit band."

"Mercy, Jack, are you still seeing that little slip of a thing?" Mrs. Mac arches her eyebrow, annoyed.

"Mama, I'm proud to say I am," Jack says and winks at me.

"That girl is not built for heavy lifting." Mrs. Mac looks at me and sizes me up; obviously, I am a girl built for heavy lifting.

"Now, Mrs. Mac, you're just a little territorial about your only son. I'm sure you'll grow to love Sweet Sue," I say, getting off this topic. Jack Mac looks at me, relieved.

Mrs. Mac goes on a long run about some sewage problem up in the hollers that she read about in the weekly paper, the *Post*. It's hard for me to read our local paper because there are so many misspelled words in it. Spelling happens to be one of the things I'm good at, so I take notice when it isn't perfect.

As Mrs. Mac loads up the table with eggs, grits (hers are homemade pale yellow, not the store-bought kind), bacon, honey, and Lord knows what-all, Jack Mac eats. For a mountain man, he has fine manners. Delicate almost. And no matter how his mama drones on, he listens intently, like everything she says is of the utmost importance. What kind of life do the two of them have up here in Cracker's Neck? I wonder how he sneaks off to see Sweet Sue, how he maneuvers spending the night away from home, what he tells his mother. This is one of the obstacles the adult child faces while living at home with his parents. I went through it until a year ago, so I know it's hard. Maybe he goes down and stays with Sweet Sue when her kids are with their father on alternate weekends. Maybe they make love in the car on some road somewhere, like down at the Strawberry Patch, or up to Huff Rock, where the teenagers go. Or maybe they meet at a hotel over in Kingsport, Tennessee, where nobody would know them.

"Ave Maria, are we losing you?" Mrs. Mac says as she pours me coffee. I'm caught, I blush, and they both notice it.

"She's off in dreamland, Mama."

"No, uh-uh. I was thinking about the Pharmacy. You know, Fleeta gets an attitude when I stay away too long."

Jack Mac rises like a gentleman as I stand.

"No, sit down," I tell Jack, a little embarrassed by his chivalry. "Your food will get cold."

Mrs. Mac nudges Jack. "See her out, Jack."

"Thanks for the coffee. And let me know how you like that new pill Doc Daugherty put you on."

"I will, honey," Mrs. Mac says as she waves me off with her spatula. "Y'all scoot."

Jack Mac is careful to let me precede him through the doorways. At the screen door it's a little awkward because I reach for it first and so does he, and he brushes my hand. "For a coal miner, you've got mighty soft hands," I tell him. He smiles. What possessed me to blurt *that* out?

I'm on the porch now, and he stands in the doorway, his broad shoulders filling it from frame to frame. He reaches up and plucks the coil on the screen door like it's middle C.

"Not really. Touch the tips." Jack Mac extends his right hand and with his left takes my fingers and touches his fingertips to mine.

"You've got calluses."

"From the guitar."

"You've been practicing."

"Have to. Pee Wee Poteet and I have an unspoken competition. Guitar versus fiddle."

"I think you'll win."

"How do you know?"

"His wife smashed his fingers in the car door last night. I had to take him some painkillers."

"Poor old Pee Wee."

"It wasn't an accident. His wife was in a jealous rage and went after him—" I stop myself. I am telling this man confidential things. I never tell confidential things!

"I like your perfume."

"It's just residual from Iva Lou," I say, turning four shades of red gingham (the curse of pale-skinned girls).

"Well, it's mighty nice, wherever it came from." I walk down the steps into the yard. The dogs circle.

"Are any of these your actual dogs?"

Jack Mac laughs. "No. They're all wild. This time of year, when the rain stops and the leaves turn, they get scared 'cause they can't find water. They know I'm a soft touch." I look down at the dogs, and for a moment I sort of like them, with their soft eyes and pink tongues.

"You ain't scared of 'em, are you?"

"Me? No. Heck no. I'm not scared of much." I guess he doesn't see that I'm invincible, like Maureen O'Hara. As I make my way back to the Jeep, Jack Mac hollers at me.

"Hey, Ave Maria, what do you think of my new truck?"

Jack Mac points to a clearing by the shed. His 1978 Ford pickup gleams red-hot and shiny in the sun.

"It's a beauty," I holler back.

"Fully loaded."

"Can't beat that." I wave good-bye and climb into my Jeep.

As I drive back to town I'm thinking about how everything at the MacChesneys' is clean.

There's a traffic jam in the middle of town. Everybody's out doing their trading. Plus, it's due date in full on the electric and gas bills. I love town when it's busy; makes me feel like something exciting might happen. Zackie Wakin, a compact Lebanese peddler-turned-local entrepreneur, is rolling racks of clothes out onto the sidewalk in front of his store. He is small at about five feet, his complexion café au lait, his lips full (sign of generosity). I've always loved his storefront: ZACKIE'S BARGAIN STORE: CLOTHES & SUCH FOR THE ENTIRE FAMILY. And he's not kidding. He has everything from toasters to gold shoes. (I know because I needed a pair of gold shoes for a pharmaceutical-convention formal once, and he had them!)

"Miss Ave!" Zackie waves me over. (He looks like a desert sheik from the movies, but he sounds like the rest of us.)

"Another sidewalk sale?"

"You betcha. Gotta clear out for the new fall merchandise. I got Frye boots coming in big next week. You keep that in mind, will ya?"

"I'll be over for my pair," I promise. Zackie beams. The man was born to sell.

The lot at the Pharmacy is full, so I double-park in the alley and leave the keys in the Jeep in case I block anyone. I see that Iva Lou is still at the gas station, and Kent is now sitting inside the Bookmobile with her. (Progress.) I examine the exterior of my building as I enter. Paint is chipping off the window casings, the sign is fading, and half of the neon mortar and pestle is flashing pathetically. I let the place go when Mama was sick. Fortunately, my customers don't care about fancy trappings; I'm always busy.

Fleeta Mullins, my only employee and the thinnest woman in the Gap, chain-smokes behind the counter. I've never seen Fleeta without a cigarette in her hand, regardless of how many conversations we've had about smoking being bad for her. I hear the start of emphysema in her cough, but she refuses to give it up. She's only in her fifties, and her face is already wrinkled, a series of tiny pleats.

"Hi-dee, Ave Maria," she barks.

"Nice do, Fleetsie," and I mean it; she just had her hair put up.

"I copied Jeanne Pruett's upsweep." Fleeta pats the spit curls gently. "I wish I could sing like her, too."

"Singing isn't the be-all. I bet she can't name all the wrestlers on the World Federation roster."

"You got you a point there."

"Busy morning." I clear the register.

"I need to declare me some sort of moratorium on these damn fund-raising jars," Fleeta complains. "I can't hardly ring up a sale without flippin' one over."

She's right. Our counter is overrun with homemade jars that have coin slots cut into their lids. Kids bring them by from school to raise money for all sorts of things. They glue their school pictures to the front of the jar with their names and a handwritten slogan. Right now the competition is heating up for Halloween prince and princess at the grade school, and I don't like to play favorites, so anybody who makes a jar can leave one. Teena Lee Ball, a cute second-grader, stands by the register. Teena Lee looks at Fleeta and thinks better of asking her for a favor, so she turns to me.

"Miss Mulligan, my mamaw said you'd put my jar on the counter 'cause we trade here."

"Your mamaw is a smart woman, and she's got a point. It's called 'turnabout fair trade.' You put your jar on the counter. Maybe we'll raise a million dollars for your campaign!"

Teena Lee smiles and shows the space where her front teeth should be. She scoots the jar in front of the others and goes.

"You're too much of a soft touch. Let me handle them kids that come in here. If it wasn't for me, people'd run all over you all day long. I'll tell them damn kids to take their jars to the Piggly Wiggly. We ain't got the room; they do. They got three register lanes over there. We've only got the one."

I lift a jar off the counter. "Did that Coomer boy ever get his kidney?"

"I think it was in the paper that he did."

I unscrew the Coomer boy's jar and pour the coins into the March of Dimes canister.

"Lew Eisenberg wants you to come see him over to his office. And I'm quitting."

"You're kidding."

"Ave, honey, I'm sick of people. I want to set home and watch me some TV. Portly has his Black Lung comin' through. It's time to enjoy life."

Obviously, Fleeta hasn't let herself make the connection that in order to collect Black Lung benefits from the coal company, her husband has to be sick. This isn't exactly the time for celebration.

"I don't want you to go." I sound pitiful, not like a boss at all.

"You'll get over it. I ain't met nobody yet who ain't replaceable."

"It won't be the same."

"It's time for a change is all," Fleeta announces like a Greek philosopher. *Change.* Why does that word send a chill through me?

Lew Eisenberg's office is next door to the Pharmacy on Main Street. I sort of dread going in there, the place is so cluttered. Inez, Lew's wife, is also his secretary. They met when Lew came down to do some legal work for Westmoreland Coal Company. Inez had just graduated high school. They had a romance and she got pregnant. Lew did the right thing and married her. (Well, the right thing for Inez, that is.)

"He's inside," Inez says without looking up. Inez still has a pretty face, but she has gained about a hundred pounds since they married. It's been frustrating for her, since she was known for her gorgeous figure when she was a cheerleader. Now she's always on a diet. She's tried Metracal shakes; AYDS, the reducing-plan candy; and Figurine Wafers (I carry all flavors)—nothing has done the trick.

Lew sits behind his desk, smoking a cigarette. His round pumpkin head looks large atop his thin frame. He has small brown eyes behind thick glasses and a space between his front teeth (the Chinese call these lucky teeth). I haven't seen the space recently; Lew rarely smiles.

"Coffee or tea or something?" Lew asks. He always sounds agitated, but it doesn't make him unpleasant. You can see he's a sweetie underneath.

"No thanks." Lew looks relieved that I don't want anything; the less contact with Inez, the better. He closes the door and sits in the chair next to me. He has never done that. "We need to talk." He is quiet for a few seconds, but it seems much longer. He stands and paces. "I finished up your mother's paperwork. Her will. The house, the Pharmacy, the life insurance—all that goes to you. Essentially, my job is done. Except for one thing." He stands at the window, flicking the blinds.

A floorboard creaks outside the office door, sounding like two hundred tiptoeing pounds. We look at each other. Lew turns on the radio for privacy—Inez has a reputation for snooping—and sits down next to me again. "There's a letter."

Lew gives me a large manila envelope. It is addressed to me in care of Lewis Eisenberg. In the upper left-hand corner it says, "From Fiametta Vilminore Mulligan." I'm one of those folks who opens her mail as she stands at the mailbox, so I rip into the envelope immediately and unfold the letter. I see my mother's handwriting. (The letter is written in English; I assume it's because Lew would have needed to read it, too.)

My dear Ave Maria,

    When you read this letter, I will have left you. There are things I could never tell you about myself. Many times, I tried. But then, I would think better of unburdening myself and stay quiet. The first thing I want you to know is that you are the best thing that ever happened to me.

At this point, my heart is pounding so hard it's moving the buttons on my shirt. I look over at Lew, who is now lying down on the floor, smoking and staring up at the ceiling.

"Did you read this, Lew?"

"Yup. Don't mind me, my back's out."

When I was seventeen, I was a very happy girl. I worked as a seamstress in my father's shop in Bergamo. My mother was beautiful, and my father a very respected man. A boy used to stop by the shop, his name was Mario Barbari. He came from a good family from Schilpario, a small town in the mountains. He was quite handsome and made me laugh. One time, my father had business in Schilpario. I begged him to let me ride along. I hoped I would see Mario, and as luck would have it, I did. Once he took care of business, Papa decided to stay in Schilpario and play cards. Mario offered to show me the town. He showed me the church, the waterwheel, the school. I felt like I had known him all of my life. I fell in love with him that day.

"May I have some water, please?" I swallow hard. Inez enters with water. Lew and I look at each other. Inez goes.

Mario came down to Bergamo to see me. My father found out about our friendship and forbade me to see him because I was too young to court. I did what no good daughter would do: I defied him and would sneak out to see Mario. I was so happy whenever I was with him. We shared such good, happy times. I knew I wanted to spend my life with him. We made a plan to run away together. He was to meet me at the Bergamo station and we would take the first train to Milan. I waited and waited but he never came. A courier arrived with a letter from him explaining that he could not meet me that day. I was going to tell Mario that I was expecting you so we could marry immediately. I am sure that he was not suspicious of my condition or he would have kept our appointment.

I knew that I must leave my home or the shame of what I had done would never be resolved. I remembered that we had a cousin in Lake Maggiore. I bought a ticket to go there, hopeful she would take me in. When I arrived in Lake Maggiore, I could not find my cousin. I had no place to go. My heart was broken. But I thought of you. I had to take care of you. Then, something very lucky happened to me. I returned to the train station. Everyone rushing around, having somewhere to go, comforted me. I sat alone on a bench. I fell asleep. When I woke up, a beautiful lady was sitting next to me. I will never forget what she looked like. She was tall, slim, and wore a blue coat. The buttons were blue jewels. And on her head was a hat, exquisite blue velvet with peacock feathers and tiny gold stars. Her face was creamy pink; she smelled like garden flowers. She offered me a sweet roll. I was so hungry, I took it. She said, "Now, my dear, what shall we do?" "I have no place to go," I said to her. "But of course you do. You're coming with me. I am going to America. You will stay with me. And when we get there, we will find you a position." I was so afraid. But this woman smiled at me and I knew we would be all right.

I am crying. Lew stands and stretches. He comes over to me, puts a limp hand on my shoulder, and pats me like an old dog.

I asked the beautiful lady what her name was. She said, "Ave Maria Albricci." I told her that she had a beautiful name and she laughed. She thought it too ornate. I told her when I had my baby I would name her Ave Maria. She laughed again. She asked me how I knew I was going to have a girl. I told her I just knew. The ride on the ship was lovely. Ave Maria had a beautiful cabin. Servants laid our clothes out. The food was plentiful, even with the war on; I felt you healthy and happy inside of me. Four weeks passed and we arrived in New York City. Ave Maria's relatives greeted us at the port. We took the train to Hoboken, New Jersey. Ave Maria bought the *Italia Oggi,* the newspaper. We read the want ads. In those days, immigrants were cheap labor and would work in exchange for room and board. "What is Virginia?" I asked the Albriccis. They laughed. I responded to the ad: "SEAMSTRESS WANTED: MINING TOWN: BIG STONE GAP, VIRGINIA. GOOD PAY."

Mama had taped the actual ad to the back of the letter to verify her story.

I knew this job was a good opportunity. I wrote a letter. The gentleman that placed the ad owned a dress shop in the town. He hired me immediately based upon my letter. By chance, his friend, a merchant from Big Stone Gap, was in New York City on a buying trip. His name was Fred Mulligan, of the Mutual Pharmacy. Would I like an escort on the trip to Virginia? I was so happy. Fred Mulligan took the train to meet me. I was surprised. He was young, like me. He understood Italian, having studied it at the University of Virginia. I liked him. He told me later that for him it was love at first sight. In truth, he suspected my condition and knew it would be easier on me if I was married. I agreed to marry him. It was an arranged marriage; I arranged it.

I never heard from Ave Maria Albricci again. I sent many letters to her family in Hoboken through the years; all were returned. I prayed for her every day of my life, though, never forgetting her kindness. Whenever I spoke your name, I thought of her and how she helped me. She was an angel.

I felt you should know the truth. I hope I made the right decision in telling you this. I asked Mr. Eisenberg to be present with you. I love you, my darling girl.

Mama

I turn the envelope upside down and shake it to make sure I haven't missed anything. A small, square lace-edged black-and-white photograph falls into my lap. In gold letters it says, "Ti Amo, Mario." On the back, in my mother's handwriting, "Mario da Schilpario Italia 1942." The picture fits in my palm. The man in the picture looks to be about seventeen. He has black hair and a trim physique. He is laughing. This is my father.

Inez stands in the doorway. "Ave, they need you up to the school. There's been an incident." The floorboards creak as Inez ambles toward me.

"Ave, you need to get up to the school. Principal called." Lew's voice brings me back to earth. "They need the Rescue Squad."

Besides being a pharmacist, I am chief of the Rescue Squad. Doc Daugherty roped me into the job a couple of years back. We're a volunteer emergency-response team—the team is the fire chief, Spec Broadwater, and me. We handle everything from car wrecks to removing buttons from kids' noses, and once we even resuscitated Faith Cox's cat.

"Spec's outside waiting fer you," Inez says, a touch too impatiently.

Spec is wedged into the driver's seat of Rescue Squad Unit One, a white station wagon with bright orange trim. I don't know why he's called Spec; he is the opposite of a speck, he's a giant, the tallest man in the Gap, at six feet seven. I climb into the car. Fleeta runs out of the Pharmacy and hands me my emergency kit through the window. Spec steps on the gas so fast, Fleeta practically loses her hand. I hear her curse at Spec in the distance as we pull away. Spec shoves a blue siren onto the roof of the car through the driver's-side window.

"Problem up to the school." Spec offers me a cigarette. I must look like I need one. My face is puffy from crying.

"It's bad for you, Spec."

"Self-medication. When they come up with a healthy way for me to calm my nerves, I'll quit."

Powell Valley High School is a stylish, brand-new redbrick structure that sits back off the main road, in a wide field. It is the jewel of this town, built with monies from the War on Poverty of the late 1960s. Spec ignores all traffic laws and careens up the circular driveway in the wrong direction.

"Problem's in the West Wing," he explains.

The principal, Dale Herron, meets us in front of the school. The kids call him Lurch. I sort of see why—he's slope-shouldered and his head juts forward. Lurch leads us inside to a rest room marked BOYS. The building is dead quiet.

"Where are the students?" I ask.

"In the auditorium," the principal says. "Miss Mulligan, I think you ought to wait out here."

"I'll handle it," Spec says, patting me like a Pekinese.

The men disappear into the rest room. A few moments pass. I hear mumbling from the lavatory. Finally, the two men emerge.

"Let's go," Lurch says, pointing toward the assembly down the hall.

We follow the angry principal into the auditorium. Every seat is filled. The teachers line the side aisles like guards. There are some whispers but not many. Onstage is a lectern and two students squirming in chairs: the student-body president, a young man with a long Renaissance curl, and the chaplain, a pudgy girl with thick glasses. Lurch takes the stage.

"Good afternoon, students. That greeting right there is for the ninety-eight percent of you who are law-abiding kids. I'll get to the remaining two percent here in a minute. I have called this emergency assembly to alert y'all that there is a sicko among us. There is a sign outside this door which reads, UNITED WE STAND, DIVIDED WE FALL. The hijinks and shenanigans of a small percentage of us will cause the whole to suffer. To fall. Mike. Brownie. Bring up the evidence."

Two young men rise from their front-row seats and disappear backstage. They enter sheepishly from the wings. Mike is a small platinum blond. I recognize him as the point guard on our championship basketball team. The other kid is mousy; his diminutive name suits him. They carry a large tarp between them.

"Dump it," the principal barks.

The boys dump the contents of the tarp. White ceramic chunks hit the stage with a clatter, making a cloud of dust. An intact toilet seat tumbles out, confirming my suspicions.

"This is what someone setting right here in this auditorium has done. Destroyed school property. Committed a crime with evil intent. How? By rigging a sophisticated round of cherry bombs to a ter-let in the boys' rest room in the West Wing."

A few nervous giggles escape the student body.

"This is no joke, people." Lurch searches the audience for the gigglers. Then he pauses. He pounds the podium. "Some unfortunate young man might have been sitting on that ter-let when it blew to high heaven. I ask you, what would have happened then?"

"Jesus," Spec says under his breath.

"Anybody actually injured?" I whisper.

Spec ignores me.

"I'm scared," a familiar deep voice says behind me.

"You should be," I whisper back. "The teacher's lounge is next."

"Dinner tonight? After the show?"

"I'd love to."

The deep voice, and now my date for the evening, is my best friend, the band and choral director of Powell Valley High School, Theodore Tipton, formerly of Scranton, Pennsylvania. Every once in a while the mines or the school will hire someone from the outside world. Inevitably, they move in and shake things up. Theodore brought our band back to life and simultaneously goosed the libidos of all the women in town. ("He's a humdinger," Iva Lou says with relish every time she sees him. "The man makes a pair of Levi's sing.") Theodore also stars as Preacher Red Fox in the Outdoor Drama. We became friends when he auditioned nine years ago and I cast him on the first round. I had to. His face reading told me that he was loyal and true and fiercely protective. I knew if I cast him we would spend lots of time together, and we have. His face is square-shaped, with a defined jaw. He has a firm chin with a dimple in it. He can look strong, like an Irish pirate, or intellectual, like a preoccupied poet. He is tall, with blue eyes and a red beard. Even though all the available women in town chase him (and a few married ones, too), he spends all of his spare time with me. We're "feriners"—even though I was born here, I'm considered a feriner because my mother was one—but that's just the start of what we have in common.

The principal wraps up the assembly with a couple more threats for the student body. If the guilty party doesn't fess up, he promises to suspend the smoking areas outside. This brings a groan from the students. The chaplain places a shoe box marked ANONYMOUS on the podium. Lurch tells the kids it will be placed in the gym so anyone with tips regarding the toilet incident can leave them in there. He dismisses the assembly. The student body rises. As the kids exit in an orderly fashion, most of them acknowledge Theodore. He is popular and respected, the perfect reputation for a teacher.

Only one student stops to speak to me: Pearl Grimes, fifteen years old, a sweet mountain girl with a weight problem. She often window-shops at the Mutual. I walk down the hall with my arm around her.

"My skin's done broke out agin." Pearl hangs her head sadly.

"I got something for that. Come by the Mutual and see me."

"All right." She shrugs. She doesn't believe me.

"Don't you know the more pimples you got now, the less wrinkles you'll have later?"

Finally, Pearl smiles. Her face, heart-shaped, with a high forehead, tells me that she is emotional yet fair. Her nose is small and turns up slightly. Her cheeks are full and round—the cheeks of a monarch—which means she can handle power.

Pearl blends off into the sea of students. Theodore takes my arm.

"I'll walk you to your car."

"Sure."

"What's new?"

"I'm a bastard."

Theodore laughs, which gets me laughing too. "Did you bust a shoplifter or something?"

"No. I didn't behave like a bastard. I mean the literal definition."

"What?"

"I settled Mama's will today. She left me a letter. Fred Mulligan wasn't my father." Theodore is surprised but remains cool for my benefit. He knows everything about Fred Mulligan and me. When I shared all those stories, Theodore always got a look like he'd kill anyone who hurt me. This new information surprises him.

Theodore leads me out the front entrance to the car. Spec sits behind the wheel.

"Get in, Ave," Spec grumbles, lighting a cigarette. "That was a waste of my time."

"See you tonight," Theodore says as he closes the door. He touches my cheek. I look up to the second-floor science lab. Pearl Grimes stands in the window, watching us. From here, in the mellow afternoon light, she has a regal countenance, like a queen looking down on her subjects. I give her a quick wave good-bye. She smiles.

CHAPTER TWO

On top of everything else, my roof leaks. It needs to be patched, and fast. The town handymen are a pair of brothers, Otto and Worley Olinger. They drive an open flatbed truck around town and pick up people's discards. Some days you'll see them with a wringer washing machine strapped to the back of the truck; another day it'll be a couple of railroad ties and a stuffed bear head. In some parts they're known as the Are Y'all Using That? Brothers because that's how they greet you when they want something from your yard.

Otto appears to be the older of the two. He is short-legged and sturdy, with gray hair and a few teeth left on the bottom. He has a distinctive nose—it has a shelf on the upper bridge, which indicates he's good with money. Worley has thick red hair and is tall and lean. His long face matches his long body. Nobody in town is exactly sure how old they are because they did not matriculate through the school system. But they seem to have been around forever.

I join them up on my roof. I manage a Thermos of coffee and a few fresh ham biscuits for the boys.

"Time for a break, gentlemen," I say as I crawl toward them.

"Miss Ave, you afraid of heights?"

"Uh-huh." I try not to look down as I answer.

Worley extends his hand to me. "Don't be. We won't let you fall. Anyhow, the ground is soft. I fell off the post office when we was fixin' an exhaust fan. Landed on my head. It weren't so bad."

"That's a lie," Otto says. "I caught you."

"How bad is my roof, boys?"

"I seen worse," Otto decides.

"I let everything around here go to hell when Mama was sick."

"It happens." Worley shrugs.

"I should be able to keep y'all busy through the winter."

"We need the work. We'll do a good job for ye," Otto promises.

There is a long silence. I've never been on my roof. I can see pretty far. Fall has definitely moved in. The treetops look like orange and red feathers to the edge of town. I wish I had brought Mama out here. She would have loved being able to see so far. I check the pocket of my overalls for her letter. I manage to carry it everywhere with me, even though I don't need to. (I've read it so many times that I've memorized it.) I wish she had left instructions. Why did she tell me this story? Did she want me to try and find Mario da Schilpario? Or did she just want me to know so I would understand Fred Mulligan? So much to think about.

"If I had a roof like this, I'd set up here all the day," Worley announces.

"My brother don't like workin'."

"Naw, I don't. I like sleepin' and eatin'. Workin' wears me out. Wind up all tarred and ferget how I spent the day."

"That's how I feel after a day of counting pills."

"Ye ought to git murried, Miss Ave. Womens ain't supposed to work like 'at."

"Otto, I ain't husband hunting. And I like my job. Okay?" I say this flatly; inquiries regarding my marital status are an everyday thing for me. Folks always want to let me know—even though I'm not married—that I'm okay, certainly nice enough to have a husband.

"Ye oughtn't wait too long to git murried. Git set in your ways and then nobody'll want you."

"What if they like my set ways?"

"She's done got a point there, Otto," his brother says.

"You ever been in love, Worley?"

"No, ma'am."

"How about you, Otto?"

Otto doesn't answer.

"Otto was sweet on a girl once. You was, brother. You was!"

"Keeping secrets from me, Otto?"

"No, ma'am."

"Do tell, then."

"I done had me a true love, but it was many, many years ago. Well, it was summer. I was 'bout fifteen. Mama done made me go to town fer jars. She was canning her some chow chow. Walkin' down, I passed a trailer. Lot of kids runnin' around. Their people, I could just tell, was Melungeon. They had that dark color, and that look of them. There was a girl there. She had her some black hair, shiny and straight in braids. I 'member thinkin' that the braids look like them garlands over the bank door. They was that long. And she had her some black eyes like coal. And she was small. Tiny, like a matchbox? Reminded me of that storybook about the fairy girl."

"Thumbelina?"

"Yeah. Thumbelina."

"What was your girl's name?"

"Destry." Otto looks away at the mention of her name. "Best name I ever heard," he says quietly.

"So what happened?"

"The summer passed. And pert near every day she walked with me. I grew to like 'at and look forward to it. One day she couldn't go with me, and I missed her bad. I knew then that I loved her. Turned out her pappy moved their trailer over to Stonega. I walked over there about five miles. I done had something to give her. My mama had a little silver ring with a red stone in it. And I loved Destry so much, I stole it and give it to her."

"How do you like 'at!" Worley said, laughing.

"You must have loved her very much to steal for her."

"That I did, ma'am. That I did."

"Mama done whooped the tar out of Otto when she found out. Beat him with a switch till it snapped in two."

"Yup, and then Daddy done came home and beat me, too." Otto reaches into his pocket. He pulls out a wad of paper crumbles, nails, and a five-dollar bill. He sifts through the stuff and pulls out the tiny silver ring. He gives it to me.

"Go ahead. Try it on."

I put the ring on my finger.

"For a big girl, you got little fingers," Worley observes.

"What a beautiful ring."

"Thank you, ma'am."

"Where is Destry now?"

"She died." Otto sighs.

"That's the sad part of the story," Worley says. He looks at his brother with great feeling.

"Yes, ma'am. She died. Melungeons git all sorts of things—they catch just about anything that's out there, and they're weak, so it tends to take 'em. She was sixteen when she died. I wanted to murry her, but she was too sick."

"Why do the Melungeons die like 'at?" Worley asks.

"Well, the theory is that there's a lot of inbreeding there. Up in the mountains, folks didn't mix with the general population. And that hurt them. Because the more of a mix you get, the stronger the blood. Or so the doctors believe."

"Where do they come from?"

"*Melungeon* comes from the French word *mélange*. It means 'mixed.' "

"I thought the Melungeons were them folks from the Lost Colony down in North Carolina."

"That's another theory."

"What's the Lost Colony?" Worley asks.

"Ye tell him, Miss Ave," Otto says.

"I think the Lost Colony was more of a tale told in the hills rather than actual fact. But the story goes that settlers from England landed on the North Carolina coast near Virginia. The ship dropped them off with supplies, and they built a colony. There was a fort, gardens, little houses, a church—things were going well. But when the ships returned from England a year later, the colony was a ghost town. Beds were made. Books were on shelves. Clothes were hanging in the closets. But no people. The people had vanished. They looked for them but never found them. There was only one clue: the word *Croatan* was carved on a tree. Some believe that a settler carved that before he was kidnapped away by the Indians. It's just a guess, though. So, a Melungeon could be a person who descends from a mix of the settlers and Indians, who hid here in these hills and never left. Your Destry could have been a descendant of those people."

"Well, all I know is I never loved no other." Otto says this with such clarity, I know it is true.

The three of us sit and drink our coffee. We're all thinking about little Destry. Otto had the real thing and lost it. I hope someday my heart will open up and have a love like that.

The open-air amphitheater for *The Trail of the Lonesome Pine* Drama was built next door to the home of the only famous person to ever come from this town, the author John Fox, Jr., who wrote the book that inspired our play. Mr. Fox was a talented loner who lived with his mother and sister. His book of 1908, *The Trail of the Lonesome Pine,* was the best-selling novel in the United States prior to *Gone with the Wind.* It's the first fact you're told on the tour of the Fox home. The town turned their home into a gift shop, where you can buy key chains, postcards, and corn-husk dolls. Next to it is the theater, and next door to the theater is the original one-room schoolhouse from John Fox, Jr.'s childhood. The state funds to refurbish it haven't come through, so you can't go inside, just look through the window. The tour buses roll in to the cul-de-sac, and it sort of landlocks the audience to spend money. Visitors peruse the gift shop and eat at the Kiwanis Club sloppy-joe stand during intermission.

I love the Drama because growing up I spent most of my summers backstage. Mama designed and sewed all the costumes for the show. There was always something needing mending or replacing, so Mama and I would walk over and tend to the problem. I always loved theater people, even though I was a little scared of them with their elaborate wigs, long black eyelashes, and bright red cheeks. The cast was always nice to me, and once they even let me come onstage with them in the finale. I never forgot the excitement of those footlights, the torches that lit the back wall and the cluster of musicians in the sawdust orchestra pit downstage. It only stood to reason that someday I would grow up and help out. Mazie Dinsmore, the grande dame director of the first season, a tugboat of a woman with the vision of Cecil B. De-Mille, spotted me early on and taught me how to direct. I served as her prompter (the girl who crouches offstage and feeds lines to the actors who forget where they are or what to say). This was an important job because more than one of our lead actors was known to hit the Old Grand-Dad before and during a performance. One night I fed a tipsy Cory Tress his line and he looked at me in the wings and said, "What?" He got a huge laugh. But those sorts of flubs are rare. We're amateurs, but we do take the Drama seriously. There was another night when a flat of scenery painted to indicate a drawing room in a Kentucky Bluegrass mansion started to teeter and was about to fall. I slipped onto the stage and grabbed it before it crushed the actors. Mazie never forgot that. She felt I had the stomach for directing. I never panicked. She thought that was one of the most important attributes in a director.

Backstage at the Drama there is always a disorganized cacophony of kids running around, musical-instrument warm-ups, dancers doing their stretches, and actors running their lines. Tonight is closing night, the last show of our season. It's a free performance for the families and friends of the cast and crew, so it's standing room only. Nerves run high when we're putting on the show for the town; somehow, performing for strangers is easier.

The play is about a mountain girl named June Tolliver who falls in love with John Hale, a coal inspector from Kentucky. He takes this wildcat girl and sends her to the Bluegrass to be refined and educated by his aristocratic sister, Helen. When she returns to her mountains after having the Pygmalion pulled on her, she doesn't fit in. In fact, she is too cultured for John Hale, who cannot believe what a lady she has become. They get past all that, though, and admit they've loved each other all along. It's a classic story, and it gets the audience every single time. My favorite moment in the play is in the first act, when June's father, Devil Judd Tolliver, finds out that John Hale is in love with his fifteen-year-old daughter. He tries to blow the coal inspector's head off. The lines go:

> DEVIL JUDD: My Juney is too young for ye.
> JOHN HALE: She won't always be fifteen, sir. I'll wait.

The actual blocking has been handed down for years, so all I do is say, "You go here," "You stand there," "Look surprised when the gun goes off," and "No chewing gum." I just follow the instructions from Mazie's promptbook. (When she died she willed it to the John Fox, Jr., Museum.) Any of the special touches we owe to Mazie Dinsmore and her theatrical vision. She put actual gunfire into the show and added the preshow of roving bluegrass musicians and singers to entertain the audience before curtain. The preshow has set us apart from all the other outdoor dramas on the circuit. Audiences love the traditional bluegrass music, and of course, they can't wait to see our world-famous backdrop: a painting, the size of half a football field, that is an exact replica of the mountain view you see behind it. It's a dazzler at twilight, when you're sitting in the audience and you see a painting of the actual vista from your seat.

The hardest part of directing is the scheduling. Because we are not professionals, everybody has a job or two outside of the Drama. I've got musicians who are coal miners and work the hoot-owl shift (midnight to lunch), teachers who are busy all day, farmers who work weekends. It's a juggling act, but it is the most fun I've ever had. I love mountain music—the Celtic Scotch-Irish sound of regret, low wailing tunes like "Barbara Allen" and "Poor Wayfaring Stranger." I always thought I loved that music because of Fred Mulligan. He was Scotch-Irish. The music was our one connection, the only mutual thing we loved. Now I must let go of that, too.

Theodore enters from stage right in full costume and beard. He crosses downstage, jumps off the lip, and comes toward me with a look of concern on his face. We have a powwow about the gizmo that leaks fake blood from his chest (he gets shot at the end of the play). Pearl Grimes is my props department, so she listens in.

My stage manager waves a clipboard in my face. "Miss Mulligan, we're ready to open the house." He calls off, "Dancers! Positions, please." The dancers take the stage. By day they are majorettes with the high school marching band, under Theodore's capable direction. Majorettes are the prettiest girls in school, even ahead of cheerleaders. Let's face it: Twirling takes skill; cheering only takes volume. By night, they're my dancers, providing storytelling through movement.

I have no twirling in the Drama, although the majorette captain, Tayloe Slagle, lobbied hard to incorporate it. I explained that historical accuracy is the entire point of doing the Drama. I don't see a bunch of mountain folk from 1895 twirling batons in the middle of a hoedown.

Tayloe enters from the stage-right wings. She takes her mark at center stage, owning it like it's the only pin dot in the universe. Bo Caudill, the follow-spot operator, widens the beam of light from her perfect face to include her body—shapely, bursting in ripe perfection in a simple red dress with a scoop neck and ruffles.

Tayloe is compact but leggy, like all the great movie stars. She has a well-formed, large head with a clear, high forehead set off by smooth, small features: a prominent but straight nose (like Miriam Hopkins), blond hair (like Veronica Lake), and wet eyes (like Bette Davis). Her right eyebrow is always slightly raised in a delicate swirl, giving me the impression she is skeptical of anything she is told.

Tayloe plays June Tolliver, the ingenue lead, the coarse mountain girl who transforms into a Kentucky lady. Tayloe won the role because she has true star quality. It cannot be invented. But it sure doesn't keep every other girl in town from trying to develop That Certain Something. We have girls who practice their footwork, suffer hours of vocal coaching, and diet down to pool-cue thin, but what they don't understand is that this luminescence is inborn and unteachable, and Tayloe's got it. All any good director has to do is exploit the obvious, so we incorporated a dream ballet into the second act, featuring Tayloe in a pale pink leotard and a wee chiffon skirt. Tickets flew out of the box office.

She's our starlet, so all the girls seek her approval and imitate her. Tayloe gives them a standard, a marker by which to judge themselves. Other skills and attributes can be appreciated and duly noted, but beauty is instantly obvious to all. I have never met a girl (including myself) who did not long to be beautiful, who did not pray for her own potential to reveal itself. When a girl is beautiful, she gets to pick—she never has to wait for someone to choose her. There is so much power in doing the choosing.

Pearl Grimes touches my arm. "I think I got a better way for the blood to spurt. I'm gonna rig a tube down Mr. Tipton's pant leg so he can step hard when he's shot."

The summer of 1978 will forever be remembered as the summer of wily stagecraft. No matter what technique we've tried—and we even called the folks up in New York City to find out how they do it—we have not been able to get Theodore shot on cue. Either the blood spurts too soon or too late. Either way, it destroys the authenticity of the moment.

"Did Mr. Tipton like your idea?"

"He's mighty impatient."

"Most great artists are, you know. Michelangelo said, 'Genius is eternal patience.' "

"Do you think Mr. Tipton's a genius?"

"Genius or not, we gotta get him shot correctly so he can die at the end of the play. It's the last show of the season. Wouldn't it be nice to go out with the right bang?"

"Yes, ma'am."

Poor old Pearl; what she's got, Tayloe is missing. She's got the thin brown hair, the thick ankles, and the weight problem. Pearl has beautiful hands, though. Pretty-faced girls usually have ugly hands. But then again, I don't know a lot of people who notice hands.

"Tayloe sure does look pretty," Pearl decides as she stands there.

"Yeah."

"That costume is mighty tight."

I'm thinking that I would never wear that dress myself. That's the difference between me and Pearl: She still has the dream of wearing it.

"She's stuck-up, though," Pearl zings.

I let the comment pass. It doesn't do me any good to try to convince Pearl that beauty comes from within and that age will eventually wither a pretty face. I get a pain in my left temple watching poor Pearl looking up on the stage at Tayloe like there is some answer up there. She is hoping that beauty will be truth. But that observation was surely made by the father of a very beautiful daughter, not Pearl's and surely not mine. Tayloe is conceited. But so what? Tayloe, not Pearl, is in the beam of the spotlight. Tayloe, not Pearl, is being examined and appreciated from all sides like a rare ruby. How Pearl wishes she was The One! Of course, I could lie. I could tell Pearl that being the prettiest girl in town is no great shakes, but eventually she would find out the truth. When you're fifteen, it is everything. And when you're thirty-five, it's still something. Beauty is the fat yellow line down the middle of Powell Valley Road. And it's best to figure out—and the sooner the better—which side you fall on, because if you don't do it for yourself, the world will. Why wait for the judgment?

Pearl squints at the stage and breathes the night air slowly like a drag off a cigarette. She is trying so hard to understand, trying to un-derstand why Tayloe and not her.

"Maybe you ought to check your prop table. Curtain's almost up," I remind her.

Pearl straightens up and goes backstage with a purpose. Having a purpose is the little secret of the nonpretties. Something to do always beats something to look at.

The cast looks terrific onstage. They've worked five shows a week all summer, yet they still have pep. They're still excited about doing the show. I'll spare you the details of the auditions and casting that take place every year from March till June. Let's just say it is highly com-petitive. Nothing like the theater to bring out the claws and pepper in people. Folks want the part they want and that's it. Never mind they're the wrong age, or can't sing, or can't dance. They'd leave notes on my

Jeep, call me at home, give me gifts of cakes and jellies—anything to sway me. I can't imagine the competition on Broadway itself could be any more brutal than it is right here. Thank goodness there are parts that actors grow into: Li'l Bub becomes Big Bub, who can then play Dave Tolliver, then, as he ages, Bad Rufe, all the way to the patriarch, Devil Judd. We've been doing the show so long, the cast members know each other's lines. We never have an understudy problem.

We do have an annoying stage mother: Betty Slagle. Tayloe's mom caused me so much grief with her many suggestions—of course all of them showing off her daughter to full advantage and forsaking the story—that I put her on the costume crew. She's busy pressing pants now, so she stays off my back.

I signal the Foxes to open the house. The Foxes are our women's auxiliary group named in honor of John Fox, Jr. (of course). They run the ticket sales, the concessions, and the rug-loom demonstration at the Fox Museum during intermission. They're a clique of young 'n' sexy divorcées and single girls. There's a sorority feeling to their activities. And they keep the history alive, so their form-fitting T-shirts say.

I cue the band to begin the overture. Jack Mac winks at me; I wink back. Now we have a secret—I've seen him in his underwear—and it's kind of fun. He nods to his boys, and they play. I'm always thrilled by the sound of those strings, mandolins so simple and clear. The soft melody sails over the outdoor theater and spills out into the dark. I take my place on the perch next to Bo's follow spot on the back wall. No matter how many times I've watched the show, I still get nervous before Curtain. I look down as the audience filters in. Iva Lou Wade comes in with a nice-looking man I've never seen before. (Where does she find them?) She wears a flowy mint-green pant set that makes her look like a Greek goddess. The gold armband completes the effect. She grins at me and I wave.

Our final show comes off without a hitch. The foot-stomp-blood-spurt cure that Pearl came up with worked (thank God). The show was perfect until Li'l Bub pulled a closing-night prank. When Theodore was shot, he threw a rubber chicken onto the stage. The crowd went wild. Theodore was not amused. After three standing ovations, Bo shines a light on me and I am motioned to the stage by my cast. Two chorus boys help me up onto the stage. Tayloe whistles through her teeth in approval. How funny that looks, as she is dressed in her Kentucky-society finale gown. I embrace each of our four leads. Then I pull Pearl from backstage. I give her a big hug for her stroke of genius, and she beams. Then I give my usual "thank you for the best season yet" speech. Sweet Sue Tinsley, president of the Foxes, walks across the stage with a bottle of champagne and presents it to me.

Sweet Sue is my age, and she was the Tayloe Slagle of our day. She is still as pretty as a teenager, small and blond, with vivid blue eyes. She's as popular now as she was in high school (accomplishment). She wasn't born with that name, though. There were three Sues in our first-grade class. The teacher got confused, so she gave each of them nicknames, which stuck. There was Tall Sue, Li'l Bit Sue, and this one, our Sweet Sue.

"A-vuh Maria, this bubbly is from the Foxes with our compliments. You're the best gosh-darned dye-rector anywhere ever on earth, and we appreciate your work so very much!" Loud applause for Sweet Sue fills the air, and enough wolf whistles cut through to conjure a Miss America pageant. For a moment I consider correcting Sweet Sue on the pronunciation of my name: It isn't A-vuh Maria like Ava Gardner, it's Ave like a prayer. Sweet Sue has been mispronouncing my name since first grade. Is she ever going to get it right? I decide to let it go when I look out over the crowd and see their warm and smiling faces. This isn't the time to be petty. I realize the pause after Sweet Sue's speech has gone on too long. Her eyes implore me to say something. And fast. She has that frozen smile and certain impatience that all pretty girls possess. *Your turn,* she seems to be saying with her eyes.

I blurt, "Thank you kindly, Sweet Sue. And thank you, Foxes." Sweet Sue is relieved as I accept the champagne.

"Hey, boys, how 'bout a song for Sweet Sue, the prettiest gal in town?" shouts our drummer from the pit.

"Thank you, boys," Sweet Sue says magnanimously. Then she leans into the pit and kisses Jack Mac long and hard. The crowd cheers. Then a chorus of "Ask her, Jack! Ask her, Jack!" The band pushes Jack Mac out of the pit, onto the stage. Wanda Brickey, who plays the mountain matriarch in the Drama, bangs the floor with her walking stick. "Jack Mac, if you don't marry this girl, it don't make a lick of sense."

The crowd calms down and waits for Jack's response. "Folks, y'all know I'm a private person—"

Before he can finish, Sweet Sue pipes up, "The answer is yes. Yes!" She kisses Jack Mac all over the face. She shouts, "I love this man!" Her sons, still in mountain-boy costume, run up to the stage. The crowd cheers. The cold bottle of champagne I hold seems as though it's in the wrong hands all of a sudden. So I make a stage-right cross and hand it to Jack Mac.

"Congratulations!" I say happily. The crowd goes wild.

Jack Mac leans into my ear and says, "Thank you."

I look at him. "Call your mother."

"Yes, ma'am." Jack Mac kisses my cheek. Sweet Sue grabs him away. "Hey, Ava, he's mine. Find your own man!"

The crowd laughs; it's one of those long, rolling laughs. Now, when you're the town spinster, jokes of this sort aren't one bit funny. Around here, being married makes you a prize. No one has claimed me, and although it shouldn't hurt me, it does. I could cry. Instead, I bend forward and laugh louder than anyone in the house.

Theodore, as if on cue, comes up behind me and puts his hands around my waist. Then he announces, "She has a man, Sweet Sue." I look up at Theodore, the most beautiful man I have ever seen. I lean against him.

"Well, I didn't mean to . . ." Sweet Sue stutters. Jack Mac cues the band, gracefully saving his girlfriend's face. He shrugs at me.

Theodore takes me in his arms to dance. The music fills the theater. Somebody's singing the lyrics, but all I hear is Theodore's voice saying, "She has a man! She has a man!" onstage, in public, and loudly for all to hear! He looks down at me and smiles. I feel wanted, claimed, and—I can't believe it—alluring. Instead of looking off as we dance, I look into his eyes, and they are as blue as the sky on the backdrop.

And then we stop. Theodore kisses me. It's not the usual friendly kiss I have become accustomed to all of these years. So at first I don't lock in. I'm confused. Then his lips, wordless and soft, persist. My spine turns from rivets of bone into a velvet ribbon spinning off its wheel and pooling onto the floor. I hold on to him like Myrna Loy did Clark Gable when they jumped out of a two-seater plane in *Test Pilot.* My waist is on a swivel as he dips me. But the kiss doesn't end. Moments later, when it does, my body feels like it is full of goose feathers. Theodore holds my face while everyone dances around us, offering looks of approval.

"You need lipstick," he says, squinting at me.

"You don't." I dab the Really Red I left there off of his face. We laugh. It's one of those shared moments that can only come between two people who know each other so well that it borders on irony. Theodore pulls me close. I rest my head on his shoulder. He smells fresh, a mix of peppermint and spice. I look across the dance floor. Iva Lou gives me a thumbs-up.

"Let's get out of here," Theodore says with an urgency I've never heard before. He takes my hand and yanks me off the stage, and I skip down the stairs behind him.

Nellie Goodloe, president of the Lonesome Pine Arts and Crafts Guild, stops us. "Mr. Tipton, I need to speak to you about candidate John Warner's visit to the Gap."

"We were just leaving," Theodore says firmly. Nellie turns to me.

"Ave Maria, tell him this is important," she says.

"It can wait," Theodore tells her with finality.

"It can't wait. I got a call from John Warner's press person, and they want a confirmation that the town is going to go all out for his campaign stump through Southwestern Virginia."

Nellie's mouth keeps moving, but I can't hear her. Her lips and hair are orange, and she has placed her hand on Theodore's chest. John Warner is married to Elizabeth Taylor of *National Velvet* fame, and they're coming to town and Nellie wants Theodore to put together a tribute salute in her honor. The town wants to show off its best asset: the Powell Valley High School marching band. They want a doozy of a halftime show. I can't contemplate all this right now. After tonight my life as it has been will be changed forever. I am a lover! In the scrap heaps of these hills of coal, someone found me. I am wanted! I have been waiting all of my life for this.

As folks sail by in a blur, talking and laughing, it occurs to me that they probably believe that Theodore and I, as close as we are, have a full relationship already. But since Theodore moved to town and we became friends, my mother had been ill, and I didn't feel right spending time away from her. So Theodore and I have had friendship without romance. At first I thought something might be wrong, but now I understand. He was waiting. Waiting for my heart to settle down from its grief, so it could make room for him!

Now the years seem wasted, like a lifetime, and I want to shove bossy Nellie Goodloe down on the wood chips and gag her with the polka-dot scarf she has tied around her neck chuck-wagon-style. Doesn't she understand that my body is filled with such longing that I have the strength to turn a truck over with my bare hands? That I have dreamed of wrapping myself around this man from the first day we met? Can't she see that I'm a ripe plum that will explode if touched? I interrupt them, and I am not one bit sorry.

"Excuse me. This is something you two can discuss later. Good night, Nellie."

I grab Theodore, and we walk out of the theater onto the street. "My house?"

"Great." Theodore helps me into the front seat of his truck, which has now turned into a stately carriage that will take me from my dreams to a real place. He climbs in and puts his arm around me as we back out. I think to myself, *Time stops when we get what we want.*

I haven't made spaghetti since Mama died. I pull out her recipe book. When she found out she was sick, she wrote everything down for me. The writing starts out in good English, then loses its clarity. She tried to finish the task when she was really sick. At the end of the notebook, most of the recipes are in pure Italian.

"Cut up the garlic," I tell Theodore. "The basil's in the window garden. I'll start the water."

Theodore goes about his chores. I notice we're not talking. Is this what happens to folks when things turn physical? Do kisses take the place of words? I think back on my past romances, all so long ago, and they seem insignificant, childish and silly—probably because they were. I wasn't a real woman then, a woman who knew herself. A woman alone in the world, free. Now I am a woman without strings, guilt, or parents, and I don't know what to say. How do I begin?

"How long have your parents been married?" I ask innocently.

"Forty-two years."

"Are they happy?"

"They're perfect for each other. He drinks and she hides it. Why do you ask?"

"We've never talked about it before."

"It seems like we have. I think you know everything about me."

"Have you ever been in love before?"

"Have you?" he asks, quite deliberately not answering me first.

This is a loaded question for me. I don't guess that I have, although there was a nice Polish Catholic guy from Chicago—I met him at a craps table during a Mardi Gras fund-raiser at Saint Mary's. I went with him for a year and a half. He wanted to marry me, but I couldn't see it. When it was over I was sad, but I wasn't broken-hearted.

"I guess I was. Once." I pick up the garlic and swish it into the olive oil in the pan on the stove.

"Only once?"

"Yes."

Theodore mulls this over, and I take a seat at the kitchen table and watch him chop some basil. I wonder if I like him there at the sink chopping. Does he fit in this house? Does he fit in my life? Will we live here in this house when we're married or in his cabin out on Aviation Road? I hear my mother's voice: "*Pazienza!* Slow down! Think, Ave Maria! Think!"

I straighten the silverware on the placemat. I like two placemats. It looks like a family lives here again. The table holds four. Children! Am I too old? Some of my classmates from high school have grandchildren. I am not too old. Thank God I have good Italian genes. No Scotch-Irish wrinkles for me. What am I thinking? What am I saying?

I catch my reflection in the steamed glass of the kitchen window. I am dewy. No! I'm soaking wet! My palms and face are sweating. I'm making myself sick and nervous. I'm a practical person, but I have always tended to daydream, and now I'm picturing myself married to this man and for some reason it's a real romance killer. I don't want to think about marriage just yet—I just want to have some sex. I need to be held! God help me!

"People are gonna talk about us," I promise him.

"Let them."

"Why are we cooking?" I'm asking this question to be coy and imply, Let's not eat, let's kiss.

"Aren't you hungry?" Theodore asks.

I nod. But I'm hungry for everything: food, him, and all that life has to offer. Everything seems possible to me all of a sudden. How will I tell him?

Theodore continues chopping. What beautiful hands he has! His large hand and squarish fingers are in total control of the paring knife. The motion reminds me of a French movie I saw in Charlottesville once. When I go on buying trips, I make it my business to see foreign movies. We don't get them down here, so they're a treat. French movies always have love scenes in the kitchen. Somebody is eating something drippy, like a ripe persimmon, and next thing you know it's a close-up of lips and hands and off go the lights and their clothes, and pretty soon nobody's talking. I check my ceramic fruit bowl on the counter. One black banana. Please don't let this be an omen.

"I haven't . . . Well, I guess what I'm trying to . . ." Theodore keeps chopping. I persist. "What I want to say is . . ."

"I'm thinking, Ave."

It may have been a long time since I've been with a man, but it doesn't take a sex goddess to figure out that thinking is not a good sign. Men don't think about sex. They think about how and where and when, but they could care less about the why.

"You don't want me," I say plainly, hoping I'm wrong. There, I've said it. The water in the pot is boiling foam. Theodore drops his knife and stirs and blows as bubbles trickle over the sides of the pot. He catches as many as he can with a spoon, but it keeps bubbling.

"Give me a hand."

"You've got it under control." I say this with matter-of-factness, but the truth is, my legs aren't working. I'm in a state of shock, from the ankles up. I just made a statement that scares me, and I need to stay very small, right here in this straight-backed chair, or I'm afraid of what I might do. Theodore moves the pot off the burner. The foam subsides. He pours the spaghetti into the colander in the sink. He shakes it hard. He leaves the pot in the sink and goes to the stove. He stirs the sauce.

"We call that sauce *shway shway*," I say, making my only contribution to the dinner.

"What is that?"

"It's Italian dialect from where my mama came from. *Shway shway* means 'fast.' Fast sauce. Instant sauce."

"It tastes great."

"Fresh basil."

Theodore pours the sauce onto the spaghetti. He pulls out plates and forks and sets the table.

"So you want to tell me why you kissed me?"

"*You* kissed *me*." Theodore looks at me directly.

"No. *You* kissed *me*." Oh God. I'm yelling.

"I went with the situation. You were kissing me, so I kissed back. And after what Sweet Sue said, I felt you needed to be kissed."

"So you were doing me a favor?"

"Yeah."

This is one of those moments when the steam between a man and a woman creates a wall. It's so thick that I can't make out Theodore's face. I do not understand him; doesn't he know how I feel? I want him. I want this. Where is the kissing Theodore? Where did he go?

"You aren't in love with me, Ave."

"What?"

"You got stirred up, that's all."

"I liked the kiss! It was nice! It was welcome."

"You said you hadn't been with a man in a long time. It's understandable. A cup of water in the desert is welcome, too."

I can't believe what I'm hearing! Theodore is comparing my aching loins to dehydration. This night is not going at all as I had expected.

"What? What?" Why is it that all I can say is *What?*

"I live alone. I like it. I grew up in a family with nine kids, and I'm still thrilled I don't have to share a bed with someone. I don't want a 'thing.' I like being with you. You are my best friend. I don't want a re-lationship."

"Everybody wants a relationship!"

"No. You want a relationship."

As we eat, I am sure he is right. It is me. I want to be loved. And I want to blame somebody because I'm not. So let me blame my par-ents. They're easy targets—one never loved me and the other leaves me scary letters after she's passed away. Let me blame life. Life keeps interfering in my plans. First Fred Mulligan was sick; then I took care of Mama, business got to booming, and I took on more and more and thought about myself less and less. Poor me. I straighten up in my chair and summon all my self-esteem in my posture. Then, very ca-sually, I lean toward Theodore.

"I can't believe you think I kissed you."

"You did. The whole town got a shock."

I don't care about the whole town. I chew in slow motion because I want to digest all of this. I initiated the kiss? I kissed him? What am I really hungry for?

"You're going to find a good man, you know."

Where? In the Blue Ridge Mountains? On the Trail of the Lone-some Pine? By the banks of the Powell River? Get serious, you trans-plant from Scranton, PA. Around here, men my age have been married since they were seventeen. Some of them are grandfathers al-ready. There are no men! You are the man! Be my man!

"You'll find somebody," he assures me.

"Somebody!" Wake up, buster! I'm not the type of woman for a Somebody. I'm picky. I take an hour to eat a tuna-salad sandwich be-cause I pick all the sweet-pickle chunks out of it before I'll take a bite. I'm vain. I cleanse and cream my face twenty minutes before bed-time, and then I hang my head upside down over the side of my bed for an additional five to prevent jowls. I'm a snob. I want a man who reads. In thirty years I've never seen a man on the Bookmobile, except strange Earl Spivey, but he doesn't count because he's a lurker, not a reader. If this mystery man isn't smart, I don't want him. Why can't Theodore see this?

"Okay, maybe not just somebody. How about a good guy, a real winner? When you kissed me tonight, you were impulsive. Daring. People around here saw you with new eyes. You watch. Something will happen."

"If you say so." I say this so weakly, it's barely audible. Theodore sprinkles cheese on his spaghetti, spins a nice mound of noodles, and eats. He chews normally. Swallows. Like everything is normal! He's ready to change the subject—like it's been discussed thoroughly and there's nothing more to say. He almost seems to be saying, "Okay, we kissed, it was nice, but it's going no further, so let's get back to our friendship."

"Somebody needs to tell Sweet Sue Tinsley she's not the home-coming queen anymore."

This is another reason I want Theodore. I want to be able to come home and dissect everybody and everything. Why can't I have this?

"She's afraid somebody will steal her man away." Theodore shrugs.

Were Theodore and I even at the same event tonight? The crowd was behind Jack Mac asking Sue to marry him; they kissed passionately, and it looked all sewn up to me. Am I so deprived of physical intimacy that I did not see this? How unobservant am I? Or am I living in some other universe, one I have created out of my own strange perceptions? I look away, out the window and into my yard, and what I see there is not the Potters' oak tree that grows over the fence but a flash of Jack MacChesney in his underwear, and how strong and bear-like he was, all man, from shoulder to foot. I shake my head to erase the picture. It goes.

"I want to have sex with you tonight." There. I just said it right out. Honestly. Clearly. Directly. Well done.

Theodore puts down his fork (another bad sign). Then he looks at me.

"You're beautiful and desirable. But it wouldn't work. We love each other; we are not in love with each other. If we had sex tonight, sooner or later we wouldn't be friends. I don't want to lose that. Would you?"

Around my fork I have twirled a mountain of spaghetti so large it is the size of a tennis ball.

I say to Theodore: "I wouldn't." But why can't I have both? The lover *and* the best friend. Isn't that the point? I know what I want. I've had many years to think about it. When I first saw Theodore at the Drama auditions years ago, my heart skipped a beat. "Kindred spirit" doesn't begin to describe our connection.

I unravel the tennis ball of noodles. It makes a square on the plate, like the frame of an open window. In the square, I imagine a cartoon, primitive and bright. A buck-toothed gorilla is being chased by an angry mouse with a giant mallet. The mouse climbs up the gorilla and clunks him on the head repeatedly. The gorilla's eyes cross, and stars shoot out of his head. The image makes me smile, so I won't cry.

CHAPTER THREE

*F*leeta is serious about quitting. I can tell because she has cleaned up the shelf behind the register. Her lifetime supply of Coke and peanuts is gone. Her bifocals are safe in their case. Her paperwork is stacked neatly in two piles. In one stack, her professional wrestling schedules. Fleeta and Portly go to wrestling matches in Kingsport and Knoxville every chance they get. Pictures of the great wrestling stars Haystack Calhoun, Atomic Drop, Johnny Weaver, and the frightening Pile Driver are in protective clear-plastic sleeves. The wrestlers' thick, clublike bodies are greased in oil. Their heads are smaller than their squat, muscular bodies; they look like apples on top of buildings. In the other stack, Fleeta's recipes. When business is slow, Fleeta rewrites her recipe-card file; she's had this project under way for about five years. In Fleeta's block print:

MAMAW SKEEN'S POSSUM

Skin your possum. Place in a large pot and boil 'til tender. Add salt and pepper to taste. Make gravy with broth and add 4 tablespoons flour and ½ cup of milk. Cook until thick. Save a foot to sop gravy!

I wonder what they do with the other three feet. I flip through the cards; many of Fleeta's specialties are included: divinity candy, a confection of whipped sugar that looks like clouds (she brings it in every Christmas), lemon squares, cheese straws, peanut butter balls, and my favorite, rhubarb pie.

"I'm putting my recipes together for my granddaughter, for when she gets murried," Fleeta says as she stands behind me. "You ever ate possum?"

"Not that I know of."

"Well, you're missing out. It's the best, most tenderest meat of all."

Fleeta grabs her smokes and motions for me to meet her in the back office for lunch. She locks the front door and flips the RING BELL sign.

Fleeta sits on a folding chair, smoking. She pours a small cellophane sack of salted peanuts into her glass bottle of Coca-Cola, stops up the top with her thumb, shakes it, and when it's fizzy chugs it back. I'm going to miss our lunches.

"Fleeta, do you really have to quit on me?"

"Honey, my mama died when she was fifty-five. I'm fifty-six. The clock is ticking. I want a life before mine's over. I will miss the money, though."

"I'll give you a raise."

"Too late for that. Come on, Ave. You got a lot ahead of you. You're gonna get murried to that Tipton fella."

"What?"

"His car was parked over to your house till all hours Saturday night, and Nellie Goodloe done spread it all over town that you and he was swapping slobbers on the dance floor over to the Drama. Now that's public. Don't hold back on me, youngun, I know you too well."

"He doesn't want me, Fleeta. We're just friends."

"No way. Shoot-fire, y'all do everything together. Y'all are each other's destinies." I start to argue with Fleeta, and she stops me. "Even when you put two rats in a box they might chew each other up at first, but give it time and they'll make baby rats."

"Fleeta, I'm eating."

"He's a fine-looking man. And he's clean. I like me a clean man. And he's got nice thick hair, and honey, after thirty you gotta put that in the plus column. He's got them nice Irish looks and features. The rusty hair, the blue eyes. The purty smile. Law me! What more do you want in a man?"

I don't answer her. *Nothing!* There's no one but Theodore for me. Why won't she stop this?

"Or do you even want a man?" Fleeta looks at me over her bifocals.

"Not just any man," I say defensively, with my mouth full of food.

"I want you to git a good man like I got. You know, Portly and I still have intimate relations. Of course, it takes a lot longer than it used to to warm up my toaster. I done gone through The Change. And that's a good word for it because everything done changed on me. I have to prepare for when he gets that look. But I'll tell you one thing—Portly has him some big clubby forearms and man-hands, you know what I'm saying, he could palm my head—really, just like a basketball. And if I didn't have those gigantic arms wrapped around me of the night, I would be one cantankerous old woman. So I know what you mean."

"How'd you and Portly meet?"

Fleeta exhales and her eyes fill with a faraway memory. She squints to make out the details of this old picture.

"Up to the school. When East Stone Gap High School was closed down, they transferred all them kids over to Powell Valley and Portly was in the bunch. First day of school, I seen him and knew he was the one. I was feeling old, though, like I'd never find nobody."

"How old were you?"

"Sixteen. And never been kissed. My mama was so proud of 'at. But let me tell you, when I snagged Portly, I made up for lost time. I remember the very first kiss he done give me. Up behind the bleachers up to the school. Hit was around five o'clock in the afternoon, after Portly's baseball practice. He looked at me. I looked at him. Course we had to take the snuff out of our mouths first—Portly and I both love our chewing tobacky. Well, we spit it out, and then we kissed, and the rest is history."

I'm so wrapped up in Fleeta's love life, I don't hear the persistent bang of the bell on the store counter. I come to and get up to answer it. The majorettes stand at the counter, some reading the *National*

Enquirer, others thumbing through *People.* Tayloe waits at the prescription-pickup window.

"I'm here for my prescription."

"I'll be right with you, honey."

"It's not ready yet?" The annoyance underscores each of Tayloe's words, and she rolls her eyes. God, she's impatient. I remember that she's just a kid, and that keeps me from biting her head off.

"No, not yet," I reply gaily.

Pearl Grimes enters the store and, upon seeing the majorettes, instantly skulks behind the hair-care rack.

"Look how fat she got!" Glenda the majorette says with authority. That's all it takes for all the majorettes to gather round *People* magazine and gloat over the picture of some formerly slim, now chunky TV actress.

"I don't know why somebody'd let themselves go like that," says another.

" 'Cause she likes to eat," Tayloe announces. It's not one bit funny, but all the girls die laughing, because in her circle, Tayloe gets to be funny as well as beautiful.

"She's not as fat as Pearl Grimes, though." A louder laugh.

I see the top of Pearl's head disappear behind the medical-supply rack. I wonder if they saw her come in. Are they that cruel? Mrs. Spivey, Mrs. Holyfield, and Mrs. Edmonds enter the store and split up to shop. Three finer Baptist women I've never known. They're also responsible for spreading more information than the town paper.

"Miss Mulligan, could you please hurry? We've got band practice. You know . . . with Mr. Tipton?" Another round of giggles. I guess they heard about Theodore's car being outside my house till all hours. Now I wish I'd had sex with him, so the joke wouldn't be on me.

I shout out from behind the counter, "It's gonna take a minute, girls." More sighs and eye rolls. They continue reading the magazines.

Fleeta comes out from the back. "Be careful with the magazines; we can't hardly sell wrinkled, used ones. Folks like their reading material virginal. And I can't blame them, as *they* are paying," she growls.

Inspired by Fleeta's choice of words, I seize my moment. I had a microphone installed in the prescription department because the store is large, and when I get busy I can call for the customer. I blow into the microphone. All the heads look up.

"Tayloe Slagle, your birth control pills are ready at the prescription window. Tayloe. Slagle. Your. Birth. Control. Pills. Come on over."

Tayloe lunges for the window and grabs the white sack.

"They're for cramps."

"Really." I ponder this possibility. The fine Baptist women look at one another and then at Tayloe with such disdain, they become a scary tableau on a stained-glass window.

"Charge it," Tayloe barks as she sprints for the door. The girls follow her.

I hear the ladies murmuring in the dental-hygiene section—mission accomplished.

Fleeta is chuckling, and of course the chuckles turn into a hack. "I'm done tarred of them girls coming in here and reading and never buying. You got 'em good."

I pick up a basket of conditioner and head for the hair-care aisle. Pearl is sitting on the floor reading labels on the backs of bottles.

"Hey, Pearl."

"I come down for the acne treatment you told me about."

"Then what in God's name are you doing in hair care?"

Pearl shrugs. Her eyes are a mite puffy, so I know she heard the majorettes.

"You wanna help me restock the shelves?"

"Yes, ma'am."

"Fleeta's quitting on me, so I'm looking to hire somebody part-time. You up for it?"

"I have to ask Mama."

"Go call your mama and ask her if you can start today."

"We ain't got no phone. And I don't know if she'd let me take a job. How would I get to and from work?"

"I could take you home after work," I offer.

"But I live up in Insko."

"I drive fast. How much you want an hour? For your pay."

"I don't know."

"Come on, Pearl. You're gonna do sales. Sell yourself."

"Well, I git fifty cents an hour baby-sitting the Bloomer kids."

"Not bad. They're a handful. I guess I gotta do better than Mrs. Bloomer."

"How 'bout one dollar an hour?" Pearl looks away, embarrassed to be talking figures.

"Only a dollar? Hmm. You're a real tail twister, Pearl. How about three dollars an hour?"

Pearl's eyes widen. "Thank you, Miss Ave! Can I start tomorrow?" Pearl straightens her spine, and I swear she grows an inch.

"You sure can."

Fleeta watches Pearl go and lights another cigarette. "Why in holy hell would you hire that girl?"

"I like her."

"She don't keep herself nice."

"You heard her. She lives up in Insko."

"I don't care. That ain't no excuse."

"I'm surprised at you, Fleeta. I thought you could see potential."

"Honey, there's potential, and then there's bullshit dreaming. I think you got a case of the bullshit dreams, if you know what I mean."

Fleeta grazes the big feather duster over the vitamins, barely tickling them.

"What I meant to say was that we could transform Pearl into a great employee if she was trained by a master."

"I told you I don't want to work no more." Fleeta lights up a cigarette and thinks for a moment. "But if you're gonna throw away all I done built up here, I'd better rethink my position. All right, I'll work part-time for ye." I am so thrilled, I hug Fleeta, who stiffens like a telephone pole. I've never hugged her before; we're both surprised.

"Three days a week and fifty cents more an hour."

"You got a deal."

"What? I'm no tail twister?" Fleeta says with a smile.

"You ain't no Haystacks Calhoun."

"No, I guess I ain't. But given the right circumstances, I might be able to take him." Fleeta chuckles to herself.

———

Pearl shows up for work the next day in her best outfit: a smock top and eyelet-trimmed bell-bottoms. Her hair is in a low ponytail. She looks neat, but that doesn't stop Fleeta from eyeing her up and down. Pearl's work life at Mutual's begins with a shipment box haul. Fleeta and I have a system. Fleeta unloads and prices items, I break down the boxes and bring them to the Dumpster behind the store. Fleeta does product placement and displays because that feeds her creative side. She gives Pearl a dirty look when Pearl artfully places shampoo bottles in a shadow-box display. I decide it's a good idea to separate the two of them during this training period; Fleeta is an old cat with well-defined territories and the claws to protect them. Pearl joins me, already full of suggestions on how to make the box haul a more expeditious process. This kid is smart, and it's not bugging me.

"I want to thank you for the job. It's really gonna help me and my mama out."

"I'm happy to have you. And don't worry about old Fleeta. She's mean on the outside but marshmallow on the inside."

"Not like Tayloe and them girls up to school. They's mean to the bone."

"Ignore them."

"I try, but it ain't easy to hide when you're the fattest girl in school."

"You're not the fattest girl in school."

"I'm pretty sure I am."

"No, you're the girl with the best after-school job." This makes Pearl laugh as we throw empty boxes into the Dumpster. "Besides, those type of girls talk about everybody. Even each other."

"You know what they're saying about you?"

"Me? Why would they talk about me?"

"They say you're a bastard, that Fred Mulligan wasn't your father."

"People say that?"

Pearl nods that they do. How naïve of me. I thought that no one talked about me in that way. I never spread stories, so I figured none were spread about me. But in a small town a good story bears repeating, even mine.

"Well, Pearl. They're right."

"They are?"

"Yep. I guess my mama came over from Italy pregnant and Fred Mulligan married her because back in those days you had to get married if you were having a baby. Only thing, my mama didn't tell me herself; she left it in a letter. I got it after she died."

"Aren't you mad about it?"

I guess I look off for a long time, because Pearl asks me again. I don't know how to answer her, because it's not like me to ever get angry about anything.

"If I was you, I'd be mad."

"You would?"

"Your mama shouldn't never have lied to you about your papa."

"Well, she did, and there's nothing to be done about it now."

Then Pearl asks me the question that would forever change my life.

"You gonna find your real father?"

"My real one?" I ask quietly. The word *real* sounds so new.

"If he's alive, are you gonna find him?"

Who has time to think about Mario da Schilpario? I'm busy. I have the Pharmacy, deliveries, the Rescue Squad, the Drama, and the Kiss.

"You gonna marry Mr. Tipton?"

"Don't tell me people are talking about that, too."

She nods; they are.

"Well, Pearl, I don't think it's anybody's damn business who I marry, or who my father was, or what size my underwear is."

"Good for you. Now you're mad!" Pearl says this with great pride.

She's right. I'm mad. But what she doesn't know, and what I don't know, is I'm just getting started.

Ethel Bartee's Beauty Salon is tucked behind the post office in a trailer. I take the back alley from the Pharmacy and cut through the loading zone to get to Ethel. She fixed the trailer up real nice with window boxes overflowing with red geraniums. The tip end of my braid is like crispy straw; I need a haircut.

The door is propped open with a drum of pink shampoo. Ethel is putting up Iva Lou's hair.

"Can you take me for a quick trim?" I ask sweetly.

Ethel, stout with a perfect bubble hairstyle that matches her shape, looks up over her bifocals as she finishes winding Iva Lou's last curl around a plastic roller.

"I guess so," she says, annoyed.

"I should've called."

"Yes, you should've. But you know I ain't the type to turn nobody away." Ethel gives me the critical once-over. "Especially not no one who needs a clip. I got two comb-outs before I can git to you, though." Ethel indicates her customers under the dryers.

"I can wait."

Iva Lou rises. "I'm gonna sit outside and let it dry in the sun, honey. It'll save you on your electric bill." Iva Lou cocks her big head full of jumbo curlers, giving me a signal to follow her outside.

"Ethel's cranky." Iva Lou lights up a cigarette. "I *heard*," she says, looking at me directly.

"Is everybody talking about it?" I ask.

"Let's put it this way. I make six stops in the Gap. It was the topic of conversation on each one." Iva Lou points her cigarette toward the trailer door. "And the two biddies under the dryer bubbles had themselves a field day before you dropped by."

For a moment I am overwhelmed by it all. I figured my paternity was my business. I lean back on the steps and close my eyes.

"You know what?" Iva Lou says brightly. "I think it's exciting news."

"You do?"

"Follow me on this. All your life you was one thing. And now you can be something else if you want! Somebody completely different. You can actually start yourself over from scratch. Turn yourself into what you have always wanted to be!" Iva Lou continues with her Knute Rockne pep-up, and I sit up and shift so I can see the back of my pharmacy. The building looks in even worse shape from here. The mortar between the bricks is chipped, leaving spaces. They look awful. I make a mental note to get them repointed. It annoys me, though. I shouldn't have to fix them; they had a lifetime guarantee.

Closing night of the Drama signals the start of the Powell Valley High School football season. My theater life winds down and Theodore's kicks in, as he is responsible for designing and executing home-game halftime shows. The fans are as competitive about the shows as they are the football games. Every year we wonder how Theodore will top himself, and every year he does. Our downtown stores are festooned with flags in our high school colors, bright Carolina blue and ruby red. Zackie hauls out an eight-foot papier-mâché Viking, spray-painted silver, letting anyone passing through town know that we are "the Vikings, the Mighty, Mighty Vikings."

Nellie Goodloe finally got a meeting with Theodore and impressed upon him the importance of Elizabeth Taylor and John Warner's visit coming up at the end of October. All eyes will be on us to deliver a weekend to remember. There is an excitement in the air anyway, as it is fall, our most luscious season. The mountains around us turn from dark velvet to an iridescent taffeta. The leaves of late September are bright green; by the first week of October they change to shimmering gemstones, garnet and topaz and all the purples in between. The mountains seem to be lit from the ground by theatrical footlights. Autumn is our grand opera. It even smells rich this time of year, a fresh mix of balsam and hickory and vanilla smoke. Friday nights are football-game nights, and Saturday nights find everyone in town over at the Carter Family Fold.

The Fold is famous because the originators of East Tennessee–style bluegrass music are the legendary Carter Family, led by Mother Maybelle Carter. She had a bunch of daughters, one prettier than the next, including June Carter, now married to Johnny Cash. Yes, it is their homestead and a magnet for bluegrass celebrity (like the great Stanley Brothers out of Dickenson County), and every once in a while somebody famous from the Carter Family does pass through, though that's not why we go there. We go there for the live music and dancing. You can eat there too—chili dogs and fries, the best anywhere. I usually go with Theodore; and ever since we didn't have sex, we're seeing even more of each other. The storm cloud of my lust has passed for now, so he's safe and I'm back to normal.

We enter the Fold, an old barn with flap sides, which are opened to the night air. The Fold is like a gypsy amphitheater—it has the feeling of a place that could be packed up and moved quickly overnight. And indeed, during the daytime when you drive by, you could mistake it for any old weathered barn in a field. But at night she comes alive. Folks sit in rows around the concrete dance floor on bales of hay. The bandstand is high and set back against a permanent wall rigged with electricals for when WNVA Radio broadcasts shows live. A colorful mix of Japanese lanterns and old Christmas lights dangles over the stage. I love the crazy-quilt mess of it; it is homespun yet dramatic. I enjoy the wondrous sight until the sound of my Aunt Alice Lambert's voice ruins it. I turn to look at her and find she is busy examining Theodore from the tip of his shoe to the top of his head. Her lips are pursed so tightly, they look like two red firecrackers looking for a match.

"So, A-vuh Maria"—she too mispronounces my name—"Hit finally come out!"

"What?" I ask, squinting up at the lights.

"The truth. You know what I'm talking about, girl." I never imagined Aunt Alice would approach me on this subject.

She senses she caught me off guard and uses it. "This changes everything. Don't it?" she snarls. "My brother's estate?"

"Your brother died thirteen years ago and left everything to my mama." I say this pleasantly, like I'm commenting on the weather.

"It ain't right. You ain't his. You never was—"

Before she can gear up, I turn and look her directly in the eye. "I am not going to discuss my business with you. Ever. So if you'll excuse me, I'm here to be with my friends and have a good time. Good night."

I can see her mouth—*Well!*—as I walk away. I've had time to think about what Pearl said and what Iva Lou implied. I guess there were signs all along that I wasn't Fred Mulligan's daughter, but for me it was just something I never questioned. He seemed like my real father. Of course, I liked my mother more, loved her more, but I thought that was because I was an only child and a girl. I figured every child liked her mother more than her father. I wasn't completely unaware something was wrong, though. I do remember whispers at family functions, the fact that my first cousins never played with me, the teasing that went on at school about my first name (feriner-sounding). But I never put it all together. I hope I figure out why I didn't. I'm angry with myself for being such an idiot.

Otto and Worley spot us.

"Want to see my snake head?" Worley asks. Before I can say no, he pulls a small jar out of his back pocket and shows me a fresh snake head, floating aimlessly, with a permanent grin and threadlike tongue, which bounces against the glass.

"I got three more of 'em at home. Caught 'em up at the Roaring Branch."

"Why did this one make the cut?"

"He had the longest tongue." Worley throws his head back and laughs hard.

"Dance with me, Miss Ave?" Otto asks like a gentleman.

"Later, Otto. I got some business to tend to right now."

Otto and Worley move off in time with the music. Theodore goes off for our chili dogs. Lew Eisenberg sits alone on a bale of hay licking a blueberry Sno-Kone.

"I got a bone to pick with you," I say to him.

"You can't make me feel worse than I already do. I'm stuck in a barn with hay up my ass. What can I do for you?" Lew says pleasantly.

"Everybody in town knows about my business. I think Inez is the leak."

Lew licks his Sno-Kone and looks off to the chili-dog stand, where Inez lays hot dogs on the grill. She is talking a mile a minute; from here we can only see her bright pink mouth moving. She looks angry, her eyebrows knit into one black V. I see my dreadful Aunt Alice with her, as well as the other ladies of the Band Boosters Club. The epicenter of the town gossip fault line rips open cellophane bags of hot-dog buns and shakes them onto the counter.

"What happened to my life?" Lew asks, and licks his Sno-Kone. "I was so happy on Long Island. Alone. All alone. I had my little practice, my little apartment, my little problems. I like things little, Ave Maria. Little, I can hide in. Instead, I've got this." He flails his arms around. "I lie awake every night and wonder what went wrong."

"I don't know what to say, Lew." And I really don't. We don't usually talk personally like this, and it's making me slightly uncomfortable.

"One mistake." I believe Lew is referring to Inez's unplanned pregnancy. "One mistake and . . . this. Inez was such a nice, quiet girl. So lovely. So soft. Like a picture. Now she's impossible. When she isn't talking, she's eating, but any way around it, that mouth is going 'round the clock."

"You have to think back and remember why you fell in love with Inez in the first place."

"She had a great body." A moment passes. "A sleek, tight, little English race car of a body. She was the TR-6 of Big Stone Gap. She could've been in a magazine." Lew looks at me. "Is that terrible of me to say?" He sighs. He really misses the old Inez.

"You're just being honest." Then we look over at Inez, completely unaware that we are talking about her. Gossips never think anybody is talking about *them*. "Do you think she knows how you feel?"

"I cannot tell you one thing that has gone through that woman's mind in five years. I would know a stranger better." He sighs.

"I bet she knows. Maybe that's why she eats so much." I'm annoyed at myself for going down this road with Lew; this is not what I wanted to discuss with him. As out of touch as he thinks he is, he reads my mind.

"What was it you wanted to talk to me about?"

I don't answer him because all I see are lovers on the dance floor. Fleeta and Portly nuzzle as though they have just found each other after having been put to sleep for a hundred years. Girls I went to high school with are out on the floor, dancing close with husbands they've been married to since we were kids. They look content. (So much for the advice "Don't marry young.") Rick Harmon, a rugged tugboat of a guy, All District Shot Put in high school, now a miner, places his hand on his wife Sherry's behind as they're dancing. She casually removes it, and they laugh privately. Worley dances with Nellie Goodloe, who waves his snake head away with a shudder. I look all around for Theodore. I want to dance. I want to be out there on the floor, gliding. Forgetting. But I can't find him in the crowd. I think he may have wandered out into the field and kept walking, never to return. He'll disappear like everything else. My heart begins to race in a way it hasn't since I pulled an all-nighter at Saint Mary's, drinking pots of black coffee and knocking back NoDoz. I put my hand on my chest and look down. My hand moves up and down against my blouse.

"You all right?" Lew asks.

"I don't feel well."

"What are your symptoms?"

"My heart is racing." I keep my hand on my chest, and as suddenly as it came, the rapid beating stops.

"That's an anxiety attack," Lew says, and swats a fly away from his glasses.

"I've never had one before."

"Welcome to the club. Once you have one, you never know when they'll strike. Part of getting older."

"I am not old!" There she is, old maid Ave Maria again, poking through the fence like a cuckoo. Not old! Not old! Not old!

"I didn't say you were old. Older."

My palpitations slow to a normal rhythm. I breathe deeply. I remember my medical training: Take in oxygen. As much as you can stand.

"Would you like to dance?" a voice says from behind me. At last! Theodore! He didn't leave me! I stand up. But I don't smell peppermint and apples: Instead it's a new smell, sandalwood and lime. Pleasant but unfamiliar.

"Would you like to dance?" Jack Mac repeats, extending his hand graciously.

I look all around for Theodore. But he is not there to rescue me.

"Okay, well. Sure."

"Have fun," Lew says, and waves bye-bye to me as though I were a child.

Jack Mac takes my hand. We shuffle into the mix and move toward the center of the dance floor. He pulls me close and rests his hand on my waist. He moves slowly, so he's easy to follow. He seems much taller to me as we dance.

"Where's Sweet Sue?"

"She took her boys over to their daddy's."

"He's living over in Coeburn, isn't he?"

Jack Mac nods.

"I remember him from high school. Do you?"

Jack Mac nods.

"Mike Tinsley was the best in everything. His varsity jacket was decorated like a four-star general's. Remember? All-state in this and that."

"Things have changed since high school," Jack Mac announces, and looks off to get me to stop yapping about Mike Tinsley. Hadn't I heard about his philandering on Sue and his terrible temper and how she moved home most weekends of their married life? Besides, don't I know that no man wants to be compared with the man who came before?

Jack Mac pulls me close; his cheek rests above my left ear.

"How's your mama?" I ask. He doesn't answer for a moment. I feel him pull away to look at me. He looks me in the eye. Then he pulls me close again.

"To be honest, I wasn't thinking about my mama right then."

For God's sake, Ave Maria! Asking a man about his mother. Who does that? You *are* an old maid! You have forgotten how to talk to a man. Say something smart.

"Could we just dance and not talk for a minute?" Jack Mac asks.

I nod. Don't talk, Ave Maria. This is a man who prefers silence. You are getting on his nerves. You don't have to think of something funny to say. You don't have to entertain. Let go. Listen to the music and dance. Just dance. That's all.

The song ends. Jack Mac bows graciously and formally like a duke. "Thank you, ma'am," he says, and goes.

I am careful to park behind Theodore's house so as not to start any more rumors. (I don't need to be the town spinster, the town bastard, and now the town tramp all rolled into one.) And Theodore is, after all, a teacher in the Wise County public school system with a sterling reputation. He flicks the lights on. His home is simple and neat. It could be any high school teacher's house, except for the elaborate display on the dining room table. The only indication that this is a dining room is its proximity to the kitchen. Theodore has removed all of the chairs and dishes. He has turned it into a workshop, where he choreographs his halftime masterpieces.

Tonight, meticulously lined up in rows, are one hundred toy soldiers; now they represent our high school marching band. A small turntable and speakers face the table on an antique server. Albums are stacked neatly next to the turntable. He's got Sousa, classical, and Al Green, the rhythm and blues singer. The table is covered in butcher's paper. Theodore has drawn the field's yard lines onto the paper with chalk. The figurines fan out in perfect lines, in the formation of a star, leading to three small paper pyramids on the fifty-yard line. The pyramids are made of tissue paper and are scaled to size.

"You're making pyramids?"

"The shop boys are going to build them. The Vernon girl is doing the craft work. Remember her? She made the giant globe for last year's prom, 'Color My World.' " How could I forget? I was Theodore's date. I couldn't believe I finally attended a prom at Powell Valley High School. I was never asked to go when I was a student. Dancing under the tinfoil stars sixteen years later was sweet retribution.

"Who's going to get them out on the field?"

"The flag girls. Two under each pyramid."

"Flag girls? Are you kidding?"

"Papier-mâché. They'll be as light as fritters."

"Great. Any blackouts?" There is a concert section in each halftime show in which the band faces the home stands and plays a number. This is traditional, but it can be dull. Theodore came up with a way to ignite the show; at the appropriate moment, the field lights shut off to reveal our lovely majorettes, with batons lit up like torches, spinning wheels of fire and spelling out words like *Win* or *Go*.

"The flag girls will have industrial flashlights under the pyramids. I'm using selections from the scores of Elizabeth Taylor's movies, starting with *National Velvet.* As the band plays the theme to *The Sandpiper,* we'll black out and the pyramids will light up. Then, as we segue into the love song from *Cleopatra,* Tayloe will emerge from behind the center pyramid, dressed as Cleopatra, and twirl fire." Theodore moves the pieces around the table to show me the chore-ography. Then he turns out the dining room light to show me the lit-up pyramids. They do give the effect of being there, right there, in downtown Cairo.

"I think this is spectacular, Theodore," I say, meaning it with every fiber of my being. "It'll knock the socks off of a movie star."

"Think so?" Theodore says as he moves the woodwinds with a ruler.

I can feel the pressure on his shoulders myself. "Elizabeth Taylor has probably had more salutes than all the presidents combined. She's seen it all! And in a million different countries. She's going to cry or something when she sees this kind of show in little old Big Stone Gap. You'll be famous!"

Theodore lights up at the mention of fame. Who among us wouldn't? What a grand concept: to be appreciated and sought after for your God-given talent. To be revered and consulted as an expert in your field. To have the awe and respect normally reserved for movie stars.

"I don't want to be famous, Ave. I just want to be really, really good."

"You are that! You are." I have no problem being passionate around Theodore. I really believe in him.

Theodore moves a line of soldiers, turning the star into a triangle. I watch him masterfully make shapes and study the table as though it's an algebraic equation. Theodore loves his work. He is forever thinking about it, studying, trying things, improving. That's how my mother was. She was never satisfied with her sewing. She ripped out as many seams as she completed, probably more. There was a level of craftsmanship, a pride in her work that I have never known. She was so hard on herself. When she sewed, she would talk to herself, criticizing her work, then mumble in approval and smile when the fabric met the thread in glorious, tiny, uniform stitches that disap-peared into the fabric in their delicacy. That was the hallmark of my mother's work: In order to be perfect, the seam had to disappear. The overall effect of the final garment was important. The line. The fit. The movement. Her work was never obvious, so it went unrecognized.

I am not an artisan like my mother, or a visionary like Theodore. I am a pill-counting pharmacist. I simply follow the orders of doctors; I don't even make a diagnosis. My work is not about expansion, it's about precision. Maybe this is why Theodore wants my input. Details. That's what I'm good at.

"To pull this show off, you're going to need a crew on the sidelines. I can get the folks from the Drama to help. I could put a crew together for you, and then you could boss us around."

"You'd do that for me?"

"Of course I would. Now, all you have to do in return is sleep with me."

Theodore and I laugh so hard at this, we shake the table and all of the soldiers fall and rattle across the table like they've just lost a war. We keep laughing until we're crying, and I'm wondering what the neighbors will say. What a boring life I'd have without Theodore. I wonder if he knows.

I gave Pearl the week off to study for her PSATs, the junior version of the college-entrance SATs. Since she's been working for me, Pearl's grades have gone from C's to B's. Dillard Cantrell, the high school guidance counselor, called me to express his thanks. She might make the honor roll next term. Girls like Pearl often fall between the cracks, he told me, and he would be personally thrilled to see a mountain girl exceed expectations.

Fleeta has the day off, and I'm running the store alone. June Walker, the most wrinkled woman in town, is driving me nuts with questions about face creams.

"June, you'll have to wait for Pearl to get here from school. She knows all about moisturizers."

"Well, she better damn hurry because I got me an emergency situation."

The Bookmobile stops outside the Pharmacy. Pearl gets off. Iva Lou waves at me from her window and motions that she will be over at the gas station. (Things must be hot and heavy with Kent Vanhook because her usual spot on the street is open.)

Pearl comes into the store with a chic short haircut and a nice outfit. Could it be a cinch belt? It is! I haven't seen her in a little over a week. What a difference. She has lost weight! Enough that you can tell! I am about to fall all over Pearl when June does instead.

"Pearl Grimes, you done dropped some weight. How'd you do it?"

"I joined Weight Watchers. And I eat a lot of Jell-O."

"Well, count me in. I'm gonna eat me a ton of Jell-O so I can drop me some weight too. Now, missie, I got me some wrinkles on my face you could hide a roll of quarters in. Which one of these here creams do you suppose I oughta slather on my mug of the night?"

"I would recommend the Queen Helene Cucumber Masque. It's thick, but it soaks in. And you get a lot for your dollar."

Pearl leads June Walker to a little makeup table she's put together. I watch Pearl the Expert as she demonstrates all the different creams on June's hand. What salesmanship. Perhaps Mr. Cantrell is right. This girl's got a future, and it ain't in Insko.

The pleasant jingle of the tri-bells on the door signals the entrance of another customer.

"Good afternoon, Preacher."

"Hello, Miss Mulligan." Preacher Elmo Gaspar, our local Church of God in Jesus Christ's Name reverend and snake handler, stands before my prescription counter and commences to go through all of his pockets.

"Preacher, you are the most disorganized man in southwest Virginia."

"Ave Maria, I know I'm a mess. But you know, there ain't no perfection in this world, only in the next."

"You speak the truth, Reverend!" June cries through her cream.

The preacher chuckles, reminding me of the light side to his character. When I was little, every Friday morning we had assembly in the elementary school auditorium. The speaker was always a minister from one of the local churches. Of course, as we grew older, we dreaded it. But when we were kids, we loved the fire-and-brimstone

Bible stories, delivered with passion and zeal by the Protestant of the Week. The Protestants were on rotation until one week when there was a cancellation and no preacher could fill in, so the spot went by default to the only Catholic priest in the area. The schoolkids used to tease me about my religion, saying Cath-licks drank blood in our service and worshipped statues. The kids were convinced when the priest showed up that he'd have horns and green skin. They were mighty disappointed when Father Rausch, a mild man with a crew cut, brought out puppets and acted out the parable of the Prodigal Son—not exactly a barn burner. I almost wished my priest had a little of the devil in him, for theatrical purposes. I wanted the Catholics to have some pizzazz. Couldn't he have explained stigmata or weeping statues? But it was not to be. We didn't have the stuff. The Protestants did.

The Protestants knew that the hard sell was everything (there has always been a heated, if unspoken, competition among the various sects), so they came fully loaded, ready to convert, with audiovisuals, pamphlets, and songs. When Preacher Gaspar came, he showed an actual filmstrip of what heaven would look like. The living room in the Palace of Heaven was made of pink and gold marble, and young, beautiful people in flowing gossamer robes were reclining on stones and staring into a bright light that came from the open ceiling. The light was God, and he was stopping by to visit the folks in one of the many rooms he had prepared for us. Then Preacher Gaspar showed us hell. It was layers of people stacked upon one another, in torment, feet crushing into faces, hands reaching out, begging for release, gnashing their teeth and wailing in horror. Preacher Gaspar left that image up a very long time and preached over, around, and in front of it, trying to scare the tarnation out of us. He succeeded because by the end of the filmstrip most of us were weeping. After we wiped away our tears and swore never to lie or steal or cheat anybody, we sang a song about the Bible.

"Preacher, remember that song you taught us at assembly when I was a girl?"

"Miss Mulligan, aren't you still a girl?" he says with a wink.

"You'll have to answer to God for lying." I hum a bit, and then in my terrible singing voice, *"The B-I-B-L-E. Yes, that's the Book for me! I stand alone on the word of God! The B-I-B-L-E!"*

"Very good." Preacher looks happy that I'm done serenading him and relieved that he has found his prescription order in his breast pocket.

I unfold the paper and attach it to my clipboard. It's from Doc Daugherty: a tincture for poison, for rattlesnake bites. I keep a supply on hand at all times; after all, it's hunting season and occasionally one of the men will get bitten.

"Going hunting, Preacher?"

"No, no. We got a revival down in the Frog Level. I'm preaching and handling. I promised Doc Daugherty I'd keep the medicine on hand."

The preacher has been handling snakes at revivals since he was very young. There's one story that he handled three rattlers at once and tamed them to sleep. Snake handling is mentioned in the Old Testament. It's a way for believers to prove their faith in God; if they truly believe, God won't let them get bitten. Preacher Gaspar's beliefs must be sincere, because in all these years he's never been bitten. He looks up at me and smiles. His expression is beatific, there is a saintly sweetness to him. He must be close to seventy now, but his face is un-lined and youthful. He still has his own teeth, straight and white. His hair, once black, thick, and unruly, is gone, but his scalp is smooth and pink, an advertisement for his good health. His blue eyes shine with a knowingness and humor that can only come from a serene and intimate relationship with God. There is no pretense to him; he is the real article, kind and good.

"You be careful now, Reverend."

"I will. I will." He turns to go, then looks back at me. "Miss Ave, do you remember the rest of that song I done taught you?"

"Reverend, I'm ashamed to say I don't."

He sings, *"God's words will never fail, never fail, never fail . . ."*

Pearl, June, and I join in, *"God's words will never fail. No! No! No!"*

Reverend Gaspar laughs as he leaves.

"Someday you ought to come down and see him preach," June says from the makeup table. "He is one of the greatest, I'll goddamn guarantee you."

Tayloe Slagle and her majorettes come in giggling and chatting. They are always loud enough to draw attention, but not so loud as to be considered obnoxious.

"What can I do for you girls?"

They swarm around the magazine rack and don't answer. If Fleeta were here, she'd swat their hands with a duster for reading the magazines and never buying them. I cut them some slack because they spend their money in other ways in my store.

Finally Tayloe asks, "Did you get any waterproof mascara in yet?"

"I don't know. Did we, Pearl?"

Pearl continues to rub cream into June's face like she's waxing a car. "Yes, ma'am. We got in the Great Lash."

"See there? One-stop shopping, girls. All your needs met right here. Maybe you ought to get Pearl to show you all of our new makeup." Pearl shoots me a look like, *Please don't mention me. If you don't talk about me, they won't notice me. I will disappear into the vat of Queen Helene Cucumber Masque.*

"Now, Miss Mulligan, let me ask you one thing." Tayloe looks at me. Even after school, without a stitch of makeup, even under my hideous fluorescent lights, she looks luminous. She sticks out her perfect chin. "Why would somebody who looks like me take beauty tips from somebody who looks like her?" The majorettes laugh loud and hard at this one. Tayloe takes my *People* magazine off of my rack and flips through it. Her casual cruelty makes me angry. Suddenly I don't want the likes of her touching anything in my store.

"Put down the magazine," I warn in a voice that startles me. "You never buy them."

Tayloe quickly puts down the magazine. I look back at Pearl, whose eyes are not filled with tears, who is not blushing with embarrassment, who calmly works cream into June Walker's face with purpose and resolve. Pearl isn't a bundle of nerves anymore.

"I'm gonna say something to you girls. And you're gonna listen." Two of the majorettes, one a redhead with Farrah Fawcett feathering, the other a brunette with a Jaclyn Smith center part, backtrack to the door to escape. "You're not going anywhere, you two." The girls stop in their tracks and turn to face me.

"I'm sick and tired of your snide comments. You're mighty proud, Tayloe. But I'd be careful if I was you. Someday you won't have your looks anymore. And all those girls, like Pearl, who weren't popular, will be the pretty ones. Why? Because they have had to work at it. So they appreciate beauty in all its forms. You only know beauty as something given, not earned. So you won't understand what's happening when your youth is gone and the pounds creep on and the wrinkles come; and you'll panic because your best days are behind you. But Pearl's best days will be ahead of her. Why? Because she had to make something out of herself from scratch. Nobody helped her. The best she got was a bunch of stuck-ups making fun of her to make themselves feel big. But trust me, that kind of power is poison. It'll turn on you. When y'all are my age, you'll be the ones envying her. Pearl will know the great power of self-acceptance and real self-love, not the shallow vanity you mistake for it. At the end of the day, Pearl Grimes will be so beautiful, she'll wipe the floor with you."

All is silent in the store except for the creaking of the spin stool June Walker is sitting on as she leans into the mirror to examine her creamed face.

"You are so weird, Ave Maria Mulligan," says Tayloe. Finally, somebody pronounces my name correctly. Tayloe and her twirlers go. Pearl continues with her demonstration.

I come out from behind the counter and stand in the doorway and watch them walk up the street. And I don't know how to pinpoint what I'm feeling exactly, but for some reason I see myself at sixteen walking away from myself. I know it's not me out there on the street, but it is, in the image of those girls, walking away getting smaller and smaller, and disappearing. For the first time in my life I feel the thread of who I am unravel. I am one of those people who swears she knows herself well, who in any given situation can be described and counted on to behave in a certain way. I never yell at people, nor do I make speeches. When things get tense, I usually make a joke, so everyone will feel at ease. But something, beyond defending Pearl, beyond standing up for what is right, compelled me to speak. Where did she come from? Who is this voice that isn't going to make nice anymore, but will tell the truth? It isn't Fred Mulligan's daughter. I think of Mario da Schilpario, my father, the man in the picture. Why have I tried to put him aside, thinking him dead, gone, uninterested in the likes of me? But suddenly I know—and I am as sure of it as I am sure of myself standing here—that my father is alive, and he is well, and I must find him. I put my hand on my chest, expecting another anxiety attack to come, but it does not. Practical Ave Maria must go. Me. The never-married town pharmacist who is never caught without her first-aid kit. Me. So responsible she carries two spare tires in her Jeep instead of one. Me. Who has double insurance on everything because she's afraid one of the companies will go out of business and leave me penniless after a flood. Me. The girl who built her life so carefully so she'd never have to ask anybody for anything. I have had it with me. Whoever I was! Get mad, Ave Maria! You're alone in this world. You were abandoned. Let that anger fuel the job you must do. Find him. Find your father!

I walk out of my store and into the street. I breathe deeply right down to my toes. I walk to the Bookmobile. I have a job for Iva Lou.

CHAPTER FOUR

It is quiet in my living room except for the sound of Theodore and Iva Lou turning pages as they read. I've never had Iva Lou over to my house. I don't know why. When Mama was alive, I didn't have friends over much. Mama ran her sewing business out of the house, so people were always stopping by anyhow—maybe it didn't dawn on us to formally entertain. Fred Mulligan hated having company. Mama had better have seen her last customer before he came home. Even after he died, she kept that schedule. When I came home from work, everything was put away. That must have been so hard for her. She was social. Mama loved people. She never knew a stranger. After she died, so many folks came up to me and thanked me for her kindnesses: girls, now women, who wore prom dresses that Mama had made for free. Brides who needed wedding gowns with extra fabric in front because they were a little pregnant and didn't want to show for the occasion. She'd never complain; she'd just make the adjustments.

Fred Mulligan, however, had boundaries in all things. He could never make his customers his friends. I think he felt he couldn't make a profit from friends, so he simply never made any. Or maybe nobody wanted to be friends with him. Anyway, it feels right and glorious to have Iva Lou and Theodore sitting in my living room, eating chess pie, surrounded by stacks of books, all special orders from Clinch Valley College, a division of the University of Virginia in Wise. Iva Lou was allowed to check out these books because she knows the powers that be at the university library. (They've shared Sanka.)

She shoves a book under my nose and shows me a panoramic photograph. "Look, here's Bergamo. It's about the size of Big Stone Gap."

I study the panorama of Mama's hometown. There is a fountain with dancing angels in the middle of the square. Buggies led by donkeys cart people around. There are cobblestone streets. Fig trees. Small stone houses. Children. I picture my mother there as a girl. It seems to fit.

Theodore and Iva Lou leave around midnight. I clean up the dishes and walk through the first floor, turning out the lights. Then I do something I haven't done since my mother died. I go into her room.

My mother's room is simple. There is a double bed with a white cotton coverlet; over the bed hangs a small wooden crucifix. A straight-backed chair and a bureau stand against the wall opposite the window. Her sewing machine is tucked in a small alcove next to the window. The closet is small, its contents neat. I sit on the edge of her bed and look around the room as though I've never been inside of it before. I used to lie in here with her when she was dying. I took my rightful place next to her, as I was all she had. When I was little and I got sick, I would come and get her, but she never took me into her bed with my father. She would always come to my room on the second floor and lie with me there. She used to tell me that she didn't want to disturb him, but now I know she could not disturb him. He knew I wasn't his, and though he could have lovingly claimed me, he did not, and she kept me quiet. That was their understanding. And it was an understanding that lasted both of their lifetimes.

My mother was an avid reader, too. Occasionally, she bought books, but usually she just checked them off the Bookmobile as I did. She loved books about romance. Books that took place in faraway places and times. Stories with costumes. When Mama designed the costumes for the Drama, she studied the period, drew the sketches and everything. She had less theatrical tasks too. Mama has made every cheerleader uniform since anyone can remember. She made elaborate square-dancing skirts. And prom dresses, of course. When a customer wanted fancy, my mother would say in her Italian accent, "Simple is better. Simple. Simple." Sometimes she succeeded, but often I would hear her clucking as she sewed sequins and lace onto dresses that didn't need the fanfare. Many times when folks dropped off their clothes for altering or mending she would convince a lady to line a cloth coat in red satin or a skirt in silk. "No one will see it, but you will know it's there and it will feel wonderful," she'd say. My mother knew the finer things, but she didn't have a life that could celebrate them. I pick up a book off the nightstand. Glamorous Gene Tierney is on the cover. It's a book about costumes from the movies of the Golden Age in Hollywood.

Mama always took me to the movies over at the Trail Theater, right next to Zackie's. I didn't know it at the time, but Jim Roy Honeycutt, who owned the place, showed movies that were ten, fifteen years old. I never bothered to ask my mother why the people on the screen were wearing funny hats and hairdos; I just accepted it. It wasn't until years later that I found out Mr. Honeycutt saved a lot of money renting old prints. That's how I fell in love with the leading men of the 1930s and '40s: Clark Gable, William Powell, Spencer Tracy, Robert Taylor, and especially Joel McCrea. Mama loved the actresses, costumed by the great designers Edith Head, Adrian, and Travis Banton. I remember their names because Mama always pointed them out to me on the screen. We would see the same movies over and over again so Mama could study the clothes. Later she would discuss them with me in great detail. The movies were black and white, but Mama could tell when they used real gold thread on Hedy Lamarr's harem pants or real sable on Rosalind Russell's coat.

My mother was a great beauty. She had black hair so shiny it seemed lacquered; she wore it simply, combed back off of her face in a blunt bob. Her skin was golden—she died without a wrinkle or a line on it. She had deep-set brown eyes with lots of lid, like a Modigliani painting. Her neck was long and so were her fingers. She had full lips and beautiful teeth; she always was faithful about going to the dentist and taking me. Her nose was regal, aquiline. Her high forehead belied a nobility; to me she was a queen. But there was a deep sadness in my mother's eyes always, a longing to be somewhere else. I used to ask her, "Why, Mama, why did you come *here?*" As though here were worse than a swamp, a place without air. But she loved the mountains. Mountains meant everything to her.

I begged her to go to Italy with me after my father died. We had the time, we had the means, and most important, we no longer had him. We were free, but we couldn't adjust to it. After he died, we could play Sergio Franchi as loud as we wanted, but we still kept it muted so we could hear his approaching car in the driveway. He wanted nothing Italian in this house, except food. He ate my mama's cooking with relish; in fact, that's when we could count on him to smile. My mother made everything fresh, from her own garden; olive oil she ordered out of New York. My father even drank espresso. Her cooking was his one concession to my mother's heritage. Though he had studied Italian in college, he refused to speak it. He preferred my mother speak English. She taught me Italian, her regional dialect; we used it as a secret language.

The summer after I graduated high school, we went to Monticello, Thomas Jefferson's home outside Charlottesville, Virginia. It bugged me when my father mispronounced Monticello—he made a soft *c*, like "Monti-sello." I corrected him, and he got so mad he slapped me. But that was the last time he slapped me. From that moment on I stayed out of his way. I gave up. Then Mama did too. For years she tried to make us get along, but it was not to be. When I look back, I realize that she protected me from him. We built our world around keeping him comfortable and not upsetting him. I never showed anger, frustration, or passion in front of him. I swallowed everything, and soon it became part of my character. I was there to amuse and entertain, never, ever to challenge or disrupt. When I was alone with my mother, I could have my feelings, but then I would feel guilty—why upset her?

My mother was Roman Catholic. She was allowed to go to mass and take me, but then we would have to attend the Methodist church with my father as well. The Catholic church here is run by a small missionary order of poor carpenter priests called the Glenmarys. We didn't even have a real church building until five years ago; the priests were so busy building churches in poorer areas, they kept putting ours off. Finally, we built it, and nothing made my mother happier than writing a big fat check to the Catholics after my father died. She gave them so much money, they finished building our church! When the Methodists, who have a grand big church, came for their share, my mother gave them a small token, citing their large congregation and huge donor list. They weren't happy about the slight, but being good Christians, they let it go.

Mama and I tried to be good Italians after Fred Mulligan died. We wanted to reclaim that side of ourselves that we had hidden. We decided to go to Italy. We had great fun planning our trip. We did our research, made all the arrangements, bought the tickets, and then, as the date approached, Mama panicked, complaining of a fear of motion sickness. She became so distraught, I canceled the trip. Then, after a few days, she became herself again. The incident upset her so badly, I never mentioned traveling again. I didn't try to plan another trip. She could not have gone anyway. She got cancer, and that changed our lives forever.

I look around this room and see that she had one of everything: one lamp, one bureau, one chair. She only ever had one winter coat. One pair of good shoes. One pretty hair clip. One child. One of everything, but only one, as if to keep her life quiet. She lived by her own philosophy: Be unobtrusive and maybe he'll let us stay. As though that was all she deserved! My mother deserved so much more! The best of everything! No gold, no rubies, no rare diamond would have ever been enough for my mother. She was a woman of great character. My deepest sadness comes because I know she lived a life where she wasn't treated that way.

You would think, after she died, I would have come in here and gone through her things, but I couldn't. And now I am putting too much importance on this room. I want to find clues to her. Figure out what she really wanted. What she desired. What she was secretly interested in. I pull the books off of her nightstand and onto the bed and begin sorting. One on breast cancer. Another on regional Italian cooking. Ingrid Bergman's life story (we both love biographies). And, finally, *Lake Maggiore and Its Regions.*

I take the book, turn off the light, and leave her room. I am never afraid in this house, but tonight a chill runs through me. An urgency. I have led a life of quiet desperation (as my favorite author, Henry David Thoreau, described in *Walden*), just like my mother had, and now I want to change. As I pass through the living room to go up to bed, I pick up a small book from the large stack Iva Lou left behind. It's called *Schilpario: A Life in the Mountains.* The checkout card in the back says, "University of Virginia Architecture Library. DO NOT REMOVE." Iva Lou really went to some trouble to get me these books. I may have to break down and buy some Sarah Coventry jewelry from her.

Once I'm in bed, I turn on my bedside lamp and look through the pictures in the book about Schilpario. The Italian Alps are pointed and snowcapped. They seem three times as high as the Blue Ridge Mountains, and more dangerous, not as soft and maternal. The roads look new but narrow. There is a picture of a race car taking the dangerous curves, showing deep, jagged valley plummets to the sides of the road. No guardrails. Just like Powell Valley! I turn the page, and there is the town. This is a long-shot vista photo, probably taken from another mountain. The houses are close together and painted in muted shades of terra-cotta, gold, and soft brown. The main street leads to a waterwheel. On the next page, a picture of the waterwheel, a point of interest for tourists. In another time, before electricity, the waterwheel provided fresh water and power to the town. Now it is a museum.

I turn the next page, and there are some dignitaries from the town. They stand in a row—all men, puffed up and proud of their little village. I glance down at the names listed under the picture. As I'm reading, I look up at the row and study one man in particular who catches my eye. It's the expression on his face. I have seen it somewhere—in my own mirror. My heart begins to pound as it did the night at the

Fold. I look down. My pajama buttons are moving, but this time I can hear the attack and the whoosh, beat, whoosh, beat of my blood as it chugs through my heart with force and fear. I breathe deeply, but I can't inhale very well, so I suck in the air in small gulps. I think of Lew, who tells me not to worry, that it's nothing. I steady my fingers against the book. They are sweating and leave small circles on the book jacket. I rub the book on my bedspread. Then I pull the light as close as a microscope and prop the book open on my knees to steady it. I count over four names; the fourth man is the man I think I know. I scoot my finger across the faces and down to the matching name: Mario Barbari, Mayor, Schilpario, 1961–present. I flip to the front of the book and check the copyright date: 1962. That's a long time ago. I pull the small lacy picture of my father out of its envelope—I keep it with me at all times—and compare the faces. Mario Barbari is small in the picture, but I can see the shape of the face, the eyes, the eyebrows—all look similar to the young man in the picture Mama left behind for me. Is he my father?

I can hardly wait for Friday because it means Iva Lou is coming through with the Bookmobile. I wanted to call her at home, but I didn't because I wanted to tell her about Mario da Schilpario's picture in person. I can't wait for her to come to town, I'm too nervous and excited, so I drive down to her first stop in the Cadet section, just south of town, where she is parked by the side of the road. Iva Lou is sitting in the driver's seat of the Bookmobile, eating a sausage biscuit. I holler from my car window, "Are you alone?"

"Nobody showed up yet. It's slow as Christmas."

I park my car next to the Bookmobile and join her. "I think I found him. Mario."

"Lordy mercy!" she shouts, and jumps up and down. The Bookmobile rocks back and forth like a boat.

"Careful, Iva. We'll flip over."

"Honey-o, don't worry. This old thing doesn't have to last much longer."

"Why? Is the county springing for a new one?"

"No. But old Liz Taylor is gonna have a fried-chicken dinner over to the Coach House when she's here to raise money for our very own library. This could be it, Ave. The Big Time."

I sit down on my snap stool. Why does this upset me? Am I that attached to this truck full of books?

"I know you love this unit, but a library! Imagine all the books we can git if we git a whole big building!"

"You're absolutely right. I am being selfish."

"The state said they'd match whatever she came up with. Can I put you down for a couple of tickets to the dinner?"

"Sure, sure."

"It'll be fun. We'll get Theodore for you, and I'll scrape up a date. Lyle Makin has been chasing me of late, and I just might let him catch me. He's nice and he's got a good suit. But, Lord, forget all that. Tell me about this man you think might be your daddy."

I show Iva Lou the book; she scribbles down some notes.

"Sanka?"

This time I accept her offer. She pulls a sack out from a shelf and offers me a pink coconut snowball from the dry-bread store. I take it, tearing off one small piece at a time as I tell Iva Lou about the night I found my father in the book. She listens intently, following my every word.

Big Stone Gap has never been so atwitter. Theodore is in constant rehearsal for the halftime show; Nellie Goodloe has taken over the organization of the library fund-raiser chicken dinner; and I'm writing letters to government agencies in Italy, gathering information about Mario Barbari. It's as though the Blue Ridge Mountains around us have been peeled back and we're being discovered by a larger universe. This is equally thrilling and troubling. There is something comfortable about life the way it has been; who am I to upset the cart?

With all that's happening to me in my private life, the responsibilities of the Pharmacy still need tending to. I'm inspecting a new shipment from Dow, Fleeta is manning the cash register, and Pearl is doing inventory on our medical supplies when the familiar mine whistle blows. The coal mines are closing for the day; soon town will be filled with truckloads of men returning home for supper. I look out over my little staff as I fill prescriptions, and I feel very secure. Then the whistle blares three times in quick succession. It's not the whistle of the day being done; it's an emergency whistle. Something bad has happened up at the mine. We kick into automatic mode. Fleeta helps me out of my white jacket and into my Rescue Squad vest, and I grab my first-aid kit. I hear a horn—it's Spec—and I jump into the ambulance. The whistle blares three more times. Spec cannot drive fast enough.

We speed up the mountainside to the mine. The road is not paved, it's pure gravel; we kick up dust and are pitched to and fro in the grooves carved out by coal trucks. The smoke on the entrance road is thick and gray, which confirms my suspicions that there has been an accident inside.

The first thing we do is pull up to the check-in hut, which is close to the mouth of the mine. Here each miner, before he starts his shift, leaves a silver tag bearing his name. He wears an identical tag on his belt, so his whereabouts are known to the company at all times. In an emergency we rely on these tags for a head count. There are three tags left on the board; only they remain inside the mine: A. Johnson, R. Harmon, and J. MacChesney. I take a breath. "Come on, Ave. We ain't got all day," Spec says as we move to join the other Rescue Squad staffs.

There are four "holes," or entrances drilled into the side of the mountain. One entrance leads the miners to their work areas; one is for the conveyor belt, which transports the coal out; and the other two are for ventilation. There is a high level of methane gas underground, and the slightest disturbance can ignite it. There is no smoking allowed inside, but pockets of deadly gas can ignite without warning. Inspectors check the methane levels throughout the workdays and nights, but the miners travel as far as five miles into the mountain; there is always the threat of danger. As we get closer the smoke becomes deadly black, so the explosion must be deep. Rescue squads from the surrounding towns pull in around us. I see station wagons from Appalachia, Stonega, Norton, Coeburn, and Wise.

Spec and I await orders from the mining supervisor, who is on the radio to survivors in the mine. The stretchers are filling up fast. Most of the injuries appear to be from smoke inhalation. Hopefully, the situation inside is not too bad. In our favor: This is a new mining site, so the construction within is modern.

Spec and I are told to join the unit from Stonega. I can't see because of the smoke, but it wouldn't do much good anyway. The supervisor shows us a map of where the explosion took place: at the third level, about five miles into the mountain.

When I trained for the Rescue Squad along with volunteers from across the county, we toured a coal mine. I remember looking forward to it, like a field trip. We dressed like the miners: one-piece coveralls; rubber knee boots; the hard hat and light; and the belt to which we attached a power pack for the hat light, an ID tag, and a mask to convert carbon monoxide to carbon dioxide in case of an explosion. Miners are required to wear safety goggles; everyone does. It is also recommended that the miners wear a protective cloth mask while they work to decrease the inhalation of deadly coal dust, but most find it difficult to communicate and work while wearing a mask, and since they are not convinced that a mask prevents Black Lung anyway, they usually skip that step.

I had romanticized the underground, thinking it would be crypt-like and eerily beautiful. Instead, it felt ominous from the moment we climbed into the transport car. The cars are shallow, tin canoes that hold about ten people. The entrance ceilings are low, so you lie down most of the trip; on a deep excursion it is nerve-racking and uncomfortable. The only person who is allowed to sit up is the driver; he operates the car on the tracks with a wooden pole connected to the electrical lines rigged on the ceiling. There is not much conversation during the ride, but there is a lot of chewing and spitting. The men chew tobacco to keep their mouths wet, as the air is very dry within the mine. The temperature remains about fifty-five degrees year-round.

I thought the interior of the mine would be black, like dirt, and well lit. Instead, the main source of light is our hats, and the walls are white. After the coal is extracted, the miners spray the walls with a white rock dust that is nonflammable, so in case of fire the mine won't turn into an oven, roasting its own coal.

Our guide explained that each car carries a work crew to a particular area. Advances in technology introduced a machine called the Continuous Miner, which actually extracts the coal from the wall. The work crew is there to load the coal onto a conveyor belt, once it has been extracted by the machine. After an area is mined, a crew places timbers on the sides and walls to create channels and shore up the walls so they don't collapse; then the roof-bolt operator and his team come in to bolt the ceiling with giant screws so the men can dig more deeply into the mine and extract more coal. The roof-bolt operator has one of the most dangerous jobs; more miners are killed by rock slides than by explosions. The guide explained that these men have superior hearing, and the slightest cracking sound is a signal to move his men out immediately. There isn't much to be done in a serious rock slide, except try to excavate the men. In an explosion, you hope they can crawl out the shafts to safety, if they can see their way through the smoke. The other threat to the miner is flooding. A man called the pumper travels through the mine during the shift and pumps out water, as there is no way of predicting underground water sources.

I remember feeling I would suffocate as the car plunged deeper into the mine, and I became more fearful as the tunnel behind us became a black river with no end. The dimensions of the mine kept changing, too. Sometimes it seemed almost large, like a cavern, and then the car would push through to a space so tiny, my arms could reach from one wall of the tunnel to the other. I never felt that I could hold my head up without getting whacked by a beam or a crossbar.

There were constant reminders of impending doom: gas meters that would sound when noxious fumes were emitted from the earth; machinery programmed for automatic use that could go off without warning and cause injury; and then, of course, the dust. You can taste it, and when you breathe it into your nose, it is a little like trying your first cigarette. At first it seems foreign and you resist it. But eventually you forget about it. Coal dust penetrates the skin and fills the lungs, causing all sorts of diseases—the least of them cancer, the worst of them Black Lung, all of them painful, protracted illnesses that cause slow death. The thing that surprised me the most was the sound inside the mine. It was deadly quiet. This was a feeling of being buried alive. I wondered how the men do it each day. I couldn't.

Coal miners in general are practical men. I get to know them long after they quit the mines and are on Black Lung benefits. That's when they need their meds, and believe me, they need a lot of them. If it isn't the lungs that go, it's repetitive injury to the joints from the picking, the loading, the hauling, and the lifting. In the same way that the mountains are depleted of coal, the men are spent by taking it from the earth.

Mining is a family tradition; usually sons follow fathers into the mines, and their sons will follow them. There are amazing stories of bravery, and I think of them as I stand and await instructions. In the 1930s, Wesley Abingdon was a local hero because he refused to give up during an accident—he took the train car, threw the men into it, pedaled out, threw the men out, and went back for more. He saved about thirty men that day, and those thirty men told their thirty families, and so on. Wesley gained saint status in these parts.

A couple of years ago there was an incident that upon repeating sounds like a folktale, but I witnessed it, so I can tell you it is absolutely true. It was late spring, and the mountains were just coming into their green. The whistle sounded, and we assembled, just as we have today, to assist in the rescue. The supervisor had determined that all the men were out but one: Basil Tate, a young miner, was still unaccounted for. The problem with explosions is that it is very hard to determine the cause until after they happen, so they are very hard to prevent. Fire and smoke are wily as well, and a good miner figures this out and works with it. The mine rescue team was deciding how to proceed, how to find Basil, when a rumbling was heard from deep in the mine. It started out softly, but it sounded like it was coming toward the exit. I will never forget what happened next. The rumble became a blast. Dirt and black smoke poured out of the entrance, and then we heard a pop. We looked up, and there was Basil Tate, flying through the air like a human cannonball. The explosion had created a vacuum, with Basil in it. Then fire propelled the fumes—and Basil—like stoking a cannon to fire. The crowd watched the spectacle in awe. Was he alive? We followed the body up over the hill and down the mountainside. Basil landed by the creek, on soft mud. We were certain he was dead. When we got to him, he was unconscious, his body contorted in an S shape. We could tell from his position that he had broken his neck and his legs. But there was still a pulse, so we wrapped him up carefully and called for a chopper from the University of Virginia to fly him out for emergency surgery. Basil was in a body cast for close to two years, and now he works the box office at the Drama. We call him the Miracle Man.

The mining supervisor, a buttoned-down city type, not from these parts, shoots me a look that says, "What are you doing here?" Spec picks up on this and tells him, "She's with me." I ask an intelligent question about the explosion, and the foreman's brow relaxes like he's decided I'm okay and can stay and be of some help. He is a foreigner, too, but that's where the similarity between us ends. His demeanor and condescension are a perfect example of why locals don't like these company men. They come in with an attitude.

As explosions go, this does not appear to be a bad one. There is no fire yet; the smoke is from a power gash near the mouth of the mine. The mining foreman is trying to explain the location of Level Three to the company man when I look up and see Jack Mac crawling out of the air vent with Amos Johnson. I hear a scream as one of the wives runs toward her husband. She is held back as the rescue team from Coeburn tends to him. I run toward Jack Mac as he turns to go back into the mine. The foreman shouts at me to stop him. Jack Mac turns and looks at me. I tell him, "Rick is still inside." Two of the company engineers try to stop him, but he throws their hands off of him and goes back into the mine. The foreman chews me out for releasing information and tells me to stay behind the line and wait for the injured.

The worst thing about these accidents is the lag time between men going in and men coming out. The waiting periods are filled with silence and some muffled weeping. For the most part, folks don't cry; accidents are an occupational hazard, and there is no sense worrying until something actually happens.

Spec is miffed at me because he's been rendered impotent by my big mouth. Spec likes to get in the middle of things, and now he is a sideliner. Twenty minutes go by. Still no Jack Mac. I feel horrible guilt about this. Why did I tell him about Rick? Couldn't I have left it up to the company men to come up with a rescue solution? Didn't I know that Jack Mac would never sit and wait for them to do something? A hand is placed on my shoulder. I turn and see Sweet Sue with a look of total terror on her face.

"Is he in there, Ava?"

"He's getting Rick out. Don't worry." I comfort Sweet Sue as best I can, and she goes to join the rest of the women behind the line. I look over at them. Their expressions range from utter desperation and fear to pure fury. They are tired of this, and they have a right to be angry. They have sharp eyes—nothing gets past them—but there is also a weariness that comes from disappointment.

Spec shouts at me to follow him as most of the other rescue squads have already departed with injured. The foreman is still furious with me for telling Jack Mac about Rick. His job is to save as many men as he can, and now it looks as though he will lose two. Spec is starting to referee our argument when we hear a woman scream, "Help them! Help them!"

The crowd hushes to still quiet as smoke pours out of the mine. Then, almost as if in a dream, Jack MacChesney emerges from the mine carrying a man. I hear someone yell, "Jack Mac's got Rick! He's got Rick!" Rick Harmon's body is lifeless. We move in to resuscitate.

Spec is terrific with CPR and oxygen, so he takes charge and I assist. Jack Mac collapses and a doctor tends to him immediately. I look over at him and see that he is out cold. Rick's wife, Sherry, runs to us with her kids. They clamor to touch Rick, believing they can bring him around with familiarity and love and kisses. But the supervisor pulls them away and we continue to pump, pump, pump. Spec looks up at me. "He's coming to."

The doctor joins us and takes over. He tells us to move Rick away from the residual smoke, so Spec and I lift him carefully onto a stretcher and carry him a few feet to a clearing. Rick opens his eyes and says, "My foot. Goddammit, my foot." I smile at Rick with a look that says, *I don't think this is a good time to be cursing God;* and he looks back at me apologetically.

"Let me take a look at it." I hadn't noticed his foot. It is mangled and bloody. I smile again and tell Rick not to worry. But I am worried; there is a deep cut across the top of his foot, and I cannot make out his toes. I fear he may lose it. "How is it, Ave?" he asks, suspecting the worst.

"It's not too bad." Rick looks relieved and closes his eyes. He passes out. I wrap the foot and ice it.

The Norton crew places oxygen on Rick and hoists him into the ambulance. The doors slam shut and they speed away. I turn to find Jack Mac, but he is gone. The unit from Appalachia has taken him to the hospital.

The supervisor grumbles at Spec and me as we pass. I stop and ask if everybody is for sure out of the mine. He assures me that they are. He smiles, not a smile of relief for the men who survived, but a selfish one. Saving lives for him is all about numbers; he has had a good day, and he knows his job is secure.

The women rush away from the roadside and get into their cars. They speed down the mountain to follow the ambulances to the hospital. Rick's wife comes toward me and I give her a hug. All I can think is how much she must love him, and how happy she and Rick were dancing the other night at the Fold.

Spec drops me off at the Pharmacy, and I tell the girls I'm going to make a run to the hospital to see how the men are doing. Fleeta and Pearl need no details; they got the rundown from the police radio. Fleeta stops me as I'm leaving and wipes dirt off my face with a tissue.

Saint Agnes Hospital was founded by Irish Catholic nuns who migrated here in the 1930s. The common wisdom around here is, "When you're sick, let the sisters take care of you." Even though the locals don't particularly care for Catholics, they make an exception when it comes to health care. The nuns built their hospital in Norton, the closest city and the location most central to the coal camps. I love the hospital because there are statues of saints and angels tucked in every corner. One time Eulala Clarkston was in for a blood clot and she swore that she saw the Virgin Mary wave at her. Sister Julia told me that, as much as they would love for the Blessed Mother to make an appearance in Norton, they were pretty sure Eulala didn't actually see her. She was on Darvon at the time and was seeing things.

Most of the miners have been released. I ask one of the nurses if there is any word on Rick Harmon, and she tells me that he is undergoing surgery at UVA Hospital in Charlottesville, and that as soon as there is word, she'll let me know. I see Spec in the hallway and compliment him on his CPR; he thanks me for helping. As I turn the corner to go, I run right into Jack MacChesney. I give him a quick hug that catches him off guard.

"Are you all right?"

"Yes, ma'am."

Jack Mac is looking at my face funny, so I assume Fleeta didn't get all the soot off of me. I wipe my face with my sleeve. Then he says quietly, "Thank you for telling me about Rick—"

I interrupt him. "The supervisor really let me have it. That guy is a real jackass." Why am I talking so loud? I'm obnoxious. Then I blurt, "Do you need a ride home?"

Jack Mac looks like he would love one and is about to answer me when we hear a familiar voice.

"Jack!" his mother cries. "Let me see you!"

Mrs. Mac is on the arm of Sweet Sue. Jack looks at me, confused for a moment. Then Sue runs to him and covers him in kisses. Mrs. Mac then takes her turn and keeps touching his face like he's five. All of a sudden I feel all the sad things I felt as a girl: I'm an outsider. Sweet Sue and Mrs. Mac embrace Jack, and rightly so, for he is the town hero now. He didn't save thirty men, but he did save one; in the eyes of folks around here, that is just as important.

I'm happy Mrs. Mac and Sweet Sue are fussing over him. He deserves it. To be loved like that! To have somebody to worry about you.

To have your mother hold your face in her hands like delicate china! I am watching something perfect and beautiful, and I am not a part of it. They are a family. I walk back around the corner and out the door to the parking lot.

All I want is a hot bath, a glass of wine, and a long phone call with Theodore, but as I round the driveway to the back of the house, I see that I have company. Aunt Alice and Uncle Wayne's Oldsmobile Cutlass Supreme is parked near my back porch. The two of them are walking in the yard surveying the trees.

"You ought to get the forestry division over here to check that poplar. It has root rot."

I want to say, *And how are you, Aunt Alice?* but instead, I shrug.

"We'd like to talk to ye, Ava," my uncle says.

I invite them in and offer them iced tea, which they decline. As we pass through the dining room to get to the living room, Aunt Alice takes into account every piece of furniture, dish, and glass. It's as if her neck were on a wire, craning this way and that, to record each item and its placement in her memory.

I can't imagine why they're here. They never visit, call, or invite me to their home. After Dad died, out of respect, Mama and I would call them on holidays, but they were always so curt, we stopped trying. Aunt Alice has not aged well. She is around sixty now but looks far older. Her short hair is permed into dry, blue, tight curls. Her small face, wrinkled from a lifetime of grimaces, squints, and frowns, has an overall sour expression. She could use some Queen Helene. Her eyeglasses are too large for her face, and she has false teeth now—I can hear air whistle through them when she talks. Life has settled in on her, and the results aren't pretty.

"What can I do for y'all?" I ask and sit. Aunt Alice sits, but Uncle Wayne remains standing. He looks awkward, as though he's uncomfortable around his own wife. He is tall and lean, with the face of a wizened marionette; its creases are deep, as have been his compromises.

Aunt Alice answers, "We come down here 'cause I ain't gonna chase you all over hell to discuss business with you. So you just set there and listen to me because I got something I need to say. Now, I know your mama done came clean with you." She used the word *clean,* implying that what came before it was dirty.

"Inez Eisenberg needs to look up *client confidentiality* in the dictionary."

"Now, Ava, you listen here," offers Uncle Wayne. "We don't want no trouble."

"What kind of trouble?" Then I look at Aunt Alice. "And what kind of business?"

Then Aunt Alice explodes. "You look here, younguns, I have stood by all my life and watched my brother, who I loved very much, give all he had to you and your ungrateful mother, and I kept silent because he wished it so, but now, now that the truth is out, you need to know that restitution must be made to me as I am my brother's only living blood relative. Blood. You know what I mean."

I nod.

"You are not blood. You will never be blood. It almost killed my mama when Fred came home with a wop. A pregnant one! Jesus help us! He shows up back here, on this here porch with a sullied feriner! She moved in here with her high-and-mighty attitude, looking down her nose at us, and took him for all he was worth. He done educated you, clothed you. You ate well and lived like a princess with trips here and yon and up to Monti-sello and so forth, and I done never even got as far as Roanoke. You done took all you're gonna take from me. And I mean that, missy."

I sit quietly and look at my hands. There are three small cuts on my right index finger. I don't remember getting them, but now they pulse a little and hurt. I must have gotten them removing Rick's gear as the Norton crew lifted him into the ambulance. There is a little bit of dried blood around the first cut. I rub it off on my pant leg. Aunt Alice continues.

"After all, that business of his made you rich. That was my pappy's building, and this was the Mulligan family homestead, and I got nothing from all of this. Do you know what it does to me to think I can't live in the house I grew up in? That some stranger is living in my mama and daddy's house, instead of me? I'm treated like this, and I am his true relative?"

"His blood relative," I say quietly.

"Damn right! And here we are! Struggling! We're on Social Security, but that ain't enough. And you're over here, rich as all get-out, and you have never lifted one finger to help us." Aunt Alice turns to look up at Uncle Wayne. His mouth moves but no words come out, just like the mechanical Santa I put in the window at Mutual's every Christmas. She stares at him to command him to speak, but he cannot. The vein in her neck is a tight, dark blue cord. Her head snaps wildly about in anger. She looks directly at me, which she has never done. I look into her eyes. Behind the bifocals, they are light brown, googly, off center, and surrounded by whites. (In face-reading, irises that float, surrounded by white, belong to folks with criminal pathologies. I'd say she's angry enough to kill right now.)

"I wish somebody had thought about me for once. Looked out for me. Nobody never done looked out for me!"

This is true. Other than those few times after Fred Mulligan died, I never looked in on them, or brought them a gift, or stopped by. But I didn't because they were the nastiest people I ever knew. Small and clannish, gossipy and mean, they didn't deserve a loving niece. Besides, they had committed the worst of sins in my mind: They were hateful to my mother. Aunt Alice never showed me any affection whatsoever. Nor could I remember a birthday gift, a card, or an Easter egg for me, ever. Really, I had no attachment to them. That is why it is so easy for me to say:

"How much do you want?"

My question catches them both completely off guard. They look at each other. Uncle Wayne is practically salivating, like I could cut them a check right now. Aunt Alice is dizzy with greed, looking around, wanting everything in this simple house, including the house itself. Uncle Wayne shifts his posture to stand up straight.

"Your aunt and I haven't actually come up with the specifics yet."

"Well, I think you should."

Aunt Alice looks at me. She doesn't trust me. Her eyes narrow.

"We've been talking to a lawyer down in Pennington, and he is advising us."

"Have him call me."

They look at me blankly. They didn't expect me to respond this way.

"I don't mean to be rude, but I just had a job with the Rescue Squad and I'm mighty tired. Maybe you heard. We had a bad explosion up at Wence. If you don't mind." I stand and motion them to the door. Aunt Alice leaves first and doesn't look back at me. Uncle Wayne, now in a gracious mode because he can taste cash, smiles weakly at me through his thin lips.

"We just want what we got coming to us."

"I hope you get what you've got coming to you."

I bolt the door behind them and go directly to the bathroom. I throw up. I am scared by how much I'm vomiting, and intermittently I cry. I flush with my left hand and lean and run the cold water with my right. As soon as I can splash the cold water on my face, vomit comes up again. This happens over and over, until nothing but clear water comes up from within me. I brush my teeth. I go to put the toothbrush back in its holder and find I can barely lift it. It is as though the toothbrush is made of concrete. I begin to cry again. I want my mother. I grip the sink. I watch my tears hit the white porcelain and disappear down the drain. "I should have killed her for what she said about you, Mama." But deep within me, I know there is a better way to finish off Aunt Alice. I just have to find it.

CHAPTER FIVE

The old wisdom that everybody needs a good lawyer is true. I have Lew. He is thorough and competent. I just wish Inez wouldn't repeat everything she hears in his office. I don't want my personal business discussed in line at the grocery store. Fleeta almost got in a fistfight when some unflattering stories were being passed around about me on double-coupon Saturday. For the most part, though, folks are more fascinated than judgmental that I turned out to be a bastard. They can't believe the intrigue of it all, or that a regular person like me could be in the center of such a tale. The truth is, most folks around here are cautious conservatives, and the Bible is a serious guidebook for them. I'm getting looks of pity and wonderment from practically everybody I run into. I can tell which of my customers are repeating stories because they cannot look me in the eye. I surprise myself, because it seems that something like this should cause me some shame. I am more relieved than ashamed, though. The relief hasn't brought me any peace of mind yet, but I am hopeful it will.

I need to speak to Lew, and I don't want Inez to hear what I have to say, so I wait until I see him leave his office to pick up his mail at the post office. I grab my coat and follow him.

Lew juggles his keys and opens his post office box. It is stuffed with mail. As he pulls it out, he drops a periodical and I pick it up for him. I tell him about Aunt Alice and Uncle Wayne's visit. Then I tell him my plan. I was up all night, scheming and drinking coffee, so I have a crazy look about me, but my mind is clear.

"You're thinking like a lawyer. That's scary," Lew says, as he makes a cylinder out of his mail and snaps a rubber band around it.

I wait for Lew to exit the post office. I buy a pack of stamps and wait a couple of minutes before I go. As I walk back to the Pharmacy, I see Inez grabbing a smoke on the stoop of the law office. I wave to her and smile. Any sign of warmth throws her off, so she looks at me like I'm the town kook, waves back, and smiles weakly.

I return to the Pharmacy. I fill all my prescription orders, check my inventory, and make my bank deposit. I skip lunch. I don't make any calls. I don't say much to Fleeta or Pearl. I do my work. And I wait. A few hours pass, and Pearl calls me to the front.

"Lew Eisenberg wants you to come over."

I hug Pearl and she looks at me oddly.

"It must be good news."

"Oh, it's not news. Not yet, anyway."

Pearl shrugs and returns to her work. She's scraping the tips off the used lipstick samples in the display rack. Fleeta is sitting on a box of new shampoos, taking a smoke, so she doesn't notice I'm leaving. As I round the corner, I feel the first cold chill of autumn. It seems like the seasons changed in the course of this one day. The cool temperature gives me a boost.

"Is your beloved inside?" I ask Inez.

She thinks this is a little too hilarious, and laughs. "Go on in," she says.

Lew is sitting behind his desk. He motions for me to sit down. He turns up the radio, so Inez can't hear us. He goes over the legalities of my plan. He says one thing that concerns me: Wayne Lambert's first cousin, Buddy Lambert, is our circuit court judge at the county level, and he is known as Judge Envelope. He can be bought, and Lew believes Wayne has probably already cut a deal. There is a part of me that agrees with Aunt Alice; Fred Mulligan's money and real estate don't really belong to me. Maybe I caused all this. Maybe my ambivalence about my father, the store, the money, and the house drew all these problems to me. Maybe Aunt Alice senses my weaknesses and knows how to hurt me the most. Her brother sure did; don't these traits run in families? I don't think she'll quit until she makes me suffer.

Fred Mulligan was the most obstinate man I ever knew. His stubbornness—not his affection for my mother—is what made their marriage last. When I was in high school, he insisted that a lemon tree could grow in Big Stone Gap. No matter how much we argued with him, he could not accept that lemons need heat and sun to grow, the opposite of overcast and cool mountain weather. When the plant didn't bear fruit, he blamed the mail-order company. The lemon tree is still in the backyard. Its branches are gray and twisted, wrapped around the drainpipe by the back-porch stoop. I'll never tear it down; it reminds me not to turn bitter.

Lew sees my uncertainty. "You're doing the right thing, Ave Maria," he reassures me.

I have to stand up for myself. There is no one here to do that for me. For the first time in my life, I truly understand *alone*. My mother is gone. There is no brother or sister for me to turn to, no husband, just my intuition.

I don't want the Lamberts to get a dime. I think of Aunt Alice mistreating my mother, and it is all the fuel I need. Lew gives me the paperwork, which I sign. He hides it in a satchel to take to court. Then Lew shakes my hand. He places both hands on mine, to give me support and courage. I want to hug him, but I can't.

I pass Inez, who is now sitting at her desk, and turn back to Lew with one final thought.

"Lew, thank you for helping me. Aunt Alice and Uncle Wayne really deserve all they're getting. It's what Fred Mulligan would have wanted."

Lew stands in the doorway. "We're happy to have been of service to you." Lew waves good-bye.

I'm out on the street, and I can hear Inez chatting on the phone already.

Insko is a tract of free land between Big Stone Gap and Appalachia that had been strip-mined. Instead of reclaiming the area, HUD put up low-income housing. When the valley floods, they move the people high up into the hills until their homes in the valley can be rebuilt. Sometimes it takes so long, folks give up and stay where they were placed.

Folks around here both rely upon and resent the government. When I was in school, we benefited from many programs. All of our vaccinations were free. Our lunch trays were filled with freebies: small bags of peanuts, a chocolate bar, or my favorite: a wedge of cheddar stamped GOVERNMENT CHEESE. They even sent entertainment from time to time. When I was in high school, a production of *Harvey* toured through, out of New York. I wasn't the only student to notice that the lead actor was drunk and actually fell asleep onstage during the second act. But we didn't care. We were looking for any excuse to be a part of the outside world, to see what folks looked like, sounded like, and wore. For fifteen cents, you could see a show and imagine the exciting lives of those actors on the stage. We were never disappointed.

Pearl and her mother live in one of the older homes at the far end of the Insko development. I have dropped Pearl off several times, so I know where to go. I pull up in front of the two-room house. I didn't call ahead because I couldn't—they still don't have a phone, and they aren't planning on getting one, as Pearl is saving for college. The aluminum siding needs replacing, and the porch is rickety and practically separated from the house. The government is not very diligent about maintenance. The windows are thin side-by-side sliders, no insulation. I can see a light on in the house. A few kids play nearby. They stop and stare at me. I fish around my purse for some gum. I find it and give it to them. They thank me and run off.

I knock a few times. Finally, the screen door cracks open about an inch.

"Mrs. Grimes?"

"Yes, ma'am."

"I'm Ave Maria Mulligan, from town."

Leah Grimes peeks out at me.

"Pearl went to fetch some leaves or something for her science project."

"May I come in and wait for her?"

"I guess so."

Leah Grimes opens the door to reveal a very clean but sparsely furnished room. There is an old bench, a small table, and a lamp. In the next room are two neatly made twin beds with old quilts on them. The kitchenette is neat. A pot of soup simmers on one of the two burners. Pearl comes in the door, breathless.

"Is everything all right, Miss Ave?"

"Everything is fine."

"Mama, this is my boss, Miss Ave."

"I know that." Leah stands tall but looks at me funny.

"Pearl is a good worker. I don't know what I'd do without her."

"I know. She's a good girl."

"Has she brought you any of that miraculous Queen Helene masque yet?"

"Yes, ma'am." Leah smiles and covers her mouth.

"I apologize if we've used you as a guinea pig for our new products, but we needed a woman with natural beauty to test it out on."

"I used to be pretty, before I lost my teeth."

"You know they can give you new teeth in town."

"Someday. Right, Mama?" Pearl says, and gives her mother's hand a quick squeeze.

"Would you like some tea?" Leah asks, finally warming up.

"If you don't mind, I've got some business to discuss with Pearl." Pearl stands up straight and acts terribly grown-up at the mention of business.

Pearl takes me on a tour of the development. About a quarter mile down the road is one of our local natural wonders: the waterfalls of

Roaring Branch. It's a magical place, natural stone steps with pure mountain water rushing over them. Folks come this way to sit and think and take in the beauty.

"You didn't know we was so poor, did you?"

"I make a lot of deliveries in these parts."

Pearl and I sit and look at the water for a long time.

"How come you drove up here to see me? Am I fired or something?"

"No. You're doing a great job."

"Thank you. I bug Fleeta sometimes," Pearl apologizes. She looks at me expectantly, wondering why I've come.

"Pearl, do you have a dollar?"

"You just paid me. I got forty-six dollars."

"I just need one."

Pearl takes out her beaded coin purse and unfolds her money neatly. She gives me a dollar bill. "Do you need more? Here. Take as much as you want."

"No, thanks. One will do it. Now, let's shake on it."

Pearl is confused, but she shakes my hand.

"Congratulations, Pearl. You just bought the Mutual Pharmacy."

"I did? But why?"

As I walk Pearl back to her house, I explain that in order to protect the business from the scavenger Lamberts, I had to sell, and sell quickly. I had to make some big decisions in a hurry. I decided to sell my business so it couldn't be taken from me.

When we get back to the house, Pearl turns to me.

"Can I tell Mama?"

"Absolutely. Just tell her to keep it top secret until I say so."

"Miss Ave, are you sure about this?"

"Yes, ma'am. By the way, just because you own the place, you are under no obligation to become a pharmacist. You go to college and study whatever you'd like and be whatever it is you decide you want to be. Fleeta and I can hold down the fort while you're gone. Fleeta will probably hit you up for a raise directly. I'm not so forward. But I do have a lot of experience, should you decide to keep me. I have a knack with the public."

"But why did you pick me? Of all people?"

"Well, let's just put it this way, Pearl Grimes. You're just about the best person I ever knew."

Pearl smiles. In the slate-blue twilight, her face is pure, unlined, and full of joy. Something good has finally happened to Pearl. At long last, somebody believes in her. Tonight in this exchange she has gained the tools with which she will build her self-esteem: She has been chosen and she has security. Maybe this is all that a person ever needs to succeed. Pearl has been picked, and that has begun to define her.

I promised Iva Lou I would meet her at the Sub Sandwich Carry-Out for a bite. This is mainly a teen hangout, but the rest of us go because the food is good. It has a nice ambiance; the plastic Tiffany chandeliers and orange Formica booths are casual and comfortable.

I tell Iva Lou about Aunt Alice and selling the business to Pearl.

"Honey-o, you ought to thank the Lord you came up with a plan like that. If your mean old aunt ever got her mangy mitts on the Mutual, nobody would trade over there. It'd close down. Ain't nobody gonna do trading with that witch."

"Lew really knows what he's doing."

"You know what I always say. A good lawyer is harder to find than a good husband. I'll have to swing by and thank old Lew my way." Iva Lou winks.

"Please. I'm in enough trouble."

"Aw, I'm just kidding with you. But what happens to you? What will you do?" Of course, I've thought about this. I've never made an impulsive decision in my life.

"I've saved a lot of money, Iva Lou."

"Good for you."

"I'll work for Pearl for a while, and then we'll see what happens."

Dickie and Arlan Baker, two Mormon fellows, join us in the booth. Iva Lou makes the introductions, as she was the one who set up the meeting. The Baker brothers look to be in their twenties. They are clean; their hair is cropped short, their skin smooth and pink. (Mama always told me to cut down on the soda pop, because it's bad for the skin. As a rule, Mormons don't drink pop; their skin is an advertisement to give it up entirely.) They wear regulation black trousers and white cotton button-down shirts. For as many years as there have been Mormons, the young men have gone door-to-door wearing the same clothing combo, passing out the same literature, preaching like the good missionaries they are. The brothers have come to the Pharmacy a couple of times, but I was always too busy to talk to them.

"Boys, we need your help out of Salt Lake City. We need to climb up Ave Maria's family tree." Iva Lou opens a spiral notebook and un-caps her pen. "There's a man over in It-lee, and we need to find him pronto. That means 'fast' in Italian."

I laugh because this is one of the first words I taught Iva Lou.

"How can we help you?" Dickie—or is it Arlan?—asks.

"This is pretty much all the information we have on Mario Barbari presently." Iva Lou gives them the book with the picture of Mario as the mayor of Schilpario in it. "Don't lose it. UVA'll have my hide." Dickie looks at Mario's picture.

"I think we can help. Most folks don't have pictures."

Iva Lou listens as the Baker brothers explain how the Mormons came to be experts in genealogy. God bless her patience. She is such a dear friend, but I'm worried. We are so caught up in how to find Mario, I haven't had time to think about what will happen if we do. What if he rejects me? How will I handle it? I'm peeling off my old life like wet clothes. It isn't easy, but I have to do it. What will my new life be? Letting go of the Pharmacy, something I thought I would never do, wasn't sad. It was exhilarating. I am becoming lighter. Will finding Mario da Schilpario be the one thing that brings me happiness? Will I truly be free of my Mulligan past when Alice Lambert finally gets her comeuppance?

Iva Lou rips the pages out of her spiral notebook. "Y'all scoot. And here's my number when you get the information."

Dickie and Arlan thank Iva Lou for dinner. They take their black valises and go.

"Iva Lou, what would I do without you?"

"Well, honey-o, somebody's got to put a fire under your butt. I see how you operate. You get all caught up in other people's dramas instead of your own. You need to be your own Rescue Squad, honey-o. Stop neglecting yourself."

"I don't do that."

"Sure you do. You ain't getting any, Ave, and that's a *big* problem."

"How do you know I'm not getting any?"

"I just know."

Iva Lou sucks the last bit of Tab through the straw. She swishes the ice around in the glass and starts chewing on it. "It ain't healthy to go without." I must look horrified because she holds up her index finger to punctuate the importance of what she is saying. "You know, I've known me a lot of men. And the one thing I've learned is that they're all different. With each new experience that I rack up, I learn something new that I take with me as I move ahead in life. Sex is the most important thing there is on this earth."

"What?" I whisper. And then Iva Lou repeats what she just said, this time with more volume. She raps the table when she's finished.

"Why?"

"Because it's the only mystery."

I don't know if Iva Lou is profound or an idiot. Or if she has searched high and low for meaning in all her romances. Sex is a mystery? To whom? Not to her. I don't understand why she is saying this to me.

"Life is a mystery to be lived, not a problem to be solved," she says. "A friend of mine gave me a coffee mug with that on it a while back, and I've made it my personal philosophy. Plus, you have to find your father before you can love any man."

"I don't believe that for a second." I brush Iva Lou off with a wave.

"You should. It's true. Why do you think I'm helping you try to find him? I know what your problem is and how to fix it. You were told something all your life that was a lie. I happen to think you knew all along it was a lie. But that is something for you to figure out on your own after all of this is over. When people live lies, they stop connecting. When they stop connecting, trust dies. Honey-o, you can't be with a man because you can't trust one. You can't get naked, and I'm using that not literally but as a figure of speech. You follow me? To my way of thinking, if you can find your father, it will be a revelation to you. You will be able to place yourself in this world. You will finally know where you belong. You ain't one of us, Ave Maria. And not because your mama was a feriner. You separated yourself from folks around here. And I don't mean that to be cruel. You've lived here your whole life, but nobody really knows you. The first time I got a glimpse of what makes you tick was that night we read the books over at your house. You were looking at those books like old Kent Vanhook looks at my ass. There was a hunger there, a desire at long last."

Some high school boys are playing a long song called "Paradise by the Dashboard Light" for the third time. Iva Lou shouts at them to pick something else, like Mac Davis's "One Hell of a Woman" (her personal favorite) or Conway Twitty's latest.

Then the bells on the entrance door jingle. They're exact replicas of the ones I have on my door at the Pharmacy. Every merchant in town has a set from Zackie's Bargain Store, and the same sweet ring happens when you go into any store in the Gap. Through the jingle, Sweet Sue comes in with Jack Mac. He sees us and walks toward us. Sweet Sue waves at us and goes to the take-out counter.

"Sue's kids with their daddy this weekend?" Iva Lou asks.

"Yes, ma'am," Jack Mac replies.

"How's your mother?" I ask. Why do I always ask him about his mother?

"She's fine."

"Tell her I was asking for her." What am I? An old lady from the Methodist church sewing circle? Iva Lou shoots me a look.

"I will, ma'am." Jack Mac looks down at the table and sees Iva Lou's open notebook.

"Y'all working on something?" he asks.

Iva Lou looks at me to answer.

"It's kind of a long story." Jack Mac looks over to the take-out window. Sweet Sue chats with Delphine Moses, the owner of the Carry-Out, as she ladles tomato sauce onto the pizza dough.

"I got a few minutes." Jack Mac sits down with Iva Lou, facing me.

"I'm trying to find my father." Why am I telling him this? Couldn't I just make up something light and silly, like Iva Lou's working on a reading list for me? Why do I have to yak about my business?

"Have you heard the story going round about our Ave Maria?" Iva Lou asks as though I'm not there.

"I've heard some," Jack Mac replies.

"We're trying to find an Eye-talian gentleman, who is our Ave's real father."

"Yep, I'm a bastard," I joke.

"No, you're not. That's a label adults put to babies. To my way of thinking, there isn't a soul born that wasn't supposed to be here." Jack Mac says this as though it's the simplest concept in the world.

Iva Lou and I look at each other.

"How's the search going?" Jack Mac asks, picking up Iva Lou's notebook and scanning it.

"Iva Lou got the Mormons involved. I guess they know how to find people."

"They sure do. Generally, they just ring your bell." Iva Lou and I laugh. Jack Mac doesn't laugh at his own joke, and I respect that.

Sweet Sue stops by our table with her carry-out sack. "Jack, let's go."

Jack gets up to leave, but for a moment I don't think he wants to go. I think he wants to sit and talk with Iva Lou and me.

"Y'all take care, now," Jack says, and follows Sweet Sue out the door.

Iva Lou rises up off the seat about three inches to catch the rear view of Jack Mac as he goes. "Nice sculpted hindquarters. Very nice. There ain't nothing like a working man."

"What do you mean?" I ask.

"I love carpenters, plumbers, construction workers, and coal miners. The Jack Mac type."

"He's a type?"

"Uh-huh. Had to narrow it down. When you've known as many men as me, you start making lists. The working man is a solid man.

They can fix things that are broke. They're practical. I like that. How about you?"

"I never thought about it." I really don't want to talk about this.

"I'll bet you haven't," Iva Lou says, and looks at me, shaking her head. "Let me tell you what. Those men that sit behind a desk all day, the office types, stay away from them. They are the weirdos of the world. They don't get out and get air and get physical every day, so their blood pools in their brains, and they get very strange sexual ideas, believe you me. Kinky. I mean it."

I try to get Iva Lou off of this subject and back to the Mormons' notes. She is talking her favorite subject, though, and is therefore persistent.

"I tried to have sex with him once," Iva Lou announces.

"With whom?"

"Jack Mac."

"Really?"

"I got nowhere. Nowhere."

"Why? You're so pretty and fun. What happened?" Why am I asking her this when I don't want to know? I do this. When folks make me uncomfortable, instead of removing myself from the situation, I try to make them comfortable.

"Well, one night, before he started going with Sweet Sue, he was up to the Fold and we had a couple of beers and a couple of dances and I was frisky, and he was frisky, so I suggested a rendezvous up to Huff Rock. I find it inspirational up there. The mountaintop, the sky, the big old rocks to lie on. You're getting the picture." I nod. "Well, we kissed a couple of times. Good kisser. Uh-huh. Good kisser. And then it was getting time to move things along toward some sort of something, and he stopped."

"He stopped?"

"I asked him why he stopped, of course. I'm not bragging, but that sort of thing never happened to me before. I said, 'Jack MacChesney, why on God's green earth are you stopping now? Aren't you having fun?' "

"What did he say?"

"Well, he looked at me with those eyes of his, and he said most sincerely, 'Iva Lou, you are a doll. But I ain't in love with you. And I'm one of those men that has to be in love to carry on like this.'"

"No!" I shriek.

"Yes. That's exactly what he said. And it was funny. My feelings weren't hurt; I wasn't embarrassed or any of that. But I'll tell you something: I couldn't believe that there was a man like that walking around in this world. I persisted a little with him, and he, very gentlemanly, kept declining my advances, so I yanked my bra straps back up and called it a night. I don't know, I guess I admired him for his principles. I didn't want to mess with it. I respected him."

Iva Lou shrugs and picks up the last crumbs of cake with the back of her spoon. "Does that beat all? I mean, did you ever?"

"No, that's quite a story." What does she want me to say?

We sit quietly for a few moments. I look at Iva Lou. As she studies her notes, she looks like a little girl. I can see exactly who she was when she was little. A curious girl with a big appetite. What happened to the girl I used to be? Where did she go?

When I was seven, Mrs. White took our second-grade class to Clinch Haven Farms. It's high up the mountains; I remember being scared in the bus. It was pretty once we got there, though. There were vivid green meadows that rolled back like folds of white icing, covered in flowers, dotted with cows, just like the picture on the milk bottle. The first thing Mrs. White showed us was a creek that twisted down the rocks and flowed into a pool. Mrs. White gathered us on the bank of the creek and explained the way water worked—how it rained and came down the mountain, making rivulets that pool and fall and then turn into rivers. We were allowed to drink of the creek. Mrs. White taught us how to kneel and, without disturbing the sediment at the bottom of the creek, cup our hands to drink the clear water off the surface. As I knelt, I examined the stones through the clear water. They were glassy brown and black stones, like the antique buttons my mama kept in a cupcake tin in her sewing closet. Then we followed the creek down to Buskers Farm and she told us how explorers always followed water. Even now, if I get lost when I'm making deliveries up in the hollers, I just remember to follow the water, and I always find my way back to town. That simple rule, for whatever reason, has stayed with me all these years and held me in good stead.

Buskers Farm was gigantic. There was an open field, a barn, and a main house. There was an outhouse; we all made jokes about it, even though some of my classmates still used outhouses.

I was with Nina Kaye Coughlin, my best friend. She had straight, shiny red hair and a turned-up nose splattered with freckles. When she smiled, her front teeth turned inward to make a V shape; it didn't look bad, though. Crowded teeth are a sign of someone with lots to say. At one point I whispered to Nina Kaye that we ought to go look in the barn. So we separated from the group and went around the back of the barn to find the door. There, in a clearing, was a hog, strung up on three long poles, suspended by the head. Its gut was split from throat to groin. Two farmhands were cleaning the open gash—I guess they were removing the organs. Their hands were full of squishy blue and red entrails. They were being careful with the parts, placing them on a small, clean tarp, pulled tightly over a barrel. The hog's eyes were wide open, staring up to the sky, as if in prayer. There was a ruby-red pool beneath the hog; his blood was so voluminous that it filled a small pit. We froze. Nina Kaye was holding my hand so tight, her fingernails made grooves on the side of my palm. Finally, the farmhands looked at us. For a moment they seemed annoyed, but when they saw how scared we were, they softened.

"Girls, we done drained the hog," one of the men explained.

Nina Kaye looked as though she might faint. We both lived in town; the only farm animals we saw were on these field trips or at FFA camp in later years. We backed away from the scene and tore around the side of the barn. Nina Kaye cried and I comforted her. "Ain't you skeered?" she said to me. "We can't both be scared," I told her.

"There you go again," Iva Lou says. "Off in space."

"Sorry, Iva."

"What were you thinking?"

"How I used to be so brave."

———

Bullitt Park, our high school football field and town park, is full of fog. It fills up with gray mist like a soup bowl some nights, especially in early fall when Mother Nature is making her temperatures drop. It's a little dreary, and tonight it's all business. After two months of intense practice, the Powell Valley High School marching band is going to run the final rehearsal of the Elizabeth Taylor Halftime Show Salute full out, no stops. Theodore is on the fifty-yard line giving some last-minute tips to the flag girls. In their gold lamé short shorts, you would never guess they were high school sophomores; they look like they could be in Cleopatra's harem.

The drum majorette blows her whistle, and the band falls into formation in the end zone, spaced across in a straight line from fence to fence. The band is magnificent in their Carolina-blue and ruby-red uniforms. From the visitors' side, the pyramid crew runs out onto the field and places the pyramids. The drum majorette barks, "Horns up!" The band begins to play.

The show is truly a wonder, but over it there is a veil of trying too hard. We are overcompensating and overprepared, but we don't know what else to do with the nervous energy that runs through us. We aren't used to famous people gracing these parts, though the great baseball player Willie Horton of the Detroit Tigers was born over in Arno. The only star that has ever passed through here was Peggie Castle from *The Lawman,* and frankly, without her makeup she didn't look like her TV self. And of course, George C. Scott (General Patton) was born in our county seat: Wise, Virginia. Until now, they were the Big Names. But we're about to top them with the biggest star of all. Everybody in Big Stone Gap has a stake in making Elizabeth Taylor's visit a success. Mr. Honeycutt has been running a "La Liz" film festival at the Trail, and this has only fed the feverish excitement. Nellie Goodloe keeps reminding us that this is an election year and the visit is really about politics. But no one seems to care about that. John Warner is a Republican, and most folks around here are Democrats, so I don't think coming through here will do his campaign much good. This is Jimmy Carter country all the way. But if anyone can sway some votes for Mr. Warner, it will be his movie star wife.

Even Tayloe Slagle is a nervous wreck. She threw up behind the bleachers before her big solo number, sending a shudder through the entire marching band. Luckily, I have a pack of Tums in my pocket— I've been carrying them around since the panic attacks started—and I run them over to her. She is embarrassed about being sick and grateful for the Tums to settle her stomach. Sitting on the ground in her mother's arms, Tayloe looks like a little girl. She is a little girl. We forget that, because kids around here marry so young. From my perspective now, at my age, she looks so small.

After he checks on Tayloe, Theodore runs onto the field, rallying the kids to focus and concentrate on the routine. You can see the fear in their faces, though. If the most perfect girl in town is a nervous wreck, it wouldn't take much for the entire band to keel over in group panic like dominoes. Thankfully, Tayloe revives quickly and returns to the field. Now she can add *vulnerable* and *indomitable* to her long list of desirable attributes.

I join Spec up in the bleachers. He just went on a Rescue Squad run to Wallens Ridge, so I'm dying to hear details.

"What happened?" I ask Spec as I sit down beside him.

"Larry Bumgarner done shot his sister."

"No! Is she okay?"

"She's fine. He missed. Put a hole in the sleeve of her shirt is all." Spec lights a cigarette.

"Why . . . why did he shoot her?"

"She was on the phone too long. He wanted to ask a gal, you may know her, she's a majorette, Bree Clendenin?" I nod. "Well, Larry wanted to ask Bree to Homecoming in the worst way, and his sister was tying up the line. He got fed up and went in the bedroom and got his papaw's gun and threatened her, and he says it accidentally went off." Spec exhales.

I look off at the mountains covered in a veil of sheer gray and decide for sure and forever that I am quitting the Rescue Squad.

Spec must read my mind. "I could have used you up there. You're good at talking sense." Spec thinks a compliment will keep me on the job. I'll let him think so. "You know, I had to ask him one thing. The kid. Larry. I had to know what in God's name was so special about Bree Clendenin that he had to shoot his sister off the phone. And do you know what he said to me?"

"I can't imagine."

"He said, 'Her hair.' He loved her hair. Does that just beat all?" It does beat all. But what did Spec think Larry would say? That he loved Bree for her character, her mind, and her sense of humor? Isn't her thick copper hair enough to drive any boy wild? Everybody knows the old mountain wisdom: Women love with their ears and men with their eyes.

I take a good look at Spec. I spend a lot of time with him, but I've never really studied his face. His profile is outlined against the concrete wall of the bleachers like a tintype. Spec has a face of contradictions. He has the high forehead of a leader, the short, turned-up nose of a procrastinator, and no chin. According to *siang mien,* he has the big ideas but no follow-through.

"Spec? Are you happy?"

Spec exhales a puff of smoke from his cigarette. The question makes him laugh, and then he has a coughing fit. The fit lasts a few seconds. He sputters and clears his throat.

"What is so funny?"

"What kind of a question is that?"

"Are you happy? That's the question."

"I don't think about that."

"You don't?" I can't believe him.

"Hell no." Spec flicks the butt of his cigarette. "Happiness is a myth."

"Why is it a myth?"

"I got murried when I was fifteen years old. I got me five kids. One a bigger disappointment than the next. Course, it's not their upbringing. It's the world. It's gone to hell, and ain't nothing nobody can do to stop it."

"If you could live your life over again, would you do anything differently?"

Spec clears his throat. The definitive set of his mouth tells me that this is a question he has thought about many times.

"I'd have married Twyla Johnson instead of my wife I got now. Twyla is The One That Got Away. Everybody got one of them, you know. That's the person that you know you ought to be with, but circumstances play out a certain way and you get sidetracked and wind up settling. I think it's hard for a man once he starts having sex with a woman regular and so young, like I did with my wife. It's hard to break it off. You get into a flow and it's comfortable and you don't know nothing else, so you can't give it up. Hell, you won't give it up. I was fifteen, and let's face it, I got me a taste of the honey and I wanted the whole hive. My wife didn't know no better neither. She just wanted to get murried and have our babies. Course I had to murry her, so that might have had something to do with the decision-making process. I made a big mistake very young, and there weren't no turning back or going forward. I got myself stuck, plain and simple. I try to tell my kids, don't never settle, but they don't even have the gumption to get off the damn couch. They're born settlers like their mama. Ain't nothing I can do about it. Life gives you what you git, and you got to live with it."

"Where's Twyla now?"

"She works at the bank down in Pennington."

A knowing smile crosses Spec's face; for a moment he has a chin.

"Do you see her?"

"We do have lunch."

"Just a meal?"

"Now you're getting personal." Spec smiles at me to let me know that I haven't done anything wrong by inquiring but he's finished talking about it. Men are like that. When they've closed shop on a conversation, there's no mulling left to be done.

Spec offers me a lift home. Theodore has to put the equipment up and I'm tired, so I accept. He drops me at my house, then speeds off to the south, toward Pennington Gap. Inside, I sort through my mail—nothing exciting, only some circulars from the Piggly Wiggly and Collinsworth Antiques. I have begun to dread the mail, though I do feel a little relief when there's no word from the Mormons. I don't need any bad news. Theodore calls for my input on the half-time show. He drills me about every aspect of the rehearsal; what a perfectionist he is! There's a knock at the door. I figure it's Spec. He probably got up the road and got a radio call and did a U-turn to fetch me. I really have to talk to him about quitting. I'm sick of running around all hours of the day and night on calls. I peek out the window. No Spec. It's Jack MacChesney, carrying two jars. Still holding the phone with Theodore on the other end, I open the door.

"Mama made her first batch of apple butter for the fall, and she wanted you to have some."

"Thank you. Would you like to come in?"

Jack Mac nods. "You're on the phone," he comments.

"Yeah. I'm just wrapping it up. Would you like coffee or tea or something?"

"Do you have a beer?"

I nod and go into the kitchen to fetch a can. I carry the phone into the kitchen with me.

"Who's there?" Theodore asks.

"It's Jack MacChesney."

"What does he want?"

"His mama sent some apple butter down for me."

"Is that all?" Theodore asks this with just enough envy to make me smile.

"No. I think he's madly in love with me and tonight we're going to make a baby."

Theodore starts laughing, and then I do.

"Look, it's rude of me to be on the phone when company comes a-calling. I'll call you later."

"You do that."

Theodore hangs up. He's never been jealous before. This is interesting. I get that little jolt of adrenaline; it's probably hormonal, but it's a catlike feeling of being in charge and on the prowl.

I poke my head into the living room to tell Jack that I'll be a second. He is standing at the fireplace, looking at a small ceramic statue of the Virgin Mary on the mantel. When my mother was alive, she always put fresh flowers near it. Since she died, I've lit a candle next to it most nights. I don't know why. I've just done it.

"That's the Blessed Mother. I'm named after her."

"You are?"

"*Ave Maria* means 'Hail Mary.' "

"I didn't know that."

"I hope Budweiser is okay. All I got in the beer department is whatever Theodore brings over here."

While I'm in the kitchen, in the reflection of the window, I see Jack Mac removing his barn jacket and folding it neatly on the rocker. He doesn't sit down. He stands and looks around the room. I pour myself a glass of water and place the fixings for his beer on a tray. I reach up into the cabinet for my mama's can of biscotti and place a few on a plate.

"The Blessed Mother is my patron saint," I yell from the kitchen.

"Baptists don't have saints," Jack replies. "All we got is Jesus."

"There's something to be said for keeping things simple," I say as I return to the living room. Jack Mac is now seated on the couch, sort of leaning forward. He places the beer, the glass, and the napkin neatly on the coffee table. I sit in Fred Mulligan's easy chair, a few feet from him, and give him the once-over. He is spiffed up. His navy blue cords are pressed; his crisp sage green shirt seems new. He's wearing cowboy boots. He looks like he's dressed to go somewhere.

"You're dressed up."

"No. I just cleaned up after work."

I curl my stockinged feet under me. I think my left sock has a big hole in it. My hooded sweatshirt from Saint Mary's is fifteen years old, and the overalls I threw on over it still have nails in the pockets from the roof patching that Otto, Worley, and I did a while back. My hair is a rat's nest of curls held up by a thousand pins. I am a mess. "I wasn't expecting company," I tell him, apologizing for my appearance.

"You look just fine," he reassures me. He points to a set of white pearl rosary beads in a small crystal candy dish on the coffee table. "Are those yours?"

I nod.

"Do you use them?"

"Not enough."

"How do they work?"

"Well, the rosary is a devotion to the Blessed Mother."

"Mary, who you're named after?"

"Right. And each of these beads is a Hail Mary that you say. Is this boring to you?"

"No, not at all."

"Each of these ten beads represents a time in the life of Jesus. The joyful mysteries, the sorrowful mysteries, and so on."

"The Cherokees have meditation beads. They sort of look like these. Mama has them. She's part Cherokee, you know. From way, way back. She had jet-black hair when she was younger."

"I don't remember her having black hair."

"That's because it turned when I was just a boy."

There is a long silence. I look at the statue of Mary on the mantel. In her blue cape and crown of stars, she reminds me of the lady in my mother's letter, the Ave Maria I'm named after. I remember the Dieter's Prayer: *Lovely Lady dressed in blue, make me skinny just like you.* I bite into a biscotti. It cracks in half loudly, and a shower of crumbs goes down the front of my overalls. Luckily, most of it lands in the front utility pocket. I brush the rest away.

Jack breaks through the quiet. "Rick Harmon quit the mines."

"He did?"

"Well, he lost the two smallest toes on that foot of his, and the doctor told him he needed to find other work. So he got a job over at Legg's Auto World."

"Good for him. That was a pretty bad injury. How did it happen?"

"When I went back into the mine, it took me a while to get to him. There was so much smoke, he couldn't see, so he was trying to crawl out. He caught his foot under a fallen rock. When he tried to get loose, it was bad."

"I . . . everybody was nervous when you went back in the mine for him," I say, speaking on behalf of the entire community.

"You . . . or everybody?" Jack says, trying not to smile.

"Everybody. Including me." I don't think I speak this man's language. There are so many weird gaps.

We sit for a moment in silence. Finally he speaks. "My daddy and I fixed the furnace over here once."

"You did?"

"Remember that summer you went to FFA camp?"

How could I forget the Future Farmers of America camp? Living with a bunch of surly girls in a cabin on a farm in East Tennessee, surrounded by farm animals that *we* had to feed, brush, and milk. Fred Mulligan thought it would be good for me. I hated it. "That was around sixth grade, right?"

"Yeah. After we fixed the furnace, your mama made us some kind of little sandwiches. My daddy was mighty impressed. I guess they were some sort of Italian specialty or something."

"They were probably roasted-pepper sandwiches. She used to take a bunch of red peppers and broil them until the skin burned to black. Then she'd peel off the charred part, leaving the soft pepper underneath, and soak them in olive oil. Then she'd slice them up thin as paper—I still can't do it like she could—and put them on the bread with a little salt."

"They were the best sandwiches I ever ate."

I want to thank him for paying my mother a compliment, but I can't speak. All of a sudden, there is a knot in my throat. So I just nod and smile. I haven't cried much since Mama died, but thinking of her sandwiches, and her in the kitchen, and now she's gone forever—tears come to my eyes.

"I'm sorry," Jack Mac says, putting down his beer, "I didn't mean to upset you."

"No, no. I'm not upset. I just haven't talked about her much."

"The wound is too fresh."

For a moment I don't understand what he means. She's only been gone a few months now, but I started to let go of her when she got really sick, which was almost four years ago. The loss doesn't seem new to me; I felt it long before she actually passed on.

"Nobody told me how much I would miss her."

"She was a fine lady," he says plainly and truthfully.

"The morning after she died, I went into her room. I had to go in there and pick a dress for her to be laid out in. So I went in her closet. And I found . . ." I am so embarrassed. My voice is breaking, and it never does. Why am I crying in front of this man? I remember myself and stop. "Anyway, I found eight new blouses. They were beautiful, perfectly pressed, on hangers. Four white cottons and four patterned gingham: red, blue, yellow, and black-and-white checked. She had made them for me. She made all my clothes. But I never remember her working on them. I thought she had stopped sewing entirely when she got sick. She had pinned a note to them. It said: 'Fresh blouses. Love, Mama.' " I laugh and Jack smiles.

"She even made my coats. I never had to buy anything, just blue jeans. And now that I've got the blouses, I won't need to shop for a long while."

"A good mother is a precious thing," he says. "You were very lucky."

I guess I was. But I know I never saw myself as lucky. I looked at my life as a series of small struggles and gentle, intermediate plateaus of peacefulness. But anything that I am, I owe to my mother. She taught me to revere gentleness. She brought out my good heart by example. She taught me how to read and to love books. All the places I went when I read, all the adventures I had, stayed inside the books, though. I never came into anything on my own, really. I never ventured far from my potential. I never tested myself and tried things. I wasn't afraid, I just wasn't particularly daring. It's fascinating that anyone would look at me and think I'm lucky. I don't have natural talents. I am so slow! I have to study things, ruminate, decide. I don't have grand thoughts that could change anything. I'm smart enough, and it is the *enough* that defines me. I am adequate. Hard-working. I have a sense of humor, but that's due to my prism, my point of view, and even that I cannot take credit for. Very often my odd sense of humor is lost on folks. I don't know what Jack is seeing when he looks at me. I'm not particularly special, and to me lucky is special. There's a lightness to it, an élan. I'm not that. I am fixture and hardware. Not a spritely thing.

"Would you like to go for a walk?" I ask. Jack Mac looks at me oddly—he wasn't planning on going for a walk. "We don't have to."

"No, no. Let's go." He waits for me to stand up. I look around for my loafers, which I spot, shoved under the dining room table. I look down at my feet. Thankfully, the hole in my left sock is on the bottom. I scoot to the dining room and slip on my shoes.

"Let me go get my jacket," I say.

"No. Here. Wear mine."

"Won't you be cold?"

"No, not at all."

Jack Mac helps me into his jacket. It is soft, and the shoulders hang down roomily over my arms. I thought I was about his size, but I'm not; I'm smaller.

"Nice lining." It's an olive-green tufted satin. The stitches are perfect harlequin diamonds.

"Your mama put that lining in."

"She did?"

Jack Mac opens the door and lets me go outside first. It is cooler than I thought. I pull the collar up around my neck. It smells like sandalwood and lime.

We walk through my neighborhood, an area called Poplar Hill, in the oldest part of town—some would say the best part of town. I live in the smallest house on the block, a 1920s clapboard cottage-style home. It is sweet: whitewashed, with a big porch. It sits back off the road, so it looks picturesque. There's a front-porch swing, and pink squares of stained glass frame the front windows. I look back at it as I walk with Jack, thinking for the first time that it is not my father's house, it is really mine.

"How's Sweet Sue doing?"

"Well, I broke off with her."

I stop in the middle of the road. This stuns me momentarily and I'm not sure why. Maybe it's because I saw them practically get married on the stage of the Outdoor Drama. I remember her terror when Jack Mac went into the mine, and how she claimed him when it was over. Sweet Sue is perfect for Jack Mac! Her kids. Her pep. Her community involvement—they seem to fit so nicely with the quiet dignity of the MacChesneys of Cracker's Neck Holler.

"She's a wonderful person, very caring," he says, and kicks a stone.

"But you were getting married."

"Not exactly, ma'am."

Does he have to call me ma'am? He's exactly my age, for God's sake. I decide right then and there to take a box of Loving Care Chestnut Brown from the store and soak my head in it. I thought I only had two or three gray hairs, but obviously I am mistaken.

"What happened?" I ask, knowing full well it is none of my business. But I feel I have to know. I'm curious. I don't think I'm being rude or forward. Plus, reading his face, I can see that the lines from his nose to his mouth have deepened in expression. These come from guilt.

"I began to have feelings for someone else."

"Dear God!" I shriek. I am a judgmental shrew, but usually I keep it under wraps. "Who?" I ask, again knowing it's none of my business.

"Well, ma'am—"

"Jack Mac, please don't call me ma'am. I'm not your spinster aunt."

"Heck, you've hardly aged since high school," Jack Mac says, and he sounds like he means it.

"Thank you. Now, what were we talking about?"

"You."

"No, we were talking about you. You and?"

"You."

"Me?" What is he talking about? Me. Me as what?

"Miss Ave?"

"Jack, no 'Miss' either. That's just one step above 'ma'am' at the AARP."

"Ave Maria?"

"Great pronunciation."

Then he begins. "We're both knee-deep in our thirties. You're all alone. You're an orphan, really. And I've got a good job. And when my mama passes, the house will be mine. And I'm in pretty good shape. I eat too much and I drink a lot of beer sometimes, but my heart's good and I'm strong. I've got some money saved. I just bought a new truck. A '78 Ford pickup. Fully loaded. And I've been thinking that I'd like a home and family. A good wife. And when it comes down to it, at our age, there aren't a lot of us left. The never-marrieds, I mean. The field sort of narrows and the pool dries up, leaving folks who have already been married, and that comes with complications. I like simplicity and I think you do, too. So, I was wondering if you'd like to get married."

"Married?"

"Yes, ma'am. I mean yes." He corrects himself. Good. He's quick.

"You're proposing to me?"

"Yes, I am."

"Is there something the matter with you?"

"Excuse me?"

"Do you know anything about women?"

"I'd like to think I do."

"In the first place, I don't know you very well. I mean, we went through school together. You have a nice mother who suffers from hypertension. You play guitar very well." Why do I feel compelled to make a list? Why do I have to be methodical? Why do I have to make *him* feel comfortable? Can't I simply respond like a woman whose head is being blown off at this moment?

"You said I was a good dancer," he says directly.

"Yes, I did." I say this evenly, temperately, as if I were talking to a child who has left too many fund-raising jars on my checkout counter. I turn away from him to think for a moment. But I realize I don't need to turn away, I don't need to think; I understand everything all of a sudden, and it blazes through me like an electric shock and spins me back around.

"I don't need an answer right away," Jack Mac says softly.

"I can give you one, Mr. MacChesney. Sir. For you to assume that I'm spent, that I'm old and without possibilities or opportunities or dreams of my own, is appalling to me. I may appear to be a pharmacist in sensible shoes, okay, maybe I have holes in my socks, but there is a river inside of me. I'm not lonely. Or desperate. Or one bit sad. I don't need to be saved!"

"You don't understand," he says with equal force.

"I get this! I really get this! If you are sincere in this strange proposal, the answer is no. I don't love you. And I'm one of those kooks who think you ought to love the person you marry."

"Wait a second—"

"And if you aren't sincere, I think it's mean. It isn't funny to play on a woman's station in life. As though she is somehow responsible for being married or being alone! Sometimes things happen in life, the pieces move around so that the game can't go your way. Things like cancer and mental cruelty and fear. So don't think it's funny to dangle some happy thing like that—like joy can be invented in a second. It can't! I am happy alone. I don't need you or anybody else! I take care of myself. And it might seem dull to you, or pathetic, but what you think of me does not change my life one way or another."

"You don't understand."

"Let me lay it out for you. I could lose everything I have, and I may. But if you think my definition of security is a mate with a job and a truck, you don't know me very well. And if I were you, I would think twice about proposing anything to anyone you don't know very well."

I turn and walk briskly up the street. He's following me. I am sweating so hard, I get a whiff of sandalwood and lime from my neck and remember the jacket. I take it off and turn.

"Your jacket."

He takes it.

"One more thing. In the future, if you want to win a woman, don't tell her you've got a new truck. Most women don't care about new trucks. It's not a selling point. Good night."

About three blocks from my house, I realize that I walked a long way with Jack Mac, and this insight alone makes me more furious. Why was I walking with him, wearing his jacket, making small talk? I don't even like him. He yups and nopes and is altogether too quiet. I hate that! Those long quiet spells he lapses into, forcing me to talk, to fill the spaces with personal stories and observations that I didn't want to share in the first place. The crust of that guy! Knee-deep in our thirties! You're the one knee-deep in old age, with your bald head! I still have some glimmers of youth around my edges; yours are gone, Jack MacChesney! Don't lump me in with you and your mother in a stone house in a holler!

I break into a run so I can make it home faster, and the nails from the roof loosen in my pocket and drop out onto the street. I know that I should stop to pick them up because they could rip somebody's tires as they drive over them, but even the thought of a blowout and subsequent three-car pileup can't make me stop. I want to go home. I want to lock my door and be alone with the only person in the world I can trust: me. As I turn my corner, I see Theodore's car parked in front of my house. Theodore is sitting on my front stoop. Beautiful Theodore who understands me! I run up the walk and throw myself into his arms. He holds me tightly.

"What happened?"

"I hate him, Theodore. I hate him!"

I sound like a twelve-year-old girl. I remember myself and sit up.

"Did he do something to you?" Theodore sounds like he could kill anyone who would harm me. He slips off his jacket and wraps it around me. He looks into my eyes. In the porch light, Theodore's face has a golden glow—sepia and stone. Strength in the features! How I love this face! This Irish face. The crow's-feet. The strong nose that tilts ever so slightly down. The chiseled jawline, an advertisement for his determination in all things. No man could be stronger in this moment than my very own Theodore Tipton. With him I can be honest, always.

"He asked me to marry him."

A moment passes. Theodore pulls me close. "And what did you say?" His tone tells me he hopes I said no.

"I said no! Of course. Are you crazy? Why would I say anything but no?"

"I don't know."

"I don't want him!"

"It's funny—"

"There is nothing funny about this!"

"About a month ago, Jack Mac stopped me at the gas station," Theodore begins.

"What for?"

"He wanted to know if we were in love with each other."

"Why didn't you tell me?"

"I didn't think about it. I get ribbed about you all the time, so I thought nothing of it."

Ribbed? Am I the town joke? I am so mad I almost forget to be embarrassed.

"What a phony Jack MacChesney is! Mr. Respectful. Mr. Perfect Manners, all quiet and calm. Who's he kidding? It's all an act! How dare he run around upsetting people!"

"You mean you. He upset you."

"Yes, I mean me!" Me. Be concerned about me. I got myself good and scared tonight. In my fury I cannot cry, so I issue orders like a commando.

"Theodore Tipton, you are sleeping over tonight." I don't care if he wants to. I need him. I need to be held. I need reassurance, the kind you can only find in the arms of a strong man.

"I think I should."

"You have to," I decide, not backing down from Furious Hill for a second.

"I have to?"

"Yes. I love you. I don't love anybody else. I'm tired of this. You need me. Just like I need you. I need my friend."

I can't see Theodore's face, so I can't read it. He just sighs deeply and we go inside.

Theodore sits in Fred Mulligan's easy chair as I straighten up the house. Headlight beams track across the walls. "He's gone," Theodore says, not looking up from the paper. Washing dishes, putting them up, sweeping, and straightening are my favorite things to do when I'm upset. I move around the living room and through the kitchen, back and forth like a pinball. I have a lot of nervous energy.

Theodore wants coffee, so I prepare the pot—we'll be doing a lot of talking tonight. When I look in the cabinet for the coffee, I find very little left in the canister. So I drag out the step stool to see onto a high shelf. There is a coffee tin at the back of the top shelf that looks like it came with a Christmas gift basket. I'm relieved. I need a cup of coffee right now. I pull the tin out. Theodore joins me in the kitchen and sits down at the table.

The tin is sealed around with clear tape. I grab a steak knife to unseal it and pop off the lid. There is no coffee in the tin. Just a bunch of letters. At first I don't think much of it: Mama was a pack rat. Of course she kept letters in cans. But from whom?

This thought makes me drop the tin. The letters shower all over the kitchen floor.

"What's all that?" Theodore asks.

"I don't know." He can tell from my tone that I'm afraid, so he helps me off the step stool and into a chair. He kneels down and gathers the letters. I look down at my chest. The utility pocket is moving up and down, up and down. The palpitations are back! I breathe deeply.

Theodore sits with me and gives me one of the letters. It is addressed to my mother, at P.O. Box 233, Big Stone Gap, Virginia 24219. At the bottom of the envelope, in handwriting, "USA." The stamp is Italian. The letter is postmarked April 23, 1952, right around my ninth birthday.

The return address is Via Davide, Bergamo BG Italia.

"Shall I read it?" Theodore asks.

"Go ahead."

Theodore unwraps the letter and scans it. "Ave. Honey. It's in Italian."

Theodore gives me the letter and I begin to read. It starts with "My dear Sister," and ends with "Your loving sister, Meoli." It's all about the goings-on in Schilpario and Bergamo. Aunt Meoli speaks of her twin, Antonietta, who is healthy and happy. There are details about cousins Andrea, Federica, and Mafalda. Comments about my mother's parents! My grandparents! An uncle had died. And then she writes that she has not seen Mario. That's all it says about him.

She inquires about me. Could my mother send pictures? Don't I have a birthday soon?

"What does it say? Honey? What does it say?"

"My mother has two sisters. Twins." I sit down on the floor. The letters are scattered all around me, filled with more shocks and surprises. I wonder how much more I can take.

CHAPTER SIX

The town paper has issued a special (lavender!) supplement with a guide to all the events involving the visit of screen legend Elizabeth Taylor. She arrives Friday afternoon, October 23, 1978, around 3:00 P.M. She is staying at the Trail Motel in their deluxe suite (boy, is she in for a surprise). At 6:00 P.M. she and her husband will be taken to Railroad Avenue, conjunct to Shawnee Avenue (Main Street), and placed in an open convertible provided by Cas Walker's grocery-store chain. At approximately 6:15 the car will follow the marching band into the ballpark. The convertible will make two 360-degree trips around the football field on the paved running track, so that Elizabeth and her husband can wave to the crowds. At 7:00 the game starts: Powell Valley vs. Rye Cove. Elizabeth will watch the game from a specially constructed platform stage, provided by Don Wax Realty, near the home stands. (This stage has been used for band-competition judges; Nellie decorated it special for this evening.) Then, the half-time show.

On Saturday morning the Republicans are having a pancake breakfast—we'll skip that. Then, starting with hors d'oeuvres at 5:30 P.M., the library fund-raiser will commence. Iva Lou made sure that our table is right next to Elizabeth's!

The beauty of Nellie Goodloe is that she wants to do everything right. The entire weekend starring Elizabeth Taylor is in her capable hands, and she is planning it like a royal wedding. The library dinner takes the place of a reception (I'm sure Nellie's own wedding was less detailed). She chose the theme "Colors" for the decorations: violet in honor of Miss Taylor's eyes, and white because it is a good contrast. The Dogwood Garden Club is doing the centerpieces; the Green Thumb Garden Club is making a floral backdrop; Holding Funeral Home is supplying AstroTurf runners for the entry and their funeral canopy in case of bad weather; I am donating the candles; Zackie Wakin is providing napkins printed with E.T. and the date in gold; and the Coach House Inn is making Elizabeth Taylor's favorite meal (and their specialty): fried chicken, mashed 'taters, and collard greens.

There's been a slight amount of tension between Iva Lou and Nellie regarding the dinner. Iva Lou has asserted herself in the dinner plans because she envisions herself as head librarian for the new facility. Of course, Iva Lou is no Nellie Goodloe; she couldn't care less about centerpieces, she wouldn't know a votive from a candelabra, or which side the small spoons go on in a place setting. Nellie, on the other hand, is the queen of etiquette. She went to Sweet Briar College and has a degree in home economics, so she brings a vast knowledge of elegant living to the Gap. Iva Lou wanted to do a barbeque. When she suggested this, Nellie nearly had a stroke; after all, you can't hardly ask the Queen of Hollywood to tie on a bib in Miner's Park and suck ribs. Nellie had to come up with a way to keep Iva Lou occupied, so she put her in charge of ticket sales for the dinner. Within several hours the dinner was completely sold out. Iva Lou unloaded every ticket. She knows a lot of businessmen, and evidently, they owe her favors.

Every detail of the planning for the pregame parade—in which Candidate Warner and Miss Taylor will ride through town in the convertible—must go through Theodore. He is in charge of everything from the Kiwanians who lead the parade to the drum section of the band that pulls up the rear. The cheerleaders traditionally ride on our town fire truck. Anticipating problems, Theodore makes sure that

Spec has our fire truck waxed and polished and that he has secured a backup truck in case of an emergency. Spec has one truck in his arsenal. If there is a fire somewhere in town between 6:00 and 6:30, the parade is ruined. A couple of years back there was a house fire during one of our pregame parades. The cheerleaders were tossed off the truck like turnips as the unit sped off to respond to the call.

With Elizabeth Night—as it has come to be known in these parts— a few days off, I stay late at the Pharmacy to catch up on my work. Pearl is out front vacuuming and dusting. I am worried but trying not to show it. I figure I'll wait until all the big doings are over to deal with my own problems.

Pearl wraps the cord to the upright vacuum cleaner around the holder, then wipes down the front of the machine with a dust rag. "Do you have a date for the Elizabeth Taylor dinner, Miss Ave?" she asks.

"I'm going with Mr. Tipton."

"He'll be the center of attention after he knocks 'em dead with his halftime show; that's for sure."

I nod and continue with my work. Pearl stands and looks at me.

"Do you need anything, Pearl?"

"Miss Ave, are you sure you want to give me the Pharmacy?"

"Yes. Absolutely. We're just waiting for the final paperwork and it will be yours. Why? Are you having second thoughts?"

"Don't you want to own this yourself? What if you get murried someday? I'm sure the place is worth something."

I smile at Pearl. I was waiting until the paperwork was finalized before I shared the scope of our transaction. She will be shocked when she realizes that we are part of a chain of Mutual Pharmacies. She won't simply own a building and its contents, but she will have a very valuable franchise to sell or keep, if she so desires. Pearl doesn't realize she's coming into some money.

"Pearl, I'm never getting married."

"Excuse me, ma'am, but how do you know that?"

"I just do."

"You shouldn't never give up."

Poor Pearl. She's a romantic. She doesn't understand what really goes on between adults. At fifteen, she could never comprehend the depth of the relationship I have with Theodore. Bells, whistles, gold bands, and a gown are not my idea of meaningful. I don't need to get married to feel whole.

"You really never tried to get murried?"

"No, ma'am, I didn't." I'm sure she heard the rumors of Theodore's car at my house all night last weekend. She's fishing. My personal life has gone beyond gossip, and now the rumor mill wants to bump me to next level: marriage. Two grown adults cannot carry on a romance in this town without a marriage license.

"I thought everyone wanted to get murried." Pearl shrugs.

"What makes you think I do?"

"You got rid of all the junk."

"What are you talking about?"

"Well, you cleaned up the back. When I first worked here, it was a mess. Now it's empty. You've been fixing things up. Otto and Worley fixed your roof. Now you're paying them to repoint the bricks on this building. You're working less. You hired me to work here, even though Fleeta can handle it alone."

"What are you saying?"

"You even gave me your business. Don't you see? Folks lighten up their lives when they're about to make a move."

"Maybe I just got tired of having junk all over the place."

"I don't think so. I think you're making space in your life to squeeze a man in."

Pearl looks at me. I don't say anything, which she takes as a sign to shut up. She wheels the vacuum cleaner to the back storage closet.

"We'll be needing a new sweeper directly," she says as she goes.

Sometimes I think Pearl Grimes is a very strange girl.

October 23 arrives gloriously without a cloud in the sky. The mountains are in the final stage of autumn, and the leaves have faded to a dull gold—the perfect backdrop for a woman who played the queen of Egypt. How I wish my mother had lived to see an actual movie star!

My mother loved Elizabeth Taylor. She would go on and on about her perfect features: those eyes, that straight nose, the just-full-enough lips, that strong chin. Elizabeth Taylor is Dresden china, the finest white porcelain set off by that midnight-black hair.

Everyone is excited, and the nervousness is bringing out odd behavior in some of our townspeople, particularly the men. Ballard Littrell, our town drunk, has sobered up. He only has one ear—no one knows how he lost the other one—so he never gets his hair cut off on the left side. But he was seen at the barber, gussying up for the evening, trying to even out the sides. Otto and Worley were seen at Zackie's store buying new shirts. They never buy anything new, so this is an important event for them. The women in town who are around Elizabeth's age, forty-five and up, took this milestone visit as a cue to upgrade their looks. Pearl noted that we have completely sold out of Black Sable hair dye and blue eye shadow.

I thought about closing the Pharmacy today, but I couldn't. I need to keep my mind busy. I am so nervous for Theodore; I want everything to be perfect for him tonight. He has worked so hard. I hope the kids don't crack under the pressure. There would be nothing worse than a fire baton going up in the air and landing on the visitors' bench instead of in the waiting hands of Tayloe Slagle. I can't imagine she'll choke, but you never know.

I decide to lock up early. Pearl is counting on it; she brought a new outfit with her to work this afternoon, and she plans to change in our powder room, then head off to the park to help Theodore set up the pyramids for the halftime show. I recruited her to work on Theodore's field crew. If there's one person who can handle a lot of pressure, it's Pearl. Just having her around is soothing.

The door bells jingle merrily. I look out the window and see a few folks milling on Main Street, staking out their spots for the parade. Two little boys stand in front of the register. They argue about whether to use their candy allowance for Good 'n Plenty or Hot Tamales. One look at their blond heads tells me they could only be Sweet Sue's boys.

"Are you the Tinsley boys?" I ask.

"I'm Jared and he's Chris," says the older of the two.

"How much money have you got?"

"Two dimes, one nickel, and one penny."

"You're in luck! It's two-for-one day. You get two boxes of candy for exactly twenty-six cents." The boys jump up and down as the bells on the door ring again. I look up and see Jack MacChesney standing before me.

"What's taking you boys so long?"

"Jared couldn't pick fast," Chris says.

"Well, go on now. Get in the truck."

"We won't get no stickies on your seat, Uncle Jack," Jared promises.

"Hey, how'd you get two boxes?"

"The lady give them to us." Jared points to me.

"Did you thank her?"

"Thank you, ma'am," they chorus, and run out. There's that word *ma'am* again. It really and truly bugs me. I must remember, these are little boys; to them, everyone is old, even their thirty-five-year-old mother.

Pearl comes out of the powder room in her new two-piece plaid suit. She looks like she's lost almost twenty pounds. She stops to check her makeup at her station but thinks better of it when she sees Jack MacChesney at my counter.

"That was mighty nice of you, Ave Maria," Jack Mac says.

"They're cute kids."

"Yes, ma'am, they are."

I straighten the folds on my prescription clipboard, flattening the creases with one of the nickels Jared gave me. I can't look at Jack Mac, not because I'm embarrassed but because I don't have anything to say. What can I say to a man whose proposal I turned down? I wrack my brain, but small talk seems teeny tiny. Jack Mac just stands there, with his hands in his pockets, jiggling coins and keys. He takes the change out of his pocket and begins sorting it. I'm glad he looks down; it gives me a chance to fix my hair. I inhale. Why does he always smell so good?

"Oh no, the Hot Tamales were on the house. They couldn't decide between Hot Tamales and Good 'n Plenty." Jack Mac looks at me, confused.

"The kids, they only had—" Shut up, Ave Maria. The guy doesn't care what their favorite candy is; he's not their father, you idiot. He's Uncle Jack, the nice man who takes them for rides in his truck and plays catch with them. Uncle Jack, who will someday be their stepdaddy.

"You going to the dinner tomorrow night?"

"Yes." Is he a loon or what? Asking me if I'm going to the dinner. He should hate me. I was so rude to him. And now he's standing here putting change in every single fund-raising jar on my counter. The coins drop into the jars, one clink, two clink, three clink; and it's a good thing, they fill up the silence.

"Well, I guess I better be going," he says, and turns and walks out.

"He likes you," Pearl announces as she rolls her lips with Bonne Bell strawberry gloss.

If only she knew. But I can't tell her.

"He looks at you like you're the most beautiful woman he ever saw. He'd dump Sweet Sue for you in a second."

"He'd be a fool if he did that."

"No, he wouldn't." Pearl can be very stubborn. "You know something, Miss Ave? If I was him, and I had to pick between Sweet Sue and any other woman in town and you, I'd pick you."

"You're very nice to say that." I wish she would stop.

"I'd pick you because there's just something about you. You're sparkly. Yeah. That's it. Sparkly." Pearl grabs her purse and goes to the door. "See you on the field."

I wear my very best coat—a red velvet swing coat—so Theodore can single me out from the announcer's booth. As I look out over the crowd in the stands, I realize that pretty much everyone in town had the same idea. We look like a hunter's convention, splashes of red and bright orange throughout the stands. Everyone wore their loudest and brightest clothing; perhaps subconsciously we are hoping Elizabeth Taylor will see us in the crowd and single us out with a smile or a wink. Fleeta flags me down from the top of the stands with a purple light wand she got at a University of Tennessee football game. She elbows Portly to wave at me; he does.

The crowd in the visitors' section is filled with overflow from our stands. Rye Cove is a small village, much smaller than Big Stone Gap. When we play them, it seems pathetic to even cheer against them since they have no manpower at all in their stands and just as little on the field. We'll beat them decisively tonight, and we should; after all, we're the side that's got the movie star.

The teams aren't on the field yet. They're lined up around the track to wave to Elizabeth Taylor. I look all around the park, and everyone is standing. There's a buzz, but it is definitely reverential. The band curves off the parking lot and onto the track, a long Carolina-blue snake, precise and pliable. And then there she is! The convertible! With her! The car harrumphs over the parking-lot median and bounces onto the track; for a moment I worry Elizabeth and her husband will be thrown off of their backseat perch. But they hang on to each other and laugh. I'm in a perfect spot to get a real good look at her.

I haven't heard this much cheering since we won the state championship in 1972. The crowd rises to their feet. The stadium fills with sound that echoes into the black mountains behind us. The chanting: "Liz! Liz! Liz!" The occasional gut holler: "I love you!" cuts through the din, all of us, yelling, whistling, applauding, thrilled! Notice us! Over here! See me, Elizabeth! We've sure been watching you all these many years! Watch us!

The convertible rolls around the track slowly. On the front grid of the car is a sign from the Nabisco distributor that reads, DON'T GO 'ROUND HUNGRY. HAVE YOUR NABS — short for Nabisco crackers around these parts. Cas Walker must have cut a deal with his distributors. I hope somebody explained to Elizabeth what Nabs are.

The convertible gingerly inches up to the fifty-yard line, where I am standing. Spec is behind the wheel. He sees me, and he knows I love old movies, so he practically slows to a stop so I can get a close-up look.

Elizabeth Taylor is exquisite. She is wearing a flowing emerald-green silk tunic and matching pants. The neckline is an off-center V, which is quite becoming. Her shoulder-length hair is pulled back into a low chignon, and she has a large yellow flower tucked over one ear. I am close enough to see into the car. She has kicked off a very pretty pair of matching green pumps. Her feet are bare, and her toenails are painted hot pink. But it is her expression, the sweet smile—not forced, genuine—that gets me. She is so happy to see us! Her eyes *are* violet! I look over at Nellie Goodloe, who seems relieved. The theme colors are a real homage now. There is something peculiar about Nellie; now I see what. She has rinsed her hair coal black. Poor old Nellie; be a leader, I want to tell her, not a follower.

Elizabeth is tiny, with delicate hands and feet, like a child's. She is a little chubby, but on her—it just softens her, so it's as though she's a little blurry, not a hard angle on her. Three of the ladies from the Methodist sewing circle stand behind me. Their comments are not as generous. Joella Reasor, who has always battled a weight problem, comments to her friends, "All my life I wanted to look like her, and now I do."

I see Theodore up in the announcer's booth, which angles out over the home section. He is in the window, examining the field from on high. I give him a thumbs-up, and he waves to me. Then I look back to the convertible. Candidate Warner gives me a thumbs-up; I guess he thought I was signaling to him. I feel a little guilty. I'd never vote for him, since I'm a Democrat. But you know what? It doesn't hurt anything to let him think I might. He smiles a big, beamy, vote-for-me smile, and I give him a thumbs-up too.

A team of folks helps Elizabeth and the candidate up to their seats. The football players take the field, but no one even notices the game. Luster Camp, a sweet soul of a man with a feeble mind, is our unofficial high school mascot. He takes his usual cheering spot in front of the home stands—tonight he's in direct view of Elizabeth Taylor's perch. Luster loves our team and leads very amusing cheers, but he isn't exactly the ambassador we want to flaunt in front of a visiting movie star. Luster, however, is undeterred. It's just another game night to him, and he's got a job to do. The crowd looks down at him as a mother does to a child who is about to embarrass her deeply in public. *Please don't,* they seem to be pleading with their eyes.

"Y'all. Y'all," Luster shouts, "it's time for a cheer!"

The kids in the stands usually cheer loudly for him, but tonight their silence sends a strong message: *Luster, sit down. Please don't humiliate us in front of Virginia Woolf.*

"Beans and corn bread got in a fight! Beans knocked the corn bread outta sight. That's what Powell Valley is gonna do tonight!"

Elizabeth Taylor laughs and applauds as though the cheer is the funniest she has ever heard.

"One more!" Luster shouts. "Two bits, four bits, six bits, a dollah. All for the Vikings, stand up and hollah!"

Elizabeth applauds again. The crowd, taking their cue from her, stands and cheers. Luster bows deeply, then disappears into the crowd in his torn raincoat and porkpie hat. I doubt he knew Elizabeth Taylor was in the crowd.

I watch every moment of the second quarter tick off, hoping it will end and afraid for it to end. How on earth is Theodore handling this pressure? I want his show to be magnificent. We just can't make any mistakes. The band empties out onto the track silently as the final seconds of the quarter pass. The teams run off the field. The band files past the home section and across to the goal line, one by one.

The announcer in the booth, who calls the game for local radio, blows into the microphone as we all look toward him.

"Ladies and gents. We got a show fer you tonight. Now we got the prettiest gal in Hollywood here, and this here show is full of all the stuff from her movies. So sit back and relax, spit out your tobacky, and let's get happy! Here we go, folks, the Powell Valley Viking marching band!"

The crowd leaps to their feet, applauding and cheering. The pyramids are ready to roll. I see the shimmer of Tayloe's Cleopatra costume from her hiding place under the visitors' bleachers. She's right where she should be. Then something very odd happens. The drum majorette blows her whistle. Not once, not twice, but four times. And then she waits and blows it again. She isn't blowing it at the band—they are frozen in position waiting to begin. Their eyes are wide and full of horror. There on the twenty-yard line, several feet from where the band is to make its first formation, are King and

Cora, the town strays, two large mutts, fed by all and adopted by no one. King has mounted Cora. Cora either senses the crowd or is through with King; either way, she does not want to be doing this right now. I can't help but think that the dogs took on all of the nervous energy in our town and now have to release it. The urgent humping is rhythmic, almost saying, *Please let this be over. Let this show be over. Let it be over now.*

Another hush falls over the crowd, and everyone looks to the queen for her response. Elizabeth Taylor is ignoring the dogs and chatting with her aide. Theodore is slumped in the announcer's booth. I look over at Pearl, who shrugs at me, wordlessly asking, *What are we supposed to do?* One of the referees can't take it another second, so he trots out onto the field to separate the dogs. Spec runs after the ref shouting loudly enough for everyone to hear, "You can't pull 'em apart, they'll bite you, you stupid son of a bitch." So we do the best we can in this terrible situation. We let them hump and we wait it out. This has to be the longest-lasting sex act on record. Finally, King depletes himself. He climbs off Cora and runs into the end zone with a gallop worthy of Secretariat. Cora slinks off into the shadows. The drum majorette blows her whistle. Finally. Finally. The show.

From the first pinwheel formation, the kids are perfect. They play the music so grandly, and what an arrangement! Seamlessly and beautifully, they rondelet through every major theme of every major Elizabeth Taylor movie. She stands and places her hands on the rail of the platform, leaning over the edge like she wants to be close to this majestic, loving salute. Then the flag girls pivot across the fifty-yard line, single file, and magically disappear under the pyramids. The three pyramids move into place and then BOOM! The lights in the stadium go out, the crowd cheers and whistles; and there in center field, surrounded by fire batons, is Tayloe Slagle, in full Cleopatra garb, including jet-black wig, posed Egyptian-style. Her figure is amazing; she is curvy but lean, just like Elizabeth Taylor when she was Cleopatra. Tayloe takes two batons and begins to twirl them like the pro she is. She twists and bends and tosses and catches and smiles, effortlessly, smoothly, and with such sass. The effect in this dark ballpark is dazzling. Pearl, who has run all the way from the other side of the track in the dark, comes up behind me, breathless. We stand and watch the show with awe. Even though we helped, we cannot believe how beautiful it is.

"She is so talented," Pearl decides as she watches Tayloe.

"Yes, she is. But baton twirling is not a skill one needs later in life." I don't know why I think I always have to teach Pearl lessons. I am not the oracle of Big Stone Gap, after all.

The lights bolt back on; everyone is cheering. The band plays off and exits the field. They pass Elizabeth's perch; she is weeping and throwing them kisses. Then the most amazing thing happens: She turns to the announcer's booth and throws Theodore a kiss. And then she bows to him! She actually bows! I will never forget this moment as long as I live.

The Coach House Inn is the only real restaurant in Big Stone Gap. We do have the Bus Terminal Café and the Sub Sandwich Carry-Out, but they are strictly casual. There is Jackson's Fish & Fry, but they only serve Sunday brunch. Punch-and-cake wedding receptions are held in the church basement fellowship rooms. So, all the rest of life's events—holidays, Lions and Kiwanis club meetings, and family buffets—are held right here at the Coach House.

The building is a simple colonial-style redbrick square, with black shutters and a sloping white roof. A sign swings from the entryway: a black silhouette of a nineteenth-century coach driver whipping a team of horses with a fancy carriage behind him. The artist who painted the coach and driver is the same one who made my nurse in a rush. The eats are terrific. The food is fresh and delectable—salty, crusty, spicy, hot fried chicken (on Sundays it's called Gospel Bird), with biscuits so light and fluffy, one person could eat a dozen. Nellie made the entrance look lovely. She borrowed the large ficus plants in brass urns from the bank, so when you enter the Coach House, you are completely surrounded by lush foliage. Edna and Ledna Tuckett, the town twins, now in their late sixties, are dressed alike in pale blue serge suits and hand out programs for the evening.

The programs are pretty; Nellie really has a knack. She is the doyenne of our Corn Bread Aristocracy. The program covers are made from lavender construction paper, with a tiny purple silk African violet glued on, framed by a small grosgrain ribbon. Inside, the agenda for the evening is laid out in a fancy calligraphy:

Welcome Candidate and Mrs. John Warner

Library Fund-raising Dinner
October 24, 1978 — 6:30 P.M.
The Coach House Inn
Invocation: Reverend Elmo Gaspar
Dinner: Chicken & Fixings
honoring the great career of screen legend Elizabeth Taylor
Aperitif: "Little Women" crabbies and punch
Salad: "Sandpiper" potato-salad
Main course: "Cleopatra" fried chicken and "Butterfield 8" biscuits
Dessert: "National (Red) Velvet" cake and ice cream
Coffee & Tea

Introduction: Mrs. Nellie Goodloe, Chair
Remarks: Candidate John Warner

The back cover reads, "Compliments of the Dollar General Store," then, in musical notes, its theme-song refrain:

> ♪Who says a dollar won't buy much anymore?
> Every day is dollar day!
> At the Dollar General Store!♪

(I guess they paid for the programs.)

Theodore looks handsome in his gray slacks, navy blazer, and pale blue necktie that brings out his eyes (classic). I'm wearing a black cocktail dress with a peacock brooch of Austrian crystals. I put my hair up in a fancy do. Through the bay windows at the front of the

Coach House I can see a few hundred dressed-up folks milling around. No alcohol allowed (technically), as this is a dry county (nonenforceable), but Nellie Goodloe has made sure there's a champagne punch with lime sherbet. Nerves have calmed down considerably, but a touch of the spirits will soothe folks even more.

Liz and her husband have not arrived yet. Theodore is instantly swarmed and congratulated for his halftime spectacular. I am so very happy for him. He beams, as would any artist, having reached a mass audience. The women in the room are dressed in their finest, and it's funny, most of them wear a bright flower in their hair. Not to be outdone, I snap a white carnation off a table arrangement and tuck it behind my ear.

Iva Lou sees me and comes right over. Her dress is a masterpiece— a floor-length gown of peach Qiana polyester. The skirt is full and flowing, with a short train at the back. The bodice is fitted tightly like a series of rubber bands. It looks very traditional, except for the fit. The little modern touch is an appliqué on the chest—a picture of three books standing upright on a shelf, outlined in seed pearls and dotted with sequins.

"Ave! Get this! We raised two thousand seven hundred and fifty dollars tonight! Isn't that something?"

"Congratulations!" I am thrilled for Iva Lou. Finally, all her connections have paid off.

"What do you think, girl?" Iva Lou twirls in her gown.

"You are spectacular."

She flashes a big grin, then sticks out her chest and points to the appliqué. "Lyle told me this dress could turn him into an avid reader. I'm gonna let him peruse my card catalog directly following this shindig. What do you think?"

"I think Lyle is the luckiest man in Wise County."

"I think you might be right. Well, if he ain't now, we'll make sure he is tonight." Iva Lou struts off toward a salivating Lyle, planting the seeds for later.

Lew and Inez Eisenberg are already sitting at their table. Inez looks pretty in her turquoise muumuu. She has chopsticks in her hair for that exotic touch. Their expressions are pleasant, but they aren't speaking; they're looking off in separate directions. I feel sorry for them. Spec picks the crabbies off a tray as they are passed. He gives one to his wife, who is sitting next to Inez. They don't have much to say to each other either.

I work the room and folks are pleasant; it's partly the alcohol and partly the presence of a television-camera crew from WCYB out of Kingsport, Tennessee. They've sent Johnny Wood, anchorman, reporter, and weatherman, to cover this event. He looks shorter and squatter on TV than he does in real life. He sweats in real life just like he does on TV, though. He seems cordial, but he's here to do a job so he hasn't time for small talk. Folks respect that and generally leave him alone. We've never been on the TV before, so we're on our best behavior.

"New dress?" Aunt Alice asks from behind me.

"This old thing?"

"It doesn't look old to me."

"You look very nice tonight, Aunt Alice." She is taken aback, and her eyes narrow suspiciously.

"Enough about that. What's going on with our business arrangement?"

"Mr. Eisenberg is handling it. You know lawyers take their sweet time."

"I just want it done." Before Aunt Alice can wind up and upset me further, I walk away. Theodore is surrounded by a fresh batch of admirers. I decide to place my evening bag at our dinner table. Iva Lou wasn't kidding; we are sitting right next to Elizabeth Taylor's table.

"You look very pretty," a voice whispers. I look up and it's Jack Mac, giving me the once-over like I'm a brand-new 1978 Ford pickup truck, fully loaded.

"Thank you." I in turn look him over, and my expression of surprise gives me away. He is crisp and classic in a navy blue suit with a barely there gray pinstripe. His shirt is pristine white, though the collar seems a little tight. The tie is scarlet red and made of fine Chinese silk.

"New duds," he says, indicating the suit.

"They're lovely." *Lovely*? I have never used that word in my life. It is a mamaw word, a sewing-circle word, an old-lady word. And besides, he doesn't look lovely, he looks downright handsome.

"My father's tie."

"That's very good silk, you know." I can't resist touching it; I love delicate silks. My mother used to smack my hands when I touched the fabric while she was sewing.

"Pap got it over in France somewhere during the Second World War."

"Take good care of it." Now, why do I say that? Is taking care of his wardrobe any of my business? What do I care if he wads it up and uses it for an oil rag?

"I wanted to talk to you about the other night." For a moment I don't know what he's referring to; it's been a while since Apple Butter Night, and I haven't had time to think about any of that. He senses this and almost drops the subject, but he can't since he brought it up, so now he's stuck. I don't help matters by acting vague.

"I never meant to insult you or upset you in any way. I'm very sorry." I don't know what to say. It's not like he shot me or anything. He proposed. His look of concern makes me uncomfortable.

"All's well that ends well. You're back with Sweet Sue, I see." Sweet Sue is working the crowd like a canteen chanteuse. She's wearing a silvertone halter dress, her hair in a golden fountain. Her eyes are painted with a dusty lavender powder. Her teeth are so white, they gleam. She looks like she fell right out of the *Knoxville News Sentinel* style section.

"Not exactly." Jack Mac says this with a smile and looks off to her and then back to me. This cavalier smirk really annoys me. Does he think he's juggling the affections of the town beauty and the town spinster? Does he see me as the pitiful one who needs the man, and Sweet Sue as the one who gets to pick? For a split second Jack MacChesney is the enemy. But I remember myself; I am not involved with this man. His duplicitous nonsense is not my problem. I am not the other woman. He tried to set that up but I did not play.

"You know, Jack, I'm just a pill-counting pharmacist. And I don't know much, I'll be the first to tell you. But from my seat, women ought not be trifled with. You have a beautiful girl over there. You ought to concentrate on her. Her alone."

Jack Mac looks at me a little confused. "You think we're together?" he asks.

"You brought her to the dinner."

"Actually, I bought these tickets when we were together, then circumstances presented—"

"You take care of her kids." Does he think I'm an idiot?

"I can't just drop those boys. I've been seeing her for over a year. They've come to know me and trust me. I won't just disappear on them."

"Okay. Fine." I roll my eyes and look away, hoping he'll take the hint and shove off. But he stays.

"You're here with Theodore. Explain the difference to me."

"Wait a second. I can see whomever I please. Okay? I haven't been going around town willy-nilly, proposing to people and then jumping in bed with ex-lovers."

"You are really something," he growls without an ounce of kindness.

"Yes, I am. I have principles!" I have my hands on my hips, and my neck is three inches off its pins, thrusting my face into Jack Mac's. He does not step back. I don't either. We are eye-to-eye, nose-to-nose. His breath is sweet, and his eyes are on fire.

"You're bitter and you're lonely. You're determined to stay that way. So stay that way. I don't have to take your bull. I won't take it. Ma'am." He turns and goes.

Theodore comes up behind me. "What was that all about?"

"What a jackass." Theodore and I watch as Jack Mac excuses himself through the crowd to get to his table.

"Nice suit, though." Theodore shrugs.

Elizabeth Taylor has just pulled up. We know this immediately because the headlights from the staff car are bright and aimed directly into the restaurant through the bay windows. The entire restaurant is flooded with light, and now with anticipation. It was one thing to see her in a convertible last night; she was still far away and dreamy as she is on a movie screen. But tonight she will be sitting in a room with us, having dinner! We're going to be way up close. It's thrilling.

Johnny Wood is giving directions to the TV crew, and the crowd, full of anticipation, chatters loudly. Theodore and I kneel on our chairs to watch her entrance over the crowd.

Several aides precede her through the entrance, clearing a path for her and the candidate. Elizabeth enters, wearing a floor-length royal-purple caftan with three-quarter-length dolman sleeves and a boat neck. Her hair is down, blown straight to her shoulders. What look like large Indian beads, in agates of gold, purple, and brown, hang around her neck like royal jewels. She is absolutely breathtaking again tonight. Nellie Goodloe greets her at the entrance and gives her a quick hug. Elizabeth points to the rose tucked over Nellie's ear; Nellie blushes.

John Warner, a former undersecretary of the U.S. Navy, looks presidential in his deep-navy-blue suit, white shirt, and red, white, and blue striped tie. He has the tall good looks of a Northern Virginia land baron. He is confident but impatient. He scoops the shock of thick gray hair away from his forehead with his hand a lot—it reminds me of President Kennedy. Folks say he's lucky to be running for the Senate at all. He came in second to Dick Obenshain in the primary last year. Then, in an unexpected tragedy, Mr. Obenshain was killed in a plane crash. The Republicans went to their runner-up, Mr. Warner, and asked him to run in Mr. Obenshain's place. He politely obliged. The papers say Mr. Warner is an old-fashioned political pot sticker; you lose a man, and he'll seal the hole. You can see he's a little put off by the attention his wife receives, but he can't exactly make her sit in the car. She brings out the voters, and that's exactly what this dark-horse Republican candidate needs to win. I wonder how he feels about always coming in second, first to Obenshain and now to his wife. Maybe he doesn't care, as long as he's in the race. He looks amazingly well-rested for a man with only ten days until the election. That's probably just good breeding. Grace under pressure is a Virginia gentleman's calling card.

Zackie Wakin strolls past the aides toward Elizabeth Taylor. He extends his hand to her. She extends hers to him, and he kisses it like a prince. The crowd woos. Zackie, the feriner peddler, charms the movie star. Zackie is small but so is she. As they stand eye-to-eye, he and Elizabeth take on that romantic Moviola glow that comes in those love scenes when the man looks down, not *at* the woman, but into her soul. Elizabeth, forever the game girl, throws her head back and laughs a few times. We can hear snippets of their conversation. She knows a lot about Lebanese culture. She accompanied Richard Burton to the Middle East when he was making a picture in the late sixties. When the aides hear her speak of a former husband, Elizabeth is hustled away, following her current husband into the kitchen to greet the staff. She turns and looks over her shoulder at Zackie, shrugs as if to say, *Sorry we were interrupted,* and waves to him.

The kitchen doors swing open, and we hear the candidate say, "I'm John Warner, candidate for the United States Senate. I'd like to count on y'all on November fourth." I read in the paper that this is something John Warner likes to do. As much as he likes the muckety-mucks out front, the folks who make the meal are the ones who vote en masse.

Theodore and I are close to the galley doors that lead to the kitchen, so we scoot to the circular windows and peer in as Elizabeth and Warner take their tour. The deep aluminum serving pans are full of golden fried chicken. One pan holds only wings; they look so succulent, I want to go into the kitchen and grab a few. Elizabeth Taylor has the same thought, and as Warner blah-blahs to the chef, she bends over and samples a breast. She holds it with two hands, pinky up, and bites into the meaty part near the bones carefully, so as not to smear her perfect peach lipstick. Warner refers to Elizabeth, and she nods as she chews. He shoots her a dirty look when he sees she's sampled the chicken. She downs a large hunk quickly to finish it off and get back to the campaigning. She swallows, but something is terribly wrong. She gags. I know from Rescue Squad training that she is choking, so I burst into the kitchen. She is holding her throat and looking helpless. She cannot speak. I can see the scar on her creamy neck from an operation she had years ago. It is still pink.

"Miss Taylor. Let me get help."

I hear the aides murmur, "Who is she?" and the staff tells them I'm with the Rescue Squad. Theodore hollers for Spec, which triggers a buzz throughout the dining room. Spec pushes through the swinging doors like John Wayne, scans the kitchen, finds Elizabeth, and runs to her. Theodore follows.

"She swallowed a chicken bone, Spec," I say.

"Jesus Christ. Run git the ambulance around tout suite." Spec tosses me his key ring. Theodore and I run through the dinner crowd, out the entrance, and into the ambulance. We speed around back, open the rear chute, pull out the gurney, and wheel it into the kitchen. Warner is yelling at Spec and his aides, but mostly he seems frustrated with Elizabeth for choking.

Spec works like a pro, lifting Elizabeth onto the gurney. He carefully straps her in and checks the wheel locks. You know, folks complain that Spec runs around town in the ambulance, using it for personal reasons, but I bet they're mighty glad that he drove it here tonight. It just may save Elizabeth Taylor's life.

Spec and I load Elizabeth into the ambulance. Warner is now extremely upset, holding his wife's hand and stroking her face. Luckily, Dr. Gladys Baronagan, the Filipino physician from Lonesome Pine Hospital, came to the dinner with her husband and was recruited to help in the emergency. I hear her tell Spec that she may need to operate.

Even in tragedy, Elizabeth could not be more beautiful. She lies on the gurney like a lavender lily. She takes pain like a trouper, and believe me, I've seen all sorts of suffering and sometimes folks act pretty crazy. But she is almost beatific, like she expects that bad things will happen, and by God, you just deal with them and go through them and don't let them kill you. Her eyes say, *I won't die. Just get the damned bone out of my throat!*

Theodore and I jump into his car and follow the ambulance up to the hospital. When we get there, Miss Taylor is whisked through admissions and brought directly to the emergency room. A small crowd has gathered but no words are spoken. It's a hell of a thing. Spec paces nervously outside the ER. We pray everything will go smoothly.

Theodore and I are starving, so we eat a variety of junk from the vending machines and wash it down with instant coffee. Candidate Warner is in a special room right outside the emergency room, so we can't see him. Several aides mill about, one more worried-looking than the next.

Finally, after about an hour, a nurse comes out to talk to us. Dr. Baronagan ran a rubber pipe down Miss Taylor's throat, pushing the bone down into her stomach, where it would dissolve in digestion. No need for surgery. Miss Taylor will be fine. Johnny Wood and his crew enter and make a beeline for the nurse; he wants an exclusive for the eleven o'clock report. She holds up her hands and asks the men to leave, telling them, "This is a hospital, not a circus." Johnny Wood shrugs and takes his crew outside. He films his story on the sidewalk.

"What's wrong with you?" Theodore asks as he turns to me.

"I'm fine," I tell him, holding my head in my hands.

"Let me see." He lifts my face with his hands and examines it carefully.

"You look pale," he decides.

"I ate too much candy. That's all."

"Let's go." Theodore laughs.

But I don't think it was the candy. I kept replaying the scene of Jack Mac telling me I was bitter and lonely until it upset my stomach. But I don't have to share that with Theodore. You don't have to tell your best friend everything.

CHAPTER SEVEN

We never saw Elizabeth Taylor again. After the bone was dislodged, she rested for several hours; then, in the wee hours of the morning, she was transported out of Big Stone Gap by helicopter to a large hospital in Richmond, on the other side of the state. She recuperated there for the remaining days of the campaign. John Warner won the election by a hair; many thought he got a lot of sympathy votes because his wife suffered an accident while on the stump for him. It's a shame that Big Stone Gap will be remembered not for the way we honored her but as the campaign stop where Elizabeth Taylor swallowed a chicken bone. Folks 'round here have a theory about it all: Maybe there's some old Scotch-Irish curse on us. After all, the coal-mining boom never made us the Pittsburgh of the South; now we've choked an international movie star; maybe we're just not meant to be part of the Big World.

After all the hoopla (which gave me a chance to put my life on hold), I face myself again. I finally sit down and write my Aunt Meoli a letter. The letter writing is cathartic. I figure she's in her sixties now, so I start the letter with a request for her to be with somebody before she continues reading the letter, in case she passes out or something. It is very hard for me to write about my mother's death, but knowing that this is my mother's sister, I give her every detail to the best of my recollection. Mama always expected the whole truth from me—how ironic—so I assume her sister would, too. I don't know why Mama didn't tell me about her family, especially since we had thirteen years without Fred Mulligan around. What was she still afraid of? Why didn't she see our trip as an opportunity to clear her conscience and share the truth with me? There were so many opportunities for her to tell me her story. When our passports arrived, she could have told me everything then. She could have told me on the plane to Italy. Pick any number of days, of moments inside those days, when it was just the two of us, here alone in this house, in private, without the threat of any outsider. She could have unburdened herself. What a gift the truth would have been! We could have flown to Italy together and re-united with the people I come from. She could have introduced me to her family. We could have stayed with them, learned about them, caught up on all the time that had gone by. I would have aunts and uncles and cousins who loved me. Look at all I missed in the bubble of a lie.

I'm about to dig into a nice slice of a chocolate layer cake that the Tuckett sisters dropped off (the other half was delivered to Theodore). I've been getting a lot of covered dishes since I was part of the team that saved Elizabeth Taylor's life. I whip up some fresh cream. I have a nice steaming mug of coffee. I'm in my softest flannel pajamas, with my feet up, when the phone rings.

It's Spec. (Who else?) He needs me to go down to the Church of God with him. I beg him to make the run alone, because I'm tired (and by the way, I forgot to tell you, Spec, I'm quitting). But he begs me, so I agree to go with him. About five minutes go by before Spec honks, and I run, grabbing my kit on the way out.

As we speed across town to the church on the riverbank, Spec fills me in. Reverend Gaspar was preaching a revival to a packed house when he took two poisonous rattlesnakes out of a cage and started handling them. One bit him.

"Relax. I gave Preacher Gaspar a serum a while back. Doc Daugherty made him take the prescription." Spec doesn't respond, he just takes a deep drag off his cigarette. This is one of those go-nowhere runs I got suckered into because Spec insisted. A snakebite is a one-man job. Wash and dress the wound, and out. I picture that moist layer cake sitting on my coffee table at home, and it makes me real cross.

The Church of God is a one-room building made of sandstone. The simple roof has a cross painted on it. The front door is painted bright red to keep the Devil out. Spec and I can hear wailing from the congregation, but this is typical for a revival. People come to cleanse themselves of their sins and seek redemption. That can get loud.

We enter through the rear of the church. Dicie Sturgill, a small sturdy woman with a shock of red hair, meets us at the back pew. She is very upset. She leads us up the aisle to Reverend Gaspar, who is lying on the floor of the altar with someone's coat wadded up under his head for a pillow. About twelve believers are laying their hands on him and speaking in tongues. I recognize one of the faces from a Rescue Squad run last year: a rambunctious fifteen-year-old trouble-maker named Den-Bob Snodgrass. During girls' PE one morning he came out of the boys' dressing room bouncing a basketball, buck naked. The girls saw him, started screaming, and ran out into the hall-ways, creating a stampede. Den-Bob was suspended, but he never re-turned to finish school. He went to work in the mines instead.

Reverend Gaspar moans softly. His wrist is wrapped in a wad of paper towel, and the blood is seeping through. I dress his wound while Spec quizzes him. Spec asks Reverend Gaspar if he took the serum. The preacher cannot focus; his response tells me he hasn't taken the serum, but I can't be sure. I ask his wife, who is crying and praying at his feet, to take a seat. She is wailing loudly, asking Jesus to save him. I tell Spec to finish wrapping the wound; maybe I can get through to the preacher. I ask the hand layers to take to their seats, as the patient needs air. They oblige. One of them puts her arms around Mrs. Gaspar and leads her to the front pew, a simple wooden bench. Spec prepares a shot to administer to the preacher. If he already took the serum, it won't hurt; and if he didn't, I pray this will do the trick.

"Reverend, can you hear me? It's me, Ave Maria. You got a nasty bite." He smiles as though he understands.

Then Den-Bob Snodgrass leaps up, pulls a pistol out of his pants, and shoots the snakes writhing in the cage on the altar. Blood and thin strips of brown and green snakeskin explode everywhere. The congregation screams out in horror.

"Goddamn rattlers!" Den-Bob cries. Two men grab him, take the gun, and hustle him out of the church. Spec and I keep our cool and continue with our business, though I feel I might throw up. I have a fleeting thought that no one ever changes; Den-Bob Snodgrass was a loose cannon before he chose the Lord, and he's a loose cannon now.

"Reverend, did you take the serum?"

He does not answer me.

"We have to take you to the hospital."

"No," he says clearly.

"We have to. You got bit."

"No!"

Spec looks at me like, *We're taking him anyway. Let's wrap this up and get him out of here.* Preacher Gaspar's face has begun to swell. As we lift him onto the gurney, a small vial falls out of his jacket. It's the sealed bottle of serum I sold him. I slip it into my pocket, hoping his wife didn't notice.

Spec barks for folks to clear the aisle. We get Reverend Gaspar outside and hoist him into the back of the ambulance. Spec drives, and I stay in the back with the reverend.

I hold his hand. He still has the strength to squeeze my hand, and I tell him to keep squeezing. He asks for water, and I give it to him. He has something he wants to say to me. First, he takes another sip.

"Why didn't you take the serum, Preacher?" I ask him.

"Faith," he says. His grip on my hand loosens.

"Hurry, Spec."

I look down at Preacher Gaspar. His expression is one of contentment. I can't understand this. He's in pain. Why isn't he crying out?

Men look so very small when they're dying. He seems like a child to me. I hold his hand and squeeze it gently, awaiting a response. I don't get one. He still has a pulse, though; he has quietly slipped into a coma.

———

Spec drives me home. We are silent most of the trip from the hospital. Reverend Gaspar died at 3:33 A.M.; some folks noted that Christ died at the age of thirty-three, and maybe there is some connection. Spec and I have never lost a patient, so we've never walked this territory with each other before. He drops me off and I walk up the steps, into my old house, but I don't feel like it's home anymore. I left all the lights on; the cake and coffee are where I left them, the whipped cream now a flat sandy pool. I take the dishes to the kitchen and throw everything out. I wash the plate and the fork and the mug. I don't cry, but I can't get Reverend Gaspar's face out of my mind.

It is a glorious late-November day, perfect for apple picking or a funeral. In a simple pinewood casket Reverend Gaspar is laid out in a white gown. Field flowers are gathered with ribbons and set about the foot of the casket. The Church of God has never been so crowded. Almost all of the local preachers from the other denominations flank the altar, including my Catholic priest, a gentle old Irishman out of Buffalo, New York.

The Mormon brothers peruse the crowd and nod to me in recognition. I smile at them in appreciation; they sent me a family tree researched by the Mormons on my behalf. The only problem was that they were off in the spelling of Mario Barbari's name. They researched the Bonboni family instead. While the Bonbonis were talented olive oil pressers, they were not related to me. I didn't have the heart to tell the boys they made a mistake, so I sat through their spiel and acted excited about the discovery.

There is much singing and revelry. Folks stand and talk about Preacher Gaspar, how he helped them find Jesus; how he prayed with them and for them; how he was a real preacher, a genuine apostle who could tell a story and make you believe it. I couldn't help thinking about his preaching at our school when I was a girl. We were a little scared of him, and also in awe. The word *faith* keeps popping up, and I remember how he said it the night he died. It sends a chill through me.

———

At the end of the funeral, after Pee Wee Poteet plays "In the Sweet By and By" on his fiddle, Dicie Sturgill gets up to read a letter that the reverend wrote to his flock in the event of his death. The very mention of this letter sends the women in the church into a wailing spell. When it goes on a tad too long, Dicie gives them a look that says, *Do you want to weep, or do you want me to read this here letter after all?* The wailing trails off to nose blowing and sniffling. Then she reads:

> My dear Friends in Jesus the Lord:
>   In my life I found Jesus, my Lord and Savior, in all things, in work and play. Jesus wasn't Somebody I turned to when I was sick or sad. I had fun with Him, too. He was with me wherever I went, whether it was to preach up at the school or fishing in Powell Valley Lake on a Saturday morning. He was always with me and I hope I knew Him well. Instead of a punch-and-cookie reception in the Fellowship Hall, I've arranged for all of you to go to Shug's Lanes and bowl the afternoon away. I want you to have some fun with Jesus. Listen to one another, laugh, and see the great glory of God in each other. It is there, my friends, believe me. Sometimes we just don't have the eyes to see it. Have a set on me.
>   Devotedly yours, Reverend Elmo Gaspar

One thing we do very well in the Gap is follow instructions. So after we put the reverend in the ground, the funeral procession headed right down Shawnee Avenue to Shug's Bowling Lanes. Midge and Shug Hall had the lanes ready, the balls polished, the Nabs out, the pop poured, and the scorecards empty.

We pour into the bowling alley, teaming up to play a series or two. No one is impatient or competitive. We each wait and take our turn and enjoy watching others play. Even the old ladies join in the fun. There are tears here and there, but mostly there is laughter and storytelling and good eats.

Iva Lou and I excuse ourselves to go to the ladies' room. You have to walk down one of the far aisle lanes to get to the back where the bathrooms are. I remember how self-conscious I was in the first buds of puberty when I made that long walk to the bathroom. One week I was a kid with a wad of bubble gum, bouncing all around this place;

within a month or two, I hit adolescence and was horrified to be on display and draw attention to myself on the way to the bathroom. Today, as Iva Lou and I make the long walk, the self-consciousness is gone. We just hope a ball doesn't pop over the aisle and hit us. Shug's is packed with lousy bowlers; balls are flying everywhere.

When we get to the back, we pause for a moment, because instead of LADIES and MEN printed on each of the rest room doors, there are two pictures to choose from: POINTERS and SETTERS. The POINTERS door has a picture of a hunting dog; the SETTERS door has a picture of a dog sitting by a hearth. "We're setters," Iva Lou announces as she shoves the door open.

June Walker is at the sink, washing her hands. "Ain't this awful about Preacher Gaspar?" We nod sadly. June continues, "You know death comes in threes, so I done guess we got two more to go."

"I don't think you have to worry about that old superstition. There have already been three deaths," I tell June's reflection in the mirror.

"How do you figure?" June asks.

"Well, there was Reverend Gaspar and the two snakes. That makes three."

As we primp at the mirror, we hear the balls rolling down the lanes toward the pins. When the balls hit the back wall of the lanes to go into the return aisle, they sound like they are going to bust right through the ladies' room wall. June can't help but jump a little with each crash. Iva Lou and I laugh. The last time I was in this bathroom I was a little girl. I had forgotten how the balls smash the wall.

I don't know why I'm not sad about Reverend Gaspar's passing. I guess it's partly because he died on the heels of my mother's death and I'm still not over that, so anything on top of it seems surreal. When I get back from the funeral, Otto and Worley are putting in my storm windows on the ground floor. I tell them all about the bowling and they laugh. I'm running out of chores to assign them, and it gets me to thinking about the future. I don't know when it happened, but Otto and Worley have gone from the town junk haulers to my home-and-business repairmen. Otto left a stack of mail on the kitchen table for me. I grab it and go upstairs. I change out of my Sunday best and into my overalls. I take the mail up to the attic, through the window, and out onto the roof. I haven't been out here since we patched the roof. Where does the time go? I kept meaning to come up here and look out over town and collect my thoughts. I guess I've been busy. Or maybe I didn't need to be high up and above everything until now.

There are three requests for magazine subscription renewals. Instead of opening them and putting them in the TO PAY stack, I tear them in half. I get plenty of magazines at the store; I'll just read them there from now on. At the bottom of the stack is an onionskin envelope with swirly blue writing: The return address is Meoli Vilminore Mai! Finally!

I'm careful to open the envelope without tearing the thin paper inside. It's a three-page letter, in Italian. I must admit, I worry about losing my Italian reading and speaking ability since Mama died; each day that goes by without her, I get rustier.

In the letter Aunt Meoli tells me how sad she is to hear of my mother's passing. She had been hopeful that someday they would reunite. She tells me my mother would be happy to know that she and I found each other. She also tells me how happy she is that I am fine and asks if I could send a photograph of myself. Visions of Italian *co-marei* gathered at the *groceria* with my picture, fighting over me as a potential bride for their toothless sons, gives me a shiver, so I decide not to send one just yet. Zia Meoli goes on about her life in Italy. Her twin sister, Antonietta, practically raised her two kids, since Meoli was a schoolteacher with a full-time job. Toward the end of the letter, I see the name Mario, so I skip past the newsy chitchat to the real reason for the correspondence. Zia Meoli tells me that she does not know my father well; he lives in Schilpario, up the mountain from where she lives. She does hear of him from time to time, as he is still mayor! She does not know if he's married, but she assumes he is not; when she last heard about him, he was known to be something of a ladies' man. She promises to try and find out more about him.

I lie back on the roof. It is quiet except for the sliding sounds of storm windows being tested from below. I know I should be happy that my father is alive and well. Instead, the news makes me cry. I don't know what to feel or how. So I cover my face with my sleeve so Otto and Worley won't hear me.

I have so many books to return to the Bookmobile that I half joked to Iva Lou she ought to just park it in my front yard. I gather them up in two carryalls and head for town. Pearl and Fleeta are handling the store today—I decided I need a few days off. I don't think they miss me much. Fleeta loves to clear the register, take the money sack to the bank, and put it in the night-drop slot. She says it gives her a sense of completion at the end of a hard working day.

The Bookmobile door is open, which is unusual. I hear giggling from inside; I think to knock but don't. Iva Lou is sitting on one of the snap stools next to Jack MacChesney, who is perusing one of the three national newspapers she has on board. The paper, attached to a large bamboo holder, is unwieldy, and watching Jack Mac try to balance it cracks Iva Lou up. I haven't seen Jack Mac since the Elizabeth Taylor Choke Night. He doesn't seem one bit happy to see me.

"Hey, y'all." I empty out the two canvas sacks and turn to leave.

"Why are you in such a hurry?" Iva Lou says with a look that means *Stay.* I look back at her with a look that says: *I'm not staying.*

"I have to check on Pearl and Fleeta. Otto and Worley are over to the house." Why do I have to justify myself to them? Can't I just drop the books and go?

"Call me sometime," Iva Lou says with a twinge of sadness. The truth is, I was looking forward to some time on the Bookmobile with Iva Lou. It would have been fun, but He is here, so forget it. All it took was Jack Mac's scowl to change my mind; I'm disembarking pronto.

Now that I've told Iva Lou I was checking on Pearl and Fleeta, I have to stop at the store; they can see where I'm headed through the windshield, and I don't want to be a liar. So I park my Jeep in front of the post office and go into the Pharmacy. Pearl and Fleeta are back by the makeup counter. Pearl is plucking Fleeta's eyebrows. Fleeta smokes.

"I'm not checking on you two. I was forced to come in here due to circumstances."

"Who you avoiding? Spec?"

"No."

"He's been looking fer ye. He done got your letter that you quit the Squad. He don't want to come over by your house, so he keeps stopping by here and bothering us."

"Did the reverend's snakebite skeer you that bad?" Pearl asks.

"I wasn't scared. It was just the last straw. You know what I mean?"

"Well, all I know is that I don't like no damn quitters," Fleeta remarks as she inhales her Marlboro deeply down to her diaphragm.

"I've been working on the Rescue Squad as a volunteer for years! I am not a quitter."

"Defensive," Fleeta decides under her breath.

I'm in no mood to argue with Fleeta. So I walk over to the post office to check my box, which turns out to be a waste. There are a few flyers for quilt shows, tours to Knoxville for the University of Tennessee football games, and several bills.

There's a truck parked next to my Jeep, so I have to squeeze in between the two vehicles to climb into my driver's seat. I hate when people park too close. There's plenty of space for everybody when you park at the correct angle. I pull my door open and I'm about to climb in when something on the passenger seat of the truck catches my eye. The word *Schilpario* pops out at me. The afternoon sun is bright, so I cover my eyes and peer into the truck through the window. It's very strange. The book I just returned to the Bookmobile, *Schilpario: A Life in the Mountains,* is sitting on the seat of the truck. Who would check that out? And why? It was a special checkout, too, so whoever borrowed it must have convinced Iva Lou to bend the rules. As I pull out, I look down the street for the Bookmobile, but it's gone. The truck is familiar. It's new. Then I remember: It belongs to Jack Mac. I don't have a good car memory, but I do remember that he pointed this one out to me long ago when I made a delivery to his mama up in the holler.

Instead of waiting to ask Jack Mac why he checked out my book, I throw the Jeep into gear and peel up to the stoplight. In the rearview I see him come out of Zackie's with a brown sack and jump into the truck. As he turns over the ignition, the light turns green. I hang a left and drive off.

Theodore and I have something special we do every once in a while. We call it our field trip. We go over to Jonesville to Cudjo's Caverns, a deep cave in the side of one of the mountains. It is full of stalagmites and stalactites, nature's majestic mineral and stone deposits—"God's Jewelry Box," or so the sign says.

At the entrance to the cave, there is a flat area where we wait for the guide, an old man named Ray. He senses when there are visitors; we hear his footsteps down the path. "Oh, it's y'all. Ye ain't been up here for a while." He chuckles. Then he leads us into the cave along a path that weaves through carved-out halls and catacombs left behind by the Indians. The rock formations that hang from the ceiling look like glittering candle-wax drips, all shapes and sizes, including some that are quite large. The ones that come up from the ground look like shimmering fingers.

Theodore and I used to keep notebooks describing the various formations. After a while, we got bored and gave it up. Still, we come back so often, the guide knows us, so he treats us to special areas of observation. Our favorite is a small crystal lake deep in the heart of the cave. Ray never takes regular folks back there because it was a sacred place of Indian prayer. It is also very dangerous; the bank of the lake is only about a foot wide, and there is one shelf of rock above it, room enough for two people to crawl up and sit. The water in the lake itself is hundreds of feet deep. Ray is afraid a visitor could fall in. He allows us to go to the lake because he knows that we'll be careful and not touch anything.

The surface of the lake is quite small, maybe ten feet across. Ray told us to imagine a deep cylinder of stone filled with water, like a tall, slim vase. I can see why the Indians prayed here; it is so quiet, the only sound you hear is water trickling down the walls. The lake reminds me of the baptismal pool at Reverend Gaspar's church. There is just enough room to immerse a body or two at a time. (I wish I would have brought him here to show him how the Indians worshipped.)

Theodore points out the far wall with the large flashlight he is holding. The water reflects off the stalactites, throwing iridescent colors all over the water-washed walls. It looks like a moving painting of blues and silvers.

Theodore, ever so sensitive, knew I needed a treat. He thinks between Elizabeth Taylor's choking and Preacher Gaspar being bitten by a deadly snake, I haven't quite been myself. He's right. I feel like the last year of my life has been one unpleasant event after another. So much for something exciting happening to me while I'm thirty-five. (Maybe I'm growing a mole or something on my face somewhere that signals disaster instead of joy.) I do have five months to go until I'm thirty-six; maybe things will change for the better—if not, I fear I will lose my faith in the ancient art of Chinese face-reading altogether. Theodore and I stay by the lake for a long time, never tiring of the color swirls nature makes.

On the way home we stop at the Dip & Cone Barn, a hamburger shack between Jonesville and Pennington Gap. Theodore orders a lot of food. We sit outside on a picnic bench even though the final day of November has a strong chill to it.

"I want to talk to you about something."

"Sure." I start tearing open the little ketchup packets. I like to have a substantial pool of ketchup before I start eating fries. I don't like to eat a couple and open a packet, eat a couple, open a packet. I like an orderly dinner setup.

"It's been a wild time," Theodore offers diplomatically.

"No kidding."

"And I don't think that I've been thinking straight." He looks down at his hands.

"About what?"

"About us." I look at Theodore and see a sincerity in his eyes that, I must confess, scares the hell out of me. He never said "us" like *us* before. We were always buddies, except for that night I threw myself at him and was rejected (a night I would like to forget).

"Remember the night of the halftime show for Elizabeth Taylor?" Remember it? Is he kidding? It was a night of nights for me.

"When those two dogs were humping in the middle of my master-piece, I wanted to quit. But I looked down at you from the announcer's booth, and you were wearing that red velvet coat, and you smiled up at me and did this funny thing where you checked your watch like, *How long can two dogs screw? It can't be forever,* and I actually felt the burden lift off of me. You saved my life that night. I'll never forget it."

"You're welcome, Theodore."

"I mean it. You're always there for me. I don't know what I'd do without you."

The only other person in my life who ever told me that she didn't know what she would do without me was my mother, when she was dying. I make note of this, in case I have to come back to it later.

"I think we should get married."

It's as though a shade, the kind on a roller in an old window, starts being pulled by the circle tab from the top of my head, slowly down my face, neck, torso, and limbs all the way to my feet. I want to stay behind this shade forever.

"What do you think?" he says after a moment.

"Oh, Theodore."

"It's what you want, isn't it?"

What I want? Can't he tell that's what's wrong with me? I don't know what I want. I have spent my entire life trying to give everybody else what they want. I'm not complaining. I like to be of service. I find great purpose in it. And no one was more surprised than me when my old routines didn't work for me anymore. Somewhere along the way, I got sucked dry and started feeling like the mountain mother with sixteen kids who wakes up one morning and realizes that she's just a vessel, a way station where life passed through before it passed her by. When Reverend Gaspar was dying, and he held my hand and muttered, "Faith," I didn't know what he was talking about. Okay, maybe he meant the traditional Jesus story, to have faith in that, but I don't think so. I think he was talking about a deeper concept. A concept I cannot comprehend. I'd like to but I haven't yet. What did he mean? Faith in God? Faith in myself? Faith in others? Faith in the unknown? I don't know. And as for the things of this world, I am even more confused about them! I don't know what makes me happy—okay, maybe Ledna and Edna Tuckett's coconut layer cake, a letter from Italy, and the lining in any of my winter coats, hand-sewn and tufted by my mother. Those things make me happy. But getting married? Is that happiness? Or is it just a container to keep happiness in? I don't know. Theodore can see that I am confused.

"I sprung this on you too quickly," he apologizes.

"No, you didn't. I've been thinking about marrying you since the day we met."

Theodore looks relieved that he's getting somewhere. If there's one thing I know about men, it's that they fear rejection.

"You know, I think you and Jack MacChesney asked me to marry you because you knew I'd say no."

"This isn't about Jack."

"No, it's not, but it sort of is. I'm the town spinster, and I've gotten two wedding proposals in the past six months. Something's up."

I eat my french fries and sip my Tab and look at Theodore.

"I want to marry you."

"Do you love me, Theodore?"

"Of course I do."

"Well, thank you."

"So, yes, you'll marry me?"

I shake my head slowly. I cannot marry Theodore Augustus Tipton. I have changed my mind. My prayer has been answered, but it was the wrong thing to have prayed for.

"Why, Ave Maria? I thought you wanted to marry me."

"I'm going to try to explain this. I hope you'll forgive me in advance if the words are inadequate, or I am inadequate."

Theodore motions to me that I should speak. I love when he does that; it means he's really listening.

"A while ago Iva Lou told me that I could never trust any man until I understood my relationship with my father. You can take your pick: Fred Mulligan or the mysterious Mario da Schilpario. Since that particular thing was said to me, I've made it my business to observe fathers and daughters. And I've seen some incredible things, beautiful things. Like the little girl who's not very cute—her teeth are funny, and her hair doesn't grow right, and she's got on thick glasses—but her father holds her hand and walks with her like she's a tiny angel that no one can touch. He gives her the best gift a woman can get in this world: protection. And the little girl learns to trust the man in her life. And all the things that the world expects from women—to be beautiful, to soothe the troubled spirit, heal the sick, care for the dying, send the greeting card, bake the cake—all of those things become the way we pay the father back for protecting us. It's a fair exchange. But I never got that. So I don't know how to be with you. Oh, I guess I could pretend, make it up as I go along and hope that I figure it all out later. But that wouldn't be fair to you. What if I never figured it out? You deserve a woman who can give all of herself to you. I think you should hold out for it."

Theodore has pressed and folded the tinfoil wrapper from his hamburger into a silver square the size of a shirt button. He stares at it for a very long time.

"Let's go home," he says. I gather up the dinner, clear off the picnic table, and toss the garbage into the can. Theodore stands by the car looking up at nothing in particular. He's going to be fine. I'm sure of it.

Pearl received the results of her PSATs, and she's in the top tenth percentile of her class. She shows me the report, but I have to grab it out of her hand in midair, because she won't let go of it as she jumps up and down. Fleeta is excited for her, even though she has no idea what the test is; she loves when anybody she knows wins.

"Pearl, congratulations! You're a brain!" I shriek.

"I knew that the day she didn't mix the analgesics in with the laxatives." Fleeta winks.

"Mr. Cantrell says I can get into a good school. Maybe Virginia Tech or UVA, or maybe William and Mary!"

"Go to Tech. They got a good wrestling program," Fleeta promises.

Tayloe's mother, Betty, comes in with a prescription slip. Fleeta and Pearl fan out to the back to do their chores.

"How you doing, Betty?"

"I've been better."

"You sick?"

Betty answers that she's not and hands me the prescription. I go behind the counter to fill it.

"Tayloe sure made a magnificent Cleopatra. We were all so proud of her."

"Some folks thought she done looked better than Elizabeth Taylor herself."

"I think I'd have to agree."

I look at the prescription from Doc Daugherty. It's for prenatal vitamins.

"Congratulations, Betty! A new baby?"

"Not mine. Tayloe's. She's done found out she's pregnant."

"Oh." I look down at Doc's prescription. Sure enough, it's T. Slagle. I don't know what more to say. This is tragic. She's a little girl!

"Can you believe it? She was on the Pill, too. But it's too late to cry over spilt milk; it's spilt and that's all there is to it. We got to clean it up and move on here."

"How's she feeling?"

"She's over the shock, but you know, the same darn thing happened to me when I was sixteen, and I got my beautiful baby Tayloe out of it. So we're trying to look on the bright side."

I give Betty the prescription. She takes it and puts it in her bag.

"Kids." Then she turns to go. "Ave Maria?"

"Yeah, Betty?"

"She's having the baby in April. Can you keep her part in the Drama open till she's back on her feet? Playing June Tolliver means the world to her."

"You tell Tayloe she can come back to the Drama whenever she's ready."

Betty brightens considerably.

"Thank you kindly."

Betty goes. She knows and I know that Tayloe's performing career is over. But Betty isn't ready to let go of all the dreams she had for her daughter. I can picture what will happen, because the outcome of this situation is always the same. Tayloe will marry, get a trailer, have her babies, and be a wife. There won't be time for six performances a week.

Fleeta comes down the aisle, having overheard our conversation.

"That damn Lassiter kid. The halfback on the team. You know, with the bedroom eyes. He done knocked her up. Boys."

Fleeta goes off to the back. I can hear Pearl, flipping the metal clip on her inventory clipboard. I join her at the makeup counter.

"Her life is ruined, isn't it?" Pearl asks.

"Of course not. It'll be hard for her, but she's a very determined girl. And her mom will help."

"I don't ever want to get stuck in a trailer," Pearl decides.

"Stay away from the Lassiter boys."

Pearl nods and goes about her inventory. I check my face in the mirror. I have dark circles under my eyes. The lids droop in exhaustion. I've lost my sparkle.

The familiar jingle of the door chimes tells us we've got a customer, but there is a residual jingle, like the door was slammed after entrance. Somebody's angry and taking it out on my door. I peer down the aisle. I'm right. It's Aunt Alice.

"Where are you, you hateful bitch?"

I look at Pearl. "Does she mean you or me?"

"I think she means you," Pearl says fearfully.

I get out of the makeup chair slowly and take that long walk down the anti-inflammatory aisle toward my aunt, who looks like she could shoot me.

"May I help you?"

She waves a letter in my face. "You done screwed me good. You think so, don't you?"

"I didn't screw anybody." I speak the literal and figurative truth, of course.

"Do you think I will sit back and accept this? If you do, you don't know me very well."

"Aunt Alice, if you have any problem with my business dealings, you need to speak to Lew Eisenberg."

"I am not talking to that feriner! I am talking to you!"

"Have your lawyer call Mr. Eisenberg."

"If I can't have this Pharmacy, I'm gonna get my house back. You watch me!"

"You'll never get my house! Never!" The tone of my voice surprises me. Fleeta ushers Pearl to the back room. That's when Aunt Alice really lets me have it.

"You're a whore just like your mother before you. You're a sponger, a taker. And you're evil. You may think you beat me out of what's mine, but I will fight you until my last breath."

"You need to leave. If you don't, I'll have to call the police."

"This is mine! This is all mine! All of it! You robbed me!" She looks like a sad six-year-old girl who didn't get the doll she wanted. Her eyes fill with mist. "I never got anything I ever wanted in my whole life!" she cries.

"You got Uncle Wayne." This is all I can say to her? Where's my fight? Why can't I defend my mother's honor? Where's the woman who schemed to protect her assets against this cruel woman? I don't need a doctor to tell me. Something is wrong with me.

I have been exhausted lately, but I blame it on the cold weather and my schedule at the Pharmacy. I started stocking ornaments, lights, and decorations (by customer request), which attract extra business. I feel bad sticking Fleeta and Pearl with longer hours around the holidays, so I cover the extra time myself. Also, folks get the flu and colds this time of year, so I'm on the run constantly filling and delivering prescriptions. Theodore and Iva Lou check on me quite a bit; they're worried, but I keep telling them it's just the holiday rush. Maybe I'm especially exhausted because this will be my first Christmas without Mama and I'm not up to facing it just yet. If I could just get some rest, I would feel so much better. It's gotten to the point where I can't sleep through the night. I haven't told anyone. But I've been thinking about calling Doc Daugherty. I just haven't gotten around to it.

I am donating several boxes of twinkling lights to the Dogwood Garden Club for the Christmas flower exhibit at the Southwest Vir-

ginia Museum. I'm late delivering them; I had some straggling customers at the Pharmacy. I drive right up on the lawn and park by the
door, too tired to walk the few extra feet from the sidewalk. I would've
asked Theodore to deliver them, but he's gone to visit his family in
Scranton for the holidays. He invited me to join him, but the thought
of a long car trip and spending time with a large family was too tiring,
so I politely refused the invitation. This Christmas, I just don't feel
like celebrating.

The entrance to the museum is actually the foyer of the only mansion in Big Stone Gap. The museum was the Slemp family home for
years, until they donated it to the state in the 1940s. Now it is a sweet
homespun museum with dioramas that tell the stories of the miners,
quilters, Cherokees, Melungeons, and families of the area. I must be
standing here a long time because two of the Garden Club members
whisper to each other to fetch Nellie Goodloe. Nellie descends the
grand staircase and greets me at the door. Her expression is one of
concern. She looks deeply into my eyes.

"Ave Maria, honey, are you all right?"

"I brought you the lights." I give Nellie the stack of lights, but I miss
her arms and they fall to the ground with a clatter.

I wake up in my own bed, in my pajamas. Pearl, her mother Leah,
Fleeta, and Theodore stand at the foot of my bed.

"What happened?" I ask.

"You fainted."

"I was dropping off the lights." I move to get up, but my legs feel
like they're filled with sand. The group moves toward me. "What's
wrong with me?" I am really scared. "Theodore, aren't you supposed
to be in Scranton?"

"I've been back a few days."

"A few days."

"It's December thirtieth, Ave," Fleeta announces, confusing me.
"Christmas is over."

"But I was at the museum two days before Christmas. What happened to me?"

"Doc Daugherty ain't sure," Pearl tells me.

"What do you mean, he ain't sure?"

"You passed out up there, and since you were close to home, they brought you here. And then Nellie Goodloe came over to the Pharmacy and told me and Fleeta. We called Doc Daugherty and he came right over here. All your vitals was okay, so he said you could sleep it off. And you did. For exactly seven days."

"Doc told me I couldn't smoke around you, so I done gave it up," Fleeta says proudly.

"Good for you." I'm glad Fleeta could take my medical emergency and turn it into a positive experience for herself.

"Do you remember any of this, Ave?" Theodore asks.

I don't. I feel refreshed, like I had a nap. I throw my legs over the side of the bed to stand, but I collapse right onto the mattress.

"You got bed legs, is all. Don't let it fret you. The movement'll come back when you start using them again," Fleeta reassures me.

"Let's go fix her something to eat," Leah announces, motioning to Fleeta and Pearl that she'll need their help in the kitchen. They go, and Theodore sits next to me on my bed.

"Am I dying or something?"

"No. Doc thinks you suffered a nervous breakdown."

"What?"

"He says he's seen all kinds of them in his life. Some folks function through them, some have blackout episodes, and some sleep it off, like a bear hibernating in the winter. You went the cave route." Theodore hugs me.

"Help me walk." I try to stand, and Theodore helps steady me. We walk slowly. We get to the bathroom, where I tell him to wait outside.

My bathroom, with the black-and-white-checked tile, seems huge to me. The skylight in the ceiling has snow on it. It must have been a white Christmas. The bathroom is cold; the fresh towels I hung a week ago are still there untouched. The soap is the same size it was before I went to sleep. This is so odd. I pull the light string next to the mirror. I look at myself.

My face looks like it did when I was a girl. I guess I lost some weight during my nap; my nose seems longer, and my jaw is sticking out ever so slightly. My eyelashes are crusted with sleep; they are gnarled and crisscrossed, but still thick. There isn't a line on my face, and believe me, there were plenty of them before Christmas.

I don't remember dreaming. Did a switch just go off in my mind, and I went to sleep? Why don't I remember anything? Where did my mind go?

"Are you okay in there?" Theodore asks through the door a little nervously.

"I'm fine. I'll be right out."

I wash my face and brush my teeth. I grip the sink, then the wall, then the door. I pull it open slowly. Theodore is on the other side, there to steady me.

"Are you hungry?"

"I've never been this hungry." He carries me down the steps to the kitchen.

hoever said "Never make any major decisions when you're tired" was a very smart person. I let January and February of 1979 pass without doing much of anything beyond the basics. Everyone in town is asking me about my Deep Sleep, as it has come to be known, but I can't tell them much. I still don't remember a thing. Doc Daugherty is checking me on a weekly basis, and he sees no lasting damage to my physical person; he is pretty certain my mind is fine, too. Pearl and Fleeta manned the store for me while I was under, and Clayton Phipps, a licensed pharmacist up in Norton, came down every Monday and Tuesday and filled prescriptions. Folks appreciated the pinch hitting.

When I do finally start back to work in March, Pearl uses my rejuvenated face as an example of the importance of sleep as a beauty must to all women. There is nothing like slumber to give the face a youthful glow. I believe this is somewhat false advertising. I believe I look so good because I didn't die. I came through something, and relief perked up my face. Either way, Pearl has been selling Queen Helene hand over fist, telling the ladies that she used it on my face twice a day, every day, during the Deep Sleep.

Pearl kept a list of all the folks who dropped by. She got the idea from Nellie, who explained that all fine families keep a guest book for visitors who pass through. I finally get a chance to look at it. Folks signed in with funny messages: Iva Lou with smiley faces; the Tuckett twins with Bible verses; Doc Daugherty with Latin phrases; the book is full and it makes me laugh. It's thick, too. Nan MacChesney came twice. I look for Jack Mac's name. He never made it over.

Otto and Worley took it upon themselves to clean out the roof gutters at the Pharmacy and my house during the Deep Sleep. Pearl tells me they were so worried that I might bite the dust, Otto cried. I give them each a bonus for their initiative and loyalty.

I learned three things about myself after the Deep Sleep. I learned who my true friends are; I learned that I bury my problems until they overcome me in a full-blown crisis; and the biggest thing of all, I learned that I wasn't happy. It's a terrifying thing to admit. It puts everyone around you in a state of paralysis, because they think that they are somehow responsible for your sadness and can fix it. Of course, they cannot. I know happiness exists somewhere; and if I knew where, I would go to it and claim it. I realize I have spent my life reacting to things and not initiating them. I let myself go somewhere along the way. And I didn't miss myself. (Does that sound crazy?) Some days I wonder if something grew inside my heart during the Deep Sleep. I want a change.

March brings the most beautiful spring I have ever seen in Big Stone Gap. Purple and yellow crocuses spring up everywhere, honeysuckle blooms and fills the air, and the mountains turn green, after being gray and brittle for all of winter.

I am finally feeling like myself again. Iva Lou is shocked when I board the Bookmobile. It has been a long time, and it feels like home.

"Hey, girl!" She hugs me, so happy to see me back on the third snap stool.

"I never did thank you for all your visits when I was under."

"Don't mention it. You had the whole town rattled." Then Iva Lou's face fills with joy. "I was gonna drop by and see you later. I had something I wanted to ask you. Lyle Makin done asked me to marry him, and I said yes!"

Iva Lou and I shriek like sophomores.

"We're gonna get married over to the United Methodist church. Reverend Manning said he'd be happy to do the service. And I was wondering if you would honor me by standing up for me. Would you please be my maid of honor?"

"Absolutely! I'd be honored, of course. But we can't call me a maid of honor. Call me an old maid of disrepute."

"That's my title. Course I'll be happy to pass it on to you when I'm a fat and sassy wife!"

Iva Lou and Lyle don't want to wait long, so the date is set for March 11. I bought a new pink dress and a matching picture hat with illusion netting and a tiny bumblebee nestled in the crown. Iva Lou asked me to wear something colorful, since Lyle likes bright colors.

March 11 turns out to be a perfect day for a wedding. The weather is warm, about seventy-five degrees and sunny. I'm glad my dress has a stole that I can take off, in case it gets hot later on in the fellowship hall.

The mail comes and I'm dressed early, so I sit down and sort through it. It's a lot of junk. One of the flyers from the Dollar General Store seems thick, so I shake it out. An envelope falls out and hits the floor. I can see that it's from Italy. Zia Meoli owes me a letter from a month ago, but the handwriting on this is not familiar. There is no return address. I remove one of my hat pins and slowly rip open the envelope.

The letter begins, "My dear daughter." I sit down in the chair, a little stunned. I hadn't made it official to myself, but I had given up on hearing from my father. Maybe that had something to do with the Deep Sleep—I needed to give up hope to move on. But I am so happy to see this letter.

The letter is short but well written, in very simple English. He tells me that Meoli's husband came to Schilpario to visit him. My uncle told my father all about me, or at least what he knew from letters. He tells me that he has no other children and no wife. He lives with his mother in the center of town. (*His mother?* I do have a grandmother! I can't believe my good luck.) Mario has been mayor of Schilpario since 1958. He would like me to write to him and has written his address on the back of the letter. I stuff it into my purse. It's a nice, friendly letter. No revelations. Why didn't my father ever try to contact my mother after he broke off their relationship? Did she mean so little to him that he could forget her so quickly and forever?

A horn honks out front. Theodore jumps out of the car and comes around to open my door. He whistles at me. "You look beautiful."

"Say hello to the Strawberry Daiquiri of Big Stone Gap."

Theodore laughs and I climb in. "What's new?" he asks innocently.

"I got a letter from Mario da Schilpario."

He practically stops the car.

I open my beaded clutch (my maid-of-honor gift from Iva Lou) and take out the letter. "It's okay." As Theodore drives us to the church, I read it to him.

There's a big crowd outside the church. Iva Lou didn't send out personal invitations, but she did run her engagement photo in the *Post,* announcing the time and date and other particulars. This is called an open-church wedding, which means everyone in town is welcome. Everyone likes Iva Lou, so she has a full house.

I haven't been in the Methodist church since Fred Mulligan's funeral. I've pretty much stuck to my Catholic church. But I know every room inside this building, including the sacristy, where brides wait before going down the aisle.

Iva Lou looks stunning in a peacock-blue gown. She decided not to wear white because it makes her look too washed-out. She, too, wears a picture hat. She is sipping vodka from a small airline-size bottle. She offers me some. I swig it—not because I'm nervous about going down the aisle but because Mario's letter has put me on edge—and I give it back to Iva Lou. She finishes it off and throws the empty bottle into her makeup case.

"You are so beautiful, Iva Lou."

"You think?" She squints into the mirror.

"You're a little piece of blue heaven."

"Thanks, honey-o."

"How's Lyle holding up?"

"He got drunk last night up in Esserville. Thank God his buddies got him home so he could sleep it off."

"Nerves."

"Uh-huh," Iva Lou agrees, as she applies a little more powder blush. Her hand is shaking, so she steadies herself.

"Don't be scared. You're doing the right thing."

"I know that. I just hate crowds. And ministers give me the creeps."

"Reverend Manning is really nice."

"I know. I just have to focus on something besides the gravity of all this. It's too overwhelming for a girl like me."

A girl like Iva Lou. What a girl she is. Always made up her own rules. Here she is, forty-plus, getting married for the first time, having tasted all the goodies in the county. Good for her. She understood what she needed and went after it. She drove the Bookmobile even though they said a woman couldn't handle it. She sells costume jewelry, for profit and to give women something small and sparkly that will make them feel good about themselves. She always paid her own way, and she owns her own home. She is very strong and also very feminine. Iva Lou must love Lyle very much, because of all the women I know, she has the most to lose.

Through the crack in the sacristy door I can hear the bellows of the pipe organ. Fred Mulligan bought that organ, and it sounds like it's been kept up to snuff.

"Iva Lou, I think it's time."

"Jesus Christ Almighty on a mountain! I forgot your bouquet. It's over there in the box."

I go to the box and remove a beautiful arrangement of tea roses in shades of pink. Iva Lou picks up her bouquet of white roses.

"Nellie. She's got the touch." Iva Lou models her bouquet. "Someday, when you get murried, you'll have to get her to do the flowers."

"Let's go."

Iva Lou and I hover in the vestibule of the church. Nellie is directing the wedding, so she'll send us down the aisle. I have to remember how these things go in the movies; we didn't rehearse. Lyle said you would only find his ass in church three times in his life: for his baptism, his wedding, and his funeral. Iva Lou dispensed with the rehearsal.

I take off with the bridal one-step, two-step down the aisle to an eight-track version of "Say Forever You'll Be Mine" from Dolly Parton and Porter Wagoner. The pews are full, and I get lots of approving glances and winks from both sides of the aisle. Joella Reasor even cranes out of her pew to whisper "Welcome back" to me. Now I know how holler folks feel when they finally make it down to town after the long winter.

As I reach the altar, I smile at Lyle, who looks very happy and extremely nervous. He pivots out ever so slightly to see Iva Lou start her trek down the great white (blue) way. I stop short when I see his best man: Jack MacChesney, polished up like mamaw's silver, gives me a wink.

I'm going to let Iva Lou have it later. Why didn't she tell me Jack Mac was the other half of this wedding party? Maybe she noticed that he didn't come to see me when I was sick. Maybe she thought I'd bow out if I knew he was involved. It's funny. I don't hate him when I look at him. I'm just glad I look good in this dress.

The Methodists like their ceremonies short and sweet. This one is practically over before it begins. I'm sure it was the longest eight minutes of Lyle's life; his face is the color of a cherry tomato. When Reverend Manning introduces Mr. and Mrs. Lyle Makin for the first time, Iva Lou weeps. Her parents are gone, too, and I know she wishes they were here to see how happy she is.

The music begins again, and though we haven't practiced the recessional, I know the proper thing to do is take Jack Mac's arm and follow the bride and groom out. I face the congregation and wait for Jack Mac to join me. He does.

"Nice hat," he says and smiles. Then he extends his arm, I take it, and we go.

Nellie has decorated the fellowship hall in a Victorian theme. There are decorative, hand-painted fans on the walls; the ceiling is festooned with a lace canopy. The tables are covered in white linen. The cake has stacked circle tiers with a bride and groom in an antique carriage on top. Silver trays lined with crisp white doilies are filled with Nellie's homemade candy wedding bells dusted in blue and pink sugar.

Lyle is relaxed now. Iva Lou is herself again, laughing and talking and making everyone feel at home. Theodore is chatting with a couple of teachers from up at the high school. I dip my cup into the bowl of champagne punch.

"Pink is your color," Jack MacChesney says.

"Thank you. Lyle's favorite color is peacock blue, so I'm the contrast."

"How have you been?"

"I'm coming back strong. Thank you for asking. How are you?"

"I'm fine myself." Jack Mac looks off. I turn to see what he's looking at. It's Sweet Sue Tinsley, escorted by her ex-husband, Mike.

"Are they back together?" I ask bluntly.

"Yes, ma'am," Jack Mac says quietly.

"You know something, Jack? I'll buy you a new hunting rifle if you promise never to call me ma'am again."

"I'm sorry. It's a habit from my upbringing."

Theodore joins us at the punch bowl. "Everybody's meeting for a potluck at Iva Lou's trailer later. Hope you can make it, Jack," Theodore offers.

"I'll be there."

"I'll get the car," Theodore tells me as he places his punch cup on the out trolley.

Theodore goes. I finish my punch and nibble on a wedding bell.

"You'll be at Iva Lou's later, right?"

I nod.

"You're gonna wear the pink dress, aren't you?"

I look at Jack Mac with a half smile that says, *Yeah, right. I am going to stay in this cinched silk cummerbund and panty girdle the rest of the day.* Little does he know I can't wait to get out of here and peel it off.

"See you at Iva's." I grab my hat off the bookshelf and go to meet Theodore.

I've never been to Iva Lou's trailer in Danberry Heights, but it's a beauty. The outside is sleek, ecru wood panels set off by crisp black shutters. Iva attached a redwood deckette at the entrance. An old-fashioned light fixture on an antique pole at the curve of the entrance casts a pretty golden glow as you enter. I arrive alone. Theodore is coming in his own car; he has a school-board meeting in the morning and might have to cut out early.

The interior decor is beige and modern—the perfect backdrop for a cool blonde like Iva Lou. The shag carpeting is a thick salt-and-pepper mix, very cozy. Iva Lou's inner circle is packed into the trailer. She has made macaroni and cheese, salad, and slaw. There are leftover mints and lots of cake—plenty to eat. She bought wedding paper plates and napkins with a bride and groom on them. Lyle is toasting pals with a bottle of beer. He looks like the lord of the manor now; he definitely fits in. Iva Lou feeds him a biscuit, then kisses the crumbs away. I'm starving, so I dig into the hot macaroni and cheese. Mama never made this dish, but I've always loved it. The soft elbow noodles nestled in butter and cheddar cheese melt in my mouth. The crushed potato chips on top give it a delicious salty crunch. I may have seconds. Sweet Sue comes up behind me with a plate of cake.

"How's it going, A-vuh Maria?"

"Great. How are you?"

"I got back with Mike." Mike Tinsley is laughing heartily at one of Lyle's jokes. He seems happy to be part of the Gap social scene again. "Yeah, the kids missed him." The space between Sweet Sue's eyebrows is knit into a little square. "I did too, of course." I smile and chew; as long as I'm chewing, I don't have to talk. I look at Sweet Sue's face. She really is very pretty. Her eyes are a clear ocean-blue. There are little crinkles around them now, but they give her a look of knowing and experience, which she wears well. I wonder if Jack Mac ever told her he proposed to me. I don't think he did, because she doesn't seem uncomfortable with me. I am most definitely not a rival.

"Well, I'll see you later." Sweet Sue smiles and wedges through the crowd to get to Mike.

"What happened to the pink dress?" I hear from the entrance to the den. Now I see why Sweet Sue scooted off like a possum: It's Jack Mac. He stands in the kitchen doorway with his arms folded.

"It was cutting off circulation. I couldn't take it another minute."

"What about the hat?"

He smiles at me and moves close, and I must say, everything this guy says sounds like a come-on to me. There's something in that slow delivery and those gluttonous pauses that makes you feel buck naked. I pull my cardigan closed and button it.

"Are you cold?"

"Ever since I had the Deep Sleep, I get shivers." I hope he buys the lie, but I don't think he does.

"Do I scare you?"

I laugh right out loud. "No, sir, you don't."

"I don't know. You get jumpy when I'm around."

"I do?" I don't notice that I do, but even if I do, I don't want this man pointing out my insecurities to me.

"What did you dream about during the Deep Sleep?" he wonders out loud.

Okay, now I get it. He's drunk. He's drunk and he's making a pass at me. He probably had the Tuckett sisters in the den and flirted with them and got nowhere, so he moved to the kitchenette, and it's my turn on the way to the living room, where he'll hit on Iva Lou's cousins in from Knoxville, and then he'll go right up to Mike Tinsley and punch him in the mouth and Sweet Sue will scream, and the guys will pull them apart, and Mike will be bleeding and he'll tell Jack Mac to stay the hell away from his woman, and Jack will tell Mike he was a no-good husband, and Sweet Sue will have to choose and we'll all watch and be horrified and hope nobody's got a gun.

"Did you dream during your Deep Sleep, Ave Maria?" Jack Mac asks me again.

I shrug as though I don't remember, and I keep eating the macaroni and cheese.

"Where do you go when you look off like that?" He totally caught me. Now what am I going to say? You know what? I'm going to tell him the truth.

"I imagined you flirting with every woman at this party and then working your way over to Sweet Sue and trying to reclaim her, and you and Mike Tinsley getting in a bloody brawl and turning the trailer over." Jack throws his head back and laughs.

"Now you know never to ask me what I'm thinking." I turn to walk away, but he grabs my arm.

"I have something in the truck for you."

"I'll bet you do." Sometimes the mountain girl in me comes out. I try to gracefully remove my arm from his grasp, but he grips it more tightly.

Then he laughs again, this time even louder.

"Are you drunk, Jack?"

"I haven't had a drop since the wedding punch. And you know how cheap Nellie is with the spirits." Okay. This is really bad. He isn't drunk. So he means everything he's saying. Now what do I do?

"Come with me."

He gets a grip on my elbow and won't let go. He guides me through the crowd in the trailer and out to the parking field. He moves fast, and I have to skip to keep up with him. It's dark, but I'm not afraid.

Jack finds his truck and reaches into the front seat. He gives me a brown paper bag. I move to the streetlight so I can see the contents. It's a book. A shiny, new copy of *Schilpario: A Life in the Mountains,* the very book I saw on the front seat of his truck a few months ago.

"Is this for me?"

"It better be. I can't even pronounce it." Jack Mac smiles at me as I open the book. "I had to special-order it out of Charlottesville. It's out of print, so they had to do a search. I thought it would be of some help to you, since you were trying to find your daddy."

I'm having a very strange sensation inside my body right now. I feel compelled to embrace him, to thank him for his kindness. But there are so many questions. When I told him about trying to find my father, he was at the Sub Sandwich Carry-Out with Sweet Sue. We didn't talk about it for very long, and why should he take such an interest in it? Why does he care? I look at his face. He cares. I have this feeling that he knows more about me than I have told him. I hug the book to my chest; the paper smells so good, and the cover is cool and shiny. And then he pulls me close and holds me. The sandalwood and lime is so familiar, and so sweet, that I breathe deeply to take it in, and also to steady my racing heart, which is in desperate need of oxygen. My heart is not palpitating; that condition seemed to correct itself during the Deep Sleep. This is a different kind of thumping, a kind I haven't felt before.

I bury my face in his chest; it seems as though there is a place carved out for me there. I can hear the Statler Brothers as they sail out of Iva Lou's trailer and into the woods; laughter and chatting underscore it; I am very comfortable right here in this moment.

A few minutes pass, and Jack Mac lifts my head with his hands. I am sleepy now; every muscle in me is relaxed.

"May I kiss you?" he asks.

I search my brain for a witty comeback, but I can't think of any. He senses I'm searching for one, and he's determined to nip it in the bud. Sometimes humor has no place in life, and this is one of those times. He traces his lips from the top of my head and down my nose until he finds my lips. Then he kisses me.

The ground under my feet is soft, and I am sinking into it. I am like a stick in a sandy creek, going deeper and farther down into the dirt, meeting no resistance but the lack of my own will.

"I think we should get back to the party."

"Why?" He kisses me again. I stop him, remembering Iva Lou, the party, and my responsibilities.

"Thank you for the book."

He looks at me, a little confused.

"Let's go back," I say quietly. We walk back to the trailer in silence.

Misty Dawn Slagle Lassiter, six pounds, seven ounces, was born at 12:03 A.M. on March 17, 1979, at Saint Agnes Hospital, Norton, Virginia. Her mama, Tayloe, is doing fine; she had an easy labor, and now she can plan her wedding. Betty came to the Pharmacy with pictures of the little one, and she looks to be a stunner just like her mother. Fleeta is concerned that Misty may develop the Lassiter underbite, but it doesn't appear to be so in the pictures.

Since I sold the Pharmacy to Pearl, I've had a different attitude about it. I don't take business problems so seriously; markups on medications don't irritate me as much; and to hell with the dusting. Fleeta and Pearl take good care of the place, but something inside me has shifted.

I am teaching Pearl the log-in procedure on medication when Nan MacChesney comes into the store. She's using a cane. Her white hair is pulled back in a tight braid. Her eyes search the store for me.

"I know you're in here somewhere, Ave Maria. I done saw your Jeep out front."

"I'm back here, Mrs. Mac. In the pharmacy."

"Oh." She comes over to the pharmacy counter. She barely reaches the top of it.

"How are you?" I ask.

"I'm all right. Can you come out of there and talk to me, please?"

"Sure." I come out from behind the counter and stand in front of her.

"Is there somewhere we could talk?" she asks me.

"There's the back room," Fleeta offers. Does Fleeta eavesdrop on every exchange that takes place in this store? I give her a look and take Mrs. Mac to the back room. I pull out a chair, but she declines, so I sit. Otherwise, I tower over her.

"Now, I know this ain't none of my business, but I got a son to worry about. I just want you to know that he is a fine gentleman and a faithful son. They don't make 'em no better than my boy. Now, I know he likes you. He thinks you're a fine woman. And I encouraged him in that, 'cause I done think you made all the right decisions in your life. You've been loyal and you've been good, and that ought to be rewarded. I know you don't see yourself as nobody's wife or mother, 'cause you've said so from time to time to me. I'm not here to repeat hearsay and gossip, I'm only going on what I know directly from your lips to my ears. But I think you need to take some time and reflect on yourself. I'm not telling you what to do, but if you let my son slip through your fingers, you'll be the sorriest gal in the world. I know what he's made of, and it's choice. He's a man of quality. So you go ahead and do whatever it is you're gonna do, but I just wanted somebody to tell you the real story about my son. You couldn't do no better."

She raps her cane on the floor and looks at me.

"Thank you for your thoughts. I know you mean well, and I intend no disrespect. I agree with you. You've raised a fine son. But I have other plans. I want to travel, see things. Try new things. Alone. Can you understand that?"

Mrs. Mac shrugs, unconvinced. "I just had to speak my mind," she says as I lead her out of the back room. She goes out the front through the jingling doors.

"What the hell did she want?" Fleeta wants to know.

"Like you don't know."

"I don't. Tell me."

"Fleeta. Come on. You're both in the DAR. That's the front burner of hot gossip in Big Stone Gap."

"Well, I have heard that somebody saw you swapping slobbers with her son at Iva Lou's trailer park and it done got around." Fleeta shrugs.

"I hate this town!"

"What do you want from me? I can't help I heard it." Fleeta dismisses me with a wave of her feather duster and goes back to work.

"Don't you think Jack MacChesney is cute?" Pearl asks from behind the counter.

"Pearl. That's enough." God knows what she'll ask me next. It's none of her business if he's a good kisser. What is wrong with these people? Do they expect me to magically transform after one kiss? Am I supposed to drop everything for Jack Mac? What about *my* plans? What about what *I* want?

Pearl smiles and concentrates on her work. I am trying to figure out which building in the Gap is the tallest, so I can jump off of it.

Iva Lou returns from her honeymoon all refreshed. There's a wedding card from the staff of the Wise County Library on the dashboard of the Bookmobile, the only sign of change since she got married. I listen to her recount the awesome beauty of Gatlinburg and Ruby Falls (one of the three natural wonders in Tennessee), and then I ask to see *The New York Times*.

"What d'you need that for?" Iva Lou wants to know.

"The travel section."

"Well, they only got that on Sundays. I could score you last week's edition. Is that okay?"

"Whatever you've got is fine." I wish Iva Lou would go and get it. She never makes a fuss when I want something. Why now?

"You going somewhere?" She sounds worried.

"I don't know yet."

"Well, don't go springing surprises on me. I'm an old married lady now, and I can't take much."

"You'll be the first to know my plans when I make them," I promise her. She looks relieved.

"I got it below, in the storage bin. I'll fetch it."

What Iva Lou doesn't know is that I am leaving Big Stone Gap. I've spent my whole life here, and it is time for a change. I want to challenge myself. I want to see what people are like from other places and get to know them. I want adventure. Yes, I would even like to fall in love. I think I should start at the beginning, in the place where my people are from. I am going to Italy. Maybe I'll like it so much I will stay there forever. I am in the last minutes of my youth; I don't want to wait any longer to be young.

I take a good long look at the Bookmobile. This may be the last time I'm ever on it, and I want to remember every detail. (Now that I want to leave, tomorrow would not be soon enough.) I want to remember the shelves made of pink Formica trimmed in green; the snap elastics that hold them in place while the vehicle is in motion; the three Murphy stools that pop up against the books when they're not being used; the Styrofoam cups; the Sanka packets; the checkout stamp; the rearview mirror Iva Lou uses to apply makeup; and especially, most especially, the smell of it.

"Here you go, Ave." Iva Lou hands me the travel section in pristine condition. She really is the best librarian there ever was. She respects library materials.

"Ave, I owe you an apology."

"For what?"

"Well, I sort of sprung old Jack Mac on you at my wedding. I never liked nobody force-feeding me when I was a baby, and I sure as hell wouldn't like it now. I should've mentioned it to you. But I guess I got caught up in all of it and just forgot."

"It was fine. Don't worry about it." What is everybody getting so worked up about? I'm not going with Jack Mac. So I walked down Iva Lou's aisle with him. So what? He kissed me once. Twice. At a party. Big deal! Women get kissed at parties all the time. I've hardly given it a second thought since then.

I get comfortable on my stool and begin to read.

"So, where you going?" Iva Lou asks.

"Italy."

"Italy? That far?" Iva Lou's eyes widen. "When?"

"As soon as I can book it."

She points out travel advertisements she thinks are effective. One catches my eye. The caption reads: "New Jersey's own: GALA NUC-CIO TOURS: YOU WON'T MISS THE BOAT. Join Gala, she makes every tour a party!" There's a big photo of Gala, who looks to be about my age. She is a very dramatic Italian woman with an elaborate hairdo, a pile of braids that curve artfully all over her head like snakes; she has big brown Sophia Loren eyes and an hourglass shape. She stands in the middle of a gondola in a Venetian canal with her arms in the air. In a flag on the gondola the tour prices are listed. They are very reasonable. I have found my travel agent and tour guide in one stop! Iva Lou is thrilled for me. She wishes she could go too, but for now she must put her dreams of Europe on hold and concentrate on her new husband.

I return home, get comfortable in Fred Mulligan's chair, and dial Gala Nuccio. The phone rings twice, then: "Frank, you son-of-a-bitch bastard, stop calling me. I am done with you! Finished! It's over!"

"I must have dialed the wrong number," I whisper.

"Who is this? No, no. Dammit. I thought this was my personal line. I have two phones over here, and I get 'em confused from time to time."

"Are you Gala Nuccio?"

"Yes. I apologize for my outburst. I never use that kind of language. But if you had been fucked over by that goomba the way I have, you'd

pick up the phone ready to bite off somebody's head too." Gala sighs.
I can hear her take a long deep drag off of a cigarette. Her accent reminds me of all the hard-boiled New York blondes in the detective
movies of the 1930s.

"Are you all right?" I ask very earnestly.

This makes her laugh loudly. "Men. You're a woman, right?"

"Yes, ma'am."

"Then you know what I'm talking about."

"Say no more," I reply pleasantly. What I really want to talk about
is planning my trip. I begin to ask questions about her tour packages,
but Gala needs to talk about Frank.

"I've been with Frank on and off for about four years. He's divorced, he's got three kids—they're brats of course. And I don't see
him enough. He says it's work and the kids, but I don't buy that line
of bull for a second. 'Lipstick on His Collar' is sort of my theme song.
You know the song?" She inhales again. I can hear her exhale the
smoke all the way from New Jersey.

"I do. It's an oldie."

"Yeah. Well. It still applies. What can I do for you?"

"I'd like to go to Italy. I speak Italian." I sound like a backwoods
bumpkin. What does she care if I speak Italian? Is there a test you
have to pass to buy a tour ticket?

"I have several tours coming up. You wanna do the Greek Isles, too?"

"No, just Italy. Northern Italy."

"Uh-huh. Venice, Milan, and up. I do that. And a side trip to Santa
Margherita on the coast. You don't want to miss that. It's scrumptious."

"Great. Maybe you can send me some brochures."

"Love to." Gala continues to puff as I give her my address and information. She is surprised that I am Italian too and live in the mountains
of Virginia. She has never heard of that before. I say that I'll tell her my
story on the long plane ride to Italy. She sounds genuinely interested.

"Hey, Ave Maria. This could be your lucky day." Gala puffs.

"Why?"

"I got a seat on my Northern Italy tour in three weeks. Think you
can pull it together by then and join us?"

I panic. There's so much to do. It's not like it's just a vacation, it's a reroute-the-rest-of-my-life trip. There's so much to settle up around here: the house, the business, and everything else. But maybe this is a sign to do it quick and clean. Maybe if I don't have much time to think, I won't ponder details. Maybe for once in my life I should just throw myself headlong into opportunity and see what happens.

"I can make it."

"Great. You're booked."

I've gone about my business quietly. I find I can get a lot done if I get up early in the morning. I've managed to pack up the house, shop for the trip, and check in on the Pharmacy without tipping anyone off. I don't want anyone else's opinion about this decision; I want it to be mine and mine alone. I wrote to Mario asking him if he would like to meet me. If so, I wanted to know a convenient time to come and visit Schilpario. I have not heard back from him. I wrote to my mother's family as well, and they are thrilled that I'll be visiting. I still haven't sent a picture. The photos that came back after Iva Lou's wedding were horrible, and I'm not showing them to anybody. The hat and the dress were a disaster, and I will never wear either one again.

I haven't told anyone that I'm leaving. I may tell Theodore in advance, but only if the time is right. My plan is to go on the trip, meet my family, and consider all my options. The only thing I am certain of is that I will never return to Big Stone Gap. This is not my world anymore. My mother is gone. The Pharmacy and now my home are in Pearl's capable hands. Spec has chosen a new captain for the Rescue Squad. Anybody can direct the Outdoor Drama. There is nothing holding me here. It's time to move on.

The front page of the *Post* has a bold headline: MOVIE STAR GIVES CHUNK O' CHANGE TO LPH. It turns out that Elizabeth Taylor was so grateful to the staff of Lonesome Pine Hospital for yanking that bone that she made a five-thousand-dollar donation to its emergency fund. I flip through the paper to the want ads. I placed one this week; I'm selling my mother's Oldsmobile Cutlass. It's amazing how much I've gotten done since I put my mind to it. I've made a list of my assets, and I plan to sell off whatever I don't need. There is only the matter of Pearl to address.

I've called a meeting with Iva Lou, Nellie, and Pearl over at Lew's office. I stop by the Sub Sandwich Carry-Out and pick up a few sandwiches and bottles of pop; we're having a working lunch. Delphine Moses throws in extra chips (she always does) and comments on how impressed she is with Elizabeth Taylor's generosity. "You just don't expect that kind of caring from a movie star," she says.

Inez looks slimmer. Pearl convinced her to join Weight Watchers, and the results are impressive.

"Inez, you look fantastic."

"Thank you, Ave. You know, I haven't felt this good in years. And I love all the little pamphlets, recipes, and helpful hints they give us at Weight Watchers. Our group leader, Pam Sumpter, is from Norton, and she lost one hundred pounds herself, so she knows how hard it is. Every week she shows us her 'before' picture. She had it blowed up large and sets it on an easel at the beginning of every meeting. I keep it fixed in my mind, and it helps me stay on program. Losing weight has made such a difference in me. I think he notices it too." Inez points to her husband's inner sanctum.

"Good for you!" As I enter Lew's office, I realize that this is probably the longest conversation I've had with Inez. She does seem like a different person. And Lew is smiling. Why shouldn't he be? He's got his tight little race car back in running order.

"How are you?"

"Better." Lew beams like a man who is getting regular attention from his wife. "And how are you?"

"I'm just great."

"You look it."

Pearl comes in, having forgotten to take off her Mulligan's Mutual smock. We hear an engine blast, followed by a fan-belt hum, and then silence, signaling Iva Lou's arrival in the Bookmobile. Then the office fills with the smell of gardenia, and we know Nellie Goodloe must be in the waiting area. Lew hollers to Nellie to come on in, as I set up the lunch.

Iva Lou breezes in and kisses everyone, but I can tell she is nervous. The girls have no idea why I have gathered them here, and let's face it, it's never pleasant when you have to make a trip to a law office. I make it as friendly and casual as I can, but food can only do so much to comfort people.

"I guess you all wonder why I have gathered you here today."

Nellie and Iva Lou nod; Pearl takes a cue from them and nods too. I find it endearing that she is acting so mature.

"Girls, I'm leaving you."

"You aren't sick or anything, are you?" Iva Lou asks worriedly.

"No, no. I'm not dying." They look relieved.

"You all know I believe in Chinese face-reading. Well, maybe Nellie, you never heard of it." She shakes her head slightly; she doesn't know what has gotten into me.

"Every face is a map. Mine tells the story of a woman who changes the course of her life the year she turns thirty-five. Now, you know, I've had quite a few whammies over the course of the last several months. It was fate at work. After much contemplation, I decided that it was time to take control of my destiny and figure out why I was put on this earth. I don't want to let life happen to me anymore; I want to choose my future."

"I did the exact same thing right around thirty-five," Iva Lou interjects. "That's when I got my two-year degree from Mountain Empire Community College and got on the Bookmobile!"

"Good. Right. See there? Iva Lou gets what I'm talking about. Sooner or later everybody has to ask the big questions of themselves. Some of us ignore the truth, and some of us gut the interior of our lives and attempt to reinvent it. I am doing the latter."

"Good for you," Nellie says because she thinks she needs to say something.

"Thank you. Now, a few months back I made Pearl Grimes here my ward. I signed over Mulligan's Mutual to her." I look at Pearl. "To you. But what I didn't tell you at the time was that I also gave you my house in the deal."

"You gave me your house?"

"Yes, Pearl. It's yours." Pearl looks at Lew, who nods in confirmation and smiles at her.

"But . . . why?"

"I'm leaving town and I thought you'd like to have it."

Pearl is overwhelmed. I know what this means to her, to live in town. To be close to the school. To have a phone. To be able to have her friends over. This is the best thing that could happen, better than owning Mutual Pharmacy. I look at Nellie and Iva Lou, who are equally stunned.

"Pearl just turned sixteen, and until the age of eighteen, she cannot fully own the properties and their assets in her own name. That's where you two come in. I would like you to be her legal overseers. Lew came up with an angle I like. You two will look over this youngun and guide her decisions regarding the business. And you will be paid for your services."

"I've never run a business," Iva Lou offers.

"You're a librarian. You're organized. You work within a system. Pearl needs a system. You can guide her."

"What about me?" Nellie says. "I'm just a housewife."

"Nellie, I picked you because you have good taste. And Pearl needs exposure to the finer things in life. You'll show her how to make a pretty store window, teach her the proper manners for business lunches, show her how to deal with all sorts of people."

Nellie's back straightens. She never realized that her skills were marketable. Now she knows.

"What about my mama?" Pearl asks.

"She is a great mother. She loves you and takes excellent care of you, and she always will. I've talked this over with her, and she's comfortable with Iva Lou and Nellie handling this stuff. When I met with her, all she kept saying is that she wants you to be happy." Pearl's eyes fill with tears.

"Yes, ma'am. That's all any good mother wants," Nellie says, backing me up.

"She's very excited about moving to town with you. You'll be closer to things that will help you develop into a self-sufficient person. She is totally in favor of my"—I look at Lew and share the credit—"our plan."

"You're moving away, Ave Maria?" Iva Lou asks pitifully.

"Girls, this isn't a sad thing. I've lived here all of my life, and it's been wonderful. But it's time to see what's out there, test my mettle, see what I'm made of. You understand."

"When do we start?" Nellie asks.

"Monday."

"Monday? Cripes, why don't you just give me a heart attack right here, Ave?" Iva Lou slumps back in her chair.

"Are you ever coming back?" Pearl asks.

"I'm sure I'll visit. I won't make like a ghost, like old Liz Taylor. I'll be back."

I motion to the lunch set up on Lew's worktable.

"Let's eat," Lew says as he stands. "We can sign the papers later."

We gather around the table. Nobody says much. We eat. Delphine can make a sub sandwich, that's for sure. Nellie unfolds a paper napkin and places it gently in her lap. She turns to Pearl, who is picking the turkey out of her sub, and gives her a napkin. Pearl unfolds the napkin and places it gently in her lap, just like Nellie.

The hardest part about packing up my house is deciding what to do with Mama's sewing supplies. The only thing I know for sure that I will keep is her button box. I used to play in it when I was little, pretending the buttons were stones when I played explorer, or crown jewels when I played princess. I've sorted out most of the plastic ones, keeping the antique and cloth buttons. Buttons are light; I can always tuck them in a corner of my suitcase, and they are very symbolic to me. When Mama made something, the last thing she did was to sew on the buttons. They were the finishing touch, the end of a creation. I just can't throw them away.

I know this should be easy. Why should any normal person be attached to bolts of fabric: scraps, ends, and odd yardage? But I am. Each piece reminds me of something she made. There's a yard of purple satin that she used to make my shepherd robe for the kindergarten

Nativity. A mint-green dotted Swiss remnant that she used to make my dress for the May Day court when I was in seventh grade. A bolt of Carolina-blue wool for cheerleading skirts and a bolt of ruby-red wool that she used in the pleats of those same skirts. Red cording and frogs that she used when she made Bobby Necessary's band uniform. Back in 1969 Bobby's mama came over all hush-hush and begged Mama to make Bobby a band uniform. He was so heavyset, they couldn't order one in his size. Mama toiled over that one. But when Bobby marched out with his clarinet during halftime, you couldn't tell that his uniform wasn't from the factory. It was a perfect match.

There are several bolts of cotton velvet in deep shades of red, blue, and gold. Mama was a big fan of velvet; she thought it was sturdy and elegant and that it "wore" in an interesting way. She used to crumple it and let it fall, pointing out how the light played on the folds, giving it a sheen and dimension. She made me so many things of velvet! Skirts, pants, coats, even a bedspread. I always had a poufy bed, with beautiful linens. Mama grew up with that over in Italy, and she wanted me to have it, too. In later years, when we went shopping for sheets, she would sniff them. She could tell the grade of cotton, the thread count, from the smell. She said she would rather have one set of sheets that were four hundred count than ten sets that were two hundred count. I've slept on the cheap stuff away from home; believe me, there is a difference.

Even my favorite bedtime story was about fabric! Mama told me the story of the Fortuny family in Italy who made their own fabrics and became world-famous for it. She told me how they invented double-sided velvet (her favorite to work with), and how they experimented with design, embroidering it, watermarking it, even burning it! I used to imagine the Fortuny factory and its workers. I pictured the men and women standing around cocoons as the silk was spun; the raw silk draped on the cutting table; the processes of soaking, stretching, pressing, and cutting. Mama told me that if you made fabric correctly and took care of it, it could last until the end of time. I guess she was right. Think of those medieval tapestries and even the Shroud of Turin. Good fabric, good care—eternity.

I know a couple of quilters up in the hollers, but I really want to bequeath this material to someone who is expert at quilting and would appreciate it. I settle on Nan Bluebell Gilliam MacChesney. She's one of the best quilters around. I wrap the fabric in burlap casings. Mama never used plastic because the fabric could not breathe. She would be proud that I remembered this. I load up the Jeep. There is barely room for me in the driver's seat once I fill it.

It's around suppertime. I don't know where the day went; I started this project at breakfast, and it seems just moments ago. The ride up to Cracker's Neck is smooth; everything is green. The MacChesney house looks so much larger in the twilight; it's a warm way station in the mountain, not just a simple stone house with four chimneys as it appears by day. Light pours out of every window, and all four chimneys puff smoke. It is very inviting.

I pull up and park. I don't see any stray dogs around; of course, it's spring and there's been plenty of rain, so the creeks up in the mountains are full. I balance one bolt of velvet on each shoulder. Jack Mac's truck is gone. Good. I can drop these off and scram.

I can see into the house through the screen door. The main door is propped open behind it. I hear talking and laughing. Mrs. Mac must have company. At first I think to throw the bolts back into the Jeep and come back another time, but it is too late. The dog stands in the doorway of the kitchen, barking like mad. Mrs. Mac pokes her head out of the kitchen door.

"Who's there? Speak up or I'll shoot!" There is a wave of loud, rolling laughter from the kitchen.

"Hold your fire, ma'am. It's just me, Ave Maria." There is dead silence. "Uh, I can come back another time. Good night." The weight of the bolts is starting to press me into the ground like a nail, so I turn to go down the porch steps, juggling the bolts. I almost push in the mesh of the screen door.

"Whoa. Hold up," Jack Mac says. "Wait a minute."

Damn, he is here. He must have parked in the back; it's dark and I couldn't see.

"I was just dropping off some fabric for your mother. It was my mother's and I didn't want to just throw it out, so I thought I'd bring it up here because she's such a good quilter." My voice broke. I hate that. Why am I overexplaining? I just want to go home. By now Jack Mac is on the porch steps, lifting the bolts off of my shoulders and setting them down on the porch gently.

"There's a lot more in the Jeep."

"I can help," a familiar voice says from inside the house. It's Theodore. What in God's name is he doing up here? I want to ask him, of course, as he is my best friend in the entire world, but I cannot, because I have chosen to project this calm, casual thing to Jack Mac, and to change course in the middle of my performance would be death.

"Hi, Theodore," I say as though it's an everyday occurrence to find him up in Cracker's Neck Holler with the MacChesney family.

"There's a lot more in the Jeep," Jack Mac tells Theodore. They follow me to the Jeep.

"You loaded all this yourself? Why didn't you call me?" Theodore wants to know. I think he's got a lot of crust. I should be the one asking questions. Like, *What are you doing here?*

"You guys need any help?" It's a woman's voice, but it isn't Mrs. Mac. I am not going to ask who she is, so I wait.

"I think we got it, Sarah," Jack Mac hollers off. Who is Sarah? What is going on here?

"It got chilly," another voice says. I look up at the porch; there, in the light, is another woman. Are they breeding slim, pretty women inside the MacChesney house? Or is this a double date? I am mortified. Theodore has a date and Jack Mac has a date, and Mrs. Mac is making them roast pork chops and potatoes, and they're all in the kitchen, laughing and talking and making plans to go on excursions together to Cudjo's Caverns or maybe to North Carolina, to Biltmore House and Gardens. Theodore is in charge of the guidebook, and Jack Mac is in charge of the parking. The girls, in their halter tops and short shorts, are in charge of nothing. They are there to enjoy. Boy, these girls are fun and ever so game! Easy to be with! Undemanding! And witty and sweet, too! And they have nice figures from my vantage point, and long hair, parted down the middle, silky and straight with no clips. These are girls who can get their hair wet and have it dry with no frizz. They're spontaneous. They don't need any time for advance planning; no, they are just ready to jump in the car, powdered and fresh, anytime, day or night, ready to just hit the open road and have some laughs. They're breezy and no-hassle and chatty and sexy and unserious, and they've probably never been depressed or suffered the humiliation of a Deep Sleep or had rattlesnake blood splattered all over them at a revival. No, these girls are the ice cream after the steak. All sweetness and light, an excellent finish to an evening.

"You got a lot here," Jack Mac says as he hauls remnants on his third trip up to the house. I lift the last heavy bolt myself, stretching it across my shoulders horizontally, yoke-style, like the Israelite slaves in *Ben-Hur*. It is the last bolt, and I don't care if it weighs two thousand pounds; I want to get this up to the house so I can get the hell out of here. Jack Mac and Theodore have different ideas, though. They run into the yard to help me with the last one.

"Let me get this," Jack Mac orders.

"Sure. Sure." I hand it over to him and Theodore. It takes both of them to carry it; that's how heavy it is. I'll bet Sarah and her slim buddy can't lift a bolt of wool.

Mrs. Mac is on the porch. The tsetse-fly twins are helping her transport the fabric in small loads into the house. I wave to her from the middle yard.

"Well, thanks, everybody. Good night," I shout gaily. I turn to get into my Jeep. I'm glad it's dark, because I think I'll start crying the second my key hits the ignition.

"No, no," chimes the Greek chorus in hot pants. "Stay."

"I can't. Sorry. I have to go."

Theodore crosses down into the yard. He says to me under his breath and firmly, "Don't be rude."

This is the kryptonite of nice girls: We don't ever want to be rude. And even though I am leaving town, I would like to be perceived as the good person I've been all these years, and not a rude lout who doesn't say good-bye properly. Besides, the Jeep is empty, and there's nothing more to do; how long can this humiliation last? I walk up to the house with Theodore.

He says: "Ave Maria, I'd like you to meet Sarah." Sarah shakes my hand. Her hand is soft and her nails are painted ballet-slipper pink. They are hands that have never lifted a four-hundred-pound man onto a gurney or patched a roof. I put my ragged nails in my coat pockets.

"Hello, Sarah."

"And this is Gail." Gail says hello. She's even tinier than Sarah, if that's possible. I feel very large, like I'm three heads taller than either of them, and two planks wider.

"Ave Maria is a very interesting name," Sarah offers.

"It means 'Hail Mary,' " Theodore, Jack Mac, and I say in unison.

"That's a Catholic prayer, right?" Gail asks, hoping it's an intelligent question.

"Yes, ma'am," I reply. I hope I make her feel good and old.

"Would you like to stay for dinner?" Mrs. Mac asks.

"I couldn't possibly. Pearl Grimes has a teacher's conference tonight, and I'm subbing for her mother, who is getting some new teeth." Nice, Ave Maria. Could you stretch the truth a little more, please? The conference, the teeth—why don't you make up a boyfriend who's waiting for you back at the house with beer and pretzels?

Theodore and Sarah look at each other confused. Oh God, no. Theodore is a teacher. He knows there is no conference.

"I'm the new English teacher at Powell Valley," Sarah says. "I wasn't aware of a conference tonight."

Sarah, the new English teacher. How literary. Does she wear short shorts to class? I wonder.

"Ave probably has a private meeting with Mr. Cantrell." Theodore comes in for the save. Just like old times.

"That's exactly right," I concur. I look at poor Gail, who is standing there, shivering. "What do you do, Gail?"

"I'm Sarah's sister. I came for the weekend to help her get settled into her new place."

"That's great." Sure, it's great. Two piranha sisters chomp their way into town and instantly find the only two eligible bachelors with a pulse and make a snack out of them. Couldn't their dates, both of them standing with their hands in their pockets staring at me like two sick fish, have waited until I left town to carry on with these girls? What am I thinking? I turned both of these men down; now I am very glad I did.

"I really need to be on my way." I check the time on my wrist. Nice. I forgot to put my watch on this morning. Maybe no one noticed.

"Thank you for the quilt pieces, honey," Mrs. Mac says sincerely.

"You enjoy them." Then I turn to the girls. "You'd better get inside. It's gotten real chilly." Wouldn't want you two tasty nuggets to catch your death and die long, hideous deaths on a respirator, would we?

Sarah and Gail smile at me and follow Mrs. Mac into the house. Jack Mac and Theodore offer to walk me to my Jeep. I thank them, but no, I don't need anybody walking me anywhere. In fact, I don't need anybody. I am Maureen O'Hara in *Buffalo Bill;* I can take anything you throw at me.

I climb into the driver's seat, shove the key in the ignition, and turn her over. I back out of the drive and off of this mountain, and I don't even check the rearview mirror. I don't cry. I don't even come close. The sexy sisters are just the goose I need to leave town. Life will go on quite nicely without me in Big Stone Gap.

CHAPTER NINE

There is something thrilling about an almost empty house. When you crave the comfort of things, as I have for much of my life, unloading them is a very freeing experience. I was always so careful in Fred Mulligan's easy chair, not to spill on it or sit on the arms or flip the footrest up and down too much. I wanted it to last. So when it is carried out of my house, I am relieved. I won't have that to worry about anymore. Lyle Makin can bathe it in beer and onion dip forever. Enjoy it. Use it. And when you're through with it, leave it in the street for Otto and Worley. Pearl and Leah will purchase all new things for this house — their new home — when I'm gone. I figure it's a bad idea for them to move in here with my old stuff. They need a fresh start; they should never feel like renters in a home of their own.

I can see the architectural bones of this house in a way I couldn't before. The floorboards are handsome and simple. The arches in the doorways are whimsical, with funny curves along the edges. The windows are very wide and eye level. It is a romantic cottage; how funny I never thought of it that way! Shorn of heavy drapes, just the rolling shades remain; I am reminded how important it is to let light play through rooms. I will remember this rule wherever I go.

I am lying on my back in the empty living room, looking up at the ceiling, a vast expanse of pure white — it seems to be a painting. My mind clears as I stare into it. I feel a moment of deep contentment, similar to what nuns and monks must feel when they pray. Being quiet is a very soothing experience.

I hear a hacking cough coming up my walk; for a moment I think it might be Fleeta with another question about accounting, but it is too deep a rattle. It must be a man. Without sitting up, I roll over, and craning my neck ever so slightly, I can see the porch steps through the mail chute in the door. It's Spec. He raps on the door.

"It's open."

Spec takes one step into the house and stands there. He is surprised to see the interior so bare, and he is also surprised to see me lollygagging on the floor like an old cat.

"Are you all right?" Spec wonders.

"Never better."

"I need you to come with me to the hospital."

"Why?"

"Otto's done had himself a heart attack."

I've ridden in the Rescue Squad wagon with Spec many times. He keeps it in prime condition. I notice that the interior has changed a bit, though. My replacement has put the clipboard in a different spot. His kit is on the hump, not under the seat, where I used to place mine. There are notes Scotch-taped to the dashboard. I never did that.

Otto asked Worley to take him to Saint Agnes Hospital instead of Lonesome Pine. The Catholic nuns appeal to his superstitious nature. When Spec and I check in, we're told Otto is in Intensive Care. The tone of the nurse's voice tells us that the situation is serious. Nurses have many excellent skills, but they are never good actresses.

Worley kneels next to his brother's bed, holding his left hand, the one without the IV, in both of his hands. It reminds me of a Buster Keaton movie, where Buster is swinging from a building, holding on to his rescuer with both hands while he flails in midair trying not to fall. Spec goes to the opposite side of the bed, close to Otto's face. I gently place my hands on Worley's shoulders. He has been crying.

"Worley, what happened?"

"My brother done ate his lunch. And then he went out back and threw up. He asked me to run him up here to Saint Agnes. And then he passed out. He didn't come to, so I put him in the truck and brought him here."

"You did good."

"Please don't let him die. Please."

I wish I could promise Worley that Otto wasn't ever going to die. But I can't lie to him, and it's not fair to give false hope where there is none.

"Worley, let old Spec take you for a cup of coffee and a chew."

"I don't want to leave him!" Worley looks at his brother with deep affection.

"If you leave for a couple of minutes, I can talk to the doctors and get some information for you. Just do what I say, okay?" Spec takes Worley away. Sister Ann Christina, the head of Intensive Care, comes up behind me.

"How is he, Sister?" She lowers her head, indicating that it was very bad, motioning to me not to ask any questions.

"Can I talk to him? Can he hear me?" Sister nods, so I lean in to Otto's ear.

"Otto, what in the hell are you doing in the hospital?"

He smiles at me weakly. His eyes are lively, though. He motions to the oxygen mask. He wants me to lift it off. I lift it ever so slightly, so he can catch some air to speak.

"I need you to tell Worley something."

"Sure."

Otto and I settle into a breathing-and-speaking routine. I push the mask up and down as he finishes a sentence. He catches his breath and continues.

"I ain't Worley's brother." I look confused. Sometimes folks go out of their minds when their bodies shut down on them, but hallucination isn't usually part of a heart attack, nor is memory loss.

"Who are you, then?"

"I'm his daddy."

I grip the stainless steel bed guard to steady myself. It is cold.

"Remember Destry?" I nod. "Destry was his mama. She died when she had him. The state wanted to take him, but Mama told them Worley was hers so they couldn't."

"He doesn't know?"

Otto shakes his head.

"You have to tell him, Otto. You have to." I say this slowly and deliberately, emphasizing the *you.*

"I can't."

"Yes, you can. You just told me. You can do this. You must."

Otto takes a long breath, and his eyes fill with tears. "I can't."

"Why can't you?" Otto closes his eyes tightly, hoping I will change my mind once he opens them. Then he opens his eyes and looks up at the ceiling. He barely whispers, "He will be ashamed of me."

And there it is. The mystery I could not solve. My mother could not bear the thought of me ever being ashamed of her, so she lied to me. A lie is better than rejection by your own flesh and blood when they find out that you are not perfect.

"Otto, you listen to me. Worley needs to hear this from you." Otto has a stricken look on his face. He's just had a heart attack, he's in pain, he's facing death, and I am refusing his final request. He is so confused. I have to make him understand.

"Goddammit, Otto. I'm a bastard. Not because of the circumstances of my birth, but because I was lied to. The lie made it wrong. You had something most people only dream of: a real and true love. And you were graced with a baby! A baby that came from you and Destry. Haven't you spent your entire life thinking about it? Thinking about her? Wouldn't you have given everything to hold her again? What is wrong with that? You loved her. That is a sacred thing!"

"I was gonna marry her," he whispers.

"Tell him that. Tell him what your plans were. Tell him what Destry wanted for him. Anything you can remember. Tell him everything. It's the best thing you will ever do for him."

Otto breathes in short bursts. A nurse comes over and gives me the eyeball like, *What are you doing in here upsetting people?* But Otto keeps his hand on mine, so she gets the message that he wants me to stay.

"Please go and get Worley," I say to the nurse. She goes.

"Now, Otto. Don't you cry. You be clear with him. He has to hear this from you. Okay?"

Otto nods that he understands. Worley comes in and goes directly to Otto's side. I pat Worley on the back and give Otto a look. Otto begins his story. I pull the curtains around the bed to give them privacy. I go out into the waiting area and wait with Spec.

"If I threw my body down and set it on fire, would it make you stay?" Iva Lou asks me over a BYOB beer at the Coach House Inn.

"Lyle would kill me." Lyle Makin goes all over town and tells everybody what a great wife Iva Lou is; she knows it as well as I do. She's stuck for life and she's happy about it.

"Yes, he would. He loves being murried."

Ballard Littrell stumbles past us to take a table near the kitchen.

"Drunk again?" Iva Lou asks Ballard.

"So am I!" He smiles, and takes a seat.

"See what you're gonna miss? What his wife has gone through. At the bottom of every woman's heartache is a bottle." Iva Lou swigs her beer.

"What happened to his ear, anyway?"

"There was a story going around that a jealous lover cut it off during a fight. But I think Ballard himself started that one around. Lyle told me that he got caught in the Continuous Miner machine up in the mines. Sliced it right off. Why do you ask?"

"It was the last open question I had about anything in Big Stone Gap."

"You know a lot of folks that are in the Drama are dropping out because you won't be directing this year."

"Come on. I'm hardly a director. I just follow whatever Mazie Dinsmore wrote in her promptbook. I am easily replaced."

"I don't know about that. Theodore Tipton quit this morning."

"No way. He's the whole show!"

"I know. Between him quitting and Tayloe Slagle having a hard time getting the baby weight off, it's gonna be a long summer. He got offered a big job."

"Really?"

"University of Tennessee wants him to be their band director."

"Fantastic!" I am hurt, though. I would like to have been the first person Theodore told. I used to be. He came over to my house after Sarah and Gail Night, but I didn't answer the door. Maybe that's what he came over to tell me.

"Funny thing is, they didn't hire him for his theatrical flair. They thought the musical arrangement of all the Elizabeth Taylor themes was genius. Imagine that."

"It was."

"Then of course, there's old Jack Mac, the best kisser in Big Stone Gap."

"What about him?"

Iva Lou shrugs.

"What have you heard?"

"He's seeing that new schoolteacher. Fleeta saw them up to the Fold."

"That's what he needs. A schoolteacher. Mining and teaching go great together."

"Listen to Miss Positive, Everything Turns Out for the Best. Law me."

"Well, it does, doesn't it?"

"You like old Jack Mac. Admit it."

I shrug nonchalantly and finish my beer.

"No, I mean you like him, in that way that I have liked half the men in Wise County. And don't lie to me."

"Let's say I did. Why would I admit it? What good would it do me?"

"To be loved is the only good anybody can do for anybody. And you know how I feel about sex. I must say, though, marital sex is a whole different animal. But it's still an animal, thank the Lord for that."

"Do you ever wonder why we're made this way?"

"Who?"

"Us. Women."

"Honey-o, I don't know. I think I understand men better than women. A man is an animal all his life. He wants to eat when he's hungry. He wants to sleep when he's tired. And every so often he wants sex when he's horny. Simple." Iva Lou looks at me.

"It's that simple?" I wonder.

"Animals. Uh-huh. Simple creatures, men. And we got the scientific evidence right here in the Gap. Anybody who says men didn't descend from apes never went out with Mad Dog Mabe. His entire body was an homage to shag carpet. That man even had hair on his elbows."

I sit outside Theodore's house for a long time before I decide to walk up to the door. A walk takes twice as long when you feel stupid. I suppose I'm going to have to grovel and beg his forgiveness for Sarah and Gail Night. I haven't spoken to him since; I know he's really angry with me. I've been dreading this moment. But I miss him desperately; we used to talk every day. Life is different without him, and I don't like the change.

"Who is it?"

"Ave Maria Mulligan. Town pharmacist."

Theodore appears in the doorway. "Former town pharmacist."

"Not until a week from Friday."

"Come on in."

Theodore lets me into his house. I never entered through the front before. I always came in the back, through the kitchen. Why didn't I go to the back of the house as I have for nine years? Why did I choose this front entrance, as though I were a salesman or a missionary? Why did I do this? Why have I put a wall between me and my very best friend?

"Did you hear about my offer from UT?"

"It's wonderful. Your work will be on the TV and everything now. You deserve all of the fame and glory in the world."

"Thank you."

"Are you mad at me?" I say in a funny voice.

"Yes, I am," he responds in a very adult tone.

"I figured. Don't I get to be a little mad because you made friends behind my back and went up to the MacChesneys' with a couple of hot dates and didn't tell me?" I whine.

"No." Theodore hates whining. Why am I playing this game with the man who knows me best?

"Why not?"

"You're a very interesting person," Theodore begins. It has been a rule in my life that whenever anybody has used the word *interesting* to describe me, it is always something bad. "You don't want to get involved with anybody, but you don't want the anybodys you know to get involved with anybody else either. Why do you suppose that's true?"

"First of all, it isn't true. People are free to do whatever they like."

"People? Is that what I am to you? A general person?"

"No, no, of course not."

"Start there. What am I to you?"

I want to tell him that he's my best friend. That if the entire world collapsed and I could only save one person, it would be him. That the thought of him leaving and taking a job somewhere else in the universe where I can't talk to him every day kills me! Why is it different when I'm the one who's going? Do I expect Theodore to sit here and wait for me while I go out and have adventures, like he's some talisman I can come back and touch to remind me that nothing has really changed? Instead, I see the wispy sisters shivering in the moonlight on Jack Mac's porch. The image makes me angry. Why am I never chosen? "Look. You don't owe me a thing. I can take care of myself."

"You don't need anybody."

"That's right. I'm very strong on my own. I don't need anybody."

"Are you sure you're not Fred Mulligan's daughter?" This comment catches me off guard, and I find it cruel. I confided in Theodore about every horrible thing Fred Mulligan ever did to me and my mama, and now he's throwing it up in my face. But I would never give him the satisfaction of knowing that he has hurt me. If you saw my face in this moment, you would think I hadn't a care in the world. This is my best area; this is where I perform at my peak. I can shut down, detach, and not feel. So, that is exactly what I do.

"You'd be the first person in the world who didn't need someone, Ave Maria. Do you think you're that person? The one girl in the world who doesn't need anybody, ever? Are you some special category of person?"

"Why are you doing this to me?"

"See, there you go. See how you operate? I'm doing something to you because I'm asking you how you feel. What you feel. It is my business. I love you."

"Sure, sure you love me." I roll my eyes like I'm five.

"You know, having sex with someone isn't the only way to show you care."

"Well, it would have been nice!" Why am I shouting at this man? Isn't he on my side? Isn't he telling me that I am as deserving of love as the next person? That it's okay to need love? That I'm allowed to be scared? But it's too late. I know Theodore is really angry because he cannot look at me.

As he paces, he says calmly, "You have big problems, okay? Big ones that you need to think about."

"*I* have big problems? What about you? You think I can't connect to people?" Now I'm shouting and I'm sure I'm scaring him. Good. My voice gets even louder. "Stop analyzing me! Stop it! I wanted to marry you for nine years and you didn't want me. Finally, finally, you propose to me, and what was I supposed to do? Drop everything and marry you in the middle of a black depression? And then what? Be happy? Maybe I loved you in the middle of my depression, and loved you enough not to saddle you with a nut case! You should have married me nine years ago when I was young and I didn't know so much! I would have had someone to love me when I went through all the worst things of my life. I've gone through all the worst things, and I did it alone. A person can't just pretend that they didn't go through it all alone. I did. I don't want any credit for it, but understand that when it comes to love, *I don't understand!* I wouldn't know what to do with a man! Hook him? Serve him? Then pray he never leaves? How do you do it without dying? How?"

Theodore goes to the kitchen. He turns in the doorway. "How about a cup of coffee?"

I sit on Theodore's futon while he fixes a pot of coffee. I look down at the buttons on my shirt. There is no rise and fall, no palpitations. Nothing but the steady breathing that comes with the unburdening of feelings locked up, locked down, and buried for nine years. It feels good. I curl up on Theodore's couch.

"You're my best friend, Ave Maria," Theodore says casually from the kitchen. "I'll never leave you."

I want to speak, to respond, to let him know that I feel the same, but I can't. So, I cry instead. I can cry here. I'm safe.

The postmaster from town calls; he has a certified letter for me. I let him open it. They're my tickets from Gala Nuccio. I am very excited about my trip, and very nervous. I have called Gala nearly every day to practice speaking Italian and to discuss the trip. She is very excited to have me with the group, since I speak Italian. Also, we've become good phone friends. She has told me a lot about her life. Her boyfriend, Frank, has finally asked her to marry him, but she doesn't see herself as Maria von Trapp, a second mother who plays puppets with her stepchildren. Gala also believes Frank still has other women. She can't prove it, but he keeps strange hours and is forever calling her from phone booths (she assures me this is a sign of a cheating man, and I think she's right). I never had a girlfriend who was Italian like me, and it is so much fun. We have similar attitudes about things. Theodore and I drove all the way over to the Tri-City Mall, to see *Saturday Night Fever.* (It's been out two years but there is still a demand in Kingsport.) I never knew people were like that. Gala assures me the movie is accurate; she grew up in the same kind of neighborhood. She finds it charming that I have a Southern accent. "You just don't expect that sound to come out of an Italian girl." I told her all about the last year of my life, and she listened carefully. She thinks Theodore is not the man for me. She likes the idea of Jack MacChesney. I told her it's too late for all of that; Jack Mac and Sarah are hot and heavy. Gala wasn't surprised that Jack Mac turned around and got another girlfriend so fast. "Men always have to be with somebody. It's just how the sons of bitches are made." Her words ring in my ears long after we're off the phone. I think she's right about that too.

I wash my face, throw on some lipstick, and grab my keys to run into town. I have already had my mail rerouted to the post office, so daily chores at my house have dwindled to preparing my meals and packing.

I need a spatula to pry all of my mail out of the post office box. I quickly shuffle through. There is a postcard from Zia Meoli telling me in a line how the whole family cannot wait to meet me. I've received a card or a letter from Zia Meoli at least once a week since I wrote to her the first time. I told her I hadn't heard from Mario da Schilpario since his first and only letter, even though I have written to him three times with the dates of my trip. I've given up on him. I would like to meet him, but if it doesn't happen, if he doesn't want to see me, I am not going to barge into his home and confront him. I wonder if he told his mother about me. My grandmother. How I wish I could meet her. It's silly, I know, but the one thing I always wished I had was a grandmother to talk to. Well, the sooner we learn that we don't get everything we want in this life, the better. I am grateful to meet my twin aunts and uncle and cousins. They will be more than enough; I guess I shouldn't be greedy.

The windows in Mulligan's Mutual have never been prettier. Nellie has painted the backdrop doors a bright lime green and placed paper butterflies on the product displays, making the windows look like a happy terrarium. The mortar-and-pestle neon sign that had burned out on the building has been replaced with a giant ℞ and it's a real attention-getter. Otto and Worley did a beautiful job on the bricks. So the place finally is up to snuff, and that makes me very happy.

Fleeta is handling the store part of the Pharmacy during the day until Pearl gets off school, and that nice man from Norton agreed to take Mondays and Tuesdays for prescription filling until a permanent pharmacist can be found. We interviewed a man from Coeburn, and he may be able to start by early summer. Nellie and Iva Lou are keeping an eye on Pearl already, though Pearl has complained that Nellie is a little bossy. I told Pearl to tell Nellie that; I'm sure she doesn't realize that she's being bossy.

Fleeta is behind the counter. I hear her explaining the difference between the chicken-wing overcross and the sleeper hold to a boy, obviously another professional-wrestling fan. Fleeta begged me to start carrying World Wrestling Federation magazines, so we did. It does bring in that young male element; they also buy a lot of candy. Fleeta is downright religious about wrestling. She has started smoking again; she said it was too hard to quit because everybody smokes in the arenas where the wrestling matches are held. Plus, her nerves get frayed during the shows when the man she is rooting for falls behind. She needs her cigarettes to calm down.

"What are you doing here?" she asks me.

"Just dropped by. To say hi."

"Shouldn't you be home, girl?" Fleeta looks around nervously.

"I was home but I already had my mail rerouted, so I came to fetch it."

"Oh."

"Is something wrong?" I ask.

"No, nothing." Fleeta puffs on her Marlboro like she's blowing up a balloon in spurts.

"You seem upset about something."

"I told you everything was fine."

Now, I know Fleeta as well as I know anyone. Something is not right. It could be something small, like she made a bet on Haystacks Calhoun or the Pile Driver and somebody's into her for twenty bucks; or it could be something big like Portly's ill. The one thing about Fleeta: She reacts exactly the same to any challenge; there are no degrees with her.

"Don't look at me like that. Don't you think you ought to be getting yourself home?"

"Fleeta. What is going on?"

"Jesus. Would you lay off?"

Fleeta has never spoken to me like this.

"You know what, Fleeta? I don't appreciate your tone."

"I'm sorry about that, Ave Maria. I really am. But I need you to just trust me on this one. You need to get yourself home."

"Is something wrong with Otto?"

"God, no. That shunt in his heart is working like a garden hose."

Fleeta clamps her little lips shut and goes about her dusting. I wait for a moment, but she isn't volunteering any further information. Something is up.

When I get home, Otto and Worley are repairing the fence in my front yard. They laugh, share tools, and consult each other about the best way to replace an old hinge. I ask them if everything is okay, and when I tell them about Fleeta, they just shrug. I ask Otto about his shunt. He opens his shirt and shows me the red staccato scar down his breastbone. (I didn't need to see that.) The doctor is pleased with the results, and Otto is feeling like his old self again. The doctor considers Otto's recovery a miracle. I think that the truth healed his heart. Once Otto unloaded the terrible burden he had been carrying all these years, the weight on his chest lifted, and he could breathe again. He doesn't huff and puff when he climbs ladders or lifts things anymore, and he gave up chewing tobacco. It's the start of a whole new era for Otto. I think he'll find a girlfriend next. He has his eye on a woman down in Lee County.

I finally found out how old the boys are. Otto is sixty-nine and Worley is fifty-five. Everybody in town is shocked by this; we thought they were much younger and closer in age. Worley has a hard time calling Otto Daddy, so he still calls him just plain Otto. The transition from close brothers to father and son has not been that much of a challenge for them. Otto always took the lead anyway; so the revelation hasn't really affected their day-to-day life. Worley seems very happy and takes every opportunity to ask folks up the mountain if they remember little Destry, the beautiful Melungeon girl. Some do, and that has brought him great comfort.

I tell them I'm going upstairs to finish packing. The house looks so cheery; Otto and Worley painted all the rooms in sheer eggshell beige, and they are pristine. All of my clothes are laid out on the bed.

Italy in April is on the cool side, so I'm packing basics in navy and off-white: simple suspender pants my mother made for me, a few pressed blouses, a skirt for church, and my red velvet swing coat. Pearl saved me all sorts of travel-size toiletries and put them in a pretty makeup bag on which she embroidered my initials as a going-away present.

I go into the bathroom. It is completely bare, except for my clean, white towels. I run a bath. I have the day free. I'm going to have a nice soak, put on my makeup, test-run my casual navy travel suit, and surprise Theodore and take him to the movies in Kingsport.

As I sink into the hot water, I look up at the skylight, which for years has been my favorite thing in this house. I could always see a patch of sky through it. I never minded if there were clouds or if it was raining; all kinds of weather had a particular beauty in that square of lead glass. I could see birds go by and watch the clouds change from billowy white to gray and then, in winter, see a sky full of snow. It was my own private clock. I'm about to turn thirty-six years old. Thirty-six! I cannot believe it. I feel nineteen some days and eighty-five on others.

I am blissfully content. I'm sure there are things I could get riled up about, like Mario Barbari dropping me as a pen pal. But I see the big picture now in a way I couldn't before. I have lowered my expectations, and that's a good thing. I can't look outside of myself for happiness, or let things like letters coming or not coming ruin my life. I am ready for a change. I just know that this trip to Italy will change my life. And I'm not going to fight it.

Since Mama died, I have prayed to her. I haven't had any sense that she's around me, but I do believe she's up in heaven. Iva Lou told me for six months after her mother died that, whenever she'd turn a light on, the bulb would blow, even if it was new. Iva Lou believes that souls are full of energy. And they channel into our energy sources to talk to us. A lamp is a perfect object for them to communicate through because it runs on electricity, and that is similar to the frequency in the afterlife. All I know is that I haven't changed a bulb in this house since Mama died.

I do say my prayers every day. Mama told me to pray even if it was just mindless repetition. "You may not need your prayers today, but trust me, eventually everyone needs to pray." I remember Reverend Gaspar's face as he was dying. "Faith," he said. I hope I find it someday.

I put my hair up in a towel and put my makeup on. I go with the full Kabuki: moisturizer, spot concealer, and base applied with a sponge. Pearl taught me how to do it, and I must say, my skin looks like alabaster. She taught me how to line my lips and fill them in with lipstick on a brush, not straight from the tube. I'm not big on eye makeup, so I don't do the shadow thing, just mascara. Pearl told me that long lashes are my best asset. Maybe she's right.

The sun pours through the skylight, giving my hair a sheen when I take it out of the towel. I dry it and it doesn't frizz. It's too early in the year for humidity. I have a three-week window in the seasonal calendar when my hair behaves. This is the first week. I'm going to miss the rest of the good-hair weeks, but I don't care—my hair can do whatever it wants on a gondola in Venice.

Mama had a bottle of Chanel No. 5 in her dresser; I dab it on sparingly. I know I can always buy another, but this was hers, so every drop is precious. I don't want to use it up. I guess I feel that when it's gone, she is really gone. I screw the cap on tightly.

When I go downstairs, Otto and Worley are in the kitchen eating their lunch. They whistle at me. I give them a look, and we all laugh.

"We just ain't never seen you all gussied up like that, Miss Ave," Otto says.

And they're right. They haven't.

"Pearl says she wants to drop some of her and her mama's stuff by later," Worley offers.

"That's fine."

"Where you off to?" Otto asks.

"I thought I'd go and see a movie in Kingsport. I'm getting jumpy waiting for Friday to get here. I need something to do."

Otto and Worley look at each other and smile.

"Did I say something funny?"

"Nah," Otto says. "It's just that you've always been so busy, running here, running there, that it's funny to think you don't got nothing to do."

"Are you all packed?" Worley asks.

I nod.

The doorbell rings. It's probably Pearl. She has keys, though. So why would she be ringing the bell?

I open the door. For a moment, I feel as though I have entered a dream. Through the screen, I see a familiar face. It's the same face that appears in an ad in *The New York Times* travel section every Sunday. The hair is different and the arms aren't extended over her head in welcome, but the same face, the same big eyes, the same big smile greet me with the same largesse and joy that's in the picture. Except she's not in the paper; she is here on my porch. It is Gala Nuccio.

"Are you Ave Maria?"

"I am."

"Oh, my God! It's me! Gala!" She pushes me into the house and embraces me. We hug like sisters, and it's so funny—she could be my sister. She's shaped like me but smaller, and she has hair that could frizz. She's much more down-to-earth and less dramatic in real life.

"What are you doing here?" I ask without letting her go.

"Before I tell you, believe me, I wanted to call and explain, but they wouldn't let me." I'm thinking, who are "they," and why would Gala come over a thousand miles to see me when she would have seen me two days from now at the C luggage area at Newark Airport in New Jersey? My nerve endings feel as though they are pushing tiny needles from the inside of my body through to the outside. I am overcome with a deep fear. Gala, my sister, can tell.

"Don't be afraid," she says, sounding like Moses if he had been raised in New Jersey. She puts her arm around me. Otto and Worley stand in the doorway of the kitchen and watch silently. Gala leans out the door and motions for someone to enter.

There in my doorway is the man in the picture: my father, Mario da Schilpario. I put one hand on my heart and the other over my mouth, as if to make sure I am still in my body and standing here. He smiles at me. Just like he did in the picture. He is about my height, and his black hair is full and curly, peppered with streaks of white. His eyes are large and brown and turn up at the corners, like mine. He has the same slight overbite I do, but he has a dimpled chin, which I don't. He is dressed impeccably, with a long-sleeved beige cashmere sweater tied around his shoulders like Jean-Paul Belmondo in all those French movies. I am stunned that my father could be so dapper. Then he says, in very rehearsed English, "I am Mario Barbari. I am happy to meet you." He takes both of my hands and kisses them. Then he embraces me. It is not a phony embrace either, and not a pitiful "I'm sorry I was never there for you all these many years" embrace; it is one of genuine joy. He *is* happy to meet me.

Finally, I am in the arms of my real father. Why, then, do I see the face of Fred Mulligan? Fred, who taught me how to peel an apple, play gin rummy, and open a checking account? Fred Mulligan, who I thought never loved me because I asked "why" too much. Fred Mulligan, who died and left my mother everything he had, knowing that someday I would benefit from that. Fred Mulligan, who didn't know how not to hurt me, because he, too, was asked to live a lie.

When I cry, Gala weeps. My father cries too, but they aren't shameful tears; they are empathetic, like he knows how important this moment is to me.

Mario looks at me with the same wonder I feel looking at him. He is much more imposing in life than he is in his picture. I take a moment to examine the details of his face in person as I have in the photograph all these months. He has a firm jaw (decisive), thick eyebrows (a healthy libido; surprise, surprise) that frame each eye from one corner to the other (a woman would kill for such perfect arches!), and a straight nose, but it is his smile, with full lips revealing perfect teeth, that draws you in. In face-reading, his is the face of a king. He isn't very tall for a man, but his posture and carriage are so regal, you don't notice.

Gala touches my shoulder, and I look at her as though I am looking into the face of an angel. I am very grateful, but I cannot thank her. How do you begin to thank someone for something so incredible? Then she says, "Would you like to meet your grandmother?"

Through the door steps my grandmother. She looks me up and down and over like she's buying an eggplant. She is tiny but broad-shouldered. She wears a simple blue serge suit. Her hair is in a white braided bun. She has a long nose and clear blue eyes. She shoves her son out of the way and says, "Ave Maria!" And then she hugs me hard, right from the gut; I think my tailbone will snap in two. "Nonna?" I say to her. She grins at me. "You speak Italian?" I nod. She is so overjoyed she slaps my arm hard. Nonna, or "Grandma," speaks in a hard-to-follow mountain dialect. She understands my Italian, though. I speak too fast when I am excited too. It is a wonder to me that she exists. I have dreamt of this all my life, and now it is real. Nonna does not stop talking. She tells me that I am her only granddaughter and she prayed all of her life to have a grandchild. She is sorry she never held me as a baby. Do Italians tell you everything they feel without censor? I think so. Then, she says, *"Dove è cucina?"* I point to the kitchen and she trundles off. Then the most magical thing happens.

Zia Meoli and Zia Antonietta walk in together. They are identical twins, and they look exactly like my mother! The same high forehead, the same golden skin, the same smile! They were ten years older than she, but their hair is still black; they wear it in the same long braid. I embrace them both at once, and I feel like I am in the arms of my own mother again. They smell like Chanel No. 5, just like Mama. They are followed by a tall, distinguished man, my Uncle Pietro, Meoli's husband. She introduces him, speaking in Italian, referring to her descriptions of him in her letters. I look off and see my father trying to communicate with Otto and Worley, using some sort of sign language. It is so funny that I start laughing; soon we are all laughing. The laughter clears my head, and I can think. I turn to Gala. "How did they get here?" She tells me she put the tour together. She reads my mind: I'm thinking, *Who paid for this?* Gala tells me someone sent the family the tickets. Who? She shrugs and looks out on the porch.

Theodore, Fleeta, Pearl, Iva Lou, and Lyle are waiting for me. They are crying, all except for Lyle, who keeps biting his lip. I go to embrace them, but none of them can wait, so we glob into one group and hug and cry. Pearl, like the great makeup artist she is, dabs the runny mascara off my face with a Kleenex.

"Thank you for this. Thank you so much." My dear friends must have pooled all their money to bring my family to me. How will I ever repay them for this priceless gift?

"Don't thank us," Iva Lou says simply.

"What do you mean?"

"Thank him." Iva Lou points to the end of my front walkway. A man stands there with his hands in his pockets, his back to us. He turns slightly and kicks a rock with his foot. It is Jack MacChesney.

"He did this for me?" My friends nod at me solemnly and look at one another.

"But why?"

"I guess you'll have to ask him that yourself, honey-o," Iva Lou says tenderly.

I turn to go down the steps that lead to the walkway that will lead me to him. I take a deep breath, but I don't move. I see him there; he does not see me yet. The mountains rise behind him in green folds that peel back, back, back, until they reach the end of the sky. How small he looks at the foot of those hills. How singular. How lonely. I know I must go to him. I look at my friends on the porch, and they agree. What can I possibly say to him? I'll think of something. I hope.

Jack Mac is deep in thought when I reach him. I touch his arm, and he looks at me.

"You did this for me?"

He nods.

"Thank you." I step toward him to embrace him. I am so full of gratitude; I want him to know that no one in the world ever did anything like this for me before.

He takes a step back and looks off into the middle distance. I am stunned that he rebuffs me. But I don't press it; he is not the sort of man you back into a corner.

"Why did you do this for me?" I ask him softly.

He looks at me, bewildered that I could ask such a question.

"This is something I planned a few months back . . ." A few months back? The night he came over with the apple butter? All shiny and dressed up like a boy attending his first Sunday-school class? The night he asked me to marry him out of the blue? Is this what he means?

"Obviously things have changed. I still wish you all the best. I'm glad this all worked out for you." Worked out for me? He didn't fix my stove or paint my fence, for God's sake. He brought me my family. Why is he so cold, and what is he talking about?

"Take care of yourself." He pats my hand and turns. He walks up the street toward town. I have an impulse to shout after him, but he is walking fast. What would I say to him, anyway? This is so strange. Where is he going? Why is he acting like this? Can't he see how grateful I am? How happy this has made me? Why won't he stay?

"Ave Maria! *Andiamo!*" Nonna calls out to me from the porch. She waves a hanky at me to come back to the house. Theodore waits for me by the gate.

"What was that all about?" I ask him.

"You are so dense."

"Can you please explain? I don't understand."

"Ave. The man sold his new truck to bring your family here. He is in love with you."

"He is not!"

"Who does something like this for somebody he's not in love with?"

"Theodore, you don't know about Jack Mac."

"What's to know? He's generous? He's a good man?"

"I'm sick of hearing about what a saint he is. Believe me, he's not perfect."

"Oh, well, if it's perfect you want . . ." Theodore throws his hands up.

"Stop! If he was ever in love with me, he isn't anymore. I was the second course between Sweet Sue Tinsley and Sarah Dunleavy. But that's okay. He was very polite about it. Now I'll be the one with good manners. I'll reciprocate. He did a beautiful thing for me and I will pay him back. I will."

"Okay, okay," Theodore says, looking toward the house.

"Come on," I growl. "I've got company. Be entertaining!"

I will not ruin this day for my family with my own problems. Obviously, Jack Mac has changed his mind about me. It is done. He's found someone new. He and Sarah Dunleavy are happy now. I can settle up with him about his truck later. *I have a family,* I think as Theodore and I climb the porch steps. They need me. And I have so many questions.

CHAPTER TEN

*N*onna has made a delectable lunch of risotto and wine and bread. Iva Lou has never had risotto before; she is surprised—she thought all Italian food had red sauce. Nonna explains Northern Italian cuisine, using Gala as a translator. I ask Nonna how she smuggled her ingredients through Customs. Nonna looks at Gala, who shrugs and says, "My Frank works in Customs."

Iva Lou corners my father and tells him how she's always wanted to have a wild international romance with an Italian gentleman, but it was not to be because Lyle Makin changed all that. (*Ciao,* Matterhorn.) My father listens intently, nodding a lot and making Iva Lou feel important. I hear my father tell her that very few Italian men live up to their amorous reputations. He convinces Iva Lou that she hasn't missed a thing having secured monogamy with a good American mountain man.

After lunch Mario sets up a card game, which attracts the men and Zia Antonietta. It surprises me that my mother and father's families get along so well. There don't appear to be any hard feelings about what happened. No anger. There doesn't seem to be any guilt either. This helps me. So much time has been wasted, it seems silly to waste more of it in sadness and regret.

As I help my nonna clear the table and set up dessert, I hear Gala telling Iva Lou the saga of her boyfriend, Frank DeCaesar, in detail. Iva Lou is fascinated by the twists and turns of Gala's volatile love affair. If there's anyone on earth who can steer Gala through the jungle of love with common sense, it's Iva Lou.

Zackie Wakin knocks on the screen door. Iva Lou lets him in.

"Zackie, did you smell the risotto from town?" I yell from the kitchen.

"No ma'am." He smiles. "Spec and me heard about the surprise you was going to get today and thought you could use some beds, since you done give yours away. If you'd like, we could set up a little hotel for ye."

He and Spec set everything up quickly. Zackie's been to Italy; he knows about *la siesta*. The family will stay for a few days; how wonderful that the boys can turn this old empty house into an instant hotel.

After we talk, the relatives are tired and beg for a nap. Everyone except Mario, who wants to go for a walk. I have been waiting all afternoon to be alone with him. I kept looking over at him throughout the meal. I cannot believe he is here. It is an amazing thing to get what you want in life.

Mario wants to see the neighborhood. We set out for a walk, but you can hardly call it that. No more than five steps from the house, he stops. He looks all around, carefully. He lingers at each house and studies the architecture. He asks me questions about the trees, what sorts of things we grow in our gardens, and what the weather is like from season to season. It's as though he is trying to place me in the world. How did his child get so far from home? And what is this place that she grew up in? As beautiful as our neighborhood is—and it is, all fresh and green and pink with the dogwood trees in full bloom—I know a better place to take him. I ask him if he'd like to go for a ride. He brightens up and says he'd love to. "Are you sure you're not tired?" I ask him in Italian. He shakes his head vigorously. Italians really are very expressive. Mario has such deliberate gestures; he is so alive. I am not used to this. I see similarities between us, though. He is stubborn like me. When his mother tried to sprinkle extra cheese on his risotto he waved his hand over the dish in a chopping motion, like he was wielding an ax. I do that sort of thing, and it always surprises people around here. These are the sorts of discoveries I will make with my family, and it thrills me.

Mario climbs into the Jeep. He adjusts the front knot on his sweater, pushes his thick hair back, and nods for me to go. We drive toward Appalachia, our neighboring village and the gateway to all the roads up into the mountains. Mario notices the Powell River immediately and wants to know where it goes and whether it floods. He makes me stop on the side of the road when we get to the coal transom, a long white pipe that transports coal on a conveyor from the top of the mountain, where the mines are, to the rail yard at the foot of them. He looks at the train cars. In his thick Italian accent he sounds out *Southern,* the name of the railroad company, stenciled on the sides of the cars. I explain that Southern is what we are around here. When we drive down the main drag in Appalachia, Mario wants to stop for something to drink. So I pull up to Bessie's Diner, the best burger joint in southwest Virginia. Bessie's is always packed.

When we enter, the dull roar of conversation trails off to a quiet din of whispers. Can they sense I just brought a stranger into town? What are they looking at? Then I see, it's not the men; they look up and see us and go back to their eating. It's the women. They can't take their eyes off Mario. One woman yanks up her bra straps by her thumbs; another wipes the crumbs from the side of her mouth with her pinky and smiles; another, at the counter, straightens her posture and gives him a sideways glance. I look at Mario. He, in turn, is surveying the women in the room as though they are each individually delectable, like pieces in a box of expensive chocolates. No woman can resist. Even a baby girl in a high chair bangs her spoon for his attention. I remember what Zia Meoli told me about Mario's reputation. I order a couple of Cokes to go, and Mario asks me more questions about geography. How far are we from Big Stone Gap? Are we going up the mountain? Do I come to Appalachia often?

Once we're back in the Jeep, I am feeling more comfortable with Mario, so I begin to ask him questions.

"Are you married?" He tells me that he is not, then he looks out the window offering no further information.

"Do you have a girlfriend?" This question makes him laugh for some reason.

He shrugs and lights a cigarette.

"Why aren't you married?" I ask him.

"Why aren't you?" he asks me.

I'm sure he didn't mean that to be as snippy as it sounds. Hasn't anybody told him I'm the town spinster?

"You are beautiful," he says simply. "I don't understand."

I think it is very sweet that he compliments me, even though it is somewhat to his credit, as I resemble him. I am happy, though, that he doesn't think his only daughter is a troll. How am I going to explain why I'm not married? I don't think there's a simple answer to that question.

"I don't know," I tell him. "It just never happened for me."

He throws back his head and laughs.

"What is so funny?" I'm getting annoyed.

"A woman can always, always, always get married," he says. "She must want it."

I don't know how to say "Give me a break" in Italian, so I begin a long-winded speech about all the reasons I'm not married. Right man, wrong timing. Love living alone. Ambivalent about children. Job all-consuming. Other interests. Taking care of sick parents. I go on and on until he stops me.

"Ridiculous," he says, and waves his hand with a grand gesture of dismissal.

The man is my father, and I cannot leave him on the side of the road. But I have just bared my soul to him, and he has waved it off like a summer fly.

"When a woman wants to marry, she lets the man know she is interested. That is all I am saying."

Now I feel foolish for being so loud and defensive and yapping on and on. He senses this too and redirects the conversation to himself.

"I am the mayor of Schilpario."

I nod.

"When you come to Schilpario, you will see that we have mountains, too. The Italian Alps. They are much higher and the peaks are sharp. The snow stays on the peaks year-round. We ski in the winter. We rest in the summer. Wild berries grow all over the mountainside—delicious, sweet blackberries. All we do is squeeze a little lemon on them and eat them. No sugar. They are sweet enough. Delicious." He smiles.

We drive up the mountain in silence. Mario looks all around and seems to enjoy the quiet and the view. He looks over the side of the mountain where there are no guardrails, but he isn't scared; dangerous heights remind him of home. We drive past Insko and up to a clearing. I want to show him the waterfalls of Roaring Branch.

I park the Jeep. We walk into the woods and up the path. I watch the expression on his face as he sees the falls for the first time. He smiles and stands still and looks at it. He opens his hands, palms up, and stands there just like my mother's statue of Saint Francis of Assisi in the backyard.

"It is beautiful!" he says. "Wonderful!"

I take him on the path that leads up the side of the falls and show him the way the water cascades over the rocks, leaving caverns of dry space in the overhang.

Then Mario kneels down next to the stream just like I did when I was little and Mrs. White took our second-grade class up to Huff Rock and taught us how to drink of the stream. My father cups his hands the very same way, and without disturbing the sediment he skims the surface of the clear water and then takes a drink. He motions for me to do the same. I kneel next to him and drink from the stream.

There is a place above the waterfalls where folks sit and have picnics. You can see the creeks connecting that feed into one small river that spills over and creates the Roaring Branch. We sit on the rocks and are quiet for a long time. In my mind I rehearse several ways to bring up the subject of my mother, but as I try them out, they don't seem right to me, so I don't say anything. Again, he senses something and solves my problem.

"Tell me about your mother," he says.

I really don't know where to begin. And I don't want to get emotional. It's too late for all of that now because it can't change anything. I want to know his side of things, but the lump in my throat won't let me make words.

"Perhaps I should tell you what I remember," he says kindly.

"Please."

"Fiametta Vilminore was a very beautiful girl from a very good family in Bergamo. She was a hard worker. I fell in love with her when I saw her at her father's shop in town." He shrugs as though this is the most natural thing in the world, to meet a beautiful girl and to fall in love. He pulls a pack of cigarettes from his shirt; he offers me one, which I decline, then he lights his own.

"She was strong-willed. Once, when I drove her up the mountain, she gave me orders about how to handle the horses. I just laughed at her. I think she liked that."

"Why did you end your romance with her?"

Mario's face changes from a slight smile to no expression whatsoever. He thinks about his answer.

"I had to," he offers. "I had a wife already." He looks at the water. His eyes follow it as it seeps over the rocks and down to the falls.

"I thought you said you weren't married."

"I'm not married now. I was then."

"Did my mother know?"

"Yes. I told her in a letter."

This explains why Mama panicked when we were ready to go to Italy. She was afraid she would see him again, and he would reject her again. And what if he rejected me? She wouldn't have put me through that. She wanted more for me. She didn't want me to be the child of a brief affair with a woman he hardly remembered. What mother would? Of course she couldn't go back there.

"What happened to your wife?"

"She went home to her parents. I wasn't a good husband."

No kidding. Somebody should tell this guy you're not supposed to date after you marry. But what good would it do now? One look at this man, and you can see that he would never change for anyone. Mario does not pretend to be a man of great virtue; I don't even get the sense he cares about that. He seems a little vain, but what great-looking man isn't? He is comfortable with himself and accepts himself, including whatever this thing is he does with women. If he weren't my father, I'd be fascinated by him. He knows himself, and he's not about to let anyone, any woman that is, possess him.

As we walk back down the mountain to the clearing, we don't say much. I wish I could hold Mario responsible for everything that has happened, but I can't. He was a seventeen-year-old boy. My mother was just a girl. I think of her; she spent her whole life pining for her first love. She was so loyal to Mario Barbari. I remember when she had a few minutes to herself, she would stack several records on the stereo, sit in her chair, close her eyes, and listen. She did not nap; she was dreaming of someone. I am sure that it was Mario. He is too compelling for her to have ever forgotten him or replaced him in her heart. For the first time in my life I am not sad for my mother. She had a beautiful dream. A dream of a faraway land and a dashing man who made love to her and gave her a baby. Maybe she knew he could never live up to what she imagined him to be. Or maybe when she realized that he was never going to come and rescue her, she did what all strong women do: She found a way to save herself. Very practical. So very much my mother's way.

I wish my mother could have told me this story herself. I find myself angry with her, not him—even though he is here and I could express my anger to him. I don't know him well enough yet to do that. My mother and I were so close, practically inseparable. It hurts me that she could not tell me the truth. Even shameful mistakes can be rectified, healed, and forgiven once they are dealt with. How sad for us that Mama could not let go of her shame.

As we drive back to the Gap, I picture the three of us: Mama, Mario, and me. What if we had been able to reunite as a family after Fred Mulligan died? What if she had told me the truth? What if we had gone to Italy, found him, and knocked on his door? Would we have fit in his life? Mama knew there was no place for us there. She knew she must stay in his memory, where she was young and beautiful and the thing men love best: undemanding. She would be the best lover in his mind's eye: the uncomplicated great love of his youth. How did she know that those memories are what warms old age? When my father speaks of my mother, a look of contentment settles into his face. He has had many, many women since. I wonder if he really cared about her.

"Did you love her?"

He does not answer me.

"It's okay, Mario. I can handle it." I pat his shoulder.

"I never forgot Etta," he says.

No one ever called my mother Etta; I am so happy he had a special name for her.

I cannot ask him any more questions right now, because I understand, just from the few short hours I have known him, that he does not have much of an attention span. He asks a lot of questions, but he doesn't stay on any one topic for very long. I can see that he is tired of this one. I change the subject as we drive through town. This pleases him.

Theodore is being a real doll and arranging all sorts of side trips for the relatives. He borrowed the school van to take my family around. Nonna loved Cudjo's Caverns. Her favorite local cuisine is soup beans and corn bread; she has eaten it every day. Mario and I are becoming good friends; everywhere we go, people tell me I look like him. We convinced Gala to stay for the four-day visit. Even though she is American, Big Stone Gap is like a foreign land to her. Worley has a crush on her, but he doesn't know it. He just follows her around like he's never seen a woman before.

Theodore and I plan a doozy of a final night for the family. We're going to take them to the Carter Family Fold. I hope we haven't built it up too much. My aunts can't wait to try clog dancing and eat their first chili dogs.

When we arrive at the Fold, the parking field is packed with cars, as usual. As we pile out of the van, my Italian relatives move slowly, like they are disembarking a spaceship. They look all around at the cars, the people, and the old barn, twinkling in the field against the blue mountains.

Iva Lou and Lyle are dancing when we get there. I take sweaters and purses and stake out a row of hay bales. Theodore takes Gala and my aunts in one direction. Fleeta takes Mario, Nonna, and my uncle to the food stand.

Sitting on the bale of hay, I realize that this is the first time since they've arrived that I've been alone and had a chance to think. It has all been so crazy—their arrival, our talks late into the night every night, the touring. I'm glad I live in a place I can show off easily in four days. The Fold is pretty much the grand finale of tourist sights around Big Stone Gap.

Nonna asked me to spend the summer with them in Schilpario. I think I will. I'm happy my new family has had the chance to visit Big Stone Gap before I move away entirely. They were able to stay in my mother's house. Even without furniture, my mother's spirit is very much alive there. Pearl and Leah will take good care of it. The fall will be a perfect time for me to relocate and find a job. Doesn't everyone start new projects in the fall?

Iva Lou and Lyle come off the dance floor. She gives him a quick kiss, and he's off to get something to eat. She waves to me and climbs up to our row of hay.

"What did you do with the Eye-talians?"

"They're having their first chili dogs."

"Good for them. Hope they like 'em."

"They've liked everything they've eaten. I can't believe it. My father likes fried chicken, and my aunts love collard greens. Imagine that."

The folks on the dance floor shift in a large circle, revealing Jack MacChesney and Sarah the schoolteacher waltzing gracefully. Iva Lou catches me looking at them.

"I hate that woman," she decides.

"Who?"

"The bony schoolteacher."

"Why?"

"She's workin' Jack Mac over. I don't like it one bit when a woman takes advantage of a vulnerable man. Unless it's me, of course."

"He likes her," I say matter-of-factly.

"It's more than that. She's going after him big-time. She was over at the beauty parlor today chatting me up about all the things they do together. They've even gone camping. It makes me sick."

"Why?" I have to admit the camping part makes me a little sick too. You can take one look at Sarah and know she is not the outdoors type. Old Jack Mac better get a lot of camping trips in before he marries her because that'll be the last time he sees her frying steaks in the great wild. She's a bait-and-trap type. Once the trap shuts, no more bait.

"You know why."

"No, I really don't. She's not in your business. You've got Lyle. So why do you care?"

"Don't do this," Iva says, annoyed.

"Do what?"

"I think it's terrible how you've treated Jack Mac. He sold his truck to bring your family over here, and you haven't even thanked him properly. What is wrong with you?"

"Iva, I've got a house full of company. I was planning on going over to his house tomorrow night. Okay?"

"You should have chased him up the street when he left your house that day!"

"He stormed off."

"You didn't even holler after him to stop him. He'd have come back."

"You don't know what he said to me."

"It couldn't have been bad. The man is crazy about you."

Poor Iva Lou. She believes in love. I want to shake her and say, *Wake up! It's me you're talking about. No man is crazy about me. How much proof do you need? I'm alone.* Instead, I turn defensive. "You don't know the whole story, so don't assume this is all on me because it's not."

"Fill me in, girl."

I whisper, "A few months back, he felt sorry for me and came over and proposed. He was supposedly broken up with Sweet Sue, but after I said no, hardly the weekend passed and he was out with her again. So it wasn't love or apple butter that drove him over to my house, it was pity. Okay?"

"Pity? Who in their right mind would ever pity you?"

"You don't know what he's like. He's very confused."

"He doesn't strike me that way, but all right, if you say so."

"I tried to thank him. I went to hug him. I couldn't believe what he had done. But he pulled away, he actually stepped back and didn't want me to touch him."

"It didn't look like that from the porch."

"I'm not lying to you, Iva."

Jack Mac follows Sarah outside to the food stand. He guides her with his hand on her lower back. She reaches back with her right hand and pats his leg. Iva Lou sees this, too, and she makes a disgusted clucking noise. "Somebody needs to tell her that flats are a no-no for girls with thick ankles."

"Let's just say he did love me once. He sure as hell doesn't anymore. Let it go."

Iva Lou can't let it go. "How do you feel about him?"

I shake my head. I don't want to get into all of this. How *do* I feel about him? All I know is that when I kind of liked him, he didn't like me. And then when he liked me, I didn't want him. I do think of the kiss sometimes—well, let's be honest, it's the last thing I think about when I'm in that weakened state right before sleep. I go right back to the trailer park, to the book, to the pools of light coming out of the windows, to the way he smelled, to the way my face fit into his chest like a puzzle piece, to his eyes that looked at me with such tenderness and with just a little humor, too. I re-create the whole picture, and then he kisses me. It's my good-night kiss, I guess, and the last thing I remember before breakfast. But this is my little ritual, and I'm certainly not going to share it with Iva Lou.

"Are you afraid of him?"

"God, no."

"I don't mean of him per se." Iva Lou struggles to find the words for the right way to invade my privacy.

"Are you afraid of having sex with him?"

"Iva Lou." My tone says, *Stop this, please.*

"Look, I'm just your friend. And you know all about me. But I'll be damned, I don't know how *you* feel about certain things. You never talk about how you feel about men. As a woman. The most fun in life for a woman is to talk about men. Look at me. It's my favorite topic in and out of the bedroom."

"I don't like to talk about it."

"Well, try. I'm a girl. You're a girl. We got our own little club; and men have no idea what we talk about. Your secrets are safe with me." From the doorway Lyle holds up a chili dog toward Iva Lou. She shakes her head and waves him off. He goes back to talking with his buddies.

"Come on. Tell me what makes you tick. Before you leave town and I never see you again." Iva Lou looks so pitiful, I almost want to explain myself to her.

"I think he's attractive. I do." I hope this will be enough to get her off the subject of Jack Mac forever.

"That's a start. Now, don't leave me hanging. Go on." I don't think I've ever seen Iva Lou this excited.

"When I saw him at the end of my walk the day my family arrived, I thought he was the most beautiful person I had ever seen."

"And you didn't throw yourself into his arms, right there and then?"

"Because he . . ."

"Follow your impulses for once! Girl, you're how old? Thirty-six? When do you think you're gonna have sex? When you're sixty? Ninety? Honey-o, get in there and have you some while you're still limber. What are you waiting for? How could you let somebody like Jack Mac slip through your fingers? I bet the sex with him is primo. I can just tell."

I wish Iva Lou would stop talking, but she can't. She is trying very hard to make me understand. I have never seen her on such a tear.

She continues, "Do you deprive yourself of a ripe strawberry or a spritz of nice perfume or a good book because you don't think you deserve them? Hell, no. Sex is no different. It is a delightful gift from God that makes life pleasant. Now, what could be wrong with that? You'll find out a helluva lot more about yourself in bed with a good man than you will traipsing off to some foreign country with a camera and a guidebook. You need to get honest with yourself. You're afraid. But you want sex. You ought to have you some sex."

On the dance floor Otto and Worley are teaching my grandmother how to clog. A supportive crowd has gathered to cheer her on. Iva Lou and I join in. Nonna's body is a small barrel, her legs thin but well-shaped. Her eyes gleam as she dances. She segues from an Appalachian two-step into a folk dance we don't do in these parts—must be Alpine Italian. Otto and Worley follow her lead, and soon everyone is spinning and smiling.

Iva Lou and I run out of breath first and sit down to watch. I look off in the grass, a bit beyond the door, and see my father talking to Jack MacChesney. My father's hands are expressive as usual. Jack Mac leans into my father's ear and says something. They laugh and shake hands. Sarah joins them—does she ever leave him alone for five minutes? Jack Mac introduces her to my father. Jack Mac and Sarah leave. My father looks around for us and cuts across the dance floor to join me.

"What were you talking about?" I ask Mario, indicating the conversation he just had with Jack Mac.

"His Italian is pretty good," my father says.

"He doesn't speak Italian."

"He just did." Mario shrugs. How do you like that? Maybe Sarah Dunleavy taught Jack a few key phrases she picked up from the *Godfather* movies. How continental of her.

"Jack Mac is a very kind man. Don't you think?" Mario looks off. Sure, Jack is a very kind man, and I'm very grateful. But he won't accept my gratitude, which makes a jackass out of me. I would love to tell my father all about Jack MacChesney and Sweet Sue and the proposal and Sarah Dunleavy and everything, but I think better of it. He would just smile and say something breezy in colloquial Italian about the salt in the cupboard or the eyes of a fish or some other image that doesn't make any sense or apply. Doesn't anybody see how hard all of this is for me?

Gala corrals us all into a group—she is first and foremost a travel director—and we head off for the van. On the drive home, everyone laughs as Nonna recounts how Otto and Worley tried to teach her how to clog. I don't feel much like laughing. I am filling up with sadness and regret. My family just got here, and already they're leaving. I don't want them to go! I wish this black road would never end and we could stay inside this van forever talking and laughing with Theodore behind the wheel and my father at my side.

When we get back to the house, Nonna gives Gala the dry soup beans and seasonings she bought at the Piggly Wiggly to take back to Italy.

"I'm gonna break it off for good with Frank tomorrow night. After I get Nonna's soup beans through Customs. Hey, he used me, now I use him."

Nonna kisses me good night and goes off to bed.

I watch Gala stuff soup beans in socks. She looks at me.

"Are you okay?" I nod. "You look sad. You're going to miss them."

"It's gone by so fast. But I don't want to complain, I sound so ungrateful."

"Believe me. It was a project getting these folks over here. What a logistical nightmare. Could they live any farther up in the Alps? They're a pack of goats, your family."

"Gala, who contacted you about getting my family over here?"

"Iva Lou."

"Iva Lou?"

"She called first. But it was just an inquiry. You know, to find out how this sort of tour would work. So I gave her a breakdown and took notes. Of course, I wasn't sure how it would work, but then I thought of it as a reverse tour and I was fine. Iva Lou didn't talk money or anything, though. That was entirely Jack MacChesney's department. He's a cute one, don't you think?"

"When did he call you to make the arrangements?"

She shrugs. "A couple of months ago. I could look it up."

"Was my trip planned before or after theirs?" I wave my hand to in-dicate my houseguests.

"After." Gala looks guilty for a moment and then continues. "I was expecting your call. Iva Lou tipped me off. I'm sorry. I lied to you, I trumped up a fake trip to make you think it was happening. But we had already planned the relatives coming over, so I saw no harm in it. Frank arranged the fake airline tickets I sent you. I'm sorry."

How could I be angry with Gala? My family is in my house, and we have had the best time.

"Don't apologize," I say to Gala. "I owe you so much more than you will ever owe me." I really mean this.

That sneaky Iva Lou. That day on the Bookmobile, long ago, when Jack Mac was there with a newspaper, that's when they found Gala. So, when I needed an international travel agent, Iva Lou steered me right to Gala. Jack Mac said he started planning this back when he proposed. And those Mormons; Iva Lou set that up to buy more time for Jack Mac's plan. Is the whole town in on my business?

Everyone has gone to bed. We set three alarms so we would not over-sleep. The Piedmont plane out of Tri-Cities for John F. Kennedy Airport in New York leaves at 7:00 A.M., and there isn't another connection, so they must make it. (I remember that *Piedmont* means "foot of the mountains." What a poor name for an airline!) I can't sleep, so I'm wandering around the house trying not to make noise. I tiptoe outside and sit on the porch. I'm anticipating how sad I will be tomorrow after everyone leaves. Yes, I am going to Italy to visit them in a few weeks; Gala took care of everything without penalty, and she invited me to stay with her in New Jersey for a week and see New York before I go overseas! But after that, what? Where will I go? Maybe I'll like Schilpario and stay there. I ponder that for a moment. How I wish Mama were here. Imagine how happy she would have been to see me with her family, knowing that I would never be alone in the world again. Even that I could not give her. Why did my mother's life have to be so hard? I breathe deeply. I will never answer that question.

Zia Meoli stands at the screen door.

"I can't sleep," she says. This makes me laugh. She sounds just like my mother. And even though you would never say my mother was a comical person, sometimes she could say one sentence in such a way that it made you laugh. Zia Meoli comes outside.

"I wanted to talk to you alone." She pulls up a chair next to me. "Please."

"How do you like him?" She indicates the window behind which my father sleeps.

"I like him." She shrugs. "Don't you?"

Zia Meoli thinks for a moment. "He's a politician," she decides.

I figure in Italy that's not a compliment. "Zia . . ." I begin, but from the look on her face, I can see that she knows what I am going to ask her. "Do you remember when Mama left Bergamo?"

She nods as though it were yesterday. "Your mother left us in the middle of the night. She did not tell us where she was going. She left a letter for me, telling me that I should not worry about her, that she would write to me."

I can tell from Zia's expression that she has replayed these events over in her mind many times. She is still bothered by them.

"Did you want to go after her to find her?" I ask.

"Yes! Of course, yes! I thought of every place she might go. Cousins. Other towns. But no one had seen her. And she left no clue as to where she went or why. I was suspicious, because she spoke of Mario Barbari often, but I said nothing because I wasn't sure. My mother, your grandmother, was destroyed. After Fiametta left, she could never be consoled."

"What about your father?"

"I think he knew what happened. See, he knew Mario Barbari. He knew his family, not well, but in business. When Papa figured out that Fiametta liked Mario, he felt she was too young to court. So he forbade her to see him. She was devastated. But our father was very strict. If anything improper had occurred, he would have made Fiametta leave our home. My sister knew this. Though it broke my heart that she did what she did, I understood. She had no choice. I would have done the same thing."

"But she was only seventeen. Just a girl."

"At that time, many Italians were leaving the country. Some to Canada, some to South America, some to Australia. All over. Many, of course, went to New York. America. I knew that if she could, she would leave Italy altogether, so as not to bring shame upon us. I also knew that when she made a decision, she would never turn back."

"Did you know she was pregnant with me?"

Zia Meoli shakes her head; she did not know of her sister's condition.

"If you knew about Mario Barbari, why didn't you go to him?"

She nods vehemently. "I went to him. I did."

"Did you know he was married?"

"I knew a family up the mountain, in a town about fifteen kilometers from Schilpario. They knew of him, where I could find him. They told me he was married. I was sure he had married my sister. But it wasn't Fiametta, it was another girl. I was told it was a match, and it did not work. The girl went back with her parents after a short time."

"How do they make a match?"

"The families come together and decide who their children will marry. Pietro and I were a match. He was one of five children, four of them sons. His father came to my father, and they discussed which daughter would be suitable for his sons. Antonietta loved a boy in Sestri Levante, near Genoa, and Fiametta was gone, so that left me. I met Pietro, I liked him very well. We courted for one year, and then we got married." She folds her arms, indicating that making matches is the most natural way to make a marriage in the whole world.

"So, what happened when you went to find Mario Barbari?"

"Oh, yes!" She remembers as she goes back to her story. I notice that Italians do digress—I am guilty of it too. In the middle of a story, one element of it grabs their attention, and then they're off the subject entirely, never to return. I am reminded of how alike we are, even though I was not influenced by them when I was growing up. These similarities, though, are deep and in our bones.

"Mario da Schilpario was very suave. The black, black hair. The black eyes. Very striking man. I figured out a way to get up the mountain without my father finding out the real reason for my trip. I was hoping that Fiametta would be there with him, and I could talk sense to her and have her come home. When I got to Schilpario, I found Mario working in the church. His family are glass and metal workers. They make stained-glass windows." Another fact about my father I didn't know!

"I knew it was him right away, because I remembered him from town; he drove a carriage down for supplies sometimes, and all the girls in Bergamo took note of him. I asked to speak with him alone. He was very pleasant, but he knew nothing of my sister's whereabouts. He had not heard from her. He asked me to understand his position; he had a wife, and they were trying to make their marriage work, even though they did not live under one roof. He thought my sister was beautiful and sweet, but theirs was a romance that could never be. Would I tell her that when I found her? I told him that was something he needed to discuss with Fiametta himself. I remember that, at the mention of her name, his eyes had great pain in them. I believe he loved her."

Zia Meoli has obviously given this a great deal of thought. But she is a woman, too, and she knows what happens to unsuspecting girls who fall for the town Lothario. At first, they accept that they are one of many, but they hope they can tame him, win his heart, and make him faithful and true. At seventeen, my mother didn't know that she would never win this battle. But she was so in love, she gave him her heart anyway. It is so ironic that I am Mario's only child. All those women, all that romance, and I am the only child that grew from it.

"So, I went back down the mountain, with no more information than when I left. I gathered my mother and my sister in a room, away from my father, and told them what I had learned. My mother was devastated; she was certain I would find Fiametta and bring her home. My mother's health turned at that time. She cried all the time, she took to her bed. The Italians would say that her blood turned. Her sadness had made her ill."

"What about your father?"

"My mother never discussed it with my father. She knew where he stood on the matter. If Fiametta had done wrong, she had to live with the consequences. One time he and I had an argument about it. He told me he knew that my sister was alive and well. He knew how strong-willed she was. Papa thought that she could protect herself. I thought he was cold and indifferent, and I was very angry with him for not setting out to find her. But he and Fiametta had always had a sense about each other; I never had that with him."

"A sense?"

"Papa knew what she was thinking. He always did. He could tell before she did something what she was going to do. It was mystical."

"When did Mama write her first letter to you?"

"It was almost a year after she left. How happy Mama was when that letter came from America."

"I didn't find any letters from your mother to my mother."

Zia Meoli shakes her finger back and forth. "Never. My mother would never go against my father! Never!"

"Did your mother know about me?"

"She was so happy. But you were only a year or so old when she died. But my mother knew your name and all of the details Fiametta sent to me."

"Did you ever tell your father?"

My aunt shakes her head sadly. "If he knew, we never talked about it. Don't judge him for it, Ave Maria. It was a different time. A girl could not leave the family home without being married, nor could she—"

"Dishonor the family name."

Zia Meoli shakes her head again. "I knew there was no dishonor. She was young. She was in love." Zia sits back in the chair, rocking a bit.

Mama in love. I wish I could have seen it.

Theodore and I see everyone off at the airport, but it is in no way a sad parting. We promise to call and write to one another, and we're all looking forward to the long summer in Schilpario.

My father tries to give me a wad of money, which I stuff right back into his pocket.

"Papa, I don't need it."

"Please take it."

"Papa, you keep it. Take care of Nonna." He smiles, and we hug for a long time. We will see each other very soon, and we're happy about that.

Theodore and I watch the plane take off. After it disappears beyond the mountains, we go to Shoney's for a leisurely lunch and relive every moment of the Eye-talian visit.

I load up the Jeep to return all the pans to the ladies in town who dropped off food while my family was visiting. One of my favorite things about Big Stone Gap is the stream of covered dishes that flows from house to house in times of joy or sadness. The ladies make it easy to get their pans back: On the bottom of each, in indelible ink on heavy tape, they print their names: N. Goodloe, E. and L. Tuckett, I. Makin, J. Hendrick, and N. MacChesney. It will take me the better part of the day to shuttle these back to their owners.

I drive up to Cracker's Neck first, starting at the top of the mountain with the first pan return. Then I'll work my way back down to town. Tufts of white smoke puff out of the kitchen chimney at the MacChesneys'. I knock at the door. No answer. I knock again. Still no answer. In a split second there is loud barking behind me, and I practically jump out of my skin. It's the family dog. He keeps barking and circles back around the house. I follow him.

Mrs. Mac is hanging out the laundry. The white sheets are whiter than the clouds overhead, and even outdoors the air is filled with the clean smell of fresh laundry. She looks up and sees me and smiles.

"Thank you for the chess pie. My family loved it."

"Who wouldn't? It's good pie."

"Do you need some help?" I ask.

"I'm all done. Come inside. I got coffee."

I follow Mrs. Mac into the house through the back porch. I have never seen this porch or entered the house this way. In fact, I didn't even know she had a room like this on the back of the house. You can't see it from the kitchen; it is off at a different angle and easily hidden.

The sunporch is lovely. There is rattan furniture with soft cushions, quilted in elaborate designs; I recognize the traditional "drunkard's path" motif on a matching chair. There are hanging plants everywhere, spilling over with blooms of pink, purple, and yellow. I have never seen an indoor garden quite so beautiful; it looks like it belongs in another house, not in this clean, spare stone house in Cracker's Neck.

"Yep, this is my favorite spot in the house. Plants need a lot of care, though."

I imagine Mrs. Mac making the sunporch her own special room, full of her feminine touches. But it is more than that; it has a spiritual feeling, like a sanctuary. I follow her through a small pantry back into the kitchen that I know so well.

"Everybody get off all right?" she asks as she fetches me a cup of coffee.

"They had the best time."

"How about you?"

"It was a dream."

"Good."

"Mrs. Mac, you probably know that Jack sold his truck to pay for all of it, and I—"

She holds up her hand to stop me. "That is his affair."

"I know. But I want you to know that I appreciate it."

"Honey, it ain't none of my business."

"But—"

"It ain't."

We sit in an uncomfortable silence for a few minutes.

"You raised a very fine person."

"Thank you kindly."

"Mrs. Mac, are you upset with me about something?"

"I wouldn't call it upset."

"What would you call it?"

"There is a word for it; let me think." She thinks a moment, gets up, goes to the cake saver, pulls off the lid, cuts a couple of pieces of pound cake, puts them on a plate, fetches two forks and two plates and two napkins, and comes back to the table and sits down with me. "I'm mystified."

"Excuse me?"

"Do you want my son or not?"

I can't answer her. Not only am I embarrassed, I realize that I am in that horrible position of having dragged somebody's mama into my confusion, a bad place for her and me.

"Do you mind if I don't answer that?"

"Suit yourself."

We eat our cake and drink our coffee. Mrs. Mac stares off at the field. She looks old to me this morning. Or maybe I'm afraid that I will miss her when I leave.

"I got a lot of pans in the car, so I better shove off."

"Ave Maria?" Mrs. Mac looks at me directly and does not blink.

"My sister Cecelia is coming to git me this afternoon to take me down to her place for a visit. I'm gonna be gone about a week. My son gets off of his shift at six sharp; he comes home here through the door no later than seven. He don't know I'm going to see his aunt, so he's gonna come home here directly, expecting dinner as usual. If I was you, and if you have one tenth the brain in your head that I think you do, you'll be sitting there on the porch waiting for him. Now, is that clear enough, youngun?"

I nod.

I give Mrs. Mac a quick hug. When I let go of her, she gives me an extra-quick hug that instructs me, *Do what I'm telling you, or I can't be responsible for what happens next.*

There are some low patches of fog as I drive down the mountain. I think of the kiss in the trailer park. It's the first time I have ever thought about it during the day. As I make the turn onto Valley Road, a cat runs out in front of my Jeep. I slam on the brakes and jump out. The cat disappears into the ditch. I'm afraid it might be injured. I cross the road and climb down the bank just as the cat slips into the dark opening of a gully. I crawl closer and brush away the leaves at the mouth of the tunnel. There are three kittens, not even old enough to open their eyes, tucked safely under some leaves. I back away and sit at the edge of the ditch for a moment, waiting for the mother. Eventually she crawls out and tends to the babies. She licks them. They seem to be okay. I start to cry. I realize what a phony I am. I told Otto in no uncertain terms that he had to be honest with Worley about his shame. And yet I cannot be honest about my own. I have chosen *not* to fall in love because I thought it would heal my mother's shame if I was a perfect daughter, virtuous and independent. I have spent my life trying not to need anyone. But I hear Mrs. Mac again in my mind and I realize I don't want to live like this anymore.

A car horn blasts behind me. It's Nellie Goodloe.

"Ave Maria, are you all right down there in that ditch?"

"I'm fine, Nellie," I call back to her.

She shrugs and drives off. I stand up and brush the leaves from my pants. By the time I reach the Jeep, I know what I'm going to do.

I drop by the Pharmacy with Fleeta's pan. Fleeta is restocking the candy.

"They done picked the new Drama director," Fleeta announces.

"Oh yeah? Who?"

"Sarah Dunleavy, that new English teacher up to the high school."

"No!" This really makes me mad. I didn't think I was territorial about the job, but her? She doesn't have any pizzazz at all.

"*Sarah*"—Fleeta pronounces it like it's a brand name for industrial sludge—"has done been greasin' the board of dye-rectors up one side and down the other. She done joined the Dogwood Garden Club, hell, she hosted their Early Bird Breakfast, she got herself into the sewing circle at the Methodist church, and she got Don Wax Realty to sponsor her tenth-grade English class on a field trip over to the Barter Theater to see a play. This gal is takin' things over. Trust me on that one. Are you chapped?"

"Yes. I'm chapped." I don't know exactly why, but I am.

"I would be, too. After all you done for the folks around here. Driving yourself cuckoo, volunteering for this and that. And this is the thanks you git. Your scent ain't even evaporated in the area, and they done filled your spot. For whatever it's worth, Portly thinks it's terrible too."

"Have we got any Coty's Emeraude cologne?"

"It's in the locked case." Fleeta points to it, pulling a key ring with ten thousand keys on it out of her back pocket and flipping through it.

"How do you know which key?"

"It's like Braille to me. I feel the grooves."

The first key Fleeta chooses fits the case.

"It's your lucky day. One bottle left."

"Put it on my tab."

Fleeta laughs and it turns into a rattle. She coughs. "That's pretty funny, bein' it's your place." I wish I could join in the hilarity, but I'm not feeling very funny right now. Sarah Dunleavy has taken my place in Big Stone Gap, seamlessly, effortlessly; it's as though I never existed. And I haven't even left town yet! I guess I'm just going to have to be a little more careful about marking my territory. I'll start with the Emeraude.

I spend most of the afternoon getting ready for the evening. I want to make sure that I am on the MacChesneys' porch by six o'clock, sitting there waiting. I'm afraid that if I'm late, and I drive up and see Jack Mac's truck, I'll throw the old Jeep in reverse and back down the mountain. I am very nervous about all of this; my last conversation with Jack wasn't a friendly one. I don't know if he'll turn mountain man on me and order me off his property or what. So I need to get there first and plant myself. That will give me courage.

I choose something very simple to wear: one of my new Mama blouses and a pair of jeans. A skirt would look like I'm trying to impress him, since I rarely wear them. This is a business meeting for me; I need to project a certain seriousness, and I have that in pants.

As I make the drive up through Cracker's Neck, I review carefully in my mind all the twists and turns of my friendship, or whatever you want to call it, with Jack MacChesney. Back in school, he was a shy, shadowy sort of figure. He didn't join a lot of clubs. I remember that he might have played baseball, but that would be all. My real memories of him started that morning when I caught him in his long johns and stayed for breakfast. That's the first time I really took note of him—sparkling, out of the shower. And I think I fell for him for real when he winked at me at the Drama rehearsal.

But I am not the kind of woman to steal another woman's man. First of all, I wouldn't do that to any woman because I sure as hell wouldn't want it done to me. And second, situations based on one-upmanship never, ever last. Those romances are not built on solid foundations; at the first sign of trouble, they collapse. Maybe that's part of the thrill, but to me no man was ever worth the heartbreak of a woman.

I am not naïve, though. I know there are the Sarah Dunleavys out there, who make a project out of finding the best men in every group and working their way into their hearts by being quiet, orderly, and not much fuss. But there isn't one among us who can playact for a lifetime. Men don't understand that, though. They think they know what they're marrying because it would never dawn on men to change their behavior for anybody. "Accept me as I am," they seem to say as they plant their feet, "or move on, girl." But women? We adapt. Adapting gets results. It worked for Mama, but that life is not for me. Perhaps that is the real reason I never married. I just couldn't adapt.

Why am I driving to Cracker's Neck? What do I think I'll find here? Maybe the subconscious lull of Jack MacChesney's kiss remembered each night before I go to sleep has imprinted itself on my heart and sent a message to my brain to face myself. I don't know. It unlocked something in me, though. This old Jeep cannot plow through Cracker's Neck fast enough to deliver me safely to the MacChesneys' porch.

My fear leaves me as I sit on the porch. I am amazed at the view, and I wish the sun would stay up longer so I could really study the landscape. Finally, after what seems like years, I can see truck lights down the mountain as they make the big turn onto the property.

The truck bounces over the pits and holes in the dirt road, kicking up a little dust. The headlights shine on me as Jack drives the truck to the side of the house. I shield my eyes from the glare but stand to greet him. The truck has the price $3,100 USED written on the windshield in white shoe polish. I guess Rick Harmon loaned it to Jack from the used-car dealership. I don't know how he can see through the big white writing well enough to drive. For a moment I panic. What if Sarah Dunleavy is in the truck with him? I wish I would have brought a cake pan; at least I could look like I have an excuse to be here, and then I could cut out, with my face intact. Too late to jump in the Jeep and get out of here, so I wait. Jack parks the truck; the setting sun shines into the passenger window, and I can see he is alone. I breathe deeply.

It takes him a moment to get out of his truck, gathering his lunch pail and boots. He comes around the back of the truck and up the walk. He looks at me funny.

"Is something wrong with Mama?"

"No, no. She . . . she went to visit your Aunt Cecelia."

"Why didn't she tell me?" Jack Mac walks up the steps, past me, and up to the door with the keys.

"I guess it came up all of a sudden or something."

"Could be," he says, and opens the door. Jack leans in and turns on the lights. Mrs. Mac has left a note on the front-hall table verifying what I just told him. He reads it and puts it back on the table.

It's as if I'm not even here. He isn't happy to see me, but he's not annoyed either. It's just a cordial indifference. How awful. Or is this a ploy to make me suffer? I've hurt him, so now he has to hurt me? Oh, God, he's going to make me work for this. I'm going to have to get down on my knees and beg this man to forgive me. I grab the rail on the front-porch stoop and hold it.

"Would you like to come in?" His voice is so monotone that there is no way to read whether he actually wants me to or is just being polite.

"Yes, I would."

I stand in the doorway awaiting further instruction. But he doesn't say a word. He just goes in and out of rooms, turning on lights, dropping off the lunch pail, putting the boots away, and moving the mail from the mantel to the hallway table. It is as though I'm invisible. I wish I were.

"Do you think Mama left any supper?" he asks me, finally. It's the first friendly thing he's said, but I don't trust him.

"I don't know."

"Let's check." Jack Mac goes into the kitchen. I could not feel more stupid than I do, standing here. He pokes his head out of the kitchen.

"Well, come on," he says, and goes back into the kitchen.

I follow him. Sure enough, Mrs. Mac has prepared a meal. The table is set for two, and there is a patio candle, a dark blue one, in white mesh in the middle of the table. The setup makes me feel awkward; it is almost as bad as parents fawning all over their pimply kids on prom night.

"Why don't you heat up supper and I'll start the fire?" He looks at me like I'm a moron, who can't figure out that if I came all the way up here and it's suppertime, we might as well eat. I go to the refrigerator and pull out a casserole that has the indelible ink and tape strip that says "mac 'n cheese." I preheat the oven.

What am I doing here? This is the worst idea I've ever had. I have to make a move to get out of here, and fast. I would rather die than tell him about the kiss-before-sleeping thing, or how I love the way he smells, or how I'd just as soon rip out Sarah Dunleavy's eyes as lose him to her. Why did I come up this mountain tonight? I should have just bought him a new truck and had it delivered and moved away and forgotten all about him. I am too old to be feeling this out of control. Why is he so calm? He is doing this to me on purpose. I bet he thinks this is funny. Mr. Never Without a Girlfriend. Go ahead, make fun of the Terrified Old Maid.

"I'm going to take a shower. You make the salad." He goes.

Where is the phone? I'll call Theodore and tell him to come and get me. I don't think I can drive in the state I'm in. This man has me completely and totally unglued. My hands feel numb, as though I could snap them off like rubber gloves. Jack Mac sticks his head back into the kitchen. I jump.

"Don't put any radishes in it. I hate them." He goes again.

Jesus, he popped his head in here and scared me like a lurker in a horror movie. He must have seen me jump, because it's the first time I saw him smile tonight. This is torture. Should I just leave? Why don't I? I can't. My feet won't move. Deep inside, I feel my core and it centers me. I breathe deeply and evenly, regulating my nerves and settling my heart. I check my makeup in the toaster. I look good. I can do this. I make the salad. I make the dressing. I find a bowl and put it on the table. I put the casserole in the oven. Then I choose a seat at the table and sit down. And I wait.

Finally, he comes back into the kitchen. He is freshly scrubbed and looks neat. He is dressed nicely, in a denim shirt and old jeans, but it doesn't look like he's trying too hard. He goes to the oven, pulls out the casserole, and puts it on the table. He takes a bottle of wine out of the refrigerator. Without asking me, he uncorks it.

"Wine?" he offers.

I put my face in my hands. "I'd rather have an aspirin." Now, why he finds this so amusing, I do not know. But he laughs like he thinks it is the funniest thing he's ever heard. He laughs long enough that I take offense.

"What is so funny?"

"You are."

"I'm mighty glad I'm so entertaining."

"You're more than that." Jack Mac sits down. What is he talking about? What does he mean? I feel like he's speaking a different language. There's a good starting point.

"My father told me you spoke Italian with him."

"I know a little."

"How?"

"From a book. I got the Berlitz book-and-tape series from the county library."

"Why?"

"I wanted to learn it."

"Because of me?"

"You aren't the only Italian in the world, you know."

"I didn't mean it to sound that way. I just assumed—"

"Well, don't."

I have had enough, and I haven't even been inside this old, ugly, hateful stone house for an hour. But I am not going to bite his head off. I am going to be dignified about this whole thing.

"Why are you being cruel to me?"

He thinks about this for minute. "Maybe it's self-protection."

Okay, now I get it. I hurt him, so he has to decimate me to level the playing field. How childish. How childish for a man with more gray hair than brown.

"I am not going to hurt you." I don't know why I say this, but it seems to me that this is the issue and I should address it.

"Too late for that."

He is really mad at me. I don't know how I'm going to get through to him. Or should I even keep trying? Maybe he wants me to leave, and his genteel Southern manners won't let him throw me out.

"Do you want me to go?" I ask very nicely.

"Do you want to go?"

I hate when people answer questions with questions. "No, I don't," I say to him pointedly. I don't know where that came from; I would have given my right leg to get out of here a minute ago, but somehow, hearing that I have hurt him makes me stay.

"Are you in love with Sarah Dunleavy?"

"Why are you asking?"

"Because if you are, I will take up your offer and leave."

"And if I'm not?"

"If you're not, I think we could work this thing out and you could get very lucky tonight, as your mother is out of town." Where did that come from? Thank God he's laughing, or I might have to ask where they keep the gun they use to shoot rabid dogs and just turn it on myself.

"Had I known it was that easy, I wouldn't have sold my truck." He gets up and pours himself a glass of water.

"Why did you sell your truck?" Now I'm standing. I think the two bites of macaroni helped me get my strength back. I'm ready for him now. So I keep going. "It was fully loaded. It was your dream truck. You loved that truck."

"Yeah, but I've loved you since the sixth grade."

He turns to me. I can't move. He doesn't either. He just stands there looking at me. Finally, he points to the floor in front of his feet, indicating that I should walk to him—he is not going to come to me. So I take those twelve steps and fall into his arms. I didn't think this moment would mean so much to me, but once I am in his arms, leaning against this place on his chest that I have dreamed of, there is nothing that could tear me away from him ever again. He kisses me, just like he has in my dreams every night since Iva Lou's wedding. I am so mad at myself for having wasted so much time.

It is early in the evening, and we still have a lot to talk about. We finish dinner (he is hungry, I am not). Then Jack wants to show me the house. He starts with the sunporch, which looks even cozier at night. He shows me his mother's bedroom from the doorway, a simple pale blue room. The parlor. The sitting room. And then he takes me upstairs to show me the attic, a room the size of the whole house. Mrs. Mac's quilting supplies are organized on simple wooden shelves, and there is a long farm table in the middle of the room, with chairs around it. Jack Mac explains that this is where Aunt Cecelia and various friends come and quilt. He leads me to the window, which overlooks the magnificent Powell Valley. I can see for miles; though it is dark, the faraway streetlights give the small pockets of the mountains a twinkling glow.

While we're in the attic room, he shows me some photographs in the family album. There are pictures of his mother when she was a girl. I think she looked like Loretta Young in *Call of the Wild;* Jack tells me his father always thought so, too. He tells me his parents had a real love affair, and how sad she was for so long after he died.

Jack shares a little about his romantic past with me, enough to help me understand but certainly not anything to make me feel uncomfortable or envious. He confides that he was worried I'd marry Theodore and he would miss his chance with me. He has a lot of questions for me, too. He wants to know where I was going when I gave everything to Pearl. I tell him I wasn't sure. I was planning to take a long trip to Italy and then decide where to settle. He asks me if I still want to live in Big Stone Gap. I'm still not completely sure, but I am starting to see that the place didn't make me unhappy; I made me unhappy. I started to view everyday things as a burden, so they became a burden. But I tell him that it had a lot to do with my mother's death.

Jack asks me about Fred Mulligan, with whom I now feel at peace. Jack remembers him as a decent man but very stern. I agree with him.

I guess I was lucky; I learned a lot from the bad stuff, too. Who would have thought meeting Mario da Schilpario would help me let go of Fred Mulligan?

I ask Jack about his father. He smiles. "The best thing a father can do for his son is love his mother. And he did that."

I think of Iva Lou telling me that Jack Mac didn't throw himself around town with the ladies indiscriminately. Maybe he's just like his father. He leads me out to the sunporch, taking the patio candle with us. We lie on the couch. He holds me. Then he tells me what's in his heart. "I'd been trying to get your attention at the Drama for years. I was always offering to stay and help with the stage crew, or I offered to bring you home a lot. Do you remember?" Now I do remember. But I never thought he was interested in me *that* way. I wasn't that kind of girl. I was always so busy. "You always seemed perfectly nice, but you never really paid me any mind." I didn't. I was friendly to everybody, but I never chose favorites. A little of that was Mazie Dinsmore's directing style that I imitated, and part of it was my own brand of shyness with men.

Jack continues, "And then there was that night, when Sweet Sue gave you the champagne and then the cast started teasing us and begging me to propose. That was just about the worst night of my life. Because I wanted to turn to you and say, 'You're the one I want.' Sue knew it too. That's when I decided to just be direct with you. That's when I came over and asked you to marry me."

"You thought I'd say yes and that would be it?"

"I thought you'd think about it. I didn't think you'd say no and get mad at me. But I didn't know what I was doing. I didn't understand you then. I do now. Things have to be your idea or they don't get done."

"But why then? Why did you ask me to marry you then?"

"Well, I thought I saw something different in your eyes up at the hospital after the explosion in the mine."

"I wanted to drive you home!" I offer.

"Right."

"But Sweet Sue and your mama . . ."

"I couldn't turn them away. And you looked at me as though you understood."

"I did," I say, meaning it.

"When I got home, I sat down and had a long, hard night of think-ing. I realized that my life was half over. Sounds simple, but it isn't. Kept me up all night. See, I went in to help Rick, and when I got to him, I realized that at my age I might not have the strength to pull him out of there. I've been in the mines since I was eighteen. That's almost twenty years. I'm not what I was."

"But you were strong! You did save him!"

"Barely," Jack says.

"What does this have to do with me?"

Jack Mac takes a moment. "I didn't want to grow old without you."

I can't speak. As the town spinster, I had no picture of my old age. Being alone gave me a certain timelessness. I don't have the deep worry lines on my face that come from motherhood, or the soft body that comes from holding a lover or a child. I have perfect posture because I never stoop or look down. I froze myself in time, hoping it would not catch me. I was so afraid to love someone for fear I would fail.

"Are you crying?" he asks me.

"I have a feeling I'm just getting started," I tell him. He laughs. "Now, tell me how you decided to bring my family over from Italy."

"See, Iva Lou kept me informed about your search for your father. When you got in touch with him, I thought I'd take you over there to meet him. So I found Gala in the paper and called to arrange a first-class trip for the two of us. Then I came over to your house and pro-posed."

"Apple Butter Night."

"What?"

"Nothing," I say quietly.

"You said no, so I was stuck with no pride and a deluxe trip for two to Italy. Iva Lou still insisted you were in love with me. So she sug-gested we send the tickets over there to bring your father and grand-mother over here. But you almost messed that up when you planned your own trip. We told Gala the whole story and persuaded her to in-vent a phony trip. You wouldn't have gotten anywhere with the tickets she sent you. They were fake."

"I know. Gala told me. But what about Zia Meoli and Zia An-tonietta and Uncle Pietro?"

"Well, you saw how things work with Gala. And Iva Lou, for that matter. They snowball. But if I was going to do this thing, I was going to do it right. I couldn't bring your father over and ignore all of your mother's people now, could I? So—"

"So," I interrupt. "You sold your truck."

"I sold my truck. The mystery is solved," Jack says simply.

Sort of.

"Why would you still go through with it after I . . ." I don't want to use the word *rejected,* so I don't.

"Look. I thought about giving up. It was too late; the plans were made. And I'm stubborn. I wasn't ready to give up. Iva Lou kept telling me you were in love with me but you just didn't know it yet. But faith can only go so far. Sometimes you need a little proof."

I never gave Jack a single sign. No wonder he walked away that day when my family came. He probably couldn't believe my reaction. I was grateful when I should have been loving. No man had ever given me such a gift. A priceless gift, really. He looked deep inside me and then set out to fulfill my heart's desire. And I acted as though he had dropped off a jar of apple butter. So he looked elsewhere for affection.

"And then Sarah Dunleavy swooped in."

"You don't know Sarah. She can't swoop. It'd mess up her hair."

"What were all of you doing up here having dinner the night I brought the fabric?"

"My mother knew her mother years ago and invited the girls to dinner. Theodore is on the Faculty Welcoming Committee. We were going to take them to the Coach House, but Mama wanted to cook. You know how she is."

"But you kept seeing her?"

"Not really. She was new in town. She called me to take her places, but I didn't call her. I liked it when you were jealous, though. It was the first sign of life I saw in you regarding me."

"What do you think took me so long?" I ask. "What took me so long to figure out I wanted you too?"

"I wish I knew." We laugh.

It takes a long time to get to Jack Mac's bedroom. (What a gentleman.) We stop and kiss every other step; sometimes we talk a bit, but mostly we just connect and connect and connect. I have dreamt of these kisses for so long that they still aren't quite real to me. I thought I had a pretty good imagination, but I am not so sure anymore. The real thing is so much better, so much more full of surprises than the stories I created in my mind's eye.

Jack's room is simple, with an old four-poster bed heaped with lush quilts, a straight-backed chair in one corner, and three windows that look out onto the long rolling field that drops off down the mountain. I won't let him draw the curtain; the view is so beautiful.

For some reason, I think of Iva Lou, and I laugh.

"What is so funny?"

"Iva Lou would give everything she had twice to know where I am right now."

"You don't want to call her, do you?" Jack Mac jokes.

"Where's the phone?" We laugh. I hope that, whatever happens, we will always laugh like this.

I am standing by his bed; he is near the windows. He comes to me and lifts me up and places me gently on his bed. He covers me in small, tender kisses—can I remember each and every one of these forever? I breathe deeply, feeling the rise and fall of my breath matching his.

When I was little and playing in the yard, I found a tiny blue egg in the grass. I looked up in the tree; there, out of my reach, was a nest in the branches. I ran for my mother. She carefully placed the egg in my hands and lifted me high off the ground and up into the tree, so that I was eye level with the nest. There were two more tiny blue eggs in the nest. Very gently, I placed the fallen egg at home with the others. This is how I feel in my lover's bed tonight. I feel that I am safe and I am home.

CHAPTER ELEVEN

J always thought that if I ever unleashed The Woman in me and gave in to my passionate nature, everybody in Big Stone Gap would know it and come running. So I am not totally surprised when I get up the next morning and no sooner do I fix the coffee than Spec is banging on the door. Iva Lou probably called my house and couldn't find me, so she called Spec, who lives in Cracker's Neck, and he's come up here looking for me. Jack is still asleep. I'm dressed, so I answer the door.

"Hey, Spec."

"What are you doing here?"

"Making coffee. What are you doing here?"

"I'm here to fetch Jack Mac. They took his mother to the hospital down in Pennington. He needs to get to her right away. It's real bad, Ave. We need to hurry."

"Stay here."

I go into Jack's room, where he is sleeping soundly, like a little boy. I kiss him tenderly to wake him, and he pulls me close.

"Jack, Spec's here. Your Aunt Cecelia took your mama to the hospital. We need to go right away." He jumps out of the bed. I help him dress, handing him a T-shirt, boxers, socks one at a time, a pair of pants. We jump into the ambulance with Spec.

Spec doesn't turn on the siren; it's Saturday morning, about seven, and most folks are on a weekend schedule. He goes about ninety, though. I sit in the back; Jack is up front with Spec. I lean forward on the seat to keep my right hand on Jack's shoulder to let him know that I am here for him. Every once in a while he reaches up and squeezes my hand. Spec looks at me in the rearview; he raises one eyebrow and lets me know he understands.

Jack doesn't say a word the entire ride. I know he has dreaded this ride all of his life. The idea of his mother in pain or sick is too much for him to bear, but he doesn't collapse. I completely fell apart when it was my mama. Jack MacChesney is not the fall-apart type.

Spec pulls into the emergency exit at the hospital in Pennington Gap. He knows it well, so he takes us through a long corridor, a back entrance to Intensive Care. Jack goes through the door first, before Spec. He sees his mother in the corner of the unit, Cecelia at her side. He breaks into a run to reach her. When Mrs. Mac sees Jack, she smiles and raises her head slightly off of the pillow.

"Took you long enough," she says.

"I came as fast as I could, Mama." Jack is close to her face, holding both of her hands.

"I done took a fall," she says as she closes her eyes.

"She passed out," Aunt Cecelia says, crying. "I couldn't get her up. It was just the two of us there, and I had to call the hospital. I got so scared." Jack is holding his mother tightly. I can't bear the sight of Cecelia's tears, so I put my arms around her gently. She looks at me, and though she doesn't know who I am, she accepts my embrace.

"She's the girl I done told you about," Mrs. Mac says to Cecelia.

"They're gonna fix you right up, Mrs. Mac," I promise.

"Do you think so?" she says with a twinkle.

I can tell that Jack wants to be alone with her, so Cecelia and I give them their privacy. Cecelia is a beauty, too, probably older than Mrs. Mac. She is taller and heavier.

"We was having such a grand time. We talked and laughed and ate. She was feeling funny last night, but we didn't think nothing of it; I thought she was just tired. But she had a bad night, she told me, like indigestion, and then this morning I went in to wake her and she was on the floor, just blacked out."

"You did everything you could. I'm sure they can help her." I try to reassure Cecelia, but Mrs. Mac doesn't look too good. Jack Mac calls for me, and a nurse takes over with Cecelia.

"Mama wants to tell you something," Jack tells me, his voice breaking. I have never heard this tone in his voice before. My heart is breaking for him. He is so sad. He knows. He knows she is going, and he is powerless to do anything about it. I know that feeling, and it is devastating.

I lean over the side of the bed.

Mrs. Mac takes a good breath. "Did you ever wonder why your mama did my mending when I was a good seamstress myself?" I shake my head; I never thought about it. "My son wanted an excuse to go to your house." She smiles. "Take care of him. Because he took good care of me."

I try to say I will, but I can't speak; I just nod and promise. I kiss her good-bye. I straighten up next to her bed; for a moment I am dizzy. This cannot be happening.

Jack leans over her bed and takes his mother in his arms. She looks like a beautiful porcelain doll, her skin a silky white, like her hair. Jack holds his mother and cries. I hear him say, "Don't go, Mama. Don't go." The nurse crosses over to help, but my expression tells her that Mrs. MacChesney has died. She died in her son's arms. And that is what she wanted.

The passing of Nan Bluebell Gilliam MacChesney took everyone in the Gap by surprise. Except Jack. He knew she would never have endured a long illness; she wanted to go quickly. And she did. My mama knew I wasn't ready to let her go, so she stayed until her passing would be a blessing, her suffering over. The terrible things that happen to us in this life never make any sense when we're in the middle of them, floundering, no end in sight. There is no rope to hang on to, it seems. Mothers can soothe children during those times, through their reassurance. No one worries about you like your mother, and when she is gone, the world seems unsafe, things that happen unwieldy. You cannot turn to her anymore, and it changes your life forever. There is no one on earth who knew you from the day you were born; who knew why you cried, or when you'd had enough food; who knew exactly what to say when you were hurting; and who encouraged you to grow a good heart. When that layer goes, whatever is left of your childhood goes with her. Memories are very different and cannot soothe you the same way her touch did. If any sense can be made of my mother's death, it would be that I was of some help to Jack when he lost his mother. I hope I have been.

Jack was so strong through the wake and the funeral. He cried a bit at the service. But I was so proud of him; he took a moment with every person who came, to let each one know how much they had meant to his mother. I fell more deeply in love with him as I watched.

I load up the Jeep to return all the covered cake pans (again!). Then I'm taking Theodore out to lunch to thank him for being such a help through Mrs. Mac's funeral.

Bessie's Diner is standing room only, as usual. I hear Theodore call my name; over the crowd I see him wave to me from a booth way in the back. I work through the crowd to get to him.

"Did you buy old Bessie a diamond ring to get this table?" I kiss Theodore on the cheek.

"Almost."

We haven't had a chance to talk much over the past week, and there is so much to tell him.

"How's it going with Jack Mac?" he asks.

"Well, he's sad. But he isn't depressed. He keeps saying he is thankful she didn't suffer a long time. He got to say good-bye to her. He's gonna be all right."

"No, I mean how's it going with you and Jack?"

"I . . . love him." I've never said that out loud.

Theodore smiles. "You do?"

"I do."

"Why?" Theodore asks kindly.

"I don't know if I can say it."

"Try." Theodore sits back and makes a pyramid out of the tiny half-and-half containers.

"I love Jack MacChesney because . . . he loves me."

"Is that all?"

I don't think Theodore understands how big that statement is, how loaded it is to me. Nobody ever loved me; yes, Mama did and some friends, but nobody Loved me. I was *chosen*. And for once, I wasn't afraid, I just let It in. How silly my fears seem now. Why did I wait so long to let go? Even Mrs. Mac knew how scared I was. She kept trying to assure me that I would be safe with her son.

"Isn't that enough?" I fire back. Theodore nods.

"Ave, I'm going to take the job at UT."

"You are?" I'm instantly disappointed, and just as quickly I am thrilled for him. "Congratulations!"

"I think it's time to move on. I need a new challenge. I need to look at myself, where I'm going, you know?"

Theodore! Don't go! I want my life to be perfect. I want to be in love with Jack MacChesney and have you, my best friend, in my life forever. I don't want anything to change! Instead, I say, "You may go. But I'm not going to let you off the hook. We'll be long-distance best friends. Okay?"

"That's what I was thinking. Knoxville isn't so far. You'll come down."

"We can talk on the phone," I say, so upbeat.

"Every day. Just like now." Theodore looks at me. "Tell me I'm doing the right thing," he implores.

"You are doing the right thing. The only thing. Sometimes you have to strip away everything to find what you were in the first place."

"I guess that's what you did too, isn't it? Who would have thought our lives were going to change like this?"

"Chinese face-reading."

"Really? Can face-reading predict what I have planned after lunch?"

"I have to bring Edna and Ledna Tuckett their pie dish."

"They can wait. We're going to Cudjo's Caverns."

As we drive to the Caverns, I think of my friendship with Theodore, what comfort it brought me all these years, how it grew as we grew. I just know he will always be a big part of my life. How could he not? He's the only person I know who likes caves.

Ray takes us up the dark path with his flashlight.

"Can we go to the lake?" I ask him.

"I got something better to show you," he promises. Theodore and I look at each other and follow him.

For ten years Theodore and I have come into this cave to explore, and every so often Ray has something new to show us. How is this possible? Does he keep things from us? Or does he make discoveries all the time and share them with us when he's ready? Is this old mountain so full of riches that they cannot be discovered in one lifetime or even two? The path narrows; I keep my hand on the wall as we climb into a new place. As we move in, I can feel the cool stream of mountain water that flows down the rocks to form the stalactites. It takes the water generations to change the rocks. And yet it is so gentle on the stones, barely a gray mist.

"There it is," Ray says. "Y'all, look."

There is a small alcove, a grotto, the back wall jagged rock that forms a canopy overhead. Moss grows up the sides where the water trickles. The guide shines his flashlight on the ground. It is covered in lavender sand, fine-grained like spun sugar. The light beam plays over the sand, making it shimmer.

"How did this happen?" Theodore wants to know. We cannot believe the beauty of the sand.

"I ain't so sure," Ray begins. "This was an ugly black pool of gunk for the longest time. I didn't go near it, because I didn't know what was in it. You never do know inside the mountain. But over the winter, it started to drain out, so I kept an eye on it. And when all the water done drained off, this is what was at the bottom. It wasn't something ugly. It was this." Ray steadies the beam on the lavender sand;

the light makes a bright circle that burns hot in the center and fades out to the edges until it falls away in a soft gloomy blue.

Ray, Theodore, and I stay for a very long time.

"I've worked in here all my life. Sometimes you just can't explain things."

Jack Mac gets home from work at seven o'clock sharp. I'm making spaghetti when he comes in. Bessie's hamburger wore off hours ago, and I'm hungry. He calls to me from the front hall and walks back to the kitchen. He puts his lunch pail down on the table and his boots on the floor. Then he looks at me.

"I called the priest."

"You turning Catholic?" I tease.

"No."

"What, then?"

"I told him I wanted him to marry us."

"I don't want to marry the priest, too. Can't it just be the two of us?"

Jack Mac laughs. "Is that a yes?"

I nod. "Isn't this too quick, though?" Old Ave Maria is back, questioning everything.

Jack Mac gives me a you've-got-to-be-kidding look that stops me from blabbering on further and ruining a very precious moment.

"I learned that it's best not to let you think about things too much," he says, and he goes to wash up.

Never put Iva Lou Wade Makin in charge of a simple wedding. In two seconds she's convinced me to wear a dress that's too tight, a hat that's too broad, and too much makeup. We argue about the blush (I don't need it; humiliation gives me the only rose hue I need), lipstick versus lip gloss (my lips are so shiny I may slide off the groom), and powder finish (I think I look chalky).

As I look at my vivid face in the mirror, it reminds me of the glamorous women of the Ice Capades, who need a lot of makeup to be seen from six hundred feet in an arena. I don't need this kind of definition in a chapel that holds twenty people tops, so I slip into the bathroom to wash my face and start over. The corals, blues, and browns of my clown face disappear in the bubbles as I scrub. It's my wedding day. Better a few hurt feelings than Jack Mac taking one look at me and sprinting from the church in horror.

While I'm in the bathroom, I realize this fiasco is all my fault. I should have planned this better. I should have had some idea of what I wanted. I never dreamt of my wedding day. Not once. Not a single fantasy. I never imagined my bridesmaids in sherbet colors lined up at the altar, my very own ladies-in-waiting. I never saw the church festooned with flowers, heard the organ music, or thought about what color sugar Nellie Goodloe's mints should be dipped in. I never thought I'd get married. But believe me, there are plenty of women who have six, seven, eight scenarios mapped out in their minds, every detail of the nuptials planned, and they're all too happy to take over your big day and turn it into a monster of lace, ribbons, and flouncy details. Iva Lou Makin is the consummate romantic.

Once I arrive at the church, I forget all the prenuptial distress. For Jack and me, this is a simple ceremony, where we will have the great honor of promising, in front of our loved ones, to be true. This thought calms me. We are having a private mass with Jack's Aunt Cecelia and our closest friends. There will be no hoo-ha down the aisle or any other grand touches. Jack and I will enter together. The witnesses are Theodore, Iva Lou and Lyle, Aunt Cecelia, Pearl, Leah, Rick and Sherry, Fleeta and Portly, Otto and Worley, Lew and Inez Eisenberg, Zackie, and Spec.

Jack Mac pulls up in his truck and jumps out. He runs up the walkway and meets me in the vestibule.

"You're beautiful," he tells me. You wouldn't think so if you'd seen me an hour ago with four pounds of Max Factor heaped on my face. I smile at my groom.

It's the strangest thing—no one cries. There is just joy, simple and unadorned, in this little chapel with the quiet priest. Tomorrow, April 29, 1979, is my thirty-sixth birthday. How did I get to this place? Who knew?

After church, we've planned a dinner for everyone in town at the

Coach House (yes, we're having the same fried chicken, taters, and slaw combo that was served on Elizabeth Taylor Night).

When we cut our cake—thank you, Edna and Ledna Tuckett, for the coconut confection—Zackie emerges from the circle around us.

"Miss Ave Maria . . . I mean, Mizriz MacChesney . . ." The crowd cheers. I look at the faces of Rick and Sherry Harmon, Nellie Goodloe, June Walker, and Mrs. Gaspar. They couldn't be happier for me. How lucky I am.

"We wanted to do something special for you and Jack Mac," Zackie says. "So we put together a little fund-raiser."

Iva Lou and Lyle emerge from the kitchen carrying a four-foot pickle jar stuffed with coins and bills. The crowd cheers again. There is a sign inside the jar: HONEYMOON OR BUST.

"We want to send y'all to It-lee. We hope this will help."

Iva Lou and Lyle place the giant pickle jar at our feet. Pearl and Leah present us with a giant congratulations card signed by everyone at the reception. I look around the room. Most folks are crying. I am, too.

Jack and I spend our first night as a married couple in his stone house on the hill. I open all the windows; it is warm and the breeze is full of honeysuckle and jasmine. My husband comes to bed.

"There's something I never told you," he begins. My heart starts to race; a thousand possibilities float through my mind, all of them horrible, like he has three months to live, or he has a second family tucked away up in Insko, or that he's been in debtor's prison.

What has happened to me? I get so afraid now. I never used to. Why am I more vulnerable now than I was when I was alone, in charge of everything? I lived by myself in the middle of town, for God's sake. I checked my own oil, lit my own furnace, caught mice. I had a routine: running a home, a business, the Rescue Squad, the Drama. I was never scared then. So much for strength in numbers, I think as I look at my husband, now that we are a family.

"The fall before your mother got really sick, I went down to your house to pick up some mending. And she was sitting in the living room. She invited me to sit down, and I did. She told me some things about herself, general things, like where she was from in Italy, how she taught herself English, that sort of thing. As I was about to leave, she walked me to the door. She told me that she was dying, and if I wouldn't mind, could I look in on you once in a while to make sure you were all right. I promised her I would."

What can I say to him? Surely he knows what this means to me. My mama picked him first, way before I was ready, back when I was afraid to. I wonder if she knows how happy I am in this moment. Though I have no proof, something tells me she does.

We cuddle down into the covers, me on my side, my husband lying next to me, on his side, holding me. He places his arm around my waist like the bar on a roller-coaster car. I am locked in for the night. We have had a long day and a lot of cake, and we are very tired. My husband tells me he loves me, and I tell him that I love him. He kisses the back of my neck and goes to sleep.

As he sleeps, I think about Reverend Gaspar and I hear him say that word, *faith*. I haven't been able to figure out what he meant that night in the ambulance until now. I don't think he was talking about faith in God. I think he was telling me that he had faith in me, that he believed I could help him. Maybe he even thought I could save him. That's why his eyes were so clear and his voice was so strong as he lay dying. He had a revelation. He knew that the great mysteries in life can only be solved person to person. We can pull each other through. He figured it out at the end of his life; I am so glad he shared it with me in the middle of mine. Maybe I can be of some use now. Maybe I can be of some good to one person. I hope that person is Jack Mac-Chesney.

The trip to Italy that was to change the course of my life has become a honeymoon. I made Jack take a leave of absence from the mines so we could spend the entire summer in Italy. My husband is a very good traveler. He's not too persnickety about seeing everything; he's loose about missing trains; he doesn't get upset when a museum is closed or a church on our itinerary is locked. He speaks Italian with a mountain twang; sometimes I have to walk away because it is so funny. He ignores me and persists. The Italians love him because he tries so hard.

We landed in Rome and have been touring the countryside north by train. There is no way for me to scientifically explain the light here, as I am ignorant of such matters. But I swear to you, the sun is hung differently. There is a peachy golden haze over Italy that makes green fields more vivid, gives brown earth a depth and people a romantic glow. I point it out to Jack, and he tells me that I'm drunk in love with the place and it is coloring my perceptions. I don't think so. I think there is something different about the light. When the sun goes down, the sky turns a vivid blue-black, the stars seem closer, and the edges don't fade out toward the horizon. The same saturated blue hems the skyline that nestles the moon. It is no wonder the Fortuny family makes fabric here. They have a different canopy of velvet overhead to choose from each night. All they have to do is look up and copy.

Of course, we cannot wait to get to Bergamo, my mother's family home, for a two-day visit, and then on to Schilpario, where Mario and Nonna live. Mario is scheduled to come down the mountain and pick us up to take us to his home. I cannot explain the deep joy I feel. My husband is sleeping next to me on the train, and I am sailing through the place I come from. There may not be a greater feeling on earth.

The train pulls into Bergamo. I wake Jack and begin yanking suitcases down from the bars overhead. We brought so much American crap for the relatives. They had time to get home and decide which items they missed, so I am loaded down with cigarettes, Bic pens, staples and staple guns, Moon Pies, Goo-Goo Clusters, and giant plastic paper clips. I didn't question their choices; I just went out and bought in bulk and loaded a trunk.

Two of my cousins, Mafalda and Andrea, are there to meet us at the station. Their happy faces move alongside the train until it makes a full stop. I hang out the window; they see me and run to our exit steps to wait for us. I don't think anybody has ever been so happy to see us.

They negotiate the cumbersome bags, leaving me to carry nothing but my new leather-bound journal, which my husband bought me in Florence.

The train station is on the outskirts of town, on a side street nestled in some trees. Andrea and Mafalda load our luggage into their small car, we squeeze in, and we're off. Andrea drives very fast, and Mafalda chides him to slow down. We take a sharp right turn that leads us to a C-shaped street that connects to the town circle. Mafalda points out the newspaper office, the government building, the church. Bergamo looks just like the picture in the book Iva Lou found at the university library. Nothing has changed. The Fountain of Angels, the cobblestone streets, the upright shoe-box-shaped houses painted subtle pastels, the little park, the outdoor cafés—they are all the same! There is only one change that I can see: The car has replaced the horse and carriage.

The Vilminore family lives in a four-story house in the middle of a block on Via Davide. Zia Antonietta, Zia Meoli, Zio Pietro, and my cousin Federica are waiting for us in front of the house. My aunts cry when they see us. They can't seem to let go of Jack, who doesn't seem to mind their heartfelt, sturdy embraces. The family home is neat and spare. Everything is white but the floor, which is made of glossy dark brown planks. Mafalda takes us up the stairs to our room, a good-sized simple room with a sleigh bed and a matching settee. The bed is piled high with white coverlets, just the way Mama liked. Mafalda tells us to rest, they will see us for a light supper later. Before she goes, she tells me that this used to be my mother's bedroom.

While Jack unpacks, I lie down on the bed and look up at the ceiling, smooth and white. The window and door frames are painted an almond color. It's the same white and the same almond trim in my mother's bedroom in Big Stone Gap. My mother may not have talked much about Italy, but she surrounded herself with details that reminded her of her home.

We lie down for a nap and wake at about seven o'clock. The sun has set; we are surprised that we slept so long. The kitchen table is set for the two of us. Zia Antonietta serves us a delicious thick soup with greens in it, and soft bread with a hard, chewy crust. There is lots of creamy butter, and good, rich red wine. Italians eat their biggest meal at noon; this supper is perfectly sized, just enough for us to feel full but not stuffed.

When we are done eating, Zia Antonietta tells us to get our sweaters, and we go for a walk, or *la passeggiata,* as they say here. We walk a short distance to the main piazza in Bergamo Bassa, where folks stand in small groups chatting. Others sip coffee in the cafés on either side of the fountain. There is laughter, and the children run and play. The people here are so animated; they raise their voices to make a point, they use their bodies for emphasis; they are so full of life and comical! It is no surprise that the commedia dell'arte theatrical tradition started here in the fourteenth century. Everyone seems to have a divine sense of humor. Zia Antonietta tells us that this goes on every night. "It is soothing to laugh before sleep," she explains in Italian. Jack thinks it's the best idea he has ever heard. Zia Antonietta points to a rim of light above the city; in the twilight it looks like there are pillars and some buildings. "Alta Città. That was the ancient city Bergamo Alta. Now it is very desirable real estate. Our university is there. Mafalda will take you tomorrow if you like."

"Why did the city move down here?" Jack wants to know.

"War. Rock slides," she explains. She sees me frown. "But that was many centuries ago. Don't worry, Ave Maria. Don't worry."

We join Zia Meoli and Zio Pietro. My uncle takes Jack off to show him something; Zia Meoli and I go for a walk, just the two of us. Zia Antonietta leaves the group and returns home up the side street.

"Where is Zia Antonietta going?"

"Home." Zia Meoli shrugs.

"Isn't she going to stay and have some fun?"

"She likes to do her chores."

"Now?"

"Yes. She prepares the table for breakfast tomorrow, and then she goes to sleep."

"Why does she prepare the breakfast?"

"That is how we do it. Antonietta never married, so she runs the family home."

That was me, I think to myself as we walk along. I took care of everything. I was so busy, I didn't think about what I was doing or where the years were going. I just did what was expected of me. I wonder if Zia Antonietta is the town spinster. Zia Meoli must read my mind.

"My sister likes to take care of us."

"She seems happy."

"She was to marry, many years ago. The third son of seven of a family in Sestri Levante, on the seacoast. Then the war came and he died. She did not want to marry anyone else. She had many suitors. But her heart was broken, and that was the end of all that for her."

I feel better that Zia Antonietta had a great love, even though he died. But I can't help but wonder what it is about these Vilminore women; do they only ever love one man their whole lives, even if they marry another like my mother, or never marry like my aunt? Are they so clear-sighted about their great loves that there is no room for any other, ever? It seems that once their hearts were unlocked, they should have remained open to the possibilities of new love. Maybe the Vilminore girls are just one-man women.

Jack is waiting for me when we return to the house. I kiss my relatives good night, and Jack and I go to our room.

We sink into the layers and layers of feather-filled mattresses. We sink so deeply we can't find each other. My mother tried to re-create this effect in America, but she couldn't. Jack, used to sleeping on hard American mattresses, is afraid his back will go out in all this softness. I pound the top mattress flat to find my husband's face.

"Thank you for marrying me," I tell him. He looks confused, like *Here she goes again, my strange wife.* "No. Really. Thank you."

"You're welcome . . . I guess."

"I like being married to you."

"Good. Because you promised to stay with me forever."

"I know. But now it seems like time is flying by; I'm not going to have enough time with you. I just know it."

"Why do you worry about stuff like that?"

I don't think he wants my answer. Because I worry about everything! I worry about Zia Antonietta, whose lover died before she could marry him. I worry that her entire life is doing dishes and sweeping without love to break the tedium! I worry that happiness can't stay; I know it is just like the Deep Sleep, it is just a phase, a time, and then you come out of it and start all over again. I worry that the joy in my heart will become so ordinary to me that I will forget how sad I was without him and I will take him for granted and start nagging him and turn him away. I worry that I'm too old to have children. I worry that coal dust is sifting like black sand in the bellows of his lungs and he'll get emphysema and die an untimely death. I worry that when we die, he'll go first and I'll be left all alone again. I worry that when I die and go to find him in heaven, he won't be there. He will have changed and I won't recognize him and then I'll be traipsing through all eternity reliving the first thirty-five years of my life when I could not love anyone.

"Stop it."

"What?"

"Stop thinking. You've got that crease between your eyes. The one that comes out when you worry."

That did it. Never tell a thirty-six-year-old that there is a crease anywhere on her. It is not something I want to hear, ever. I rub the crease away. "That's my third eye."

Jack laughs so loud, I pull the sheet over his head. "Shh."

"What is a third eye?"

"In face-reading. It's the all-knowing eye of your mind. It's where you create the pictures that become the reality of your life."

"Put a pretty picture in there then," Jack says simply.

Oh, if it were only that easy; I look at him pityingly. When it is all said and done, he is still a man, and men just don't understand.

Mario Barbari stands outside the Vilminore homestead on Via Davide like he owns the entire block. He is dapper in navy slacks, a navy cashmere V-neck sweater, tucked in without a wrinkle (of course), and his signature ecru top sweater, tied in a knot and draped over his shoulders. He is having a smoke—so European. I don't stand on ceremony. I race down the sidewalk and throw myself on him. "Papa!" He hugs me and we kiss. He is so happy to see me. I'm so glad I like my father. I really do. He's a character, all right, and his cologne could ignite downtown Bergamo, but he is truly an original. I love to be around him.

"So you get married and you don't even wait for your own papa to give you away."

"You didn't miss much. I had on too much makeup, and I couldn't breathe in the dress."

"I'm sure you were lovely," he says, flicking his cigarette. Is this guy a movie star or what? My father embraces my husband as men do, with a quick hug and big slaps on their backs and arms, and then the two of them load the car. My family gathers on the steps of their home and waves us off into the distance, past the end of the block; Papa drives like a maniac. We're like a silver pinball whipping around the curves of the town circle surrounding the Fountain of Angels, past the park, and then to the road that leads out of town. SCHILPARIO NORD 7 KM, the green-and-white sign says. We're on our way to Grandmother's house.

Jack and my father talk about the difference between the beds in Italy and the beds in America. Jack tells Papa that he is shocked that his back is fine after sleeping on all those feathers. Papa explains that the body heat is evenly distributed when you sleep on feathers, or straw for that matter, so the muscles in the body stay the same warm temperature, and the result is you wake up without kinks and spasms.

"Look at me. I am old. And I am well rested. Yes?" Jack nods; Papa looks good for his age. Papa winks at me in the rearview mirror. He is fifty-four, but not fifty-four in Big Stone Gap years. His hair is long and thick and layers back in soft waves—the only aspect that shows his age is the white streaks throughout. His carriage is upright and youthful. And his skin is still magnificent. He looks about forty. I hope I have his genes.

About halfway up the mountain, Papa peels off into a ravine. I think we're going to land in a forest, but the road clears, revealing a chalet jutting out from the mountain. Papa looks at us.

"We rest." He parks. We get out of the car and go into the chalet.

The chalet is a restaurant. It is midafternoon and too early for dinner. Papa nods to the owner, who is restocking the bar. He brings us each a glass of bitters, which my father throws back in one gulp. Jack shrugs and throws his back. I follow. Bitters, I know from the Pharmacy, are herbs steeped in a fizz, a tonic. They are usually medicinal; I have never heard of them being used for social purposes.

"Cleans the blood," my father offers.

The owner brings out a tray with three small silver bowls and three tiny silver spoons. He places the summer blackberries before us. Papa squeezes fresh lemon over them.

"Go ahead. Eat." Jack and I eat, and we can't believe how sweet the berries are. Papa is pleased.

"Now we go," he says, and we are done. He nods to the owner. He leaves no money. I thank the man behind the bar, and he waves us off with a smile.

The road to Schilpario is really twisty, and my ears are popping as we ascend. I ask my father how high up we are, but he isn't sure. Then, with a flick of his wrist, he careens us off of the road to a scenic overlook. The protective railing is old and crumbling, and my heart beats faster when Papa parks too close.

"Come," he says, and gets out of the car. "Look." Jack and I join him at the edge of the mountain. I look down the precipice; layers and layers of jagged rock, gutted by time, create a deep gulch for miles to the bottom, which from here looks to be about the size of a quarter. I get dizzy and have to step back.

"Too far down, eh?" my father says. I nod.

"Let me tell you a story," Papa begins. I ask Papa and Jack to step back. I can imagine a strong wind kicking up and blowing them both over the side, never to be seen again.

"This is a story told to me by my father, Gianluca Barbari. His father, my grandfather, owned a carriage and two horses. He used to take people up and down the mountain to town. They paid him very well, so he kept a very elegant carriage. One morning the town widow called to arrange a ride the following day down to Bergamo.

She wanted to leave before the sun rose, and my grandfather agreed to take her. He woke that morning in the dark, fed the horses, hooked them up to the buggy, and went to pick up the woman at her house. She came to the door in a beautiful gown of pale green satin. Her shawl was embroidered with tiny yellow and gold leaves. She wore a beautiful hat with a green plume. My grandfather remembered a beautiful necklace with a diamond the size of a stone. It shimmered in the lamplight. Grandpapa helped her into the carriage. He remembered that she smelled like roses and that she smiled very happily. They began their trip down the mountain. This is the place where my grandfather used to stop and rest the horses. The woman wanted to stretch a bit, so my grandfather helped her out of the carriage. He was right over there watering the horses when he heard a sound like the sound when you shake out wet laundry before hanging it on the line. So he turned to look. The old lady had jumped off the mountain. Her skirts made the terrible sound as she fell. My grandfather ran to the edge, but she was gone. He shook terribly, and he had a moment where he thought that he too would jump. But he had eight children to feed, and he could not do it. So he went back up the mountain and directly to the police station. Grandfather knew the policeman and hoped he would believe his story. The policeman said it would be difficult to prove Grandfather's innocence because the widow had no relatives in town; she was alone, so who could corroborate his story, or at least offer information as to the woman's mental state? No one. My grandfather now worried he would be thrown in prison, unjustly accused of pushing the old widow over the mountain. But then the policeman had an idea. 'Let us go to her house and see if there are any clues that would help us ascertain if she was crazy, or in a weak state of mind.' When they reached the widow's house, the policeman was going to break the lock, but he did not have to. The front door was unlocked. The policeman went in, asking my grandfather to stay outside. He said the minutes while the policeman was inside the house turned his hair from black to white. The policeman came out holding a letter. The letter said that the authorities were not to blame Gianluca Barbari for her suicide. She said it was her choice entirely. She was ill and had no one in the world and wanted to die. Please give whatever was in her house to the church. Then the policeman handed my grandfather the fare for the trip, explaining that the widow wanted to pay him. My grandfather returned home and told his family the story. He was so grateful that the widow had left behind a letter clearing his name that he commissioned a stained-glass window to be made for the chapel. My grandfather's brothers had a small glassworks business. They made the stained-glass window and installed it in the choir loft. The window is still there." My father promises to show it to us.

We are high up in the Alps, and though it is summer, the breeze is very cool and sends a chill through me. Jack and Papa lead me back to the car. We drive the rest of the way in silence.

There is no grand entrance into the town of Schilpario. You happen upon it, almost by accident. It has not changed, either; it looks like the pictures in Iva Lou's books. It is just much smaller than I expected. I am not disappointed, just surprised. The main drag is a narrow street, lined on one side by shoe-box houses. These homes have different details from the ones down in Bergamo, though. There are Alpine touches: dark wood trim in gingerbread curves, small porches, and colorful shutters of soft beige and pink. The stucco on the outside is painted more vividly than down in the town. Perhaps the people of Schilpario paint the houses light colors so they are not lost altogether in the mountains and can be found by travelers as they pass through.

The town is nestled into the side of the mountain; houses dot the hillside above us; narrow streets make veins that lead to the main street. Papa drives us through the town and up to the waterwheel, which spins clear, icy mountain water over its flaps. Everyone who sees us waves and smiles. I get the feeling my father is well-respected here. Papa does a U-turn and returns down the main street, pulling over to park in front of a bright green shoe-box house. Nonna appears in the doorway. She is surrounded by people—I assume I am related to all of them. As they gather around the car, Nonna shoves them aside and hugs me and then Jack. She grabs my hand to inspect my gold wedding band.

"*Sposa bella!*" she says to me, and hugs me so hard I hear my clavicle crack. She leads us inside. Nonna has prepared a feast of risotto, salad, and roast duck, which Jack flips for. Jack and I and Papa sit at the table. It seems there are four people serving to each one sitting at the table. We are waited on like royalty. I notice my father is treated reverentially; and I also notice that he expects it. He is the only son in this household, and he is the mayor of this town, so he is held in very high esteem. I look at him and admire his self-confidence. He wears it so naturally.

The women won't let me help clean up, and they look at Jack as though he is from Mars when he rises to help with the dishes. Nonna wallops his back with her hand so hard, he sits down and doesn't try to help anymore. Nonna brings out biscotti, berries, and espresso at the end of the meal. We eat everything. She is pleased.

Two of Papa's old pals, actually first cousins, drop by to check out the Americans. Papa and Jack invite the men to play cards. Jack asks me if I'd like to play, but I decline, not because I don't want to play cards but because I know it's a men-only thing. My cousins look me up and down like a new appliance. I return the favor by examining them just as closely; it breaks their concentration, and they stop staring at me. They aren't aware of how well I speak Italian, so one of them whispers "nice ass" to the other as I leave the room, figuring I don't understand. I can't resist, so I lean in between them and say, "You have nice asses too." At first they are taken aback, and then they laugh heartily.

Nonna serves our breakfast, hard rolls left over from the previous night's dinner, soft butter and berry jam, and a large mug of steaming milk with espresso in it. We can't figure out why, but this combination is satisfying. Jack and I decide to eat this very thing every morning when we return home. How do the Italians know how to live? We don't understand it. Everything tastes better, even hard rolls and butter! And the pace is so easy. Work a little. Take a nap. Work a little more, eat a little something, take a little nap. And so on, day in and day out. Lots of play time: cards and socializing and long walks. It is a heavenly existence in the Alps.

Papa wants to take us to the chapel with the windows his grandfather created. We walk up the narrow street and turn onto a small side street where the chapel sits, like any house, except the details are simpler and the door is painted bright red—just like the Church of God in the Gap. Maybe they have to keep the Devil out in Italy too. We enter the tiny chapel. A priest is tinkering up at the altar.

"Ave Maria, this is Don Andrea, our priest," Papa says.

"Ave Maria," he says. "I never met an Ave Maria before."

"Don't you say your rosary?" I ask him. At first he doesn't get the joke, and then he smiles.

"This is my husband, Jack." Don Andrea shakes his hand.

"They just got married, Don Andrea. This is my daughter; I told you all about her."

"Oh, yes, yes." The old priest understands everything now.

"We're going to take a look around," Papa tells him. Jack studies the architecture. I ask Papa to show me the Blessed Mother window. He leads me up to the choir loft and points to it. It is very small, about the size of a book. As I lean in to examine it, a shiver goes through me. The lady in the glass wears a long blue gown and a hat with gold stars and peacock feathers, just like Ave Maria Albricci, the woman who helped my mother on the boat to America. She has a serene countenance. She stands on what looks like the waves of the ocean.

"Are you all right?" Papa asks me.

How can I tell him about Ave Maria Albricci? Even Jack was confused when I told him about her. He shrugged it off, like angels appear to people every day and save them. But this is too strange. In this sea of coincidences, I am beginning to understand that we don't control our destinies; they are mapped out for us as surely as we are born.

"Papa, I want to get married again," I announce to my father. Sometimes he looks at me like I am a little nuts, and this is one of those times.

"Who will tell Jack?" my father asks with a wry smile.

"Not to a different man. To Jack. Again. Here. I want you to give me away."

My father shrugs, like it isn't the worst idea he's ever heard.

So on Sunday, June 3, Jack MacChesney and I are blessed all over again, by Don Andrea, at La Capella di Santa Chiara in Schilpario, Italy.

My father is nervous as he walks me down the aisle, but very happy too. He serves as Jack's best man, and I ask Nonna to stand up for me. She is very embarrassed, though; she thinks she is too old. But I make her do it, strong-arming her the way she commands everyone else.

Men don't like church weddings the first time around, so you can imagine the begging I have to do to get Jack to repeat the vows. But I realize something important about him in all of this, something that I never knew before. No matter what I ask of him, no matter how corny or difficult or plain old-fashioned undoable it is, if I ask, he will do it for me. He loves me so completely that he cannot deny me anything. I pray that I will never abuse this gift. But knowing me, there will be times I come close. I just hope he understands.

The best summer of our lives comes to an end. We say our good-byes, but they aren't really binding, as Papa plans to visit us the next spring. Jack and I promise to spend part of every summer for the rest of our lives here in Schilpario, my father's home. Good-byes are not sad to me at all anymore. I have learned to enjoy what leads up to them too much to worry about finalities.

I am anxious to get home. I have missed the Blue Ridge Mountains. Jack laughs about this.

"Mountains are mountains wherever you go," he says.

"No. Our mountains are home," I tell him. I can't explain it to him, but Big Stone Gap has gone from the place I was running from to the place I most want to be. I have seen where I come from, but now I know where I belong. Home is with Jack MacChesney in that stone house on the hill.

———

The plane ride home is bumpy. I am sick most of the way, as is Jack. But I think he gets sick when he sees me get sick. What is the old expression about true lovers: When one gets cut, the other bleeds? When we land at Tri-Cities Airport, I am not sad. I am looking forward to returning to Cracker's Neck and waiting for the seasons to change and bring us our first autumn together.

Well, it wasn't airsickness back in August. Almost a year to the day after our American wedding, April 28, 1980, Fiametta Bluebell MacChesney was born to two very happy parents. This is all so new to me, and I have no words to describe it.

I do know, and I will explain to my daughter, that she is a very lucky girl. She need look no further than her own family to inspire her to cut her own path in life. We're calling the baby Etta, the name my mother's true love called her. I hope that she has my mother's heart; it is evident to all, in the two days she's been on earth, that she has already inherited her stubbornness. Most of the time, when I hold her, I think of Mama. I feel her around me now, guiding me. Finally, my mother's choices make sense to me. Now I understand how she found the courage to leave her family and start a new life with me. A baby gives you the strength to do just about anything.

Etta has Nan MacChesney's eyes. They say all babies have blue eyes, but I see the green there already, and they have a knowingness and a humor that can only have come from her no-nonsense grandmother. How sad I am Etta will never know her grandmothers! Why am I making a list of all the things our daughter won't have? The only thing I know for sure is that I will worry about this little one until the day I die. Jack agrees with that; he says I've been practicing worry for thirty-seven years, so I'm mighty good at it.

And what about Jack MacChesney, my husband and the father of our daughter? Will he teach her to play the guitar and whistle?

The moon is just a sliver the first night home with our baby. I'm tired, so Jack relieves me and I doze off to sleep for twenty minutes or so. When I wake up, the house is quiet. I can't find Jack and Etta inside, so I go to the backyard and circle around to the front of the house. There they are. Father and daughter. Sitting on the porch, looking at the moon. I stand there for a very long time. I don't know why. She starts to fuss and I know she is hungry. But I can't move. I want to watch the two of them forever—a daughter learning to trust, and a father doing the thing he does best: protecting her.

ACKNOWLEDGMENTS

I am filled with gratitude to Suzanne Gluck, my longtime friend and now agent, who encouraged me to write this book in the first place. My thanks to Suzanne's right arm, Karen Gerwin, and to her left, Caroline Sparrow; to Laura Davies, ICM's answer to international coffee; and to Lorie Stoopack, my answer to domestic caffeine.

I have been graced with a great editor in fellow Virginian Lee Boudreaux; also at mighty Random House: Ann Godoff, Pamela Cannon, Beth Pearson, Andy Carpenter, Todd Doughty, Amanda Maher, and Sherry Huber. At Ballantine, my thanks to Gina Centrello, simpatico Italian girl and paperback whiz.

My undying gratitude to my fellow writers whose advice, criticism, and encouragement were invaluable: Tom Dyja (whose faith in me was ever true), Michael Patrick King (everyone needs such a champion), Ruth Goetz, Rosanne Cash, Susan Fales-Hill, Richard Kirshenbaum, Lorenzo Carcaterra, Charles Randolph Wright, Kare Jackowski, and Mary Trigiani.

I owe a great debt to all my teachers in the Wise County public school system whose love of books and reading opened up the world to me.

I am grateful to Brownie Polly III and Brad Cavedo for sharing their memories of the Gap; June Lawton, who introduced me to the art of Chinese face-reading; and Gina Casella for her Italian flavor and flair.

My thanks and love to: Ruth Pomerance, Caroline Rhea, Bob Kelty, Greg Cantrell, Mary Testa, Sharon Watroba Burns, Nancy Ringham, Dana Geier, Jake and Jean Morrisey, Beata and Steven Baker, E. J. Jones, Joanne Curley Kerner, Sharon Hall, Todd Kessler, Chris Sarandon, Wendy Luck, Dee Emmerson, Cynthia Olson, Constance Marks, Susan Toepfer, Adina and Michael Pitt, Rosemarie and Anthony Casciole, Marisa Acocella, Nancy Josephson, Jill Holwager, Danny Greenberg, Jeanne Newman, John Farrell, Craig Jacobson, and Lou Pitt and the Pitt Group.

I am very lucky to have been influenced and mentored by Monsignor Don Andrea Spada, Mario Mai, Lucia Spada Bonicelli, and Michael A. and Yolanda P. Trigiania. Their impact on my life is incalculable.

In movieland, endless thanks to my magnificent men of the Shooting Gallery: Larry Meistrich, Jim Powers, Todd Steiner, and Mark V. Lord.

My eternal thanks and love to my father, Anthony, who found Big Stone Gap, and my beautiful mother, Ida Bonicelli, who made our home there; also to my partners in crime on Poplar Hill, and my brothers and sisters: Mary Yolanda, Lucia Anna, Antonia, Michael (and wife Lisa), Carlo (and wife Tina), and Francesca (and husband Tom). My thanks, too, to the Stephensons—sometimes you get lucky and marry a good bunch.

Big Stone Gap

Adriana Trigiani

A Reader's Guide

A Conversation with Adriana Trigiani

Iva Lou Wade Makin, Big Stone Gap's favorite librarian,
sat down at the Mutual Pharmacy cafeteria/fountain with Adriana
Trigiani for an interview. Iva Lou had a chili dog, Ms. Trigiani
had a diet pop. They both had a lot of laughs.

Iva Lou Wade Makin: First things first, girl. What's it like to live in the big city after you've lived in a small town?

Adriana Trigiani: It's noisier in New York City than it is in Big Stone Gap. And you can get a newspaper everyday, not just once a week. And you'd think that you have your anonymity in the city, but you really don't. People get to know you in your neighborhood. I look at Manhattan as if it's made up of a lot of Big Stone Gaps that hook together and make a city. It feels like home; it is home.

IL: I loved your book. Especially the way I looked in it. By the way, I stopped selling the Sarah Coventry in seventy-nine.

AT: I'm sorry to hear that.

IL: Most people around here think you got things purty accurate, except for the geography. You moved places around — like the Roaring Branch. Did you mean to do that?

AT: Fiction gives the writer license to invent, rearrange, imagine. I moved things in my imagination, so it's a mix of the real and true and the Big Stone Gap of my heart, which is a kind of Brigadoon to me. It's not a physical place, as much as it's an emotional place; a place I grew up in with my family and friends. When I called your Book-mobile "a glittering royal coach," I surely meant it.

IL: I was surprised by that. I've been trying to git the county to give it a paint job for about five years here—your description did not help me acquire those funds.

AT: Sorry.

IL: Now, honey, we need to get down to the brass tacks. Everyone in town agrees that the people in your novel are based on real people. We're trying to figure out who is who. Obviously, I am me. But who is Ave Maria?

AT: Ave Maria is the woman you can count on. She's your best friend; the person you go to for advice, the person who has a cool head in a crisis. Maybe she's a loner and lives a life of service and not of intimacy. She's the woman that you wonder about. You hope she finds a nice man. You hope she's happy; she certainly seems to be. That's what the novel is about. A person may appear to be one thing, but inside of them there's a river of complexities and fears and desires. When you find that out, there is no end to the depth of emotion. The book is really about the interior life and feelings of that woman you know; perhaps she even reminds you of yourself.

IL: Yeah, but who is she?

AT: She's herself.

IL: Yeah, but who? People round here think it could be . . . (Iva Lou turns off the tape recorder.) Okay, we're back on folks, I apologize, I didn't want to name no names.

AT: That's a good idea. Besides, she isn't just one person. She's an amalgam.

IL: How about Theodore?

AT: Well, he's based upon a friend of mine who is from Scranton and is a great artist. Our dynamic is a lot like Theodore and Ave's. So it was fun for me to access the way we communicate and explore how we're present for one another in our friendship.

IL: What about Jack Mac?

AT: He too is a combination of ideas of men. But I would have to say that my husband reminds me of him; though I was surprised by the direction the character has taken in this book; and I think all my readers will be surprised when they'll find out where he goes in the sequel. I think this is what is so powerful about fiction. The writer enters a world to record the story, the action of that world, and it is full of twists and turns and revelations that surprise even the writer.

IL: You sayin' you don't have control of the story?

AT: A lot of times I don't. I have control of how I'm telling it, but not why. If I have an idea that I want to use, sometimes it feels like I'm shoe horning it into the book, so I step back and let the world of the imagination take over and guide me. And that place, inside all of us, where creativity is the engine, and where ideas are born, never lets you down. You simply must listen.

IL: I read a lot o' books, honey, but I never knew *that* was going on behind the scenes.

AT: It's an amazing process. It's not pretty. It consumes me.

IL: Sort of like how I feel when I'm reading a good book.

AT: Yeah.

IL: I've loaned out your book a lot, and if you don't mind, I'd like to ask you the most commonly asked question I git from readers. Why would Ave Maria, a pharmacist, go with a coal miner?

AT: How snobby!

IL: I thought so too.

AT: Well, I guess the readers have a small point there. Here is this woman who went off to college and returned home, while Jack Mac had his life in the coal mines. What would they have in common? And of course, Jack is with Sweet Sue; their relationship seems like a match, she offers him an instant family.

IL: Yeah, but Sweet Sue is in it for herself.

AT: She's a young divorced woman with two kids. I could see why she would appreciate a man like Jack.

IL: Yeah, but she wasn't right for him. Ave was!

AT: Sweet Sue is a woman for whom things seem easy—she's pretty, she's fun and bubbly. She never seems to have a bad day. Of course, we know that couldn't possibly be true, but this is Ave's book, not Sweet Sue's.

IL: Thank you Lord for that.

AT: What I like about Jack and Ave is that they don't seem right for each other. But, as it is in real life, there is a connection that can not be denied by either of them. Sometimes the power of what we feel overwhelms all other decisions; our hearts rule our heads. Now, the sequel dives into that very issue: What happens to Jack and Ave; how do they make this marriage of opposites work?

IL: Honey, I thought *Big Stone Gap* was a book about falling in love. Sounds like *Big Cherry Holler* is a book about staying in love. One more thing. I love the Mario da Schilpario revelation because I think there is nothin' more fascinatin' than a family secret revealed.

AT: The revelation of the relationship between Mario and Ave was the foundation upon which the story turned. Ave had this very difficult and painful past. She grew up in a home with a father that ignored her and was irritated by her presence; and a mother whom she adored and who tried to compensate for the lack of a loving father.

I believe that in order to be alive in a marriage, truly alive and there for the person we are with, we have to understand where we come from. The marriage (or lack of one) you saw as a child shapes your adult life. It's what you know; so that is the place from which you make your daily decisions about how you will be in a relationship.

If you noticed, both Jack and Ave were attached to their mothers. They both needed to let go of their parents in order to find each other. Ave thought the answer would be to find her real father. What Mario shows her is that the answers were inside her all along.

I believe that when we talk about how hard marriage and relationships are, we are really talking about our parents' marriage and how we perceive it.

IL: So the past is important in dealing with the present.

AT: Absolutely. And the best places where these themes can be explored in depth are in books and of course, in other art forms, such as painting, music, theatre, film, and television.

IL: Honey, we understand you're shooting the movie right here in Big Stone.

AT: Yes we are.

IL: Can I be in it? I always saw myself as a star, and now I want my chance to shine in the spotlight. Do you think you could hook me up?

AT: Anything for you, Iva Lou.

READING GROUP QUESTIONS AND
TOPICS FOR DISCUSSION

1. Why do you think the author set *Big Stone Gap* during the late 1970s instead of today?

2. The coal mines are the site of danger and oppressiveness, while the caverns Ave Maria and Theodore visit reveal the beauty hidden deep in the earth. How does this dichotomy reflect Ave Maria's inner world during her yearlong crisis?

3. As the novel progresses and Ave Maria learns more about herself and her past, her feelings for Big Stone Gap change from contentment to disassociation to joy. Have your feelings for your hometown changed as you've changed? How?

4. Ave Maria refers to herself as a "ferriner," but when she visits Italy she realizes that her home is in Big Stone Gap. What other works have you read in which the hero or heroine must travel to find his or her home in the world?

5. Ave Maria's description of some events, such as kissing Theodore after the Drama and Jack Mac's reaction to her gratitude for bringing over her Italian family, differs from other people's perspectives. Do you believe Ave Maria's interpretations? Why or why not?

6. Theodore and Ave Maria have romantic feelings for each other, but never at the same time. If their feelings had been more coordinated, do you think they would have entered a lasting marriage? Do you think their "best friend" relationship will endure after Ave Maria and Jack Mac's wedding?

7. When did you suspect that Ave Maria would fall in love with Jack Mac? What were the clues that the author left?

8. Jack Mac tells Ave Maria, "Stop thinking." Is Jack Mac correct? Does too much thinking lead Ave Maria into making the wrong choices? Are her emotions a trustier guide or equally unreliable?

9. A common theme in literature is that the heroine (e.g., Snow White, Cinderella, Jane Eyre, Nancy Drew) must lose a parent or parents before she is free to discover who she really is. Is this merely a literary convention or does it have roots in real life? Does it apply to male characters as well? How much significance does Mrs. Mac's death have to Jack Mac's personal development?

10. Ave Maria feels relief and not much surprise when she learns Fred Mulligan is not her father, and later she recognizes aspects of herself in Mario. Though Fred is not her blood kin, what traits did he pass on to Ave Maria while he raised her? How much of Ave Maria's personality was shaped by nature and how much by nurture?

11. When describing her friend Iva Lou, the majorette Tayloe, and Sweet Sue, Ave Maria focuses on the power of beauty and desirability, but she also cautions Pearl that beauty fades while character endures. How does Pearl synthesize the importance of character with the force of beauty?

12. Both Ave Maria and Worley discover their fathers aren't who they thought they were, but Worley learns of his true parentage when his father is still alive. Do you think Ave Maria's expectations of love and marriage would have been affected if she had learned the truth about Mario before her mother died? How?

13. Ave Maria is named for the mysterious woman who took Ave Maria's mother under her wing. Do you see another meaning in Ave Maria's name? Does it tie in with her developing belief in destiny and faith?

14. *Big Cherry Holler*, Adriana Trigiani's next novel about the people of Big Stone Gap, jumps forward eight years into Ave Maria and Jack Mac's marriage. Knowing these two characters as you do, do you expect the path of true love to run smooth for them? What quirks do Ave Maria and Jack Mac bring to the relationship that could cause bumps or, conversely, even out the way?

A LOOK INSIDE

Big Stone Gap

THE MOVIE

Dear Reader,

Historically, novelists have a fraught relationship with the screen adaptations of their books. Rarely do you hear an author say that she loves the movie version of her novel—usually, we cross our fingers and hope for the best as our dear friends in Hollywood try to deliver their version of the story we conjured in our imaginations. This time, with *Big Stone Gap*, we cut out the middlemen/women: I wrote and directed the film version of the novel.

Big Stone Gap was published on April 3, 2000. We went into production on the movie in mid-October 2013 under the leadership of Academy Award–winning producer Donna Gigliotti. A year of post-production followed as the movie was edited, set to music, color-timed, looped and perfected in sound, and offered up in the marketplace for distribution. Altar Identity Studios, which produced the film, found the perfect partner in Picturehouse. We all agreed that *Big Stone Gap* needed to be seen in theaters, to be experienced in community. In 2015, theatrical distribution is nothing short of a miracle for a filmmaker. It was a long, winding climb up a mountain road to get here, but worth every step.

Visually lush (photographed by the great Reynaldo Villalobos), dramatically arresting (what a cast), and funny, the movie conjures a time when movie entertainment was pure escape, when you could steal into a theater and fall into a story and emerge a couple of hours later rejuvenated, if not redeemed.

We believe the story of *Big Stone Gap* is timely. We embrace the notion that, like Ave Maria Mulligan, you must know what you come from in order to build your own life and take a risk in love. We live in perilous times, and we believe the fictional people of a real town might shed some light on what matters. At least, that was our hope.

I was encouraged to make the movie in my hometown, surrounded by the brilliant talents, commitment, and support of our cast and crew, my family, the kids I grew up with, and an eager mayor and a hardworking town manager. All of southwest Virginia pitched in, including the surrounding communities in Wise and Lee counties. It didn't hurt that six governors, four state senators, and one delegate fought for many years to have the movie made in the place where the story was born. The people of southwest Virginia wanted us to come home to make the movie, and it's always a good idea to work where you're wanted. We felt the love, and you can see it on the screen.

I grew up in Big Stone Gap and am deeply grateful and proud that our movie was made and shot entirely on location in Virginia. The music was composed by John Leventhal and features many local artists, with music recorded at the historic Maggard Sound in Big Stone Gap.

You have followed the life of Ave Maria Mulligan—a lonely town spinster who finds love and, in so doing, her life—through the series of books. I hope that you will have a seat in the audience to see Ave's story on the screen.

I've excerpted some scenes from the screenplay here in this special edition of *Big Stone Gap*. When you have everyone over after the movie, please make the recipes we enjoyed while we were on location, and if you'd like to Skype me in, please email my assistant at adrianaasst@aol.com. Thank you always for your love and support; they sustain me and keep me working hard for you. See you at the cineplex and at the library!

xoxo,
Adriana

Big Stone Gap Screenplay

IVA LOU AND AVE MARIA ON THE ROOF

One of the great gifts of living in the mountains is the visuals—the divine vistas, scope, height, and colors, greens and blues so intense you are enveloped by them. I wanted to show the audience the mountains from high in the air, so from that desire came this scene. It turns out that just a speck of the scene made it into the movie, but if you love Iva Lou's wisdom and Ave Maria's fundamental common sense, this outtake will appeal to you. We'll make sure it's in the bonus material when we release the movie on DVD. —A.T.

In this deleted scene, Ave Maria (Ashley Judd) and Iva Lou (Jenna Elfman) have a heart-to-heart on Ave Maria's roof.

EXT. AVE MARIA'S HOUSE - LATER - NIGHT

Ave Maria lies on the roof in her party dress. Iva Lou parks
the Bookmobile in front of the house. She sees Ave Maria on
the roof.

> IVA LOU
> Body on the roof! Body on the roof!
> Don't jump! It ain't worth it!

Iva Lou goes into the house. Cut to:

> IVA LOU (CONT'D)
> Oh Lord. Oh Lordy mercy.

She flicks on lights all the way up the stairs to the second
floor. Ave Maria lies on the roof and stares at the sky. Iva
Lou climbs out the window and crawls to Ave Maria.

> IVA LOU (CONT'D)
> I'm skeered of heights.

> AVE MARIA
> You'll get used to it.

> IVA LOU
> What are you doin' up here?

> AVE MARIA
> Stewin'.

> IVA LOU
> Honey-O, I been stewin', too. I'm
> worried sick about you. You done
> give enough of your life to your
> mother and to Frederick Mulligan
> and to this town, too. To Theodore.
> I mean, you've been out of high
> school for twenty-two years and you're
> still goin' to football games every
> Friday night so you can help him
> set the batons for the halftime
> show.

> AVE MARIA
> I like to be useful.

IVA LOU

How about taking care of you for a
change? Do your nails. Your hair.
You get yourself a push-up bra.
When a girl's boobs are high, so are
her spirits. See, you just act like
you are happy and pretty soon you
will be. You start living your life
like it is where you want to be and
you will have everything you dream of.

AVE MARIA

I don't dream, Iva Lou. I have
lists of things to do. I've got
pills and potions, but there's
nothing I got in all the Mutual
Pharmacy that can fix my life. I am
alone. You want to know the truth?
I was trying to recollect one nice
thing that Frederick Mulligan said
to me in all the years I knew him.
You know, Iva Lou, he looked
through me like an empty jelly
glass. He never saw me. Wasn't
interested. And that made me think
I wasn't worth his attention.
That's how I got to being useful.

IVA LOU

Why do you do this to y'self? It's
the past. Let it go.

AVE MARIA

I come up here and remembered. He
said, "Sometimes folks think the
mountains are walls and they should
never go beyond them. You should
never be afraid to go over the
mountain."

IVA LOU

Are you?

AVE MARIA

Terrified.

>   IVA LOU
>   Maybe that means you're in the
>   right place. You just need you the
>   right person. Did I ever tell you
>   about the date I had with Jack Mac
>   years ago? Anyhow, we were over at
>   the Carter Family Fold and we had
>   fun dancin' and then we went to my
>   truck and had a beer. I was frisky
>   and he was frisky, so I suggested a
>   rendezvous up to Huff Rock. So we
>   drove up there and got out on the
>   rocks and did us some star gazin',
>   which is a better prelude to sex
>   than a steak-and-tater dinner from
>   Skoby's, in my opinion. We kissed
>   for a while and then it was gettin'
>   time to move things along and he
>   stopped.
>
>   AVE MARIA
>   Why?
>
>   IVA LOU
>   I'm not braggin', but that sort o'
>   thing never happened to me before.
>   I said, Jack MacChesney, ain't you
>   having fun? And he looked at me
>   with them gray-blue-green-brownish
>   eyes of his and said, "Ma'am,
>   you're a doll, but I'm not in love
>   with you. And I'm one of them men
>   that has to be in love to carry on
>   like this."
>
>   AVE MARIA
>   He's not the answer, Iva Lou.

JACK MAC AND HIS MOTHER—THE KITCHEN

This scene wasn't in the original screenplay. In production, the writer/ director has to live in the moment with the actors, and when she sees something happen—a connection, a spark—she must be open to follow it—to seize it—to write something new on the spot to enrich the story.

Patrick Wilson and Judith Ivey lit up the screen when they were to-

gether, and yet they didn't have a scene that celebrated that connection. So I went off in a corner and wrote one for them—and here it is. And when you see the scene in the movie, they are sublime. —A.T.

Nan MacChesney (Judith Ivey) sits down with Jack (Patrick Wilson) for a much-needed mother-son conversation.

INT. MACCHESNEY HOME - KITCHEN - DAY

Mrs. Mac is bringing some fresh laundry in from outside.

                    MRS. MAC
          Son, have I been a good mother?

                    JACK MAC
          Yes, ma'am.

                    MRS. MAC
          Good answer.

                    JACK MAC
          Why do you ask? Is something wrong?

                    MRS. MAC
          I have a forty-year-old son who has
          never pulled the trigger. And I
          don't mean that one. This is one of
          them moments I wish your daddy was
          alive.

                    JACK MAC
Just say it, Ma.

                    MRS. MAC
I don't want you to murry Sweet Sue
Tinsley. I never taught you the
difference between lust and love.
See, true love energizes you. Lust,
and all the other kinds of love,
exhaust you.

                    JACK MAC
Mama, all right.

                    MRS. MAC
Listen to me. Clearly, I have
failed you. Of course, anything and
everything that goes wrong with the
children is the mother's fault. So
let me embrace my failure. Why
aren't you marrying a nice girl
rather than a hotsy-totsy flaunter?

                    JACK MAC
I'll marry whomever I please.

                    MRS. MAC
That there is the issue! What
pleases you don't always serve ye.
Who is going to take care of your
heart instead of your . . . Well,
my point is, you can have both.
John Gilliam MacChesney, you can
have good and better sex with
someone who really loves you and
loves you your whole life long.

                    JACK MAC
I know that, Ma.

                    MRS. MAC
Then explain this to me. Explain
what you are doing with your life.

                    JACK MAC
Mama, look at me. Everything has
passed me by. When I was young, I

had a handle on things. I knew
exactly who I was and what I
wanted. But I work in the dark. And
I have been for twenty-two years. And when
I come out of the mine, I don't
want complications, I want simple.

                MRS. MAC
Well, that is a word I would use to
describe Sweet Sue.

                JACK MAC
I know you don't like her, but I
love her boys and she's nice to me.

                MRS. MAC
Well, you told me. If that is your
choice, Sweet Sue will never know
my true feelings. Can I fix you
some supper?

                JACK MAC
No, thank you, Mama. I got plans.

AVE MARIA AND THEODORE TIPTON—AT CARMINE'S

Ashley Judd and John Benjamin Hickey were dazzling together on camera. I love this scene because it has, at its heart, two lonely people who have tried to have a relationship but, for reasons they could not name, somehow couldn't take their feelings to the next level. Mr. Hickey played Theodore with a ferocious intensity and a whimsy I have never seen in a movie before, and Ms. Judd, the consummate actor, played to the revelation in this scene with a big, wide-open heart. The end of the scene feels like a valve blowing off a steam pipe—quiet but powerful. —A.T.

INT. CARMINE'S DINER - DAY

Theodore slides into the booth across from Ave. She tries to
leave. He stops her.

                AVE MARIA
I don't want to talk to you.

THEODORE

We are going to talk.

AVE MARIA

You're in love with Edna. Or Ledna.
You've been sneaking up to Coeburn
for years and that's why you never
made a move on me.

THEODORE

Is that what you think? Those girls
were in town to interview for a
couple of teaching jobs at the high
school. That's all. Mrs. Mac knows
their mother from the Southern
Baptist Summer Conference, so she
made breakfast. It's all very
innocent.

AVE MARIA

It doesn't matter.

THEODORE

You're sitting here crying. Of
course it matters.

AVE MARIA

It just reminded me of what it was
like before you came to town. I was
never invited anywhere. I'd deliver
prescriptions and before I knocked
on a door I'd hear laughter and
conversation coming out of a house
and wonder why I didn't have a life
full of that particular kind of
joy. I felt left out.

THEODORE

I wouldn't leave you out, ever. It
was business. Ledna wants my job.

AVE MARIA

Why?

THEODORE

I was offered the band director job
at the University of Tennessee and

I'm going to take it.

                    AVE MARIA
We should get married right away
and move to Knoxville.

                    THEODORE
But you're going to Italy.

                    AVE MARIA
I never said I was going to stay
there forever.

Ave Maria leans back in her seat. Theodore turns and faces
her.

                    THEODORE
We can't do this anymore.

Ave Maria takes a moment to breathe.

                    AVE MARIA
No, we can't. It's exhausting.

                    THEODORE
We have to stop pretending that
we're . . . you know . . .

                    AVE MARIA
A couple?

                    THEODORE
Exactly.

                    AVE MARIA
Then why did you ask me to marry you?

                    THEODORE
Because I love you.

                    AVE MARIA
I know. I love you, too.

                    THEODORE
You don't want me. I'm a bad bet. I
have quirks. I'm persnickety. I'm
churlish. I'm moody and cranky and

> impossible. I have a terrible
> background. Half my family drinks
> and the other half hits the people
> who drink.

Ave Maria takes this in. After a moment, she has an epiphany.

> AVE MARIA
> Theodore. Do you like men?

> THEODORE
> That, too.

Leah Grimes (Jasmine Guy) and Fleeta Mullins (Whoopi Goldberg) chat at Iva Lou's wedding reception.

Hope Meade's Wedding Mints

One 8-ounce package cream cheese
¼ teaspoon peppermint oil or other flavoring
Two 1-pound packages confectioners' sugar
Food coloring of your choice
1 cup granulated sugar

In a medium mixing bowl, cream the cheese. Add the flavoring and mix well. Add the confectioners' sugar, mixing until creamy. (If using a food processor, blend in half the recipe at a time.) If you want to use more than one color, separate the dough. Using your hands, mix the food coloring into the dough. Until ready to use, wrap the dough in plastic wrap to prevent drying.

Pinch off enough dough to fill a plastic or rubber 1-inch candy mold. Before placing the dough in the mold, dip it in the granulated sugar. After you've molded the dough, pop the pieces out onto wax paper and dry thoroughly. You may freeze the mints or keep them in the refrigerator in an airtight container for several weeks.

Makes about 4 dozen mints

Cousin Dee's Peanut Butter Balls

One 1-pound box confectioners' sugar
One 18-ounce jar crunchy peanut butter
2 cups graham cracker crumbs
2 sticks unsalted butter, melted
One 12-ounce package semisweet
  chocolate chips
2 ounces paraffin wax

In a medium bowl, blend the sugar, peanut butter, graham cracker crumbs, and butter. Roll the dough into bite-size balls.

Melt the chocolate and wax together, either on the stove or in the microwave in 30-second increments. Stir.

Dip the balls into the melted chocolate and wax and place on wax paper. Chill for about 15 minutes, or until the chocolate hardens.

Makes 3 to 4 dozen balls

Leah Grimes's Soup Beans and Corn Bread

SOUP BEANS

> 5 cups dry pinto beans
> 1 cup diced baked ham
> Salt and pepper to taste

Rinse the beans under cold water, then place them in a large pot and cover with 3 inches of water. Stir in the ham, season to taste, then bring the mixture to a boil. Reduce the heat to a simmer and cover the pot. Stir frequently; you want a thick, stewlike broth. Add water if the beans and ham are too thick.

While the beans are cooking, make the corn bread.

CORN BREAD

> ½ cup shortening
> 1 cup buttermilk
> ½ cup whole milk
> 2 large eggs
> 1 cup yellow cornmeal
> ½ cup all-purpose flour
> ½ teaspoon salt
> 1 tablespoon baking powder
> ½ teaspoon baking soda

Preheat the oven to 450 degrees.

In a cast-iron skillet, melt the shortening over medium heat. As it's melting, whisk together the buttermilk, whole milk, and eggs in a medium bowl and set aside.

In a separate medium bowl, mix the cornmeal, flour, and salt. In a large bowl, mix the ingredients of the two bowls. Add the baking powder and baking soda. Stir to combine. Pour the batter into the hot skillet; stir in the shortening and batter until well blended. Move the skillet into the oven and bake about 20 minutes, or until golden brown.

Makes 6 to 8 servings

Ave Maria visits the home of Pearl Grimes to deliver some surprising news.

Ave Maria's Summer Pasta with Mint

1 pound spaghetti
1 pound fresh or frozen peas
¼ pound salted butter
1 cup grated Parmesan cheese
½ teaspoon salt
¼ cup olive oil
½ cup breadcrumbs
1 bunch fresh mint, torn (reserve a few whole leaves for garnish)
½ lemon
*½ teaspoon freshly grated black pepper or ½ teaspoon red pepper
    flakes*
½ cup shredded Parmesan cheese

Boil the spaghetti, following the package directions. When the pasta is al dente, throw in the peas. Boil the peas with the pasta for 1 minute (30 seconds longer if you're using frozen peas).

Drain the pasta and peas (never rinse!) and return to the pot.

Throw the butter on top of the pasta and peas, then sprinkle the grated Parmesan cheese and the salt on top and toss until the butter has melted through. Drizzle the olive oil over the mixture. Add the breadcrumbs and toss.

Add the mint, squeeze the juice of the lemon half over the pasta, then add the pepper of your choice, and toss through the pasta and peas. Before serving, garnish with the shredded Parmesan cheese and the reserved mint leaves. It never hurts to give the finished dish a splash of olive oil before serving.

Makes 4 to 6 servings

Big Stone Gap local Rickey Wiles makes his cinematic debut as Earl Purvis.

Earl Purvis's Pineapple Upside-Down Cake

(by Big Stone Gap's Rickey Wiles)

PINEAPPLE GLAZE
½ stick unsalted butter or margarine
¾ cup firmly packed light brown sugar

One 20-ounce can sliced pineapples
One 10-ounce jar maraschino cherries

CAKE

1 large egg
1 cup granulated sugar
½ stick unsalted butter
2 cups all-purpose flour
2 teaspoons baking powder
¼ teaspoon salt
2 tablespoons pure vanilla extract
¾ cup whole milk

Grease a cast-iron skillet or a 9-inch round cake pan. (If using a cake pan, line it with parchment paper.) Preheat the oven to 350 degrees.

For the Pineapple Glaze: In the skillet, over medium-low heat, melt the butter, then stir in the brown sugar. Arrange the pineapple slices and cherries on top. Turn the heat down to low until the cake batter is ready to be poured on. Keep an eye on the mixture to make sure it doesn't burn.

For the Cake: Add the egg, sugar, and butter to a medium mixing bowl. Beat until fully mixed. Stir in the flour, baking powder, and salt, then add the vanilla and milk. Beat until blended. Pour the cake batter over the pineapples and cherries. Bake for about 30 minutes, or until golden brown.

Do not let the cake cool. Immediately put a serving plate on top of the skillet or pan and turn it over, releasing the cake. Serve warm or cool.

Makes 6 to 8 servings

PHOTO: © TIM STEPHENSON

ADRIANA TRIGIANI is beloved by millions of readers around the world for her fifteen bestsellers, including the blockbuster epic *The Shoemaker's Wife*; the Big Stone Gap series; *Lucia, Lucia*; the Valentine series; the Viola series for young adults; and the bestselling memoir *Don't Sing at the Table*. Trigiani reaches new heights with *All the Stars in the Heavens*, an epic tale from the Golden Age of Hollywood. She is the award-winning filmmaker of the documentary *Queens of the Big Time*. Trigiani wrote and directed the major motion picture *Big Stone Gap*, based on her debut novel and filmed entirely on location in her Virginia hometown. She lives in Greenwich Village with her family.

adrianatrigiani.com
Facebook.com/AdrianaTrigiani
@adrianatrigiani

ABOUT THE TYPE

This book was set in Electra, a typeface designed for Linotype by renowned type designer W. A. Dwiggins (1880–1956). Electra is a fluid typeface, avoiding the contrasts of thick and thin strokes that are prevalent in most modem typefaces.